D0816911

ABOUT THE AUTHOR

Laurel Archer has been a canoe guide and instructor since 1988. She is a Paddle Canada instructor and a Master Instructor for the Recreational Canoe Association of BC, teaching all levels of lake, moving-water and canoe-tripping courses. Her love of travelling waterways of all kinds in varied types of craft has also led her to become a certified lead sea kayak guide and whitewater kayak instructor. She currently teaches courses in all these disciplines for the Canadian Outdoor Leadership Training Program (COLT) at Strathcona Park Lodge on Vancouver Island. She also is a contractor for several commercial guiding companies and paddling clubs that offer canoeing and kayaking courses and trips, and volunteers her services to community and conservation organizations. She is a patron of the Canadian Parks & Wilderness Society's Boreal Forest Program and a member of the International Explorers Club.

Beyond her work as a professional outdoor educator and paddling instructor and guide, Archer spends part of the year writing. *Northern Saskatchewan Canoe Trips: A Guide to 15 Wilderness Rivers* was her first published book. She freelances for a number of magazines, and her stories have appeared in well-known anthologies. Archer has a BA in Communications and a Masters in Distance Education, which have been useful but never quite motivated her to work indoors on anything like a regular basis.

In her spare time, the author canoe-races competitively, paddling in events and on waterways all over the globe. A long-time resident of Saskatchewan, Archer currently lives in the Comox Valley on Vancouver Island, where she paddles all year round. She has been known to hike, but prefers to use gravity in her favour whenever possible.

Northern British Columbia Canoe Trips
   Volume One
by Laurel Archer
Price $29.95 (CAD)
ISBN 9781897522134
Format: paperback 6 x 9 inches
304 pages

This first volume of the guidebook series *Northern British Columbia Canoe Trips* describes in detail eight northern BC paddling routes over eleven rivers, and is designed to provide canoeists with all the information they require to plan a river trip appropriate to their skill level and special interests.

Each route includes:
- a summary of the main attractions of the trip
- where to start and where to finish along the river
- trip length in days and kilometres
- required maps
- suggestions about when to go
- star ratings for difficulty and for historical and recreational value

Northern British Columbia Canoe Trips: Volume One covers numerous routes never documented in any publication before, including the Taku, Jennings, Omineca and Gataga rivers, among others, as well as more well-known favourites such as the Fort Nelson and the Dease. The book provides paddlers of all types with a variety of river trips to choose from based on comprehensive and comparative information, as well as detailed and specific navigational notes to aid them along their chosen route.

FROM PAUL TO SAUL

JOEL MCNENNY

iUniverse®

FROM PAUL TO SAUL

iUniverse books may be ordered through booksellers or by contacting:

iUniverse
1663 Liberty Drive
Bloomington, IN 47403
www.iuniverse.com
1-800-Authors (1-800-288-4677)

ISBN: 978-1-5320-4079-5 (sc)
ISBN: 978-1-5320-4080-1 (hc)
ISBN: 978-1-5320-4078-8 (e)

Library of Congress Control Number: 2018901587

Print information available on the last page.

iUniverse rev. date: 02/28/2018

Dedication

This work is proudly and humbly dedicated to Jasmine Liên McNenny and Joshua Tri McNenny. I have experienced no greater joy than watching you two grow into the magnificently beautiful people you are. May you always dance in the miracle.

Acknowledgments

My list of people to thank is so extensive I am not going to attempt to name them all.

I'd like to thank all of my friends and family who volunteered to read the book in its various incarnations and offered their thoughts on how to make it better. To my parents, my STAG brothers, my dear friend Keith Stults, Sharon Burns, and with a special shout out to my brother, Jay, I can only humbly say "thank you." I listened to your opinions and advice and will always be grateful for it. Much respect to you all.

A sincere thanks to Cara Lockwood whose insights and expertise were always spot on and who made a good story so much better. "Thank you" is too small a concept for the ways I am indebted to you.

I'd also like to single out my dear children, Josh and Jasmine. Jasmine was always the first to read anything. Her awareness brought color to a black and white sketch and her loving patience encouraged me to continue. Josh lived with me through most of the writing process and had to put up with me when I was acting the irrational artist. Many thanks for their love and understanding.

Finally, I'd like to thank all of the non-fiction writers who have written on this subject. With great respect, I have attempted to take your warnings and put them into story form. I hope I have done your ideas justice.

Part I

Chapter One

"Joshua!"

Time was running out. The way up was perilous; he was under enemy fire and the jagged rock cliff was almost insurmountable. His only advantage? He had been there before, fifteen times before. He had learned from his mistakes. Now he knew exactly where the footholds were. He needed to stay far to the right where a crevice made it difficult for the Babylonians to get a bead on him. Most importantly, he had to keep moving.

"Joshua!" The voice came from far outside the battlefield.

He continued his climb, his men cheering him from below. Arrows crashed against the rocks. One pierced his left leg, sharply registering pain, but he continued scaling the cliff; his ascent was confident and sure.

"Joshua?" She was opening the door.

There was no getting around it. He hit the pause button and his Israelite avatar froze, precariously dangling by one hand.

He removed his VR helmet. "Yes, Mom?" Yet, he knew what it was about.

His father had mandated it at breakfast that morning. "Get out there. Meet some of the guys. You don't want to wait 'til church." There was the illusion of a consensus and now his mother was following through.

"Think you've been up here long enough? It's almost noon."

With more fanfare than he intended, Josh stood, stripped off his gaming headset and dropped it into a nearby chair.

"I'm sensing a mood here," his mother said. He stopped. "Sit down." She pointed to his couch. Josh looked at his mother. His whole life he had never thought of anyone more perfectly beautiful. Her dark, bold eyes appeared animated and her soft bronzed skin glowed from an inner light. In kindergarten, he had declared to the whole class, "My mommy's a real live angel." He wanted to crawl under his desk with embarrassment when the other kids laughed and the teacher corrected him. Yet, the thought never left him- she was an angel.

"Your father and I are aware of how hard all of this has been. We understand, we really do. But it's been a week. A week you've spent hiding... sorry, unpacking.... Look around, your room's perfect. A palace fit for David, but you can't stay up here forever."

"But, Mom, just walk down to the pool and introduce myself? I can't do that. Maybe Stephen or Dad could, but not me."

She sat silently for a moment. "You're right, and we're not asking you to be anything but who God made you to be. So, let's not look at this as you going to the pool and introducing yourself. Let's look at it as you 'taking a walk', and leaving it up to God."

She took his hand, and he felt the familiar tender warmth. How many times had this happened in his life? Surely hundreds more than he could remember. Her voice was gently soothing; her guidance resolute and loving. The scared boy in him wanted to reach out and rest his head on her chest, but the growing young man resisted.

"I'm going to let you in on a little secret. When your father first learned of his promotion, he wasn't too thrilled about it. He and I had been talking about him leaving DHS and going back to work at Grandpa's church. But the Apostles assured him this was God's plan. So, if this is where God's taken your father. We should rejoice in that. To love God with all our heart and soul means we need to *be strong and courageous. Do not be frightened, and do not be dismayed, for the LORD your God is with you wherever you go.*"

"Joshua 1:9."

His mother held her smile. "That's right... Joshua. God has a plan for all of us. I don't know what great things He has in store for you but I'm certain it doesn't include hiding in your room. *For we are his workmanship, created in Christ Jesus for good works, which God prepared beforehand, that we should walk in them.*"

"Ephesians 2... um... 10?"

"Triumphant, my smart young Joseph."

Moments later, dressed in his bathing shorts, a T-shirt honoring the *King David* gaming series, sandals, his beach towel draped across his neck, and smelling like sunblock, he opened the front door of what had been declared to be his new home. Immediately he was struck by the stifling overpowering force of the humid August heat. It must be a hundred degrees. He would get heat stroke before he even reached the pool!

He considered simply standing there for a while but he knew he was being watched.

The housing development his parents had chosen, the Gardens of Galilee, was one of the most prestigious in all of Columbus, Ohio. A village unto itself. From the air, it appeared as three concentric circles. At the center was the community pool, complete with lanes for the real swimmers and an array of slides and water toys for the children. The first annulus was an assortment of shops, coffee houses with outdoor patios, and, most popular, Wendal's Sports Bar and Grill. The annulus beyond, and with the greatest gap, held the houses, huge, auspicious Romanesque edifices with massive columns. The lawns were exquisitely manicured by a team of in-house landscapers. The development held hundreds of homes with room for hundreds more. Surrounding all of this was a state-of-the-art security fence monitored 24-hours a day by the community's own mini-police department. It was far more grandiose than his home in Canton; it was also coldly foreign.

Josh walked to the end of the driveway. His lot was toward the north, in one of the newly developing blocks. Walking due south all roads led to the community areas. He again envisioned himself walking past the rows of lounge chairs filled with mothers and children, all of them stopping in their conversations to watch the "new kid" walk by. He pictured what it would be like to walk up to the boys his own age and...and...what? "Hey, I'm the new kid. You guys wanna be friends?" His parents just didn't get it. It's not that easy. There were rules, and Josh was not at all confident he knew what all the rules were. But wait, what if he went to the right? To the right was a growth of trees. He could take a nice leisurely walk in the woods. No shops, no pool, and most importantly, no people.

Sounded like a plan.

As he approached, he recognized "woods" was a bit of an exaggeration. He was not at all sure what the proper name for the cluster of scraggily trees before him should be, but compared to the forests surrounding his old house, these were pathetic.

As he entered he instinctively slowed his pace. He found it difficult to see clearly. It was not the standing trees but the fallen ones and the numerous bushy thickets that gave the appearance of skeletal remains. He was struck by the smell of rotting leaves, a smell quite unique to Ohio in mid-August. The incessant humidity permeated the heavy layer of naturally composting leaves elevating a pungently sweet scent in the air. It was a comforting odor reminding him of family camping trips.

Snap!

Josh froze, his mind leaping to survival mode. There was something moving down the slope.

Snap!

Oh, please Lord, no! He crouched down. Whatever it was, he wanted to see it before it saw him. There it was again. Too far away to make out but it was bigger than a squirrel. A lot bigger. Josh planned his exit, back up the way he came… double time.

Snap!

That one came from his left. Was that something else? Now Josh felt terror. What was he doing there? He should be safely back in his air-conditioned house leading the Israelite army against the sinister Babylonians.

Down the hill, he could make out a person. He squinted trying to bring the image closer. It looked like it was a boy around his age. A kid? That was worse than an animal. Still the kid had not seen Josh. Should he begin moving back up the slope? If he did, it would create noise that might draw attention. On the other hand, if he didn't move at all, he was a sitting duck waiting to be discovered.

O LORD, be my helper! He prayed as he focused on the young boy surveying the slope. He decided as soon as the kid looked away he would start making his way back up the hill to freedom. And… if the kid saw him… he would mad dash it back to the house.

SMACK!

From out of nowhere, Josh felt the stinging sensation of a slap on his back and heard a victorious shout.

Josh rolled over to see a stocky kid standing over him like a successful hunter over a kill. When their eyes locked, the boy's smile vanished and his face drained of blood.

Josh leaped to his feet.

"Who the hell are you?" demanded the boy.

Josh, bristling at the profanity, could only mutter, "Um…um…."

The boy sized Josh up. He was a head shorter than Josh but bulkier. His cropped hair was a fiery red. He was dressed from head to toe in camouflage. The green and black face paint highlighted his steely green eyes. Josh decided the boy was shaped a bit like a jelly bean with appendages.

"Who's this?" the voice came from the first boy, who had made his way up the slope.

"Says his name is Um-um," the shorter boy said.

"Josh… actually."

"I'm Matthew," the second boy said, offering Josh a heart-bump. Matthew was several inches taller than Josh, thin, but his developing muscles were clearly defined. He wore an earth tone pair of shorts, a brown shirt, but no face paint. His dark skin provided a natural camouflage. His welcoming smile was in direct contradiction to the other boy's sternness. "He's Luke. We're playing *Capture the Flag*. You live in The Gardens?"

"Um… yeah, just moved in…. up there."

Luke turned and yelled, "Time out! Time OUT! We found… someone."

Josh prayed the leaves would roll into a tidal wave and sweep him away. Seconds later, like a herd routed, five more boys arrived from various directions. They were all dressed in forms of attempted camouflage yet no one was as decked out with the seriousness of Luke.

"What's up?" one of them asked.

"We found this… kid," said Luke.

"Who're you?" asked another.

"Josh." He suppressed a wave of agitation. "Look, I was just taking a walk…"

"Yeah, well, these're our woods," Luke coldly stated.

"That's enough, Luke." The voice came from above.

All heads turned upward. Josh looked closely and saw a shadow high in the trees. The shadow dropped down to a branch, revealing another young boy. Momentum carried him over to a sturdy limb on another tree where he gained speed with several long arcing swings. At his highest peak, he launched himself in the air, grabbing yet another branch, where he swung twice before letting go and sticking the landing like a gold medal winner.

To Josh, it was the most amazing display of gymnastic skills he had ever seen but no one else took notice.

As the boy rose to his full height, Josh was immediately mesmerized. Unlike the others in their camo, this boy was wearing nothing but a pair of dark shorts. Josh was struck by the muscular definition of the young man and was glad his own shirt hid his still boyish physique. The boy's mat of auburn hair was haphazardly curly, as if it had never felt a brush. The only thing covering the kid's feet were several layers of multicolored dirt. What struck

Josh the most, however, was the young man's face; it appeared to sparkle with electricity.

"Hey, I'm Peter," the boy said, extending a heart-bump to Josh.

"Josh."

"Yeah, I know. I was up there. Heard the whole thing." As he spoke, he shimmied up and sat on a nearby branch. "I heard you were moving in. My mom met your mom. I live down the street from you."

"You were up there the whole time?" Matthew asked.

"Solomon, oh…and by the way…." Peter pulled out a handkerchief from his back pocket widening his grin. "I believe we won!"

"What? Jesus Christ!" Luke cried.

"Ah, c'mon, joes," proclaimed Peter from his perch, "The name of the game is stealth. It's not that difficult. *I can do all things through Him who strengthens me.*"

"Shit, this time it wasn't fair. This guy interfered," declared Luke. The boys erupted into various expressions of opinion on the subject. Josh just wanted out of there…. five minutes ago! A second later, Luke stormed away. "I'm not playing anymore. Too damn hot anyway."

"Hedge, Luke," Peter said cheerfully. Then he turned to Josh. "I believe some introductions are in order. Let's see, you met Matthew already. And that's Jude, John, Phil, and the Miller brothers: Noah and Gideon." As each boy was introduced, he nodded and offered a heart bump.

"So, what do you say, joes, shall we go another round?" asked Peter.

"Luke left," said Noah.

"But we got Josh," said Peter.

Josh's brain ignited in panic, his mind searching for exit words. Before he could say anything, however, Luke, who had not walked away so far as he could not hear, turned around. "I'll play. I'm the only one who's got a chance against Pete anyway. Better chance than this scrawny…"

"Luke," Peter interrupted with a smile. "Glad you're back."

"Yeah, solomon," Josh said. "I gotta go anyway."

"Really?" Peter asked and Josh could tell Peter knew he was lying. "Next time?"

"Yeah, solomon….um…nice to meet all you, joes. Moving in and everything, you know. Hedge."

Josh walked as quickly as he dared without looking ridiculous and made a bee-line up the slope. He could vaguely hear the boys continue to discuss whether his involvement could be defined as interference.

Josh felt a familiar sense of panic like an evil slime monster crawling up his chest from his belly. His jaw clenched involuntarily as he galloped his way back to his yard.

He could not go home yet. It was way too early and, besides, he was not in any shape to go in smiling. Yet, there was no way he was going anywhere else. That was all the adventure he wanted for one day. He needed someplace to hide.

Josh noticed a sliver of shade to the left of his house. With great stealth, he made his way to where several small bushes withered in the heat. He stood between two of them with his back to the house and squatted down. If he stayed tight, he could not be seen.

For the first time since leaving the fiasco in the woods, Josh allowed himself to breathe.

What, in the name of righteousness, was that? Absolute complete babel! A guy takes a walk in the woods and comes across Peter Pan and the Lost Boys? The only one missing was Tinkerbell. And *Capture the Flag*? On a hot afternoon? Without it being a youth activity? Those guys were playing in the woods by themselves. Never in his fourteen years had Josh heard of such a thing. During the summer, if a normal kid was not at church camp or youth group, he would be at the pool or in the house gaming. What kind of guys get dressed up like soldiers and run around the woods by themselves… in this heat?

Luke looked like he could have killed Josh and never given it a second thought. And what was with all the profanity? Luke had used "hell" at least twice and Josh was sure Luke took the Lord's name in vain. Who does that? And the others said nothing. *As for those who persist in sin, rebuke them in the presence of all, so that the rest may stand in fear.* Were they even Christians? They had to be, of course, but they were unlike any Christians Josh had ever met. Christians back home did not talk like that. *Set a guard, O Lord, over my mouth; keep watch over the door of my lips!*

Then there was the craziest thing of all. Peter! How was that move out of the trees even possible? And all the other witnesses watching like it was no big deal!

Well, it wasn't human.

The panic-inspired slime monster had returned to sleep and Josh felt his breath normalize. This, however, simply opened the pipes. He took one quick glance to be sure he was alone and then allowed the tears to flow freely.

"None of this was fair!" his head shouted in defiance.

His life had been fine, close to perfect. He had his two best friends, Jesse and Jared. He had been surrounded by his cousins, none of whom would ever be running around the woods half-dressed. They were all just normal kids who went to church and school. Then came that fateful day when his father announced his promotion and Josh's whole life collapsed.

Josh punched his fist into his hand. It felt good. He punched his thigh. That felt better. He punched it again. Then again. He felt awash in a wave of guilty pain.

Josh stayed in his fetal position until the shadows grew long. Somewhere in there, he dozed off. He was startled awake by one of the landscapers trimming the bush at the end of the house. The man showed no sign of noticing him. Josh slid his back up the wall and then, with as much dignity as he could muster, he walked from his hiding place. His stiff muscles screamed in protest even as he felt unbalanced from a rush of blood to his head.

He slipped into the house and up to his room.

"Hey, honey, how did it go?" his mother called. "You were gone a long time. Did you have fun?"

"Oh, sure, fine. I'm gonna take a shower. I'll tell you about it at dinner."

Later, after grace, he told his story. "On my way to the pool I decided to poke my head into those scrawny woods down there. I was walking around when I found a bunch of joes playing *Capture the Flag*. They all stopped… and… I met them. Most of them were littler kids."

"Younger," his mother corrected.

"Younger. I don't remember most of their names. Three of the guys were my age. Matthew's tall though so he might be older. He was solomon. There was this other guy, Luke. I didn't like him; he seemed really mad."

"Do not judge by appearances, but judge with right judgment," said his father.

"Yes, sir, thank you. Then there was this other guy, Peter, he-"

"Oh, yes, I met his mother."

"Yes, he told me. You should've seen it. He jumped out of a tree like-"

"You never made it to the pool?" asked his dad.

"No, the joes were playing in the woods."

"Capture the Flag? I remember that game. We used to play that at YF." His father smiled.

"They still do… sometimes," said Josh.

With that, the conversation surprisingly moved on.

Josh went to his room after dinner. His parents were convinced he had done what they wanted him to. He knew this was a bit of a deception but he trusted God would understand. His parents sure didn't.

He spent the evening playing online with Jared and Jesse and soon he felt right there with them again. By the time he went to bed, the afternoon nightmare was a distant memory.

Chapter Two

Tonight was it. From the moment, her father entered the house, shuffled by everyone without responding to their greetings and made straight for his man-cave, she knew the curtain was up and it was time to implement The Plan.

She was awash in a wave of fear but she could hear Coach Jude's voice in her head, "Don't ignore the fear. Don't feed it either. Just allow it to flow and dissipate naturally."

Her father stayed downstairs but his presence remained. Her mother busied herself, to the point of obsession, preparing the evening table. Her brother, Benjamin, covered in his VR headset, was lost in a distant adventure. Maggie could do nothing more than sit and wait.

Tonight was it, she again resolved. This would be the last night they would play out their macabre theater. It was time to start being the family they pretended to be, the family everyone thought they were, the family God wanted them to be.

Eventually, her mother called Benjamin and Maggie to the table and walked to the top of the basement stairs. "Micah? Micah? Dinner's ready."

There was no response. Her mother hesitated before returning to the kitchen. Maggie and Benjamin silently waited. It was obvious her mother had run out of things to do but she kept herself busy rather than sit.

After several long agonizing moments, he could be heard on the basement stairs. Seconds later, waving his scotch glass in the air and wearing a resplendent smile, he arrived. When she was a child she used to laugh and cheer at his grand entrances; now, at thirteen, she barely looked at him.

Inevitably, before her father would sit, he would find something to complain about to her mother. This night it was a supposed blemish on his fork. Her mother hurriedly retrieved another one. They said their formal grace in robotic unison. Upon the "Amen" they could serve themselves. There was no conversation unless it originated from Daddy. "How was camp today, Benjamin?"

"Good, Daddy."

A long pause.

"Well, did anything happen?"

"No, not really."

"Is that so? You'll take your bath right after dinner. And hurry, because your sister needs to take one after you."

"I took a shower after practice this morning." It was the first words she had spoken since he came home.

"And you'll take a bath tonight."

Maggie stared down at her food. It looked disgusting.

Daddy did not ask her about her day, or her mother's, instead he went into a long rabbling story about lunch with three of the elders and how the waiter had spilled pasta sauce all over Chuck's new suit. Maggie half-listened. His banter and stories were nothing more than an over-rehearsed improvisation.

When he had run out of material, there was silence in the room as each of them focused on their food, waiting for the next cue.

Her father took several long gulps of his drink. "Okay, Benjamin, you're finished. Upstairs and get your bath."

The blood drained from Benjamin's face. "But… dessert?"

Daddy's face rolled into a contorted look of disgust. "Dessert? Dessert's a reward for a good day. Since nothing happened to you today, there's no reason to celebrate. Now get upstairs."

Tears welled up in Benjamin's eyes. He sat helpless, knowing crying would only solidify Daddy's edict. In stepped Mother. "Micah," she said in her most soothing voice, "I told Benjamin we had a special dessert tonight. His favorite, baked banana splits."

Her father slammed his hand on the table causing all the dishes and plates to jump. His face turned ferocious. "What in the world are we having banana splits tonight for? Those are for birthdays and…" His thoughts swam upstream. "and… stuff."

"I know, but it's been a nice summer. School starts next week, I thought…"

"Well, that's your first mistake." But he was the only one who laughed at his joke.

"How about this?" her mother asked meekly. "If Benjamin promises to be careful, he could eat the dessert after his bath."

There was a long pause. Her parents stared at each other. Her mother looked away first, head bowed. "Fine," said Daddy, "after the bath then. I don't want to see one tiny speck of dirt on you, young man. Not one, and next time I see you hiding behind your mother's skirt, I'm gonna.... *act like a man, be strong*, saith the Lord. Do you hear me?"

At that moment, Benjamin would have agreed to selling his right arm. "Yes, sir."

"Now get upstairs. Spoiled lil' moby." As Benjamin whizzed by his chair, Daddy swung for his butt but missed.

While her mother brought the dishes into the kitchen, Daddy declared his need to "baptize" his drink.

Maggie sat alone at the table. So far things were typical. Part of her wanted to fast-forward through all this preliminary stuff. The other part of her hoped something would happen to throw the whole night off whack and she could cancel The Plan altogether.

Eventually, Daddy half-stumbled back up the stairs and managed to find his way to his chair. He reached out to tousle her hair but ended up missing and wiping her face with his sweaty hand. He sniggered as if it was the funniest joke he had heard all day.

Her mother came into the room carrying the tray of desserts. Benjamin, now in his pajamas and smelling of soap, came bounding downstairs. For the next few minutes, the spotlight was on him. He gleefully gobbled his ice cream while Daddy made a few comments about his lack of table manners and his apparent destiny of forever being a moby. When he was finished, Benjamin kissed his parents and flew up the stairs.

"How long are you gonna baby that boy?"

No response.

"Woman, I'm talking to you."

"He's only ten," her mother answered.

"And in Moses' day he would already be in military training. You're spoiling him."

A heavy silence hung in the room. Maggie stared at her dessert. Even as it melted, it looked plastic.

"And how many times do I need to tell you? Never, ever, contradict me in front of my children! *Be subject to your husband!*" SLAM! Her father's hand smacked the table again. He turned to Maggie with a contorted grimace. "Get upstairs. Take your bath."

Upstairs, she shut the bathroom door, turned on the water, but never got in the tub. She kept the water running as much to drown out the screaming as it was to create the illusion of a bath. She stared into the mirror. The image in front of her was murky, but only partly due to the steam. In one way, she recognized herself- her hair, her nose, her eyes. And yet the image kept wavering, like ripples in a pond, morphing from one persona to another. In one, she appeared years younger, an innocent terrified little girl; the next instant her face was older, stern and confident, like a warrior's. As she waited, she became transfixed by the transformations dancing in front of her. With a deep determined breath, she imagined the warrior, shield and sword at the ready, standing over in defense of the frightened child cowering within her.

Several months ago, she attempted to talk to her mother, but it was like swimming upstream against a powerful current. She could feel the fear emanating from her mother. A deep uncontrollable fear. Her mother quickly killed the conversation with *"Let no corrupting talk come out of your mouths, but only such as is good for building up."* One night, impulsively, Maggie told her babysitter, Rebecca. Rebecca said she would do something, but she never did. As a matter of fact, she never came back to babysit again. It was then Maggie realized she would have to solve the problem by herself. That's when she came up with The Plan.

It came to her from a television show, *Meet the Connells*, a popular sitcom about the everyday trials of a typical family in Christian America. In this particular episode, the little boy had to go to the bathroom but he had tied the drawstring on his sweat pants so tightly he could not get them undone. There he was, dancing around trying not to pee his pants, while his mother was frantically untying the knots, screaming at him to "Stand still!" The audience roared. As he watched, Benjamin rolled on the ground holding his gut; her parents found it hilarious, as well. Maggie, on the other hand, was not so much focused on the humor but on the idea... her grandmother had given her a pair of drawstring sweat pants for Christmas...

"Fine, flee to your mother, fucking Jezebel!"

Maggie was yanked into the present by her father's booming voice. The fight was over so much sooner than she had anticipated. Frantically, she turned off the water, and dashed back to her room.

She tore off her clothes and slipped into the drawstring pants. She lay down on her bed and sucked in her stomach to a painful level. She pulled the drawstring as tightly as she could and then tied it off. With trembling fingers, she double-knotted it.

What was that? Was he on his way up?

"Come on!" her mind screamed at her fingers. "Tie! For God's sake!"

Like admonished children, her fingers began to work faster. She pulled each knot tightly. When she had tied the final one, she slipped her nightgown on and climbed into the sheets. As she waited, she listened to the sound of her heart reverberating from one end of her comforter cocoon to the other.

She could hear him on the stairs. Then his shadow passed along the bottom edge of her door as he shuffled by to check on Benjamin. Seconds later, the heavy shadow was back.

"This isn't gonna work!" her mind argued. "Just bail out before it's too late."

He rapped on the door gently as he pushed it open. "You asleep?"

She said nothing.

"Rough day. Office…money… and then…. your mother… Mind if I climb in?" But he did not wait for an answer. At one time, she had been comforted by the presence of his big warm body. Now it just seemed slimy and gross. His breath reeked.

He slipped his arm under her so that she was forced to have her head on his chest.

"Daddy?"

"Yes, dear," he said as he rubbed her shoulder.

"Can we talk?" It was as if her voice was coming from somewhere else. Outside of her body.

"Of course."

She tried her best to control the quiver. "I love you, but… I'm not gonna let you do this anymore." There, she said it. The warrior inside her was standing firm.

There was no reply. She felt his hand go down her leg, pulling up her night gown as it went. When his hand came to her sweat pants, it hesitated for a second before continuing upward. She felt his fingers reach beneath the drawstring, then retreat and go to the mound of knots.

"Daddy, did you hear me?"

The only response came in the form of a distracted grunt. He pulled back the comforter exposing the extent of the problem and let forth a gasp. He began working the knots but quickly had to fall to his knees by the bed. Propped up by his elbows, he tried using both hands.

"Daddy, listen to me."

But he wasn't. He was completely consumed by the obstacle. "What the hell?"

He got off the bed and turned on the overhead light. The brightness shocked her senses and warped his face into that of a demonic ghoul.

He leaned over and grabbed her by her waist, pulling her to him.

He made it through five knots, but there was a dozen more. With the earlier knots she had more string to hold on to and pull tight, making each preceding knot harder and harder to untie. Her father's frustration was reaching frightening levels as he grasped and clawed at the blockade in front of him.

Two more knots and he threw it down in disgust.

Maggie tried again. "Daddy, please, please, you're hurting me…"

He tried different angles. Ironically, Maggie was reminded of how on the sitcom this was the part where the audience laughed the loudest when the mother was frantically trying to untie the knots. Yet there was not the slightest amount of humor now. Her father was furious and she was paralyzed with fear.

The knots were almost impossible at this point. "Who the fuck would do such a thing?" he screamed.

What had she been thinking? Tie herself up in a pair of sweat pants and reason with him? It seemed like such an insane plan now. It seemed so…so… childish.

Enough! shouted the warrior within her. She didn't need a plan. She didn't need a gimmick. She just needed to put an end to this babel!

She stood up and made for the door. The warrior was leaving.

She was suddenly grabbed from behind by his heavy arms. He grunted as he held her against his hip as easily as he would a toddler. He walked over to the desk and rummaged through the top drawer. "Ah ha," he cried in triumph.

"Dad, stop it, you're hurting me."

He made no response but threw her on the bed. He grabbed her by her sweat pants. In his hand was a pair of scissors. They were her first-grade scissors, the kind with the blunted top and so dull they barely cut construction paper. But it was obvious what he intended.

"Dad! Stop it. STOP IT!" She yelled at him as if scolding a small child. He paused for a moment and she felt a twinge of hope she had reached him. But then he bent back over his work.

His hands were slimy and sweaty, his breath atrocious and his mind transfixed by the task at hand. In his eyes, she was not his daughter anymore; she was just a piece of meat wrapped in a package he was having a hard time opening.

In disgust, she kicked at him and missed. She shifted and kicked again. This time she made contact to his cheek. His response was to become even more violent. He grabbed the drawstring and thrust the scissors, driving them into her stomach. They were too dull to puncture her skin but the pain felt like they had. He began sawing at the string.

"Stop it! Get off me!" she screamed.

She continued to try and break through but to no avail. He had turned off his senses and was completely, though drunkenly, focused on the progress the little overworked scissors were making.

Finally, the string broke. Maggie immediately felt a physical relief that the drawstring was no longer cutting into her hip but also realized the situation had been raised to a whole other level.

He had always been drunk but had never acted like this. He had been kind and loving. Afterwards, he would talk to her about how much he loved her and how important it was to keep "the secret" or she would be taken away from him and Mommy and Benjamin and placed in some horrible house where they tortured children. She had always seen him as an important man and with that there was a great deal of pressure on him. He told her there was so much at stake, not only for the family but for the Final Great Awakening. He needed her and loved her. That is what she believed. Even after she had realized what they were doing was wrong, a sin, she felt that he loved her. It was a love that had gotten off the Godly path but it was still love.

Now as he stood victoriously over her, she could see the awful truth. He wasn't a good man overtaken by evil, he was evil that knew how to put on a Sunday morning smile.

Well, it was time to wipe that smile off. She pulled her feet to her chest, and with a thrust that had been coiled her whole life, she kicked him.

She was shocked how easily Daddy flew backward. He staggered, arms wheeling, and smashed into her dresser, causing her trophies to tumble over. One of them landed squarely on his forehead, creating a gash above his eye. He stared bewilderedly at the blood.

She felt separated from her body. As if her mind had left her head completely and was just floating above her. She could see herself but could no longer feel. It was more than mere numbness, it was a complete separation of mind and body. She found it fascinating and then she found it fascinating that she found it fascinating.

She grabbed an old stick. It was her prop for when she played a shepherd in a Christmas play. She had kept it because she liked the way the wood shone. She held it over him. They locked eyes.

He held his arms up to ward off the blow and begged. "Wait, please… I'm… I'm… bleeding."

Maggie hesitated. This was her great big scary Daddy. The one they were all terrified of. He was a child, nothing but a fucking whining selfish child.

She should kill him. But she couldn't. She grabbed him by his shirt and did the best she could to help him to his feet. He let her guide him out of her room. In the hallway he slurred, "Goodnight." And stumbled away.

She sat on the edge of her bed. She felt for the first time in her life she was seeing clearly and she was done. This was never going to stop. He'd sleep it off tonight, but he'd be back. How could she even face him the next morning? She knew what to expect from him. A practiced smile, a warm morning greeting, and an attitude that nothing had changed.

But something had changed.

She had discovered the warrior within her.

She found her backpack in her closet and loaded it with a few changes of clothes. She packed her bathroom supplies in the side pocket. She changed into a pair of pants and even though it was too hot, an oversized hoodie. She quietly slipped into Benjamin's room and kissed him on the forehead. "I love you," she whispered.

She went to her parents' bedroom. The door was wide open and her father was draped across his bed the way he had fallen. He was making a disgusting gargling snoring sound. His blood seeped into her mother's favorite bedspread. She did not worry about waking him. She found his wallet on his dresser. That was all she came for.

Her last stop, before leaving, was in her father's study where she spiked a handwritten note through the gymnastic trophy that had slit open his head. The note read simply: "If you follow me, I will tell. Don't doubt it."

Chapter Three

Josh awoke the morning after his encounter with the boys to an unusual sight: his father's smiling face. It was not at all uncommon to have his father wake him up as his father was a big one for "rising and shining." What was unusual was the smile. Then it came to him why his father was showing that side of himself. Josh rolled over and groaned. "No, I thought we were gonna do this later in the week."

"This is a better day for me. Now rise, shine and give God the glory. Tour begins in half an hour."

The tour was his lesson on the Columbus transit system known as the ET. His father thought it was important that he personally take Josh and his mother to allow them to get acclimated. His father explained that this was how everyone got around in the big city. "There are no school buses for high school. You have to get there by yourself." His father showed him the map one night and it looked like a clutter of spiders with crooked legs scattered in all directions. Josh thought a lesson might be a good idea.

But that was not why his father was grinning.

His father was normally a reserved man. Around his extended family he was the "quiet uncle" who rarely contributed to the conversation- with one notable exception. Every year, from long before Josh was born, the whole family would get together for a vacation. Most often it had something to do with water, either condos on the beach or cottages on a lake. Uncle Tim, the guy who rarely said anything, would step forward and insist the family make a stop, or three, at the historical sites. Once there, he would lead the family in a well-researched tour filled with intricate details. Those family tours were his father's pride and joy.

It was obvious his father was in his "tour director" mode. It was bad enough they had to learn how to get around a new city. Now they were going to look like tourists doing it. After the previous day's chaos, this was complete babel. Josh knew, however, there was no point in even attempting to argue or delay; when his dad made up his mind to do something, he got the job done.

Half an hour later, he rode with his parents in an SV to the small ET station just inside The Gardens of Galilee security fence.

His father's recitation did not even wait for the car. "Since the Final Great Awakening began, Columbus has more than quadrupled but it's a different kind of city thanks to the Apostles' foresight. Take the ET, for instance. When the technology for these elevated trains was developed, a lot of cities just treated it like a glorified subway but the Apostles in Columbus had a different vision. They saw how the city's priorities were changing. It was no longer sufficient to take people from one station to another like the old COTA system did. It was more important to bring people where they needed to go and that's just what the ET gave them. Now everyone's connected to the locations they most need; that's why the map looks so complicated. In the old days, there would be one color for one line but now we have one color with four tiers. We'll travel on the fourth tier…"

"I don't get it, if all the tiers go to the same places…" his mother said.

"But they don't, see?" his father said, patiently pointing to the map. "Sure, all the tiers can take you downtown, and to the train stations and airports, and places like that but the stations on a tier are linked to where a person is mostly needing to go. For instance, if a guy works security or something, he's probably on tier two. Tier two links to his neighborhood, his work, his church, and the most likely shopping centers. We're on tier four. There are a lot of ministers and government officials in The Gardens of Galilee so our tier is linked to the government buildings, the influential churches, and other places we need to go. We're blessed because there aren't nearly as many people on tier four as there are on the other ones."

When the train arrived with a slickness of perfectly engineered technology, Josh followed his parents aboard. He had envisioned it would be a glorified subway filled with numb morning passengers on their way to work, the kind he had seen in movies. What he walked into felt more like a lounge in a five-star hotel. On the walls hung monitors providing the Good News for the day. Instead of rows of benches and poles, there were slick leisure chairs arranged casually around coffee tables. In the back were several refreshment machines serving a variety of coffees and other drinks. All that was a bit shocking but what most threw him was the attitude of the other passengers. Each of them waved and said "Good morning" in some form or another as his father led them to an empty set of seats. It was like walking into church; all that was missing was an usher.

His dad made an announcement that he was showing his family around their new home. Josh scolded his dad for embarrassing him in front of total strangers. But his father said, "They aren't strangers. They're our neighbors: this is our community."

As the train zipped off in a burst of speed seemingly defying the physics of inertia, Josh stared out the window, hoping no one would try and talk to him. His dad could be as excited as he wanted, but these were not Josh's neighbors and this was not Josh's community. As the train carried them high above the city, Josh observed the massive urban sprawl below him. At first it was ovals after ovals of housing developments behind security walls. The borders, however, quickly grew indefinable as the metropolis grew tighter. The largest buildings were the stadium-like structures that served as the sanctuaries for the churches dotted about. Josh was surprised many of them seemed as big as his grandfather's church. He was willing to bet however, they were not nearly as nice.

Suddenly, the train stopped at a busy terminal. The thing sure was smooth. Josh had to give it that. A large gold banner draped across the station front read: *All who believed were together and had all things in common; Acts 2:44.* Below the words was the logo for CATS, the Christian American Transportation System.

"Believe it or not, you can travel to anywhere in the country right from this spot. Isn't that amazing?" asked his dad.

Amazing, can it take me home?

As the train left the station, his father moved closer to him. Uh-oh, could it be he had sulked too hard?

"Look, son, I know how difficult this is for you. I do. Canton's my home, too. I grew up there, lived there most of my life, and I'm a tad bit older than you." His dad paused hoping for a smile, Josh obliged him... a little. "But look out there, that's Columbus, Ohio... A righteous city. *For he was looking forward to the city that has foundations, whose designer and builder is God.* Joshua, Columbus offers so many more opportunities. Columbus is where Apostles live and we'll be living among them. We're going to be members of the American Harvest Church. Do you have any idea how famous that church is? The place is miraculous! Wait until you see it."

"It's solomon, Dad. God's Will be done."

"No, Josh, it's more than that. You should be excited. This'll be a great place to live and every year we'll invite your cousins and friends and host an OSU/Michigan party, just like we promised. It's going to be... triumphant." His father nervously chuckled.

It was one of those awkward moments that was all the more unbearable since Stephen had gone away to school. Josh decided to let his father off the hook. "Place sure is big."

"It is, but it's really easy once you figure it out. You know, Columbus was once considered a liberal city. There were whole areas where there was nothing but libs. But, after the FGA, the city not only came back, its thriving! I mean, don't get me wrong, there're still some dangerous places and I don't see any reason you need to ride on any tier lower than four." He stopped to be sure Josh understood that was an order and then continued. "But for the most part, it's a safe and blessed place to live. Take High Street for instance."

"High Street?"

"Yeah, at one time nothing but bars and drunks all over the place. Well, today, as the saying goes, 'the party remained when the sin was disdained.' The whole area's been renovated as a symbol of God's grace; there's still taverns but now you can get a decent meal. There're theaters, concerts, museums, all kinds of unique shops. Old-fashioned street trollies take you around. Every corner has something going on, street musicians, comedians, dancers and at night... especially, on a Saturday after a Buckeyes win, the place goes berserk. We should go sometime."

"Yeah... yes... sounds fun." But it didn't and he wondered if such statements qualified as lies.

Soon they arrived downtown and exited the ET.

Josh felt dwarfed by all the skyscrapers around him. As his father led them into a nearby building, they had to pass under a humongous hanging that read: *Let every person be subject to the governing authorities. For there is no authority except from God, and those that exist have been instituted by God. Romans 13:1.*

His dad led them away from the main pedestrian traffic and over to one side where a single guard stood. When the guard saw them coming he stood to attention. Josh's dad greeted the officer and introduced him as Christopher.

Officer Christopher led them to a private elevator where they were shot to the thirtieth floor. The elevator opened to an elaborate office where a young pretty woman was seated at a desk. His father introduced her as his secretary. She smiled sweetly as she shook Josh's hand. Once through the secretary's office, his father led them into his own office. This was the rest of the floor winding all the way around in a loop made entirely of windows. By doing so, Josh's father's office offered a panoramic breathtakingly fabulous view of the massive city.

"This is your office?" Despite his sour mood, he could not help but be impressed.

"Miraculous!" his father said, trying unsuccessfully not to sound like a giddy kid.

"You can see everything." Josh looked over to see his parents holding hands. They so wanted him to be happy, and here he was, disappointing them again. He forced himself into a better mood. "It's great, Dad, really."

"Wait until November 11th. There isn't a better location to watch the 'Red, White and Boom' fireworks display than right here. And over there, that's the 'Shoe,' where the Buckeyes play. That's **the** Ohio State University. Maybe someday your school."

"I heard that's pretty tough to get into."

"Hey, you're just starting high school; if you buckle down… show God you're ready. *I can do all things through Him who strengthens me.* Speaking of school, look way off to your left there. See that growth of trees on the hill. Just on the other side of that hill is Alum Creek Dam and the American Harvest Church. Do you know the American Harvest School is almost as famous as the church? The Youth Director, Mrs. Marone, started a high school program. It's called Josephs of Tomorrow.…"

"Dad, we talked about this. My scores aren't high enough."

"Well, I spoke with Mrs. Marone and set up a meeting for you and your mother next Friday."

"Dad!" He shot a glance at his mother who shrugged unknowingly. He snapped his attention back to his father. "What're you doing?"

"Mrs. Marone assured me they prayerfully consider each applicant."

"But I don't… it'll be too hard!"

"Nonsense. What have we been talking about? Hard work is righteous work."

"I know but…"

"Honey," his mother interrupted, "it doesn't hurt to talk to the woman. We'll find out about the program and make a prayerful decision from there. Okay?"

No, not okay at all. He did not know much about the program, but he knew enough. This was the kind of program Stephen could get into; in fact, it was the kind of program his cousins would thrive in, but not Josh, the unspoken disappointment that he was.

Josh spent the rest of the tour in a funk. Why did his parents do this to him? Couldn't they just accept the fact he was not Stephen and never was going to be?

After the tour, they lunched at an outdoor café. From there his mother and Josh took the ET home by themselves as his father went back to work.

In the afternoon he played games online with his friends in Canton. They asked him how things were going. "Miserable." They offered him some useless encouragement which simply irritated him. "Can we just play?"

The only good news he received that day was his father's announcement at dinner. "Your mother and I were talking. If you show us you know how to handle the ET then maybe, and right now that's a firm 'maybe,' you can take a train up to Canton some weekends... by yourself."

"Really? That'd be solomon."

That night he lay in bed. Maybe this was not going to be as bad as he thought. Once he finished disappointing his father by not getting accepted into the Josephs for Tomorrow program, he'd go to a normal high school. He could still communicate with his friends during on-line gaming. Heck, that's what they did most of the time anyway. Then if he could go up and stay with them on the weekends, maybe even the summers, it would almost be like he was still there.

One thing he was sure of, he didn't need any new friends... especially not the weird kids in Columbus.

Chapter Four

"Good Morning! And welcome to your Good News for today. President Apostle Wilson has declared today a day of blessings and anointings. These are your top stories. In Pakistan, a jihadist terrorist attack was thwarted by our glorious Christian American troops. Some three hundred terrorists were killed. By an Act of God, there were no American casualties.

"Reverend Zacharias Robertson continues his blessed ministry in the African country of Uganda. Despite the dangers and threats posed by radical atheists and jihadists, Reverend Robertson held another crusade where it was reported over a thousand people were healed and nearly thirty thousand led to the Lord.

"But first, when we come back, we'll offer you the Good News of the stirrings of a real spiritual awakening in Russia…"

Josh kicked himself for not turning off his alarm system. He tried to go back to sleep but to no avail.

So, he lay in bed planning his day which was going to be a good one. After all, he had fulfilled his sonly duties yesterday. In another hour, he may crawl out of bed. Then it was on to video games, which he would play until lunch. After a quick meal, it would be back to gaming for the rest of the afternoon, followed by a family dinner, and on to gaming until he fell asleep. He was unsure how much time Jesse and Jared had but he knew they would join him as much as they could. It seemed like the perfect summer day and there were only a few of them left.

The thought caused his mind to drift to the thing that was terrifying him the most: church. Never in his life had he walked in anywhere that people did not know him. At times he hated that, but now he realized how comforting it was. In a few days, he was going to go to his new church. A multitude of faces looking at him, thinking whatever thoughts they were having. They didn't know him, and, for the first time in his life, being a Conrad was not going to help.

He felt the familiar lump rising in his throat and the wave of near nausea rolling over in his gut. He did not want to do any of this. He just wanted to go home.

There was only one solution to his wandering, suffering mind. He pushed back the covers on his bed and dropped out of his loft to his deluxe gaming chair. Whatever he had to face he would face later; for now, it was time to lead the Israelites to victory.

Just as he slipped on his VR helmet, there was a knock on his door.

Oh, no.

"Honey, you awake?"

"Yes, Mom."

"You have a visitor," she said, as she opened his door.

It took a moment for the sentence to register. Then, "Wait...what?"

"Peter's downstairs. One of the boys you met the other day?"

Josh's mind was still unable to grasp the situation.

"Should I send him up?"

"Um...no.... Mom?" He looked at her pleadingly. The voice in his head was screaming out excuses. *Tell him I'm asleep. Taking a shower. Sick. Yeah, sick as a dog.* He knew she would never go for any of that. Josh resisted the urge to drop to his knees and beg. His mother said she would let Peter know he would be right down.

A million angry thoughts churned through his mind as he hopped up, threw his pajamas into the laundry chute and slipped on a pair of shorts and a T-shirt. Why was this happening? Had he done something wrong?

He flipped up his sheets in what would have to pass as a made bed and headed downstairs.

As he entered the kitchen, he encountered Peter and his mother sitting at the kitchen table. They were conversing and drinking.... tea?

"There he is," his mother announced.

"Hey, Josh," Peter said with his big goofy grin. Peter was dressed in what looked like the same ragged shorts he had on the other day. He did have a faded T-shirt on but his hair was not yet combed and amazingly there were still no shoes on his feet.

"Hey," said Josh.

There was an awkward silence as his mother seemed reluctant to give up her conversation. "Peter and I were talking. We thought the two of you could hang out today. Maybe go down to the pool."

What is this? Now his day was being planned by Tarzan here?

"We don't have to," Peter said. "I just stopped over to welcome you officially. You didn't stay long the other day."

Josh could see the look of puzzlement on his mother's face. Time to get this guy out of the kitchen. Josh went with the only thought that came to mind. "You want to see my room?"

"Sure," Peter said. He turned to Josh's mother. "Thank you, Mrs. Conrad. Thanks for the tea and conversation."

His mother giggled. She actually giggled like a little girl. What was it about this guy?

"C'mon," Josh ordered. Peter did not take notice of his tone but his mother did.

When Peter entered the room, he was duly impressed. "Nice. Huge. My room's about half this size."

Josh let Peter soak it in. If there was anything positive at all about the move, it was his room. It was three times the size of his old room with a fully stocked kitchenette and his own bathroom containing a sunken spa tub. His bed was a walk-up loft providing ample living space. His closets were concealed as walls but would instantly slide open when the weight sensors were triggered. On the walls, Josh had meticulously placed his 3D posters. There were several praising his favorite movies. Other posters proudly displayed his loyalty to the *King David* gaming series and one to his favorite band, The Foundation. Josh had spent hours sweating over every detail. What he was particularly proud of was his state of the art VR deluxe gaming system set up prominently in the middle of the room around a series of large couches and gaming chairs. Peter, however, looked right past it.

Might as well get it over with. "You a gamer?" Josh asked.

"I play a little. I like being outside better."

Josh did not know how to respond.

There was an awkward silence. "I'm sorry for coming over like this, if you want me to go, I'll…"

"Oh, no." Josh knew his mother would kill him if Peter left too quickly. "It's solomon."

There was another pause.

"Moving must be a lot of work," said Peter.

"Yeah, did you ever have to?"

"Nope. Grew up my whole life right here in The Gardens. Hey, you want to meet someone?"

"Who?"

"You'll see. He's in the woods. Solomon?"

The idea sounded horrendous to Josh but the next thing he knew he was following Peter out of the house. He tried to keep up with him but Peter did not really walk. He more hopped, skipped, jumped, and returned. Josh felt as if he was training a puppy to walk on a leash.

Boy, this kid's babel.

Josh's shirt was soaked with sweat before they reached the edge of the woods.

"C'mon!" Peter called as he increased his pace.

Dutifully, Josh followed him but he was not going to run. This was babel. Nobody lived down there.

Josh noticed there was a well-worn path leading down the slope and off to the left, but he also noticed Peter was not taking it. He seemed to prefer finding his own way through the bramble and trees.

Josh, then, saw it: something massive. As he approached, he saw it was a tree. The most enormous tree he had ever seen. It looked completely out of place in the scrawny woods, but there it was having taken root hundreds of years ago. Josh assessed the diameter must have been at least six feet. It rose out of the ground for a good fifteen feet and then its six main branches separated. Each of those massive limbs was a tree in its own right as it zig-zagged its way upward separating into a kaleidoscope of twigs and leaves.

"Wow!" Josh gasped involuntarily.

"Meet Elmer," Peter declared like a circus announcer.

"Elmer?"

"Yeah, been a kids' fort for years!" Peter was on the move again, rushing to the base of the tree. "Over here." Peter stepped into a nearby bush and emerged with the end of a thick rope.

Oh, no. They were going to climb up there? Using a rope?

"Come on, it's really not as hard as it looks."

Josh followed instructions and, gratefully, found it to be rather simple. Once on top he could only marvel. From one end to the other, in not always straight, but, obviously, solid rows, a hodgepodge of planks of wood were nailed down to create a solid floor. There were no walls or ceiling, but there were occasional boards nailed throughout that were either intended to block the sun or be steps to the higher branches. Whatever they were for, they were amazing. Josh stood in awe, marveling most at the fact that the boards were in various states of deterioration, which indicated multiple additions from numerous generations of neighborhood kids that had used this very site for a fort. Triumphant.

"Check this out," Peter said as he walked over to one side. There he grasped a pole that was connected to another pole that had a blue plastic tarp attached to it. "If it rains when we camp out, we pull this across."

"You camp out here?"

"Yeah, all the time. Mostly Matthew, Luke, and me. You should join us. You camp?"

"Major. A few times a year the whole family goes someplace. Niagara Falls, Upper Peninsula, or sometimes just to Mohican State Park."

"Hey, yeah, I've been there. My YF goes there."

"Mine does... did... too."

There was a silence where Josh became aware of a slight cool breeze trying to bring relief.

Peter said, "I tell you, this has been my spot since I was just a little kid. My mom's big on the 'boys should be playing outside' thing, you know."

Josh did not but nodded.

"Luke and I grew up together. Matthew came when I was about nine and now you." Peter smiled broadly, offering a heart-bump. "Welcome."

"Thanks."

"You're gonna love living here. Columbus is a righteous city. Mom said your family's going to American Harvest. That's where I go. Greatest church in the world and that's not a biased opinion. You going to school there, too?"

"Yeah."

"You're gonna love it. It's a righteous school, best in the..." Peter stopped and smiled. "This spokesman is not a paid actor... Sorry, but it really is a great place. I've been going there all my life. It's totally triumphant, an anointed church during the Final Great Awakening. The whole place is bathed in the Spirit. Wait until you see all the pictures and plaques in the entrance. You'll like the guys, too. I know Luke can come across a little tough but he's solomon. His dad's... rough on him. He's ex-military, one of the elders of the church. My dad was never in the military, went straight to college. I think it'd be solomon, going overseas, helping with Jehovah's Revolution, doing some good. Your mom said you've got a brother at West Point?"

Josh nodded.

Peter whistled appreciatively. "I've got little twin sisters. They're alright.

They're getting girly. My dad's a lawyer, his office is at American Harvest. He's busy but we do stuff together sometimes. My mom volunteers at the church. I guess you could say we're just a typical boring family. What about yours?"

Josh wanted to ask, *If your family's typical and boring, how does that explain you?* but instead he answered the question, "Well, my mom used to teach at my home church; I don't know if she will here or not. My dad's Director of the Midwest Region of Homeland Security."

"I know, I heard. An Apostle."

"Oh, no. He's never been anointed. He was in the military though. Two tours in Israel. Then, he became an agent for Homeland Security."

"An actual agent?"

"Yeah. Went overseas a couple of times. He was working out of Cleveland and then, last winter, he got promoted and we had to move to Columbus."

"You don't sound very happy about it, if you don't mind me saying."

"I guess I'm not. I'm gonna miss my friends and family."

"Your family?"

"Aunts, uncles, grandparents and especially my cousins. See, back at the beginning of the FGA, my grandfather started a Bible study in his basement. That was when the Spirit was just starting to be revealed and people had to be cautious. But, my grandfather was anointed and his little group grew into the biggest church in Canton. My grandparents had six kids. My four uncles… then, my aunt, Sarai, and finally my dad. The whole family except my dad works for the church and they all have families. I have nineteen cousins."

"Nineteen?" exclaimed Peter.

"Yeah, and we're close. We get together all the time for vacations, parties, holidays, but now…"

"Well, it's not like Canton's in Israel."

"I know, but… I don't know… I had a good life, solomon?"

"Yeah, I can imagine. It'd be rough."

Josh was caught off guard. Here he had just met this crazy guy a couple days ago and now he's talking to him like he was a friend. Yet, surprisingly, it did not make him uncomfortable. The guy seemed normal when he wasn't prancing through forests or swinging from trees.

"Miss your brother?"

"No, I mean, not really. Don't get me wrong, he's a good guy but we were never close. It's hard to describe. I think it was the age difference. He was always this guy I tried to keep up with and never could. He wasn't nice about it either. I think he thought it was his job to toughen me up."

"Not solomon. So, what's it like being the son of a DHS Director?"

"I guess I don't know yet. He was just promoted. But my dad? He's my dad, you know. He's quiet most of the time. I've heard whispers that something happened when he was an agent. I asked him about it once and all he said was '*the secret things belong to the* LORD *our God, but the things that are revealed belong to us and to our children forever.*'"

"Deuteronomy 29:29."

"He's always been closer to Stephen. In a way, it's been like my parents split us up. My dad for my brother and my mother for me. Now that Stephen's at school, my dad's trying to do stuff with me but we don't have that much in common. He thinks the highlight of a father/son experience is following the Buckeyes together. He doesn't game with me anymore at all. Says I'm too good at everything. There's nothing we do together we both like equally... except maybe the family camping trips. Those are always fun."

Their conversation was interrupted by Matthew and Luke making their way through the woods.

"Shhh," encouraged Peter with a devilish grin. "Wait here." He effortlessly and in silence shimmied up a limb and then jumped over into the waiting branches of a nearby tree.

A few tense moments later, the two boys were at the base of Elmer. Josh hunched down and remained motionless.

"Hey...hey Pete!" Luke called. "You up there?"

"He's probably messing with us again," Josh heard Matthew say.

"Pete!" Luke hollered louder.

"Maybe he went to that new guy's house."

"Yeah, maybe. Did you like that guy? I thought he was kind of a pe..."

Suddenly, the small woods erupted in an explosion of branches and leaves as Peter, looking like a California surfer, rode one of the thin trees down as it was forced to bend under his weight. As he neared the ground, he leapt from the tree and it sprang angrily back into its upright position.

"Jesus Christ! You scared the shit out of me," exclaimed Luke.

"I told you he was messing with us. *A fool gives full vent to his spirit!* You Pharisee!" Matthew called. By this time Josh could hear Peter cackling uncontrollably. Josh dared to lift his head so he could see and witnessed Luke jumping at Peter, tackling him and rolling around in the leaves. Josh was struck with feeling like an interloper.

"You've got to teach me how to do that," Luke said. Seconds later, Peter bounced back up onto the platform, followed by a more methodical Matthew, and finally, Luke. When Matthew saw Josh on the platform, he smiled and heart-bumped him; when Luke saw Josh, he exclaimed, "What the hell's he doin' here?"

Josh prayed to miraculously teleport back to his house.

"Josh's gonna join our club," said Peter.

"What?"

Matthew gave Josh a smile and a nod. "I don't see anything wrong with it."

Luke protested, "But we don't know him. What if he's a...."

"A what?" Peter asked.

"I don't know. A morit, or something."

"Come on, Luke. Look at him. What's wrong with him?"

Luke looked Josh up and down with an evaluative stare. Josh thought about reminding them all he was sitting right there, conscious of everything going on.

"All I'm saying's that it should be a club decision," said Luke.

"And it is," said Peter. "All in favor of Josh joining the Brotherhood of Elmer say 'Aye.'"

Matthew and Peter immediately said, "Aye."

"Those opposed?" asked Peter.

Silence.

"Welcome to the club." Peter and Matthew enthusiastically heart-bumped Josh. Luke turned and took a seat.

For the remainder of the afternoon, the new friends got to know one another. At one point, Matthew left to return with a knapsack full of food. "My mom slapped together some sandwiches for us." Matthew was the youngest of seven children and the only boy. "I will not leave the path of righteousness for I have seen the horror of the wilderness," he said solemnly with his hand over his heart. They all laughed at his mock suffering. His father owned a security company that specialized in housing developments, including The Gardens. Matthew's mother had been a doctor before she gave it up to have children. It took Luke some time but he eventually warmed up and shared that he was an only child. His dad was in the First Israeli War and earned a Purple Heart. "My dad's a war hero." He said nothing about his mother. Josh found himself again sharing his own story.

As he grew more comfortable, Josh said, "So, I have a question."

"All one in Jesus," said Peter.

"What do you joes know about the Josephs of Tomorrow program at...?"

"You made it into JOT?" Peter asked, shocked.

"No... I don't know... I have a meeting with my mom and the director."

"Mrs. Marone?" asked Matthew.

"Yeah, I guess that's her name. I was just asking if you joes know anything about it."

"Well, yeah, we happen to know a great deal about it," Peter answered. "We all made it in."

"JOT opens doors. With it we'll be able to get into any college in the country. Our path to a good career will be laden with gold," said Matthew.

"Yeah, but what's it like?" Josh appreciated their enthusiasm but they weren't speaking to his concerns.

"It's boot camp," Luke answered. "Or at least as close as a public school can get."

"Come on, Luke," Peter said, "that's not what's it's about. And it's not about paths of gold to find a good job. It's about girding us with the spiritual armor we need to bring Jehovah's Revolution to the whole world. *There will be one flock, one shepherd.*"

"Sounds hard," said Josh. He was anxious to cut to the chase.

"It will be. *And let us not grow weary of doing good, for in due season we will reap, if we do not give up.*"

Josh was left with a feeling of dread. He did not want to show any weakness in front of these boys, and yet at the same time, unlike them, his fear far outweighed any kind of enthusiasm.

The conversation shifted to music, movies and television. Josh was disheartened to find the only gamer in the group appeared to be Luke. The idea of spending an afternoon with the guy playing video games, for some reason, seemed like a scary proposition. As dinner time arrived, the boys received texts to come home. Peter and Josh ended up walking out of the woods together.

"You going to church Sunday?"

"Yeah. My dad's being introduced."

"Solomon. Rolling out the red carpet for the new DHS Chief. Tell you what, after the service meet me at the Jonah fountain, you can't miss it. We can go to YF together."

"Sounds triumphant, joe," Josh said. "Thanks... and hedge."

"Hedge over you," Peter called as he skipped away.

Chapter Five

No amount of orientation could have prepared Josh to experience his first day at the American Harvest Church. All those years of going to his family's church now seemed like a bunch of little kids playing house. It was not just the visual enormity of it all, as Josh and his parents walked through the main gates, but the tidal wave of sensory input. Music came from a multitude of directions, vid clips of the Apostles giving welcoming messages beamed from giant screens, blowers and fans kept the hot humid air moving, and, behind it all, the ocean of voices greeted each other with a warm, affectionate Sunday morning tone. The smells of coffee and baked goods being offered from street carts almost overwhelmed all his other senses. Above him, hung between two massive wooden pillars, stretched a golden banner under which all walked: *Obey your leaders and submit to them, for they are keeping watch over your souls. Hebrews 13:17.*

Josh found himself swooning. His parents were standing together, holding hands, and he involuntarily stepped closer towards them.

A youthful neatly polished man with a wide smile and dazzling teeth approached them from the crowd. "Hi, are you the Conrads?"

"Timothy Conrad," his father answered, shaking the young man's hand. "And this is my wife, Naomi, and son, Joshua."

The young man somehow smiled even wider. "Mr. Conrad, it's an honor to meet you. Ishmael Martin, I'm your usher for this morning. Mrs. Conrad, blessings in the name of Jesus Christ. And, Joshua, right?"

For a split-second, Josh thought the guy was going to tussle his hair. Instead, the two young men shared an awkward handshake.

"Solomon, it's an honor to meet you all. So, we reserved a few seats in the front of the sanctuary for you. Pastor Mike will introduce you during the service. Afterward…"

Josh tuned him out. If his day had been scheduled for him he did not really want to know about it. Tagging along behind his parents while they were paraded around like celebrities was just something he would have to endure.

"And you, little man…" Ishmael said, drawing Josh's attention back to him.

Josh couldn't believe his ears; the kid couldn't be more than four years older than him!

"After lunch, we'll hook you up with some of the youth. They have activities all afternoon leading into YF. You did bring a change of clothes and swimsuit?"

With a smirk, his mother handed Josh the small bag she had been carrying. Inside was everything he would need for the day.

They all climbed into a waiting SV with Ishmael in the driver's seat. Josh realized this had to be Ishmael's greatest gig to date. To be the personal escort of the Director of DHS and his family must have been quite the popular draw.

Ishmael cautiously guided the SV through the congested streets until he parked in front of the sanctuary in a spot marked "VIP."

As Ishmael led them inside, Josh was blown away. Other than a few Cleveland Cavaliers games, Josh had never been inside anything so massive. The foreboding dome roof, retractable during fair weather, loomed over them. From its highest point, draped a massive banner with a portrait of Jesus with the American flag laying across His shoulders. Tens of thousands of people were filing through the dome's floor and balconies, some were stopped in conversation, others were walking around in long living rows resembling slowly slithering snakes. The crushing enormity of it made Josh feel like a baby ant at the bottom of a gigantic anthill.

The house band was long into its set. The volume was thunderous and the musicians were stomping and dancing in joyous ecstasy. As he walked, Josh felt awash in every bass beat as it thundered through his chest, and yet, at the same time, his limbs and head grew increasing lighter. The duality of sensations made him dizzy. It was more than dreamlike, as he filed past a sea of unfamiliar faces. It was as if he had invaded someone else's dream.

They were led to the front row… middle. Of course, Josh thought gloomily. As they stood in front of their seats, Josh found himself awkwardly shaking hands with the people around him. Everyone within hand-shaking distance was eager to greet him and tell him how "blessed we are to have your father here." Josh never felt comfortable shaking hands with adults so he was more than relieved when attention turned away from him and his parents and back to the stage.

A man, Josh's mother identified as Pastor Mike, dressed meticulously in a navy-blue suit walked to the pulpit. His skin was almond-color and his polished head, sporting a band-aid on his upper forehead, glistened in the bright lights. He was not an overly tall man, but he was big. He looked like he could have been an offensive lineman. He stood for a moment silently commanding the congregation's attention. When he spoke, his voice was thunderous, as if insulted by the microphone attached to his lapel. He welcomed everyone and thanked the band. He spoke a bit about upcoming events and then, with great fanfare, he introduced the "New Director of the Midwest Region of Homeland Security and his blessed family!" Josh was familiar with the routine having taken bows for being a Conrad all his life. Stand, nod and smile to the speaker, turn in the opposite direction of his mother, smile and wave, smile and wave, slowly making a 360-degree turn, smile a little extra as he passes his mother, come around, smile and wave at the pastor again and return to his seat. Other than the loudest applause he had ever been subjected to, everything went fine.

From there, Pastor Mike rendered a glorious biographical depiction of the whole Conrad family. It was interesting to Josh to hear someone far removed from his family and Canton deliver the story. Josh could not decide if it was merely the pastor's exuberance or the growth of a legend, but the way this pastor told the story made his grandfather, and the whole family, larger than life.

Pastor Mike began with the famous "Basement Bible Study." His portrayal of Josh's grandfather reminded Josh of a painting he had seen of John Brown, the famous abolitionist. John Brown was depicted with a wild fiery determination holding a Bible in one outstretched arm and his rifle in the other. That was quite the contrast from the gentle Grandpa Gabe that Josh knew. Josh's strict yet sometimes goofy uncles were described with an equal amount of gusto, giving him the image of them standing together in superhero-style tights. Even his aunt, who was probably the quietest person Josh knew, was declared to be a warrior for Christ. "To the Conrads… the Holy Spirit was doled out like Easter candy!" Pastor Mike declared.

Next, the pastor's attention centered on Timothy Conrad. He gave a short biography of how God had led the youngest son away from the Mountain of

Religion into the military. He talked about how Timothy had served with the "courage of Christ," and embellished Josh's father's military exploits to the point of action hero status. From there, the pastor spoke of his father's time as an agent and how difficult it is for the DHS undercovers to live in that "cauldron of sin" without becoming a part of it.

Finally, the pastor spoke of Timothy's wonderful family beginning with his "beautiful wife, Naomi, a dedicated Joseph with the longest committed church résumé I've ever seen." The pastor spoke about Stephen who "begins his second year as a West Point cadet." Then Pastor Mike took a dramatic breath and introduced the Conrads other handsome son, Joshua, "who, I am told, is a strong candidate for the Josephs for Tomorrow program." The murmurs of approval felt like electrical shocks. Someone behind him patted him on his back which made his skin crawl. Josh wanted to melt into the pew.

For the next half-an-hour, the house band and choir kicked it into high gear. It was called "praise music" for a reason. In addition to singing along, members of the congregation found ways to individually show glory to God. Some simply held their hands up towards heaven, in a gesture known as "hugging God." Others danced in place as there was little room to move around. For those on or near the aisles, they would often step out of their pews and go all out with a praise dance. Again, for Josh, the only unfamiliarity was the sheer enormity of the circumstances.

Eventually, the congregation sat back down attentively ready for the sermon. Pastor Mike stood to the podium and mopped his brow. After a long dramatic pause, he began to preach. "This past week, among many trials and tribulations sent by Satan, I asked God what He wanted me to say this morning. I prayed, 'Lord, I know I'm to welcome the Director of DHS. What message do you have for me to give?' The Lord directed me to Nehemiah, chapter four."

Pastor Mike read a passage unfamiliar to Josh. It was the story of a group of Jewish people who returned from Babylon and were attempting to rebuild the walls of Jerusalem even as they were surrounded by enemies. When he was finished, Pastor Mike gently closed the Bible, took a long cleansing breath, and raised his head to the congregation.

As he preached, he stepped away from the podium and walked freely on stage. "So, here we have a small assembly of God's people who've returned from exile in Babylon. Upon their return, they set out to rebuild Jerusalem. Now, the people around the area saw the returning exiles as weak and few in number. Here, God's enemies thought, were these peans coming back to their decimated city and trying to rebuild it. They thought God's people were babel, out-of-touch with reality!"

Pastor Mike's speaking style was greatly different than his grandfather's subdued delivery, but Josh found himself enjoying the sermon. He liked the enthusiasm. The pastor said everything with the excitement of a football coach in the locker room.

"Then, they started laughing at them… taunting them. They were roaring when they saw God's people trying to use the charred ruins as materials to restore the buildings. And howling when they saw God's people believed the makeshift wall could serve as a defense. There the enemies were… mocking them… ridiculing them… insulting them… does any of this sound familiar? So, God's people prayed, *Hear, O our God, for we are despised. Turn back their taunts on their own heads.*"

"Amen!" the congregation shouted.

"Let not their sin be blotted out from your sight, for they have provoked you to anger in the presence of the builders!" Another wave of joyous shouts crashed from one end of the giant sanctuary to the other.

The pastor took a deep breath. "God's people prayed fervently… and they went to work, as well. They worked with all their hearts and souls and minds, committed, resolute, ever-enduring, ever-toiling… until lo and behold, the wall was already half-way up. For *I can do all things through Him who strengthens me.*

"When the enemies heard of this miraculous construction, they were furious, because the walls were going up… and the gaps in it were being filled. Yes… the gaps…for you see it isn't enough for the walls to simply be high. They must also be complete… thick with no holes, no gaps. The people had to worry about an army coming over the hill but they also had to worry about a stealth attack… spies slipping through the gaps in the wall.

"Nehemiah, being wise with God, posted guards in full armor near families. And he said to the nobles, officials and all the people, 'BE NOT AFRAID! *Remember the Lord, who is great and awesome, and fights for your brothers, your sons, your daughters, your wives, and your homes!*' So, it was… while the engineers, the laborers, and the women all worked tirelessly, they could do so without fear. For, Nehemiah had established Watchmen to protect them."

Here Pastor Mike stopped, his shoulders dropped from an inner exhaustion. When he spoke again, his voice was softer, drawing the congregation in. "Well, it's twenty-five hundred years later, and we're on the other side of the world, but we too are rebuilding a holy nation. We're toiling tirelessly for the Lord and we can do our work because we have Watchmen guarding our gaps."

Ah, so that was where he was going with this. Josh liked the set up. He was sure his grandfather would approve.

"It wasn't always thus, was it? Just a couple generations ago our fathers and mothers faced a far different America. A 'United States of America,' controlled by the Devil, and run by atheists, humanists, secularists, racists, and adherents to false gods and false doctrines. The good Christians of this country found themselves hiding in basements. But it took brave men and women. Men like Gabriel Conrad, to go into the basements and say, 'Come out, come out. We, the Christian Americans, did not conquer the wilderness to get lost in it! We conquered the wilderness to take dominion over it!' They became spiritual warriors, training themselves in the Word, girding themselves with the armor. They stepped out, Josephs of all kinds and colors, marching determinedly up the Seven Mountains, and they took dominion."

Josh felt catapulted from his seat by the tumultuous roar of celebration. All around him people shouted, "Praise Jesus!" "God Bless the Christian States of America!" "Glory to the CSA!" "All One in Christ!"

"Now, this generation works on rebuilding the walls of our nation. Yet, how can we focus on our work? How can we go about bringing this nation back to God when we have to worry about our enemies attacking us? What of our gaps? Gaps still in every one of the Seven Mountains. Hackers infecting our Net with viruses. Musicians creating satanic beats and slipping blasphemous messages into the lyrics. Sports heroes faking their commitments for a paycheck. Heretical interpretations of the Bible displayed in movies and television. Liberal educators hiding amongst our teachers. The black market and all the products being sold far from the oversight of CAP. Satan is using every tool he has available to continue to attack this great nation, to weaken our resolve, to threaten our liberty, and... to attack our families.

"Ah, but He has placed Watchmen... Men who are standing guard over our gaps... over our families... over our children, so that we may remain safe. And, in that, is the absence of fear. In that absence is our freedom. For we are now free to focus on God, free to walk His righteous path, free to rebuild this nation and free to take Jehovah's Revolution to the Whole World! All... One... in... Christ!"

The pastor accented the last four words by pointing to Heaven as he pronounced each. Even before he was finished, the congregation was again on their feet, clapping, laughing, and shouting.

Finally, it grew quiet enough for the pastor to have one final word. "Today, as you greet our new Watchman and his beautiful family. I want you to keep this verse in mind. Romans 13:4, *For he is God's servant for your good. But if you do wrong, be afraid, for he does not bear the sword in vain. For he is the servant of God, an avenger who carries out God's wrath on the wrongdoer.*"

The sanctuary again erupted into a spontaneous explosion of applause. Josh looked over at his dad whose crimson face maintained a smile through a clenched jaw. *He's embarrassed!* His always dignified father, rubbing shoulders with Apostles, was thoroughly embarrassed.

The praise continued for another few minutes and his dad took it with a smile. Finally, the pastor led the congregation in the singing of several more songs concluding with "America the Beautiful." Next to him, his mother had closed her eyes and raised her hands in praise as she sang. Her shining face elevated towards Heaven. Josh took his mother's hand and together they hugged God.

When the service was over, Ishmael, miraculously appeared. "We're gonna go through the side doors. Follow me." Ishmael began to lead his VIPs through the crowd. What he had not anticipated was everyone wanting to personally greet the new DHS Director and, equally as popular, his wife.

Ishmael tried not to show his irritation but Josh could see how exasperated he was in his powerlessness.

Once outside, they could move a little quicker to the waiting SV.

Just then, Peter and Matthew, their arms waving wildly, pulled up in an SV of their own. "Josh, hey, Josh... come on!"

Ishmael glared at the two boys with disapproval. Peter hopped out of the SV's driver's seat. As Peter approached, Ishmael said "Excuse me" and stepped out to cut him off. The two talked for a bit. Josh could not hear what they were saying but in the end, it was Peter who patted Ishmael on his shoulder, as if Peter was the elder.

Ishmael returned to the SV. "Apparently, there's been a change of plans. The young man over there, Peter, would like to take Joshua with him. Our Youth Director, Judith Marone, has asked to speak with Joshua."

Mrs. Marone? Why would she want to meet with him now? Without his parents?

Josh turned to his mother. She took a long look in his eyes. "Not a good idea to turn the Youth Director down, is it?" Josh nodded his agreement. "He can still come to lunch at the pastor's house?"

"I'm sure he can," replied Ishmael.

His mother turned to him. "You okay with this?"

"Yeah, I guess."

Ishmael walked Josh over as if transporting a prisoner. "His mom said he needs to be at Pastor Mike's house for lunch."

"No problem," Peter said, climbing into the driver's seat. Josh took a seat in the back.

"Does Mrs. Marone know you're driving an SV?" Ishmael asked.

"Of course!" Peter shouted as he steered the SV away. "NOT!" he added as he and Matthew burst into gales of laughter.

A second later, Peter shouted, "Welcome aboard, Matey!"

"You looked like you needed rescued," said Matthew.

Peter wove the SV through the crowd and traffic. He quickly pulled off the main street and headed down an empty maintenance road.

"Is that what you're doing?" called Josh.

"You betcha!" Peter answered as he accelerated down a hill far faster than an SV was designed to travel. The body of the SV began to shake. Matthew cut loose a victorious howl.

"So, I'm not meeting with the Youth Director?" Josh shouted.

"Of course, you are. We're just taking our time getting you there." At that, Peter made a sharp turn to the left onto what appeared to be a walking path and entered a wooded area running adjacent to the lake's edge.

"Get ready for your unofficial tour!" Matthew bellowed. Peter drove the SV along the outskirts of the church property, at times right up against the security fence. Josh found himself flipped from one side to the other as Peter navigated the vehicle like a derailed roller coaster car. One minute, Josh was truly terrified, the next he was merely petrified they were all going to get in trouble.

They made a loop at the back end of the parsonage's lawn, which was covered in rows of neatly set tables beneath an immense sun tarp. Workers were busy setting up for the upcoming lunch. A few looked up, saw the out-of-place SV, and waved.

"Are we allowed back here?" Josh asked.

"Not really," answered Peter, as he cut tight to the right.

Matthew turned around in his seat to face Josh. "See, Peter here gets away with everything 'cause Peter's Justjudy's darling."

"Silence, Pharisee, I am not."

"Justjudy?" Josh asked.

"That's how Mrs. Marone signs her name," answered Matthew. "Says it keeps her humble. Wait until you meet her. She's intense. Short. 'bout five foot nothing, but nobody messes with Justjudy. Nobody."

"She mean?"

Peter shook his head. "No, not mean. Dedicated. You aren't gonna find anyone more dedicated to the Awakening."

Peter drove up a hill that looked out over the whole church property. At the top was a pavilion, picnic tables, and a small parking lot for SVs. No one else was there. Peter pulled to the curb and stopped.

"She's without a doubt the greatest person I know," Peter said. "But she doesn't put up with bullshit either. Lukewarmers are useless."

"Lukewarmers?"

"Yeah, you know, *because you are lukewarm, and neither hot nor cold, I will spit you out of my mouth.*" Josh was familiar with the passage. Was he a Lukewarmer? No way. With a family like his, how could he be?

The boys took seats on top of a picnic table. Josh gasped. There before them, spread out like a fantasy kingdom, lay the whole church. Josh estimated he could fit ten of his family's church into this place. Alum Creek to the south created a resort like atmosphere with the lake and private beach for church members. The main sanctuary was plainly visible and even from this distance and height, it appeared enormous. Peter and Matthew pointed out the three schools on the grounds. They then showed Josh where the other main buildings were: the nursing home, medical clinics, the two mini-malls, health center, and the "business district" with the banks, insurance companies, attorneys, and whoever else could afford the donation. Peter tried to pinpoint his father's office for Josh but Josh could only helplessly nod. Off to the right and looking a slightly shinier green than all the rest of the church's lawn lay the grounds of the parsonage. Surrounding the entire property was a state-of-the-art security fence with gates at each of the 12 entrances. Josh had seen countless movies and news stories of churches this size but they had always seemed a million miles away. Now he was standing in one; more than that, he was attending one.

"Miraculous, isn't it?" Peter whispered.

"It's triumphant!"

Peter gazed over the scene. "This is one of my favorite spots in the whole world. When you stand here and look at that, there's no doubt the world is in God's hands and He has a plan for this nation and everyone in it. *For we are his workmanship.*"

"Amen," Matthew said.

Peter clapped Josh on his back. "This place'll prepare us to bring the Gospel to the whole world. *And I have other sheep that are not of this fold. I must bring them also, and they will listen to my voice. So there will be one flock, one shepherd.*"

Josh allowed the words, expressed with conviction, to hang in his mind. He felt hypnotized by the grand carpet before him. Prepare him to bring the Gospel to the world? Josh was not ready for all that. He just wanted to get a good start on high school without embarrassing himself. Still, if any place could prepare someone for Jehovah's Revolution, it had to be this place. He was so lost in his thoughts he nearly jumped when Matthew asked, "Think we should get going?"

"Right you are, my boy," Peter exclaimed, and stomped to the top of the picnic table. There, he pulled out an imaginary sword from an equally imaginary sheath and raised it high in the air. "Let us deliver this gallant knight to our fair queen!" He then leaped off the picnic table and half-dove, half-somersaulted to the SV.

Matthew turned to Josh and warned with a grin. "Get out! Get out now. The guy's babbling babel."

Chapter Six

Slowing only when the church crowd demanded it, the boys made another mad dash in the SV. They went by two gigantic fountains. One was in the shape of a giant fish with Jonah in its mouth, the other was a group of Puritans raising their hands up to the "living" water spouting high into the air.

Peter took what he called a short cut through a walking path that was clearly labeled "No SVs." With a precise dramatic flair, he pulled it tightly against a curb in front of a large office building. "Here we are, gentlemen."

Josh found his hands were shaking as he climbed out. As they entered the building, Josh read the plaque that hung from its side: *Let the elders who rule well be considered worthy of double honor, especially those who labor in preaching and teaching! 1 Timothy 5:17.*

As they went inside and down a hallway, Peter assured Josh, "It's solomon. Trust me."

Peter knocked as he opened the door and led Josh into a spacious office. It was divided into two sections. The first was a group of couches and leisure chairs around a short table in the middle. In the back was a large desk where a woman was rising from her chair. The first thing Josh noticed was she was short, very short. What had Matthew said? "Five-foot nothing." The second thing Josh noticed was her build. She was shaped very much like a well-constructed snowman with legs and arms....and breasts. Big breasts. Warnings went off in his head. He forced his eyes away and prayed she had not noticed him looking. Above all else, it was her head that appeared to be a perfectly formed snowball with puffy cheeks. Professionally dressed in a black suit, she walked forcefully to the boys.

"Sorry we took so long," Peter said.

"Yes, well, I had to explain to Security what you were doing. I had no explanation for your driving, however. You do know you're on camera? And what am I to say when they ask if I gave a fourteen-year-old permission to drive an SV?" As the lady lectured she forced her forehead to create burrows and inflated her cheeks.

Peter and Matthew cackled. The lady turned her comical face to Josh and he forced a nervous smile. Her face returned to normal and her hand came out. "Judith Marone." Her handshake was overwhelmingly strong. "Come on in; have a seat."

Josh went around and sat on the couch. Mrs. Marone took the chair to his left. Matthew and Peter were together on the couch across from him. For the first-time Josh noticed the painting on the wall. It was a large picture of Jesus, finger pointing towards Heaven, sitting on a rock, surrounded by a group of followers.

"What do you think of that?" Mrs. Marone asked.

"It's nice."

"I didn't ask how it felt. I asked, what do you think about it?" Her face was serious but not unfriendly. Josh decided he liked her eyes and the way her forehead was shaped; it gave her face the look of a koala bear. "Well?"

"It's a painting of Jesus teaching his followers."

"More."

Josh was not sure what she wanted. He looked at his friends across the table who were smiling at him.

"Don't look at those two. Look at the painting. How many followers?"

Before he finished counting, he figured out the answer. "Twelve. The Original Apostles?"

"Is that a question or an answer?"

Josh gulped. "An answer."

"Right. And?"

"And they're listening to Him."

"What's He talking about?"

"I don't know." *Lady, it's a painting, not a video.*

"Yes, you do. Figure it out. Look for clues."

Was this a test? This seemed like a test. He studied the painting intently. The Apostles were all holding walking sticks. Jesus was pointing to Heaven or... maybe He wasn't. His arm was angled lower, pointing to the mountains in the distance... the seven mountains in the distance.

"It's Jesus giving instructions to his Apostles to go forth and take the Seven Mountains."

Matthew and Peter cheered like he just scored a winning touchdown. Mrs. Marone reached over and tapped his hand. "Very good. Do you know what they are?"

"Families, the media, sports, arts and entertainment, education, business, and government. They're the seven areas of society over which God has given Christians dominion." He felt sure if it had been a test, he just passed.

Mrs. Marone said, *"For God did not send his Son into the world to condemn the world, but in order that the world might be saved through him."* She studied him for a long moment. At the point it began feeling uncomfortable she said, "So you're Timothy Conrad's son."

"Our new DHS Chief!" exclaimed Peter.

Mrs. Marone seemed disinterested in the comment. "I know your father."

"He told me he spoke to you."

"No, I mean, I met your father once at a youth seminar when we were in high school. We ended up in the same small group. I knew God was gonna use him in big ways."

Josh grappled with the idea of his dad and this lady meeting each other when they were his age. Adults should not make such revelations without warning.

"He tells me you're interested in the Josephs of Tomorrow program?"

"Yes," he answered, trying to sound enthusiastic.

It was no use, she could see right through him. "It's a tough program but you don't choose JOT. God chooses you."

"God's Will be done."

Mrs. Marone smiled approvingly. "So, what do you think of our church? A bit bigger than your grandfather's, isn't it?"

"It sure is."

"It's not the size that makes it different. It's the passion. See Josh, I grew up in the same area as you did, only I grew up in a tiny town that made Canton look like the big city. I'd sit there in my house surrounded by strip mines and cornfields, watching TV. I'd watch the men and women who put their lives on the line to bring this country back to God. Then I'd go to church and we'd pray and give special offerings to different causes. And that was it. I'd go to church and school but the Awakening was something that was happening somewhere else. Follow me?"

"Yes, ma'am."

"But this church, Josh. This church has been on the front lines of the FGA before we even knew there were front lines. It fought its way through to become the most prominent church in Ohio. Senators, congressmen, judges, mayors, police chiefs, the governor and, yes, even the head of Homeland Security are members of this church. But it didn't get there easily; God tested us at every level. It was that testing that made us stronger. And do you know what got us through?"

"Faith?"

Mrs. Marone smiled. "I knew you were gonna say that. And don't answer a question with a question. No. Faith is for the churches that sit on the side lines, praying. What does it take for a church like this? Commitment. That's what this church is all about. We know we have the Truth. We don't need faith; we need commitment. Do you see the difference?"

Josh nodded.

"See, that's just what I'm talking about. You're sitting here giving me the 'right' answer. I don't want the right answer; I want the committed answer. Are you committed?"

Peter's warning that she did not like "Lukewarmers" was ringing in his head. Yet, it was obvious she had the gift of sight. She could see right into his heart, so it would do no good to sound too excited. Instead, he found himself compelled; his mind ordering him to open the gates. "Well, when you grow up in a family like mine, I guess I've always felt committed. But… in truth, I didn't really want to move here. I had friends and stuff but now… now, I'm thinking maybe this is God's way of telling me to grow up." As he spoke he kept his eyes down, far away from the boys. Josh was surprised by his words but they had the ring of truth.

"*When I became a man, I gave up childish ways.* You know, I felt the same way. After college, I went back home and got a job as a teacher but I soon realized God had bigger plans for me. I'm not sure if He's done with me but I do know this little farm girl is now the Youth Director in the largest, most important church in all of Ohio. God's Will be done."

"God's Will be done," all the boys repeated.

Josh's phone toned.

"Your mother reminding you of lunch?" she asked.

"Yes."

"I promised I'd get him to Pastor Mike's," said Peter.

"Of course, I imagine they're making a big deal of your father's arrival."

Josh started to answer but was cut off by Peter. "You should've seen the crowd around his dad. We had to cast a fishing line in just to get Josh out."

"Well, don't let me get in the way of your lunch plans. Are you staying for YF this evening?"

"Yes, ma'am."

"Good. It was a pleasure to meet you." Mrs. Marone stood and extended her hand to Josh. She turned to Peter, "I trust you'll get your stolen SV back without a scratch on it."

Peter's grin widened two times. "Oh, it'll be back, but I can't promise no scratches."

"Seriously, young man. Drop him off and bring the SV right back."

"Aye, aye, captain," Peter said and saluted grandiosely. Mrs. Marone rolled her eyes at him.

Outside the building again, Peter turned to Josh. "You're triumphant, joe!"

"Yeah," said Matthew. "Solomon."

Josh was not at all sure what they meant but he was glad to have his new friends' approval.

Eventually, after yet a third roller coaster ride around the outskirts of the church, and receiving more than one annoyed look from security officers, they made it to the parsonage. They dropped Josh off explaining the pastor lunches were by a rotational invitation and it was not their families' turn.

After the morning's events, it felt strange entering the formality of the luncheon as Josh found his mother and father sitting at the pastor's table. With formal manners, he apologized to the table for being late and sat down.

"Honey," his mother said, "I'd like you to meet Pastor Mike's wife, Mrs. Steward."

Josh nodded to the lady across the table. Her beauty was dazzling. Her dark hair was in a bun high on her head which accented her long thin neck, her skin was infused with a golden hue. She offered him a pleasant smile but it was her rich deep dark Asian eyes with long elegant lashes masking a hidden sadness that drew his attention. She seemed about to say something but was interrupted by a young boy, the spitting image of Pastor Mike with hair, running up to her to ask a question.

"How'd your morning go?" Josh's mother asked.

"Good."

"Josh met with your youth director this morning," his mother explained to the table.

As everyone nodded their approval, Pastor Mike spoke, his tone more conversational than it was from the pulpit but still held everyone's rapt attention. "Yes, Mrs. Marone. This church is so blessed to have her. I've known her for years. Her testimony's living proof everything happens for a reason. God's reason. When she and her husband discovered God didn't have a family in His plans for them, instead of crying out 'Why me?' She simply said, 'Here I am Lord!' Her commitment to the Mountain of Education is unsurpassed. The Josephs of Tomorrow program is something quite unique and is garnering a great deal of attention nationwide. I fear we may end up losing her to Washington. God's Will be done."

After the luncheon where his father spent much of the time answering questions to which Josh paid little attention, he took a trolley with a whole slew of other kids to the Youth Center. There he found Matthew and Peter. Luke was there, as well, distant but not unfriendly. Peter took Josh around and introduced him. At first Josh felt embarrassed, but the way Peter spoke made Josh feel not so much as the "new kid" but more like Peter's long-lost friend returned.

The rest of the day was a blur. The youth were divided by grade level and then subdivided again and again. Josh stuck close to Peter and Matthew as they moved through the various activities. Then they were at the beach. Josh was quickly aware of the body differences as the boys took off their shirts. Both Peter's and Matthew's were well-developed, the sculpture of their muscles easily differentiated and their abs were chiseled below their rib cages. Luke did not take his shirt off. When he got wet however, the shirt did little to hide his extra rolls. Josh removed his shirt and felt like every eye there could notice his skinny arms, noodle-shaped legs, and boyish stomach. He quickly hit the water and got in up to his neck. There he could enjoy the water without looking like an out of place fifth grader. Soon he was in a game of keep-away. Josh did his best not to make any major mistakes and got through it without being singled out. Just the way he liked it. When it came to anything sporty, Josh was very content just to blend in.

After the beach, things became a bit more comfortable. Despite the differences, the number of students, and the fact he knew virtually no one, the afternoon and evening were spent in a comfortable surrounding participating in familiar activities. There was a volleyball game where Josh held his own, though that was primarily because "stretch" Matthew and "ninjaman" Peter were both on his team. Their victory was followed by a Bible study and discussion led by an Associate Youth Pastor. Josh stayed quiet, but he enjoyed the conversation and began to see the "crazy Columbus kids" were all pretty normal after all.

The ET ride home was the perfect end to the day. His mother and father had long left and so he rode the ET with the others. Luke sat quietly, not looking happy. Matthew talked incessantly about the girl who performed some songs that evening. "Her voice," he exclaimed, "Angelic." Peter was as fresh and lively as if he had just woken up. He never sat for long, moving from person to person asking about their day. It was obvious he knew many of them but most surprising was the way he was received by the adults. Josh would never dream of speaking to adults that way for fear he would come across as a morit. Yet, Peter spoke to everyone with a genuine sincerity that seemed appreciated. He was the way he was… with everyone, and, judging from his popularity all over the church, people admired him for it.

Josh sat silently, reliving the whole day in his head. What a wild roller coaster of feelings. He had been so nervous at the beginning of the day, clutching his mother's hand. Then the raucous service and sermon, the "rescue," Justjudy, and finally a fun-filled afternoon of swimming, games, and Bible study. Now he was riding home, without his parents and with his new friends. For all his worries, and the ups and downs of the day itself, he had to admit, ultimately, it turned out to be pretty triumphant.

Chapter Seven

Maggie left her house that last night with the determination of a warrior and absolutely no plan.

Her mind traversed between it all being a dream to having reality never appear more real. She assumed it was only a matter of time before she was caught but she was determined to make that eventuality as distant as possible. For her, each moment she stayed free was an arrow shot at her father, and when she was caught, she vowed, she was not going to go quietly.

Her first obstacle was getting by security but they were focused on in-comers not out-goers. The ET, with its identification requirements, was out of the question. Instead, though the night was terrifying, she walked, avoiding cameras, guards, police and anyone else she saw. At first, it was one walled housing development after another but that quickly gave way to a sea of buildings and streets that had no end; a maze without an exit.

By the time the sun came up, she found herself in a different world. A world that had been far beneath her when she had passed over it on the ET. At its best, her concept of this area of Columbus had been something out of the *Christmas Carol* with the grave robbers singing merrily in their poverty; at its worst, her vision was of raging street gangs tearing each other apart. What she found were people... living.

By late afternoon, she had her eyes fixed on a plan. In this area of the city, while the apartment buildings all seemed occupied, Maggie noticed the numerous office buildings left abandoned. Many times, the first floors were utilized for various nefarious purposes, but no one seemed to be occupying the upper floors. Maggie watched one building for a long time until she was sure. When she was, she bypassed the stairs and scurried up the pipes. She slid in the top floor window and found it to be just what she had expected;

nothing but a big open floor with abandoned office furniture. She moved the heavy desks in front of the doors and then used some of the worn partitions to create a cocoon to sleep.

There she spent several days, mostly on the roof, eating her small supply of food and only venturing below when she absolutely had to use the toilet. She spent most of her time terrified. Terrified of being caught, of not being caught, of the noises around her, of the silence around her. There was a war going on inside of her. A war between the terrified little girl who just wanted to surrender and the warrior who vowed to fight to the end.

The nights were the worst as the noises from the street transformed into something menacing. When she was able to drift into unconsciousness she was often yanked awake by vivid nightmares. Conglomerations of all her childhood fears mutating into a demonic caricature of her father.

Perhaps it was because the area was slow to rise, or perhaps because she felt empowered every time she survived a night, but she found the mornings to be the best times. Like a baby squirrel climbing out of the tree for the first time, Maggie began to explore her surroundings. She had stolen her father's ATM card and was able to obtain some paper money but she was still terrified to transact any business. Would these dilapidated businesses even take paper money? She had learned about it mostly at school as her parents would always simply swipe their cards across the machines. She had never even seen the real thing until one evening her father had taken a withdrawal and let her push the buttons for the security code. A code she had not forgotten. Not too smart, Daddy-O.

She lived those first few weeks in a state of numb defiance. As scared and miserable as she was, she leaned on the warrior within. To give up would be to give in to him, and that would be completely unacceptable. She trusted no one, and so, spent most of her time wandering the streets, looking through the slew of garbage for items she could use and watching people from the perch of her rooftop.

Other times she escaped to city parks. There, she could see an array of green from the deep jade of the pine trees to the light olive of the milkweed. If she tried hard, she could hear the leaves rustling together just under the steady hum of the nearby city. And if she closed her eyes, focusing completely, she could smell the scent of dirt, not the man-made kind she lived in, but the kind that plants grew in, the kind that reminded her there was something beyond the city.

One cool autumn day, Maggie was sitting on a park bench, when a young girl ran by her on her way to the playground. The girl looked to be about ten... poor, homeless, yet playing with the enthusiasm of any child. The girl stood before the parallel bar. She tried hopping up. She was unsuccessful. She tried again. Nope.

"Put your hands closer," Maggie called.

Her voice startled the young girl. "What?"

"Your hands are too far apart. Wait. Is it okay if I show you?"

The young girl smiled brilliantly. "Sure!"

Maggie glanced at her things she had collected. She was not going far, they would be okay.

"See, if you put your hands too spread out, you can't balance. You have to keep them closer, like this." Maggie expertly performed the mount, paused for a moment, then flipped herself over the bar and back up.

The young girl was flabbergasted. "Wow, can you teach me to do that?"

"Well, first we need to get you to make a proper mount."

"Mount?"

"You know, getting up on the bar. That's called the 'mount.'"

"Are you a real gymnast?"

"Used to be."

The young girl's face lit up even more.

"I'm Maggie."

"My name's Emily. It's actually Elizabeth Emily but I just go by Emily. You live around here?"

"Around. You know."

"Yeah."

"Here, I'll spot you. We'll go slowly." Maggie showed Emily where to put her hands and then confidently spotted her to the mount. From Emily's smile, it was obvious Maggie had won her over.

Emily showed herself to be a quick study. She had the two inborn traits all gymnasts need: the desire to perform perfectly and the lack of good sense to listen to fear. After mastering a few tricks on the bar, Emily noticed a beam on the other side of the playground. "Can you do the beam too?" Emily asked.

"Sure, all four food groups." Emily looked at her blankly. "Sorry, gymnast joke."

As Maggie began going over the basics of the beam, she was interrupted by Emily shouting, "Hey, Jake!"

Maggie was struck with fear. Behind her was a boy, taller than her, older, walking towards them. She had not seen him coming and now he was between her and her things.

"It's okay. That's just my brother." Maggie felt a little relief but her muscles remained coiled. "Maggie's teaching me gymnastics," Emily shouted gleefully.

"I saw. She a good teacher?" Jake asked, nodding towards Maggie. His smile was gentle but, she reminded herself, that meant nothing.

"The best."

"I was just showing her a few things. Nothing dangerous."

Jake laughed. "I got news for you. You could teach this girl to jump out of an airplane without a parachute." He paused. "So, do you know a lot about gymnastics?"

"Some."

"Do you do the stuff yourself or are you just a coach?"

"She does it herself," Emily piped in. "And she's really good too."

"That true?"

"Well, I used to be a lot better. Look, I've gotta get going," Maggie said and moved to leave.

"No!" protested Emily.

"Hey, don't go on my account. I'm just keeping an eye on her."

"Well…"

"Oh, please, Maggie!" begged Emily.

"Well, okay."

"Yippee!" Emily shouted and jumped up on the beam again.

Maggie had thought Jake would leave but he didn't. He announced he would keep watch over her things. This caused her concern until she saw him take a bench far from where she left them.

At first, Maggie felt self-conscious about having Jake there watching. She eventually realized, however, what she was doing. What did she care what he was thinking? After that she gave him little thought, especially when the two girls moved to a grassy spot to work on mat skills. Just doing the tricks again was rejuvenating. For the first time since she had runaway, she found herself having fun.

After spotting on what may have been Emily's one hundredth round off, Maggie declared she was tired. "It's getting dark anyway," she explained to Emily's sour face.

"This was the best day of my life," said Emily.

Maggie pointed out that they obviously did not live far from each other and so they were bound to bump into each other again, but that was not good enough for Emily. In the end, Maggie found herself agreeing to meet Emily two days a week at noon. Her payment would be in smiles.

For the first time in a while, she glanced over at her things. She was shocked to see two other boys with Jake. When did they get there? Were they trouble? Is this where she gets robbed or ….? Damn, she left her knife in her backpack. Had she been taken in? She looked over at Emily who seemed disinterested in anything but her pouting. So, Maggie came up with a plan. She would walk in that direction, maybe a little small talk, but stay far away from them and work her way over to the bench. Once there she would decide if she would just grab her stuff and bolt or get to her knife to defend herself. God, she hoped it would not come to the latter. As she walked, she forced her strides to be as normal as possible. At first, they did not see her coming but eventually Jake noticed her. He said something to the other boys and they walked away trying not to show they were glancing back. What did that mean? Jake stood up as she came closer. She nervously took a step back. He smiled.

"How did it go?"

"Um, good. I've gotta go."

"Yeah, I'm sure. I'd like to talk with you for a minute, if I may? About a job."

"A job? Well, if it's to teach Emily gymnastics, you're too late. And I'm pretty sure she negotiated a better deal than you ever would."

There was a moment of silence as Jake needed to replay the statement in his head. He chuckled. "Yeah, I bet she did. No, this is another job. And I promise it'll not interfere with any previous commitments."

"What kind of job, then?"

"Did you see those guys I was with?"

"Yeah."

"Well, we're sort of a group and we do things…to make money."

"A gang?"

"Not in any formal sense of the word. More like a family that looks out for each other."

"Sounds like a gang."

"Would it help if I tell you there are only seven of us and one of them is Emily?"

Maggie did not respond to the question. Instead she asked, "Drugs?"

"We smoke a little herb when we can get our hands on it but that has nothing to do with the job."

"Anything to do with… the other thing?"

He stared at her.

"I'm a girl, you're a boy, duh?"

"No, no, no. Nothing like that." She cross-examined his eyes. "I promise," he assured her.

Maggie knew she needed to be wary. She had not run away from one rapist just to get entangled in another, but there was a genuine sincerity in his voice that eased her fears.

"So, what's the job?"

"We need a gymnast," he explained and then provided the details. There were four of them: Jake, Thad, Seth and Mickey. Mickey was a computer genius, able to hack into anything. "He could bring on Armageddon if he wanted to." Mickey did all the background stuff, he found out the security systems, found ways to get into them, and set it all up. Jake, Thad and Seth would break in and get whatever they were looking for like money and jewels but mostly technical stuff they could turn around and sell.

"So, if Mickey turns off the alarms and you three steal whatever, what do you need me for?"

"'Cause sometimes the only way to get into the building requires skills none of us have. We've had to turn our back on jobs 'cause, even though Mickey can kill the alarms, we can't get into the building, not without bringing attention to ourselves anyway. We need someone with gymnastic skills. Someone small, like you…. the split's five ways. No bullshit."

Emily, sullenly dragging her feet, arrived by the bench.

"Hey, Em, you worn out?" Jake asked.

"No."

"Maggie tells me you hired her to be your gymnastics coach."

Emily's mood instantly changed. "Is that what I did?" Maggie smiled.

"Thad has something for you. I was gonna eat it but it was way too sweet for me."

"Candy? Where is he?"

"He's up ahead. I told him to walk slow so you could catch him. I'll be along in a minute. I want to finish talking to Maggie."

Emily called back as she ran away. "Okay, but if she becomes your girlfriend, she's still my gymnastic coach first."

"Em, it's nothing like that." Jake tried to hide his embarrassment beneath a jovial laugh.

Maggie angrily gathered her things. She knew it. Everything's a charade.

"Wait, look, I'm sorry about Em. She watches too many romance shows. We've been looking for someone with your skills for a long time. Seriously, this is just a business proposition."

She stopped. She wanted to believe him but alarms were sounding throughout her body.

"I'll make that clear to Em. No one's gonna mess with you. I swear. Come on. You're alone, aren't you?"

"No...yes..."

"I thought so. Loners don't last long, and girl loners last even less time."

Though she was just a newcomer to the streets, she knew how true his words were. It was a world she did not understand. She was hiding as much from this world as from the world she left. She was tired of hiding. She needed natives to show her how to get things; how to find the places that will sell with no record, how to find food without going through trash bins. She needed them but she'd be damned if she was going to let him know that. "Okay, I'll look at what you've got, but if I don't like what I see, I'm gone, got it?"

Jake smiled. "Sounds perfect."

Maggie had no idea what Jake said to the guys but it was obvious he said something. When she was introduced to everyone they greeted her with professional respect. Thad was the friendliest. Maggie placed him at about seventeen. He had a gentleness about him, like a frog on a Lilly pad content to watch the world go by. He showed a genuine love for Emily, teasing her at times in the nature of a brother. Mickey, the great computer geek, was not the scrawny, sloppy, socially awkward nerd she had anticipated. He was a big guy, more like the power forward type. His demeanor was aloof but friendly. Seth was younger, around fifteen. He was thin and it sometimes seemed he did not have complete control over his gangly growing body. At first, she thought he was annoyed with her but she quickly realized he had a sullen attitude with everyone.

There were three others living in what was dubbed "The Office." There was Emily, of course, who was overjoyed with Maggie joining the team. Emily had no memory other than the streets and she took it upon herself to teach Maggie the ropes. She steered Maggie to the businesses that would sell them things out the back door. Emily pointed out which soup kitchens, food pantries, and clothes donation sites would give away things without asking any questions. She showed Maggie the shortcuts, the safe zones, and the areas to stay far away from. To Emily, they were just tricks but, to Maggie, it was all vital information.

The two little boys running around were Seth's twin brothers, Barak and Asher. They were the youngest of the group and completely unsupervised. Each morning they would set out to seek adventures. They prided themselves on their abilities to steal and sometimes returned in the evenings as victorious hunters with whole meals and tales to tell.

The Office was the entire third floor of an abandoned building. The old office partitions created a maze of bedrooms and living spaces. There were two restrooms on each corner. Inside one, the group had set up their kitchen. Water and the chemicals for the bio toilets were items that were often on everyone's "shopping list." There were no baths. The group stayed clean by finding ways to hose off and maintaining a steady supply of shower-towels. Barak and Asher avoided the concept completely.

It took just a few weeks for Maggie to officially move in. It started with her hanging out with the group more. As the evenings wore on, Jake would volunteer to walk Maggie home. She enjoyed the walks, but, as the weather grew colder, it became an inconvenience for them both. So, she started to have sleepovers with Emily, which soon led to her moving into a room with her.

When she did, she was surprised to find she would be asked to pay rent. Members contributed a part of their take to the common fund. The money was used to buy supplies they could not steal but part of it also went as a payment to the local gang, the Kellies. From what Maggie could observe, the money seemed to serve the purpose of the gang leaving the young group alone.

That is how Maggie, just months after running away, ended up in the shadows of an alley waiting for the signal to spring into action as "the Night Warrior." She was dressed from head to toe in black. Her head and lower face were covered in a mask so only her eyes were visible. Oh, if Daddy-O could see what she was doing with all those gymnastic lessons.

The trick in front of her was daunting. She would need to vault sprint to get the momentum to reach the first storm pipe. From there she could climb to the window sill where there would be a bit of a jump to the ancient remnant that was once a fire escape. After that it was gravy, but there was no time for do-overs.

Any second, Jake would signal her Mickey had the power down. Once that happened, it was up to her to get inside, locate the master keypad, and be ready to punch in the stolen code when the power came back on.

In the distance, she saw a single light flash. Ready. All the lights in the area, including the street lights went dark. Set. Two blinks from a flashlight. GO! She started the timer on her watch.

A focused athlete, she leapt into action. The launch to the drainage pipe was flawless and she used the thick pipe like a vault as she catapulted herself to where she could grab a window ledge. She easily pulled herself up and positioned her toes on the edge of the narrow shelf. This would be the tricky move. She had to jump, twist, and grab the edge of the fire escape. She had one shot with a twenty-foot drop should she miss.

She paused, taking a deep concentrating breath. When she was ready she coiled and sprang. To her pleasant surprise, she found the edge right at her eye level. The adrenaline sure was flowing. She was so high she could grab the rails instead of the platform. Seconds later, she was racing across the roof of the building. At a ventilation grate, she knelt and pulled the power screwdriver from the makeshift utility vest Jake had designed for her. The sound of the tiny whirling engine seemed loud in the still night. With the grate off, she slid into the dusty tunnel, using a penlight to cast a small beam. Mickey had assured her it was only thirty feet but it felt more like thirty yards as she scurried through the filthy pipe. At the opening, she punched open the grate and dropped to the floor below. Once inside, she dashed down six flights of stairs, springing through most of them, until she was on the first floor. She worked her way through the maze of desks to the back of the office. The pad was on the wall.

Her watch beeped. She had made it.

The security light popped up followed by the low hums and clicks of various office equipment restarting. Maggie flipped open the pad and typed in the numbers.

They were in business. She ran to the back doors and opened them. Jake, Seth, and Thad were waiting. Each boy had his assignment. Maggie ran back upstairs to clean up her mess and replace the ventilation grate. When she finished, she met the boys outside the back door.

"We good?" Jake asked.

"Good," everyone reported. Jake reset the security and they all took separate routes back to the Office. An hour later, they were gathered together again at their kitchen table. All except Jake.

"The safe up front had a few hundred," Seth said.

"I didn't get anything," said Thad.

"What the hell, Mickey? That was the big haul?" Seth snapped.

"Jake's not back yet."

At that moment, Jake strolled through the room carrying a small satchel and a massive grin. He walked right up to Mickey. "You were right."

Mickey smiled. "How much?"

"Thousands!"

"What?" exclaimed Thad and Seth.

"Check this out, manos!" Jake turned over the small satchel in his hand and dumped its contents. Money rained down saturating the picnic table.

Maggie and the boys gleefully clutched the piles of bills.

"I don't get it; how did you know?" Maggie asked.

"I've been monitoring this guy for a while," answered Mickey. "He was into some shady real estate deals. Things were starting to heat up. He was taking off before they took it all from him."

"But we took it from him first!" declared Seth.

"And better than that," Jake added. "Thanks to Maggie, we were in and out cleaner than we've ever been. We couldn't have done it without her."

Maggie felt fully accepted that night. She had earned her spot with the group on her own terms. Now living amongst these thieves, in an abandoned office building, in a grungy crime-ridden part of Columbus, she felt safe.

Chapter Eight

When Josh was just a little joe, Stephen had taken him on an amusement park ride. He had not wanted to go at all but Stephen had ridiculed him into it. The two of them were strapped into a small cage and then spun around and around, upside down, sideways, diagonally, and ways that made Josh feel his convulsing stomach was being catapulted from his head to his feet and back again. From the moment it started, Josh hated the sickening sensation and begged his helpless older brother to make it stop.

It was the exact same feeling he had with the Josephs of Tomorrow program. All week long leading up to the meeting with Mrs. Marone, his mother kept finding information. "Their acceptance rate is only ten-percent. Ninety percent of JOT graduates go to Ivy League schools like Liberty and Harvard."

Josh knew she meant well but none of that information was helpful. The only thing worse than the embarrassment of being turned down, would be to make it into the program. First, it was for the smart kids. Josh was average… at best! He had always done well in social studies and Bible classes but that was because he liked the stories. When he looked at the class list, he gagged. Every course was accelerated; there was no way he could handle that. *Strike one*. Second, JOT students arrived at school two hours before anyone else to undergo what was referred to as calisthenics but Josh saw it for what it was… athletics! *Strike two*. Third, JOT students did not even get summer vacations. Instead, they maintained almost the exact same schedule through a combination of summer school and church camp. Gone would be any plans to spend the summers in Canton, even the weekends would be in jeopardy. *Strike three*.

The only plus Josh could see was the fact that his new friends were in the program. Yet he felt equally sure they would not be his friends for long once they realized he could not keep up. Then, there would be the inevitable disappointing of his parents. Josh knew it was wrong but he secretly prayed God would not let him into the program. Then he would just go to normal school and be a normal kid… failing no one.

He lived the week in a chronic state of anxiety. So, when he was back in Mrs. Marone's office, it was with a sense of relief. Time to get this thing over with. This time he sat where Peter had been and his mother sat in the sofa across from him.

His mother took note of the "beautiful painting."

"Yes. That's a painting I show the students," said Mrs. Marone. "I like to get their interpretation of it. Your son did quite well the other day."

"Really?" His mother smiled.

"Yes," Mrs. Marone said. "Joshua, would you like to explain the painting to your mother?"

"It's a picture of Jesus giving instructions to His disciples before sending them out to take the Seven Mountains."

"Oh, yes, I see," his mother said. "It's a very powerful message."

"I believe it encapsulates the true purpose of the Josephs for Tomorrow." Mrs. Marone summarized. "It's our full expectation that each student, sometime during the course of the four years, will have a personal revelation from Jesus, directing that student to one of the Mountains. All the training we do to the students' bodies and minds is just getting them ready to receive that message." There was no smile in Mrs. Marone's voice. She was as professional as she was serious. Josh saw this was not lost on his mother who was silently nodding.

Silence reigned in the room as Mrs. Marone cleared her throat. "Your son is not qualified for JOT."

Josh's small puddle of disappointment was washed away by a sea of relief.

"His grades are too low, his test scores are average, and his activities are subpar."

His face burnt with embarrassment. Though he wanted to see his mother's reaction, he had no courage to look at her. He did not want to see her disappointment.

Mrs. Marone was not finished. "However, I have prayed about this matter, and God has selected your son to be a Joseph of Tomorrow."

Josh felt the ride take a wicked turn.

"That's wonderful!" his mother exclaimed and beamed proudly at Josh.

Josh forced a smile but begged inwardly for her to decline. *But I don't want to be. Please don't make me! Mom! Mom! MOMMY!* It was pointless. His mother was not in sync with him.

"I see Joshua's not overjoyed with the news," observed Mrs. Marone.

"You are. Aren't you, Joshua?"

What Josh wanted to do was leap over the table and bound out the window like the lion from the *Wizard of Oz* but there was no escape. He took a deep gulp, and forced his squeaky voice to say the words. "It sounds really hard. I'm afraid I won't keep up." There, he admitted it, now there was nothing to fear… except… everything.

His mother looked at him with loving disappointment.

Mrs. Marone dismissed his words with a scowl. "*The fear of man lays a snare, but whoever trusts in the* LORD *is safe.* We don't let our students give into their fears, Joshua. Here, we don't let Satan win… ever."

"Yes, ma'am."

As Mrs. Marone walked the two of them to the door, she turned to Josh and, in a whisper, she declared, "Welcome to the Awakening."

Three days later, dressed in the JOT uniform of khaki pants, white dress shirt, red tie with an embroidered gold cross and blue sport coat, Josh rode the early morning ET like a dead man walking. Matthew and Peter talked excitedly. Luke sat as glumly as Josh.

Staying close to Peter, Josh muddled through the morning calisthenics that were led by a former drill instructor who truly loved his job. After the required showers, where he did his best to remain completely invisible, he followed his three friends as they made their way through the hallways. Josh noticed Peter moved with the gracefulness he had when he was prancing through the woods. He had greetings for everyone, even the upper classman. His wishes of good luck to the football players were with the same enthusiasm as his congratulations to the chess team. Everyone in the hallway seemed so focused on greeting Peter and Matthew they barely noticed the "new kid" following along behind them. That was just fine with Josh.

They came to the "Great Hall" auditorium where Peter insisted they take seats in the middle of the middle section. The auditorium was abuzz with adolescent chatter.

"Are these all freshman?" Josh asked.

"No, it's all the JOT students. We'll meet like this every morning."

Matthew leaned over and smiled. "It's the Justjudy Show."

Soon a tall thin student, who looked years older to Josh, walked to the podium amidst a thunderous applause. When he got to the stage, he held up both arms and shouted into the microphone, "Good morning, Josephs!"

The auditorium burst into a unified shout. "Good morning, Joseph!"

"For those of you who do not know me, I'm Jabin Griffith this year's Joseph's of Tomorrow president, and I want to welcome all of you to a brand-new school year!"

Again the auditorium applauded. Josh felt a chill run down his spine. Fear? Or the Spirit? He could not be sure.

"Let us pray."

Instantly, every head was bowed.

"Dear Lord Jesus, thank you for allowing us to begin another year. And thank you for JOT. No matter where we are, whether we're just starting out on this righteous journey or beginning our last year on it, we know that You are in control of our walk. We know if we just keep our focus on You then no matter what we are asked to do, no matter how fast we are asked to run, no matter how high we are asked to climb, or how many verses we are asked to memorize we do it all to honor You. In Jesus Name we pray, Amen."

Josh lifted his head. There was no stopping this. He was on this ride until the end… whatever that might be.

"And now, it's my blessing to introduce a true Joseph for Christ. Someone whose heart's filled with the Holy Spirit. A spiritual mother to all of us. Fresh from a summer of being the keynote speaker at the National Youth Conference in Washington D.C. where President Wilson himself anointed her an Apostle."

It was like Josh was pushed up by a wave, a wave of chaotic jubilance as every student leapt up in an explosion of shouts and applause. The noise was so loud and so long, Jabin was forced to yell his final line. "A woman we're all proud to call both teacher and friend…Mrs. Judith Marone."

The lights danced all around the room as the speakers blared a popular praise song. Mrs. Marone walked out on stage to a chorus of applause and shouts that grew even more immense. Beside him, Peter and Matthew were hollering and shouting as loud as anyone. Josh felt crushed by the energy but he maintained a steady applause. Mrs. Marone gave Jabin a hug and then stepped up to the podium. The applause continued until she put her hands up and asked for quiet. "Thank you! Thank you all. And thank you, Jabin, thank you for those kind words. And thanks to our tech team for the wonderful introduction. Wonderful, thank you."

As the students sat down, Mrs. Marone walked around the podium. "But let's just remind ourselves of something. This isn't about me. I'm just a humble servant of Jesus Christ. And while that is a reason to rejoice, it's also a reason to get serious. What does Jesus ask of us?"

"Our best!" The students shouted in unison.

"That's right! Not just our lives…that's easy to give up. But our effort. That's what Jesus asks of us every day. Our absolute best effort."

With that, the room grew dark and the screen lit up with a movie clip. It was from an ancient 2D movie. The scene it showed was a football practice where one of the players made a statement about the team not being very good. The coach heard the comment and pulled the player out. He ordered the player to get on the ground supported only by his hands and feet. Then another player laid on top of him so that they were back to back. The idea was for the player to see how far he could bear crawl with the other player on his back. Beginning at the goal line, the player said he might be able to make it to the forty-yard line. The coach blindfolded him and told him he wanted him to "give it all to God." So, the blindfolded player set off. As he was going, the coach was constantly reminding him that he had promised to give it all to God. As the player started to falter, the coach began to yell at him, "Really? Is that all you have? Is that all you got to give?" The coach continued to yell, shouting for the player to "give it all to God! Everything you have! All to Him!" As the player kept going, and the shouting became more and more intense, the other players stood up to watch the unfolding miracle. Finally, the player flopped to the ground, his muscles having arrived at total exhaustion. When the blindfold was removed, the player discovered he carried the other player from goal line to goal line.

When the clip was over, there was a stunned silence throughout the auditorium. Mrs. Marone, in a whisper, proclaimed, "God demands our best. Not just on the football field, not just in the classroom, not just in our churches but in every single thing we do. Every. Single. Thing. Give it all to God and Jesus promises us, we'll be able to move mountains!"

When the theater calmed after yet another explosion of adolescent energy, Mrs. Marone concluded by asking everyone to bow their head in prayer. "Dear Lord Jesus, we beseech you to transform us into living swords. Make us righteous weapons for Your Word. Forge us in your holy fire. Sharpen us to a razor's edge. We will strengthen our bodies for you, develop every muscle for strength and endurance. When we're asked to run one mile, we will run two. When we're asked for a hundred push-ups, we'll give You two hundred. We'll strengthen our minds. When we are asked to write a ten-page paper, we will deliver twenty. When asked for four books, we'll read eight. And we'll strengthen our souls. We'll learn Your Word with diligence. We'll take it deep into our souls, make it our solid foundation. Whatever you ask of us, Lord. We will make our bodies Your temple, our hearts will sing Your praises, and our souls will become living sacrifices to Your glory. Amen."

As he recounted the day in bed that night, he had little recollection of the actual events and more a feeling of spending the entire day as an airbreather at a coral reef. There were strange activities going on all around him in a sea of unfamiliar faces. He had to continuously resist the impulse to push it all away and return to the world he knew. If it had not been for Matthew and Peter he was sure that he would have had a complete meltdown.

Unfortunately, surviving the first day was just the beginning.

Each morning began with a grueling ordeal of military-like exercises complete with perfectly formed lines. The students were separated by both class and gender, yet all wore the standardized blue shorts and red shirts. This was one place Josh decided it was better not to stand next to his athletic friends. Instead he stayed in the back middle where he could blend in and not attract any attention to himself.

After the morning workout, the students were required to shower. Here Josh became even more invisible as he did his best to hide his thin developing boyish body from all the young muscular men. He undressed in the furthest corner of the locker room and his shower in the group stall was no longer than thirty seconds. Then he would slink back to his corner and quickly clothe himself.

From there, they attended the Justjudy show, and that, despite her intensity, was the most relaxed part of the day. She had a variety of teaching methods which always gave her presentation an air of originality. Short videos were accompanied by the latest popular music. Other times guest speakers would take the podium, and often, the students themselves would become involved in skits and presentations. Every morning was a different theme; most often it was about working hard for the Awakening and being open to the Spirit.

Then the real school day started. The pace was high-speed and unrelenting. Every class demanded more attention than Josh could provide. Within a week he already felt in danger of drowning. After school, there were supplemental small groups and tutoring sessions to keep everyone up to speed. As a result, Josh left his house at five every morning and did not return until dinner, where he would quickly wolf down his sustenance only to hit the homework until he passed out.

The one class offering any kind of respite was American History. He had always enjoyed history but he especially appreciated this class because it was taught by Mr. Dillon, a young skinny bearded man who looked like he had just stepped out of a civil war photograph. He had a habit of casually climbing on and off the back of a chair. What Josh liked most about Mr. Dillon was the way he taught. He spoke with a deep respect for his subject matter but created a relaxed informal atmosphere in his classroom.

Mr. Dillon also always spoke as if he was addressing Congress. "Now then, my fellow Americans, as we have learned… well, judging by your test scores… most of us have learned, the Pilgrims, the original Christian founders of what is now America, came here on a mission to establish a New Israel. A New Promised Land for God's Chosen People, or perhaps a better way of saying it, a Land for the people who choose God. It was a second Exodus and just like the Israelites, they had a covenant with God. Everyone remember what a covenant is?"

"An agreement," someone shouted. Mr. Dillon's class was the only class anyone would dare speak before being called upon.

"A contractual agreement," corrected Mr. Dillon. "The Israelites had a covenant with God through the Ten Commandments and the Jewish law, whereas the Pilgrims had the Mayflower Compact, which, as I am sure you all remember, began with the words….?"

"In the Name of God. Amen," Peter called out.

"Exactly. The number one overriding fact…resolute… 'In the name of God. Amen.' A powerful declaration… BAM! 'In the name of God. Amen!' That's who they had their covenant with-God. Not 'we the people,' or some obscure reference to an unnamed 'Creator' but God, the one true God that made heavens and earth, who sacrificed His Son to pay our debt of sin.

"Now, in this next unit, we're going to learn how the Puritans had their vision usurped by a group of liberal Unitarian Universalists who almost destroyed this country. But, more importantly, I'm gonna give you the straight poop about a huge mistake the early promoters of a Christian nation made. See, initially, they tried to make the claim that the 'Founding Fathers' were Christians establishing a Christian Nation. It was not until this was exposed as a lie of Satan that the true history was revealed. When that happened, the Final Great Awakening truly commenced. God was waiting for us to get it right, to get our history right, His-story right. The Bible teaches us, *Righteousness exalts a nation, but sin is a reproach to all the people.* And that includes in our history, as well. We have to learn to expose the devil wherever he may be hiding, even if it's in our own history, even if it's about men we once held… aloft." As he said "aloft," he raised his hand with Shakespearean flair. "At the heart of it all was a term called 'religious liberty.' Do we remember how the Puritans defined that term? Joshua?"

"The freedom to worship God according to the Bible," answered Josh meekly.

"Right. And how do we define that term today…religious liberty?" Mr. Dillon asked, climbing onto the back of a chair.

"Same way," Josh answered.

"Exactly. The same way." Mr. Dillon leapt from the back of the chair and nearly kicked up his heels. He moved to the side to draw attention to the screen, where a portrait of George Washington appeared.

The class booed.

Mr. Dillon smiled. "Yes, good old Georgie. Now, Georgie here was once asked why he got involved in the American Revolution. Why would he put it all on the line to create a new nation and he answered…"

A quote popped up over the portrait, it read, "The establishment of civil and religious liberty was the motive that induced me into the field."

Mr. Dillon read the slide emphasizing the words "religious liberty." "So, it looks like old Georgie is fighting for religious liberty too, doesn't it? But was he? Was he fighting for the freedom to worship God according to the Bible? When asked who this freedom to worship applied to, he stated…"

Another slide popped up on the wall. It read: "if of the denomination of Christians; or declare themselves Jews, Mahomitans or otherwise."

"Mahomitans is what they called the jihadists. Think about that for a second. He's saying, even as long ago as the 1770s, that America's doors were open to terrorists. Seriously? But look what he tags on the end, 'or otherwise.' What do you think he means by that?"

"You could be any religion at all?" answered Ruth. She was one of the popular girls who was far too pretty for Josh to even look at. Not that she ever noticed him as she had her full attention on Peter.

"Exactly. Satan is so patient. It took him over a century and a half but he twisted the definition from its original Godly intent to a muddled mess of accommodation. By the time of the American Revolution, the words had come to mean allowing all religions an equal place in America. Does that sound like a Christian teaching to you? Have any of you read anything like that in the Bible? Of course not. What does the Bible teach?" He paused and looked around the room. "Start with the Ten Commandments…" he hinted.

"*I am the Lord your God; thou shalt have no other gods before me,*" Peter recited.

"So, by the time of the American Revolution," Mr. Dillon concluded excitedly, prancing around the room, "when the Founding Fathers were doing their whole Constitution thing, they had already broken the first commandment. They were no longer in covenant. The Founding Fakers wrote the Constitution outside of a Covenant with God. This caused all kinds of problems because we were not the righteous nation we were intended to be. Slavery, for instance. If the founding fakers had truly been doing God's Will, they would have abolished slavery right off the bat. But they didn't, so we were not a completely righteous nation. As we shall see in a few months, this led to God's judgment, something officially called the American Civil War. But, through it all, God never abandoned us. He waited patiently for us to come back to Him, back to HIS original intention. Back to HIS original covenant with this nation. Back to November 11, 1620. Back to that tiny little ship filled with true Christians who knew, before they went ashore to start a new nation, they had to make a declaration. They had to declare to the world they would be establishing this new nation…" Here Mr. Dillon threw both arms in the air like an orchestra conductor and the whole class shouted. "In the name of God. Amen."

The class burst into applause and laughter.

Mr. Dillon was a demanding teacher, as all the JOT teachers were. They had to be with Mrs. Marone at the helm. Patrolling the school with megaphone in hand, she expected nothing but excellence from everyone. She could pop in on a class at any time, causing nervous tension among both the students and the teachers. At any given moment, she could stop anyone in the hall. When she did she would order everyone in the vicinity to freeze and then subject the targeted student to a ten-minute public lesson about grades, attitude, or most likely, work ethic. When she finished reaming the student she always concluded through her megaphone. "There's to be no gossip of this incident. *Do not associate with a gossip.* Learn the lesson being taught then go and have a blessed day."

It did not take long for Josh to realize any regular trips to visit his cousins and friends in Canton were out of the question. He would be blessed just to make it for the holidays. Even more so, his thoughts of staying connected through on-line gaming seemed childishly naive.

As busy as the JOT program kept them, Saturday was the only day with any amount of free time. Mornings were spent in required Bible classes but in the afternoons, they were on their own. As long as the weather was even remotely nice they would meet on top of Elmer. There was no talk of playing *Capture the Flag* or any other summer game. This was the only down time they had and they used it to lay around and do nothing.

One crisp November day, Luke was the last to arrive to Elmer. His cheeks were red and streaked with tears.

"Luke?" Peter asked.

"It's solomon," Luke said in a voice that was anything but.

"Grades?" Matthew asked and Luke glared at him. "C'mon, joe, it's solomon. We're brothers, aren't we?"

"Yeah, Luke, c'mon, we're here, joe," said Peter.

"It's nothing. Justjudy hates me, that's all."

"That's not true," declared Peter.

"Oh, yeah? She never wanted me in her program." Luke wiped his eyes. "My dad made her."

Josh could not picture anyone making Mrs. Marone do anything but he also considered Luke's dad being an elder.

"I don't get it. Did she kick you out?" Peter asked.

"Not yet, but I've got to get my grades up by the end of the semester or I'm done."

They sat in silence for a moment.

"Hey, joe," encouraged Matthew. "We'll get it done."

Luke rolled his eyes. There was another silence where Josh wished someone would say something.

"What'd your dad say?" Peter asked finally.

"Among other things…flunk out equals military school." Luke curled up into a fetal position and put his face on his arm. No one could think of the right words to say. After a long uncomfortable minute, Luke took a deep breath and lifted his head. "Fuck it. I'm headed to the military anyway. I never wanted to be in her fucking program. I even told my dad that but he puts me in." Luke slammed his fist into his thigh. "Dammit, I told them it would be too hard, but do they listen? NO! Fucking assholes."

Josh sat as still as he could and hoped Luke's profanity was not directed towards his parents.

Later, Josh and Peter walked together back to their houses. "Can't we help Luke somehow?" Josh asked.

"Luke gets a lot of help," Peter answered. "You know how Mrs. Marone's always telling us to give it all to God. Well, Luke is. He's never been good at school. He tries, he tries hard. He has to. His dad… but it just doesn't come easy. Then he gets mad and that just makes it worse."

"I wish we could help him."

"I think the best thing that could happen to him is that he gets out of that house." Peter's eyes showed deep concern. "Look, you have to promise me never to tell anyone this, solomon?"

"Solomon."

"One time, a few years ago, I went over to his house. I was about to ring the doorbell when I heard all this yelling. In truth, I peeked in the window. I know I shouldn't have but I was a kid. Anyway, I saw his dad and… and I've never seen anyone that mad before. I mean the guy was like an animal or something. His face was all red. No. It wasn't just his face, it was his whole bald head. And then, I saw him hit Luke's mom. He didn't slap her either; he hit her with his fist….and Luke… he comes dashing at his dad with a knife in his hand."

"A knife?"

"It was a table knife, probably wouldn't cut butter, but he starts hacking away at his dad's shoulder. His dad grabs him by the neck and slams him up against a wall. Then, his mom gets up on her knees and starts screaming, begging him to hit her not Luke."

"What happened?"

"I got out of there. I've never been so scared in my whole life." Peter paused. "I've tried to bring it up but Luke doesn't want to talk about it. He'll bad-mouth his dad all day long but if anyone even hints his dad isn't the greatest man in the world, he'll go ballistic. I'm pretty sure things like that are still going on in that house."

By this time, they had arrived at Josh's driveway.

"Algebra test Monday and a busy day at YF tomorrow," reminded Peter.

"Ouch, why do they give us tests on Monday? They know we don't have time to study on Sundays!"

"*Share in suffering as a good soldier of Christ Jesus.* I'll pray a hedge of protection around you. See you in the morning, joe."

Chapter Nine

Life in the Office settled into a normal routine. Each morning, over breakfast the group would meet and discuss the tasks for the day. The jobs were based on need and divvied out by skills, abilities, and, when it came to Barak and Asher, interests. For the youngest two were undoubtedly the first to leave the meeting with agendas of their own. Mickey took on all computer related tasks spending the rest of the day on the second floor where he had quite the elaborate office. Maggie did not understand all the technological gizmos he had running but he assured her it was necessary to "keep me as invisible as the wind." The "guys," Jake, Thad and Seth, spent most of their time working the streets.

The three were well known and well respected. They always seemed to have a dozen deals being negotiated. The boys were the go-to suppliers for technology. "If we don't have it, we'll get it," they would assure their potential customers.

Maggie loved the daily life. There was always something to do; something to focus on which left little time to ruminate about the past or worry about the future. Day to day survival was the focus, even as they sat in the evenings in their "living room." There, the conversations were primarily centered on the needs of the group and the adventures of fulfilling those needs. Little was said of any past lives.

One thing Maggie did learn was that, next to her, Mickey was the newest member of the group. He came from a suburb near Dayton and found himself on his own when his parents were "taken." He had a deep, seething hatred for anything having to do with the government and as a result, the subject was rarely discussed.

In fact, in direct contrast to her childhood home, there were two subjects that were all but taboo around the Office. The first being the government except as an obstacle to be avoided. The second was anything having to do with Christianity. No one answered questions with Bible phrases. In fact, there was not a Bible present at the Office at all. Out of everything, the living conditions, the food, the gangs, all of it, that Maggie decided, was the most shocking difference. Not that she minded it. The thought of a loving heavenly father had become as foreign to her as a loving earthy father.

During any down time they did have, Emily and Maggie spent it doing two things. The first was gymnastics. The guys even went so far as to help them set up a mini-gym on the fourth floor for bad weather days. The second thing was to play school.

One day, Jake came to her after class. "I see what you're doing."

"What?" Maggie asked.

"Playing school. That's just your way of getting her to learn stuff."

"Shhh, don't tell her."

"Oh, I won't, believe me. Think maybe we could get Asher and Barak to attend?"

"They did the other day."

"Really?"

"They lasted five minutes, declared it recess, and we never saw them again."

Maggie worried about the twins. They were urban jungle boys. Occasionally, she heard Jake warning Seth. "The boys are wild, you need to set some boundaries." To which, Seth would shrug his shoulders helplessly. The only guidelines Seth presented to the boys were to stay away from drugs and gangs. The boys themselves were adorable, which they used to their advantage. Maggie loved it best when they would get dressed up in their "rich kids' clothes" and return at the end of the day triumphantly carrying bags of fresh fruit cleverly swiped through one of their multitude of schemes. They were young and cocky... confident and naïve.

One day, Asher came back sporting a big grin. "I got you something, Maggie."

Maggie and Emily were setting the table for dinner. "Oh, yeah? What's that."

Asher's face was streaked with dirt which made his smile even more brilliant. He reached into his pocket and brought out a ring box in his filthy hand. He handed the box to Maggie. "Here."

Emily whistled. Maggie opened it.

"It's a diamond ring," he announced proudly.

Just then Barak burst into the room, completely out of breath. "Maggie, Maggie, I got something for you."

"Wow, you guys know it's not my birthday."

Victoriously, Barak handed Maggie a long thin box. She opened it to reveal a shiny glass bracelet.

"Those are real diamonds."

"Mine is, too," Asher said.

"I can see that." Maggie smiled. "Where did you find these?"

"In a store," Asher said.

"An empty store," added Barak.

"Out of business," said Asher.

"Back door was wide open."

"Wide open."

"We could just walk right in."

"Walked right in."

"The place was cleaned out but I found the ring."

"And I found the bracelet."

Listening to those two was always like watching a tennis match. Maggie said, "Well, I don't know what to say. I'm really touched."

As the boys walked away Maggie could hear them argue. "Mine had more diamonds," declared Barak.

"But mine was a ring," countered Asher. "Rings mean you love someone more than just bracelets."

Maggie and Emily watched them until they were out of earshot. "You know, they both say they're gonna marry you when they grow up," said Emily.

"Well, I'm glad I have a long time to make up my mind."

At Mickey's insistence, whenever they could, they ate together. "It's good for group unity." All Maggie knew was she liked it. Sure, they were a hodgepodge of people, with the oldest, Mickey, only being twenty-three, but they were a family, a group of people genuinely caring about each other.

Other than in her nightmares, her real family felt like a distant memory, a whole other life. She worried about getting discovered and being returned to them but as time went on, it seemed less and less likely. For one thing, Mickey reported there was no on-going investigation. She was not even on any missing person's list. That did not surprise her; her father would never have contacted the police and her mother was too weak to do it either. Still, she could be picked up and then discovered. So, Mickey came up with a solution. He gave Maggie a new identity. She was now Margaret Anderson from Cleveland. The forged documents would never pass muster for church membership but they gave her a comfortable cover. Her fears decreased even further when she discovered her father had been transferred out of state. With a new name, no one looking for her and her family far removed, she felt as safe as she would ever be.

The one thing she loved above all else was the nights she could don her working clothes and become the Night Warrior. Adrenaline did not just flow through her on those nights, it replaced her blood completely. Every one of her senses was heightened to a point of primitive acuteness. Scaling the buildings, stealthily slinking in the shadows of the roof tops, and slipping her way into the buildings were the most alive moments of her life. Some nights, when the swirling memories prevented her from sleeping, she would slip out for parkour practice. She would spend hours working her way around the rooftops, honing her skills, but more importantly, reveling in the freedom.

All in all, Maggie loved her new life.

Chapter Ten

As the weather turned to winter, it was to Josh's great delight the boys gravitated towards hanging out in his room on Saturday afternoons. He had no siblings running around, a mother that doted after them, and a huge room perfect for four teenage boys.

One frigid afternoon, Peter, Matthew and Josh were casually lounging around on his bedroom furniture snacking on an assortment of fruit his mother had prepared.

"She likes you, you know," Peter said to Matthew.

Matthew picked up a handful of blueberries and feigned ignorance. "Who?"

"Oh, give me a break, you know exactly who. That angelic voice!"

Matthew broke into a grin. "Ada? I've known her since fifth grade."

"So?"

"So, she's like a sister. Besides, JOT forbids relationships."

"I know, but she does like you."

Matthew realized his smile was giving him away so he quickly diverted the conversation. "What about you, Peter?"

"Me? What?"

"Me, what? Don't give me that stuff. You've got a virtual harem around you."

"A harem?" Peter laughed and looked at Josh who could offer him no support as Matthew was speaking the truth. "Like you said, that's a no-no in JOT. Besides, I think about what Paul wrote in 1 Corinthians: *The unmarried man is anxious about the things of the Lord, how to please the Lord. But the married man is anxious about worldly things, how to please his wife, and his interests are divided.* Girls are a distraction."

"Can't argue with that," Matthew said, throwing a blueberry into the air and catching it in his mouth. "They distract me every time they walk in the room."

The conversation was interrupted by the voice of Josh's mother.

"Joshua?"

"Yes, Mom?"

"Luke's here. I'm sending him up."

Two seconds later, Luke arrived at the door. He had taken to wearing a military jacket. He also kept his hair just shy of shaved. Shaven heads were against the dress code, but Luke managed to push it as far as he could. He was carrying a bowl of grapes and a backpack, grinning widely.

"Your mom sent some more fruit," he said, as he grandly placed the bowl on the table.

"What's with the grin?" Peter asked.

"I got something," Luke said and removed his backpack. He took out a rectangular black box that was wrapped in old fashioned electric cords. "I found it in my dad's stuff in the attic. Think it was my grandfather's."

"What is it?" Josh asked.

Luke removed two contraptions that looked a little familiar. "It's an old game system and games. Only get this, these were before the FGA." The boys waited for the punch line. "Don't you get it, peans?" Luke exclaimed and then lowered his voice to a whisper. "These games are not CAP-approved."

Impossible! The little symbol of the Christian American Party was everywhere. There was not an item in any store or a package in any grocery that did not have the CAP stamp of approval. Josh grew instantly curious and frightened at the same time.

"Those are illegal," Peter said.

Luke was bringing the games out of his bag with his hand. He stopped. "Jeez, Pete, why don't you say it a little louder. Josh, get the door."

"My mom'll think that's weird."

Luke looked exasperated. "Seriously? Solomon, just keep your voices down." Luke overturned his backpack and dumped the contents to the floor. A dozen plastic cases fell out, products from another time. "Most of 'em are old sports and military games. It's all just 2-D but still fun."

Sports and military games, so far, no big deal.

Luke quickly dug through the pile. "This one," he said, holding up a case with a picture of a soldier shooting a machine gun on it. "I was playing this last night. You won't believe the shit you see. When you shoot an enemy, you see the bullet go into the guy's body and explode his heart. Or if you shoot him in his head, his brain blows up."

He had Josh and Matthew's attention; Peter remained unimpressed. "What about that one? The one with the scary woman on the front."

Luke picked up the case and covered it with his hand. "This one," he said, looking over to the open bedroom door, and then whispering, "Black magic."

"Oh, no way!" Peter said, jumping out of his chair.

"Jesus, Pete, don't be a girl!" snapped Luke.

Josh was not sure how to feel; he was as curious as he was scared.

"Playing with magic opens the door to Satan," Peter said.

"Oh, come on. It's just a video game. You know, electronics, computer programing, and it's ancient at that."

"It's wrong," Peter said. "Besides, you say you took this from your dad? What happens if he finds out?"

"Who cares? I'm gonna flunk out anyway. No way am I gonna get my grades up."

Silence.

"I don't know what to say, joe," Matthew said.

"Yeah," Josh heard himself say.

"Oh, silence, Pharisee!" shouted Luke. "You're just as stupid as I am. Just because Justjudy likes you."

"Luke!" Peter shouted.

"Well, it's true!"

"This isn't Josh's fault," Matthew said.

"It's nobody's fault," Peter said. "It's God's plan. You know that, Luke. *Many are the plans in the mind of a man, but it is the purpose of the LORD that will stand.*"

Luke vigorously wiped his hands over his face. "Yeah, I know." He heart-bumped Josh and said, "Sorry, joe."

Josh bumped back. "It's solomon."

"Now, how about these games?" said Luke, anxious to change the subject.

"Fine, but not the one with the magic," Peter declared.

It took some time to figure out how to hook up the ancient system to the modern technology but soon the screen was alive with a battle. Josh had to admit it was intense even if the graphics made it look cartoonish. On the other hand, he could see why games like these went out of business, there was no way CAP would approve of this level of blood and gore.

Peter was thinking the same thing. "I can't believe they let little kids play these games."

"Fucking libs didn't care," Luke chimed in as his avatar bayoneted an enemy soldier.

"I sure wouldn't want my kids playing this," Matthew said.

"Yours and Ada's?" Peter teased.

"Silence, Pharisee!" retorted Matthew with a grin.

For the rest of the afternoon, the boys played their vintage treasure. It was not lost on Josh that this was the first time he spent an afternoon gaming with his new friends. It was fun but it also seemed out of place. With the intensity of the JOT program, the hours of exercise, the daily grind of academics, playing video games was plain childish.

Several weeks later, semester grades came out and Luke disappeared for two days. On the third day, they each received a text from him. "Elmer's even."

"What's that mean?" Josh asked.

"It's something we used to do back in middle school when we thought we were a real secret club," answered Peter. "We'd write in code, sort of, and challenge ourselves to figure it out. He wants us to meet him at seven o'clock at Elmer."

That night, just after dinner, Josh met up with Matthew and Peter on their way to Elmer. The temperature was in the low teens and even with all of Josh's winter protection, the biting January freeze chilled him to the bone. Peter, on the other hand, bounded through the snow like a spring fawn.

When they arrived at Elmer, they found Luke was already there contorted into the smallest ball he could for warmth.

"Okay, Luke, explain to us why we're all out here freezing our butts off," Matthew said, through chattering teeth

"I needed to say good-bye this way. Tomorrow morning... military academy."

Silence engulfed the tree fort. No one had words.

Luke took a deep breath. "Look, this isn't supposed to get all intense or anything. And I know we can't stay here long before we all freeze to death. But, I just needed to be here one more time with you. You're like my only friends."

"We're more than that. We're your brothers," said Peter.

"Besides," Matthew said, "it's not like its forever. You'll be back in the summer…"

Luke shook his head. "Military camp. My dad's decided you all are a bad influence on me. Ha! That's a laugh." He paused. "So, I was hoping you'd join me in something that will never go out of style." Luke reached into his jacket and pulled out what looked like a small flat thermos. "We'll seal the deal in the way of men… whiskey."

Small paper cups appeared in his shaking hand. He handed one to each of them. Luke carefully poured the contents of the flask equally into the four cups. Josh saw he ended up with about half a cup. He had tried wine at Thanksgiving a couple of times. And his father had shared a beer with him once but this would be his first taste of the hard stuff. It didn't smell too good. He wondered if he should sip it or down it all at once.

Luke held up his cup. "So… I don't really know how to do this but I'd like to make a toast. To brotherhood."

They all tapped cups and then, with quite some fanfare, they downed the contents. Josh had never tasted anything that burned so much. Peter and Matthew danced about in theatrical pain. Luke stood tall and laughed but his cheeks turned a bright crimson color plainly visible by the starlit sky.

The boys' guffaws echoed in the cold winter air.

Then, Peter had them all huddle up. "Joes, and I don't think this is the whiskey talking." The others chuckled. "Luke, Matthew, we've grown up together. We've seen each other cry, get mad, and laugh for hours. I know God has plans for each of us. Big plans. We just have to focus on Him and follow His path. But you… I don't think any man is closer to anyone than the joes he grew up with. And Josh. How solomon are you? I mean, you move in what…. seven months ago? …And I feel like I've known you my whole life."

"Me, too, joe" Matthew said as he heart-bumped Josh.

Then, Luke did something Josh did not see coming. He hugged him. A great, big, masculine bear hug. "Sorry I gave you such a hard time, joe."

Peter nodded solemnly. "*So the soul of Jonathan was knit to the soul of David, and Jonathan loved him as his own soul.* That's what God means by friendship, our souls are knitted together."

For the final moment, they stood silently in a group embrace.

Luke was the first to break the huddle. "Well, joes, I'm about to freeze my ass off. Besides my dad doesn't know I left. So…"

As Josh and Peter walked towards their houses, Josh asked what Peter thought.

"Luke doesn't realize this yet but I think this is God's plan to get him away from his dad."

It would be years before any of them would see Luke again.

Chapter Eleven

Maggie slipped further into the shadows of the rooftop overlooking her target.

Two nights ago, the boys had approached her hesitantly with the idea. They assumed she might have a problem with the target being a church. Silly assumption.

The church was downtown. It was not as big as its infamous off-spring Christian Heritage but, in Columbus, the Hillside Evangelical Church had been one of the first to claim the Awakening.

What Maggie did not tell the boys, she was somewhat familiar with the church, having gone to services there more than once. Now, staring at it from her hidden perch she could almost see the lost little girl she had been, standing straight and tall in her Sunday morning dress, smiling brightly and saying all the right things.

The front was covered in ornate columns leading to the looming statues of Jesus on one side and Mary on the other. The figures were covered by concrete awnings. She used to think how nice it was for the builders to protect Mary and Jesus from the weather. Even as a little girl, Maggie had liked the church, it had old-school personality. Now... she was going to rob it.

The church was well-maintained, and updated with great security, save for one oversight. An old electrical wire was running between two nearby buildings and right over the ancient roof. Jake got hold of a zipline trolley. She just had to time it right and she would drop down right on the top of the building where she could climb up the bell tower and get to the window. Once inside she would work her way to the basement, taking the route Mickey had mapped out to avoid any of the night time security crew.

The trick to the roof was an adventure but not very difficult. She could easily control her speed so she could technically come to a complete stop before dropping onto the large roof. But where was the fun in that?

A light blinked in the distance. Time for the Night Warrior.

Like a fox from the shadows, she jumped up on the ledge and attached the trolley. Without hesitation, she was off, gliding down the wire over the busy street fifty feet below her. As she approached the church she built up momentum. She could feel the cool evening air blast its way through her clothing. Damn, how she loved the adrenaline.

Without slowing she dropped to the middle of the roof, inertia carried her forward. She went limp, coiling, then sprang up to slow her momentum. When she hit the roof again she was in full control, managing a few tumbles on the dusty roof before sticking the landing.

It was a spectacular move, not that anyone was around to see it.

Maggie looked up and into the face of a grey-haired security guard, an unlit cigarette dangling from his mouth. "Wh… wha… what the hell are you?" he sputtered.

For a split second, the whole world stopped. She had one thought. Abort the plan and get the hell out of there. But she couldn't go back the way she came. Damn!

She flipped into flight mode.

Sprinting to one of the edges of the building, she peered over. It was the rear of the building. Not encouraging. If she jumped she would be a splat on the sidewalk.

Shit.

She turned around. The man's senses appeared to be returning. "Okay, now… let's just calm down a moment… solomon?" The man turned and closed the maintenance door he had used to gain access to the roof. He noticed her studying the door. "You don't want to go that way. You'll run right into three armed guards and they ain't as nice as me."

The guard, in a near crouch, was slowly moving, like a zoo keeper trying to rein in an escaped animal. "You're just a kid, ain't ya? Look, I'm not sure what's goin' on, not even exactly sure how you dropped outta the sky like that, but technically, you ain't really done nothin'. Hell, I'll be in more trouble than you, seein' as how I was up here to cop a smoke. So, I'll make you a deal. You come with me, nice and quiet, and I'll get you outta here without no one knowin'."

Shit, shit, shit. Like any animal she was down to her final option. Fight.

After all, she had done it before. But this guy was not a drunk pervert. He was stone sober and armed.

Goddammit!

She ran to the other side. It was the front of the church. Oh yeah, that's right. Now this had potential.

"Look, I really don't want to have to call someone. But they ain't no other way down."

She pounced to a crouch on the edge of the building.

"Now, hold on… let's not do anything stupid here…" The man was frightened, that empowered her. She jumped off the building, down to the top of the concrete statue holder. She was pretty sure it was Mary under there.

The officer peered at her from atop. It was then she realized he did not want to call backup. He really was afraid of having to explain what he was doing on the roof.

"Hey," she called up to him. "I'll make you a deal."

The man chuckled. "I'm not sure you're in a position to deal."

"If I make it down without breaking my neck, you let me go, no report, nothing. If I don't, I guess you call anyone you like."

"That's not a 'deal.' What's in it for me?"

"A story to tell your children."

"Ha! Have to be my grandkids at this point."

Maggie began her descent. She checked every toe and hand hold twice before putting any weight on it. Who knew what parts of this old building were about to give. The lights from the street appeared to be light years away. Don't think about that. Focus on the task at hand. If she did not, she'd see those lights soon enough.

She worked her way to the front of the statue. She had been right, it was Mary. Her stone-cold face offered no empathy towards Maggie's predicament. Maggie shimmied her way down Mary's legs until she was using her feet as hand holds. Her own feet, dangling in the air, went searching for the next foothold but there was nothing else below her. Now what?

She saw her only option. There was a large column a few dozen feet away. The concrete was made rounded, giving it the impression of a pole being slammed against the corner. She could shimmy down it… maybe all the way to the ground. She just had to get to it.

"Alright," she heard the security officer say. "Just get back up here before you kill yourself."

She looked up and offered a smile he could not see through her mask. *Oh, you ain't seen nothing yet, old man.* Using only the slim edge of the building she worked her way, one hand hold at a time, along the thin edge of the ornate roof. At moments she felt the old bricks give, as she inched her way along. As her fingers began to ache, it was with a sense of relief when she was clutching the concrete column. The relief did not last long, as she found herself having to keep every part of her body pushed up to the column with all her might. Her single chance was to keep moving but only one body part at a time. Inch by inch she crept her way down the column.

As her muscles shook from the strain, she began giving odds on which of her limbs would fail her first. As it turned out, they all did at once. She clawed at the wall but she was falling fast. Out of control, a ball of pure panic shooting up her throat, she dropped.

And landed in heavy canvas. What the hell was this? Then it dawned on her, she had landed on a long walkway awning that kept the churchgoers out of the weather. She couldn't believe her luck! She had not only not died, but hadn't even broken a bone.

The awning began to sink lower and to one side. With a crash, the structure collapsed with Maggie wrapped up in it like a wad of gum.

It took seemingly forever to get out of the entanglement. When she did she looked up to see the security guard staring down at her. He saluted her. She waved and disappeared into the night.

"What the fuck, Mickey?"

They were all back in the office. The young ones were asleep. Jake was not happy.

"Jesus, Jake, keep your voice down. I'm in charge of the security systems, you know… computer stuff. How the hell should I know some guy was going to be up there? He wasn't supposed to be."

It was a game of flaming hot potato, and Mickey had given it right back. Jake needed somewhere else to go. He turned to Maggie. "And you! What the hell do you think you're doing?"

"Um… getting away." She saw Thad cover a smile.

"Risking your life." Jake was moving closer to her. She felt her pulse rush.

"I did what I had to do. Same as anyone."

"No, not the same as anyone, cause most people would have turned themselves in and those that didn't, would be splattered on the street. That was a ridiculous chance you took." He was now mere feet from her.

"Oh, come on, it wasn't that extreme." She tried a laugh, but he kept coming.

"We saw you! We all saw you!" Jake was in her face. Too close... too close.

She placed her hands on his chest, then slowly pushed him to the proper distance. "You saw me get away. Would you rather I get caught?"

"Yes! Maggie, if it's between that and dying..."

"Hey, I didn't die. Besides, I think it probably looked scarier than it really was."

Thad could no longer restrain himself. "I thought it looked amazing. You were like this little bug, only you were going backwards, and..."

Jake stomped his foot, grabbed an empty chair and tossed it into a wall. "What the hell are you talking about? You were just as scared as the rest of us."

"Yeah, and I was. And I want to say to Maggie, if you ever do anything like that again, I will swat you down myself. But you have to admit, she pulled it off."

Jake screamed and stormed out of the room.

"What the hell's up with him?" asked Maggie.

Thad looked to be sure Jake was out of earshot. "Oh, he just hates it when things go wrong. He'll get over it. Maggie, I'm telling you... oh my god..."

Seth leaned into the conversation. "That was the most amazing thing I've ever seen. Wait until I tell Barak and Asher. I'm gonna bring them there, right to that spot, I'm gonna show them what you did."

"Seriously, though," said Thad, "What were you thinking?"

"I was thinking I could do it. And then I think I got lucky. Let's not tell the twins this one. They don't need any more inspiration."

The boys made her relive her great escape again and again throughout the evening. Each time the story was told it became embellished. She imagined it would not take long for the heights to be doubled and "while bullets rained down on her, she..." That is how stories are created. That is how legends are made.

Later that night Jake asked to speak to her... on the roof. "Sorry, I yelled like that, but you have to understand... that terrified me. I thought we were going to lose you."

"Really? I still don't think it was..."

"Maggie, it was crazy! And it's not the first time. I see you, even when we're practicing. It's like you don't just get something right, you have to conquer it. You take too many risks."

"I appreciate the concern."

"I'm not sure that's enough. Can I ask you something?"

"Maybe."

"In all the months you've been with us, you've hardly said anything about your fam…"

Maggie cut him off with the wave of her finger. "Don't go there… don't even think about going there…"

"But Maggie, I'm worried about you… maybe there's a reason for the risks… maybe…"

"Knock it off. There's nothing to worry about. I get it, less daredevilry stuff. I'll take care of it."

Jake took a deep breath. "Look, Maggie, I know you sneak out at night to play Catwoman."

"So? And it's 'Night Warrior.'"

"Whatever. It's dangerous. Not only for you, but the whole group. Why? Can't you sleep?"

"Say one more thing, Jake… just one more."

"Oh yeah, the warrior that you are. Well, look my little lady friend, like it or not, you've got people who care about you now. That might be a strange feeling for you, but it's true. And we need you to take care of yourself. What would I have done if you fell? What would I have told Emily?"

He was tearing up. Big bad Jake, who was always trying to order everyone around, was about to go "wah-wah." He really cared. She was not at all sure how she felt about that. She knew what she should feel, and wondered why she didn't. As close as she had come to all of them, there were lines she did not let them cross. She told them nothing because there was nothing she wanted them to know. "Okay, seriously. I'll bring it down… a notch."

Jake rolled his eyes. "Or two. Thank you."

Jake knew she did not like them, but he insisted on one every once and a while. This was one of those moments. He gave her a hug. Big brother Jake.

Chapter Twelve

For two years, not a day went by that Josh did not have to consciously put down the evil slime monster wanting to crawl up his gut. Sure, behind it all was the fear he would ultimately fail out of JOT but the daily terror of avoiding Mrs. Marone's megaphone lessons was what was really debilitating. He was caught by her only once. In his panic, he could not remember what his grade in Creation Science was and she blasted him for it. He vowed never to get caught again. As a result, he became as invisible as possible, staying in the middle, slinking from class to class. Above all, he maintained rigorous attention to his studies. Somehow, he was able to make it through his sophomore year.

The week before his junior year, Josh was called to Mrs. Marone's office. She had only given him a day's notice of the meeting. He was quite grateful as that allowed just a day of stewing in his anxiety. As he walked into her office and took a seat, he paid mental tribute to the painting on the wall.

"I've got a problem I was hoping you could help me with," began Mrs. Marone.

"Sure," he answered. She was asking for his help?

"My problem is this. My numbers in JOT are too large. I have a big batch of freshmen this year. Now, it's always been my policy to give those freshmen a chance to prove themselves so, when I need to make cuts, I look at the upperclassmen, to see if there are any weak links."

Josh's heart dropped. He knew it was by the skin of his teeth but he had thought he had passed. Where had he miscalculated?

"I looked thoroughly at my current students and I saw there are two young men who are friends but aren't really good for each other."

Now, Josh was officially confused.

"One of those boys was born to be an Apostle. The other is this shy boy that seems to need the other boy. I almost never see the shy boy but when I do, he's always standing really close to the leader boy. The leader boy's doing all the talking. The shy boy just stands there, like without the leader boy, there would be no shy boy. It's a very unhealthy relationship. Now, I'm not in the business of breaking up friendships but I am in the business of turning out the best leaders I can for God's army. So, I'm not sure what to do. Any ideas?"

Josh swallowed hard. He avoided her eyes. "Maybe you should remove the shy boy from JOT."

"Mmm, it sounds like you're saying I should break these two up, is that right?"

"Yes, Mrs. Marone."

"Okay, I'll let the leader boy go."

Josh replayed her words in his head. "The leader boy?"

"Of course, were you listening? God chose the leader boy to be an Apostle when he was still in the womb. JOT isn't making him a leader; I'm just giving him the credentials. Since my job is to give God the best Josephs I can, if I keep the leader boy and let the shy boy go, I give God one Joseph. But, if I remove the leader boy and separate him from the shy boy, then kick that shy boy in the gluteus maximus and show him what kind of a Joseph he really is, I give God two Josephs. Strategically speaking, what would be the better move?"

"You can't do that!"

"Oh, but I assure you, I can."

"No, I'm sorry. I didn't mean any disrespect. I meant you can't do that to Pe...I mean, the leader boy. JOT is...might be everything to that joe. He may have been wanting to be in it since he was a little kid. It wouldn't be fair to kick him out if he's doing the work."

"This isn't about doing the work and it isn't about being fair. It's a simple strategical decision. How would I be serving God best, by providing Him one officer for His army or two?"

"Maybe the shy kid will grow up and be a Joseph anyway," he stated meekly.

"Not likely. More likely, the shy kid'll take the message he's no good and end up playing video games the rest of his life." Josh looked at his shoes. "Nope. The way I see it, there's only one solution."

"Mrs. Marone. Please, you can't kick Peter out. JOT's Peter's whole life.

He loves it so much. He loves you so much. You can't…I mean…please, don't," Josh tried futilely to hold back the tears. "I'll quit."

"That's not a solution. I just explained that," she said sternly, handing Josh a box of tissues.

"Please don't kick Peter out of the program."

"Why not?"

"Because it would kill him."

"Peter? Come on, do you even know your friend?"

"I don't…I don't know what you want from me."

"I want to deliver two Josephs to God."

Josh nodded helplessly.

"*And I heard the voice of the Lord saying, 'Whom shall I send, and who will go for us?' Then I said, 'Here am I! Send me.'* Is that what you're saying, Joshua? Are you waving your hand up to Heaven and saying, 'Send me!' or are you hiding in the background hoping others'll do it for you? I didn't pick you for this program, Joshua. It wasn't your parents, it wasn't your name, and it wasn't your friendship with Peter. It was God. God Himself chose little invisible Joshua Conrad to be a Joseph. You can't hide from God. *No creature is hidden from his sight, but all are naked and exposed to the eyes of Him to whom we must give account.*"

For a long moment, there was silence in the office, save Josh's sniffling.

"*A rebuke goes deeper into a man of understanding than a hundred blows into a fool.* Now, your junior year things are gonna get real… very real. And I'm not holding your hand anymore. Understand? Seriously, Joshua, when I see you, do you know what you remind me of? A moby. Knock it off. I've arranged your schedule so that you have only a minimum number of classes with Peter. Oh, don't worry, you're still in the same homeroom. I wouldn't want you to go cold turkey or anything." Her sarcasm was counteracted by the mention of Peter not only still in the program but still in his homeroom. "I need to see you stepping up this year, Joshua. No one can carry you up the Mountain. You must listen to God and go up the Mountain He reveals to you… in the way He reveals it to you. Do you understand?"

"Yes."

"*Do you think that I have come to give peace on earth? No, I tell you, but rather war.* This isn't a game, Joshua. It's a war. And you need to start looking at it that way. Mr. Dillon says you're a good history student. Is that true?"

"I like his… I mean, yes, Mrs. Marone."

"Do you know how old a soldier had to be to fight in the First American Revolution?"

"Sixteen, we learned that in class."

"You learned that. And how old are you?"

"Sixteen."

"Time to get serious, don't you think?"

"I will, Mrs. Marone, I promise."

Josh left the office feeling like a soldier preparing for battle, determined to give God his all or die trying. It wasn't long however before he felt trapped in a bombarded foxhole. The level and intensity of the work quadrupled. The papers and projects blasted him from all sides in every subject. Each day was a whirlwind of fear-filled chaos beginning with morning calisthenics and ending in an evening of struggling to both finish and comprehend the mound of work. At night, he would flop into his bed only to be awakened by the Good News Network encouraging him to get up and serve God another day. It was a treadmill stuck on high with no way off. The only benefit he could see so far was the nights he stood in front of his mirror and flexed. His muscles were growing, becoming pronounced. At least he did not look like a scrawny kid any more. Through it all he had two anchors in the way of Peter and Matthew. At school, he rarely saw them as he maintained a low profile but in the neighborhood, they were always there for him with patient encouragement.

Then, of course, there were the Saturday afternoons on Elmer that they all held as an almost sacred ritual.

It was on one such chilly but bearable, April afternoon when Matthew dropped a bombshell. "Can I tell you joes something?"

"All One in Jesus," Peter said.

"Ada might be pregnant."

Stunned silence hit the tree fort. Pregnant? Had Josh heard that right? Ada and Matthew's growing friendship had been obvious but Josh had been so busy he never gave it much thought. Clearly, there was a great deal more going on around him than he realized.

"What do you mean 'might'?" asked Peter.

"Well, I'm trying to get my hands on one of those home tests but she's worried because she hasn't had her... you know."

"And, you and she…?"

"Obviously, or we wouldn't be worried, would we?"

"Ouch."

Josh did not know what to think. He knew Matthew could be in serious trouble but Josh's sinful nature was interested, as well. It was the act he fantasized about late at night when he struggled with Satan's temptations. What had it been like?

"I'm just so worried," lamented Matthew. "It's all I can think about. I mean, we'll both be out of JOT; you know Mrs. Marone won't tolerate it. We all pledged, remember? But, I'm gonna marry her. I mean, if God's given us a child, we're gonna raise him as a family."

"Of course, you are, joe," Peter said. "And it'll be solomon, too. You love her, don't you?"

"I do, Peter. I really do but if she's… people are gonna… she's gonna…"

"Wow, joe," Peter said holding up his hands. "Getting a bit ahead of ourselves, aren't we? This isn't the first time something like this has happened…"

"In our church?" Matthew shot back.

"Maybe, but it seems to me the first thing we need to do is confirm if she's pregnant or not."

"Good luck with that. It's not something you can just walk into a drugstore and buy, you know."

"Well, it just so happens," said Peter. "I might know of someone, who might know of someone…"

"Of course, you do." Matthew laughed.

The following Saturday Matthew was the last to arrive. When he did he was despondent. "The good news is she's not pregnant. The test was negative. The bad news is Mrs. Marone found out, about the pregnancy scare…the whole thing."

"What?" Josh asked.

"As far as we can figure, Ruth told her. I can't believe Ada told Ruth, of all people! I'm out. We're out! Both of us."

"CHURCH?" Josh gasped.

"No, no, JOT."

"How was Mrs. Marone?" asked Peter.

"Oh, it was a righteous rebuke. Right in front of my parents. She pretty much matthew 18'ed them too. Believe me, the gloves came off. Then, right at her most feverish, she suddenly stopped, smiled, and she was talking normal again. She went on about how people make mistakes and our sin certainly wasn't beyond forgiveness either by God or the church community. She said she could tell Ada and I love each other and that, while she doesn't condone the sin, she'll continue to love the sinners."

"Solomon," Peter said.

"Yeah, then she talked a lot about those who are anointed for leadership and those who are anointed for something else. She said a good Joseph always has his eyes on God and I took my eyes off Him. So, I'm out." It was the final two words that broke him. He buried his face in his arm and sobbed.

Peter reached out and put his arms around him. "God's Will be done," he comforted gently.

When Matthew collected himself again he continued. "We go back to regular school starting Monday. What's gonna hurt the worst is having to watch what Ada's gonna go through. People are gonna see her… you know… but she's not like that. I'm gonna marry her after high school and I am not gonna do anything that'll hurt her again."

Though nothing was ever said, Matthew started to spend less and less time with the boys. His new schedule was completely different and the only activities he shared with them were Saturday afternoons. Those became more infrequent as Matthew set out to prove to everyone, especially Ada's parents, that he was sincere in his feelings for Ada. Although almost always chaperoned, now that they were out of JOT, they began to openly date and talked of marriage.

Josh, for his part, barely had time to miss Matthew. The world around him grew tighter and tighter as he struggled through his spring semester. It all came to a head during final exams. Josh was given his calculus exam and his brain became covered in a sheet of impenetrable ice. He had thought of little else for a week and now he could not recall a thing. He fumbled around with the numbers and symbols but knew he was not even being consistent. He struggled onward, hiding his tear-filled eyes from the other students. In the end, he knew, whether he failed the exam or not, there was no way it was going to raise his final grade to where it needed to be. That realization caused him to crash and burn. His mind became mush, and it was all he could do to hold it together, let alone perform well on his remaining exams.

On Elmer that Saturday Josh could do nothing more than cry. "This is tough," Peter said, lobbing a small stone into the trees.

"Not for you, it isn't," said Josh, sounding angrier than he intended.

"Oh, okay, Luke," said Peter and laughed.

Josh couldn't help but smile…. meekly. "I'm gonna fail. I know it."

"You don't know that yet."

"You don't understand, Peter. I never belonged in this program. If God chose me, He made a mis…"

"Easy, Josh," interrupted Peter. "Let's not end up in the wilderness here. In the program or out of the program, God's Will be done."

"I know but I fail at everything."

"Really? Give me that list."

"You know what I mean."

"No, I don't. Just give me the top ten."

"Well, JOT for one thing."

"You don't know that yet but fine, I'll put it on the list. Next?"

"You don't understand. I'm a Conrad. My grandfather's an anointed pastor. My father's a director of DHS. My brother's graduating from West Point! And I can't even get through high school."

"Mrs. Marone teaches us it doesn't matter who our families are."

"Mrs. Marone doesn't have to attend a Conrad family reunion."

There was a pregnant pause, followed by Peter bursting into wild laughter. The force of his cackles was too much for Josh who felt his hopeless mood dissipate. "I'm serious, joe. You don't know what it's like. I can see myself standing in front of my uncles, 'and how are things with you, Josh?' 'Oh, I flunked out of the most prestigious high school program in the country, thank you, and, how are you?' And they'll be like, 'Your cousin, Abby, just got accepted to Liberty.' My grandfather will make some embarrassing comment and everyone will hush him up, apologizing with strained smiles. That's the worst of it. It's not what is said but what isn't. And I've been failing like this my whole life."

"There you go again, joe. What's this 'whole life' stuff? The only thing you've done your whole life is tried to live up to what you think other people want from you. Is that what God truly wants for us? As long as you know you're right with God, it doesn't matter what others think."

"Yeah, I know."

"Josh, I'm your best friend so I'll give it to you straight. You know it up here," he said, pointing to his head, "but not in here." Now pointing to his heart. *"An intelligent heart acquires knowledge, and the ear of the wise seeks knowledge.* These aren't just words for our heads they're the living words of Almighty God. And he's telling us, He holds each one of us in the palm of His hand and he's saying 'Relax, I've got this.'"

Josh sat in silence. So, he was not only failing high school, he was failing God? Great… just great.

"Josh, you didn't know me when I was a kid. I went through a period around fifth, sixth grade when I had to be the best at everything. I was running around trying to be David, Solomon and Paul all rolled into one. I had to win every game, every argument. I was driving everyone babel. Then one day, Mrs. Marone matthew 18'ed me, and I mean, like the wrath of God Himself. For a month, all I could do was watch. I wasn't allowed to play any games or sports but I had to go and sit on the sidelines. I had to sit quietly in class and not say a word. If I forgot, I got a whole day added. It took me forty-five days to get off punishment. At first, I resented Mrs. Marone for disciplining me like that. I didn't think it was fair. After all, I was just trying to give it all to God. But, eventually, I began to see what she wanted me to see. I noticed it first while watching a soccer game. Everyone on the field plays a part in every play whether he touches the ball or not. Then I saw how everyone, the players on the bench, the coaches, and even the fans on both sides, all contribute to everything that's going on. And then I saw that applies to the classroom as well. I could see how every comment leads to the eventual outcome and how even the students who don't say anything contribute. Then I saw it also plays out in every informal conversation. As a matter of fact, it plays out all day… every day. It showed me how life is like a river and every drop of water contributes to that river. I began to think about that drop of water. How it gets tossed about by the current; how it dances all the way to the ocean. It has no control over where it's going, it's just one droplet of water in a whole river and yet it dances and bounces up into the sun."

Peter's voice trailed off and there was silence. "Jehovah's Revolution is our river, Josh," Peter said finally, "And we must do our part. God's asked our generation to take dominion over all the nations and that's an incredible responsibility. A responsibility we must face with no fear but with that responsibility comes an even greater privilege. Our generation's gonna bring the whole world to Christ, and then we're gonna see Jesus come back. We're gonna witness the end of history. It'll be the greatest party of all time. The concerts, the rallies, even the Super Bowl are gonna seem like sandbox parties compared to a world-wide celebration of Jesus' return. You and I are gonna be a part of that. We're riding a river to the greatest event of all time! It doesn't really matter whether you're sitting in the White House or cleaning toilets, we all got the same invitation. *Blessed are those who are invited to the marriage supper of the Lamb.*"

Chapter Thirteen

It was a hot July evening when Maggie's happy life was shattered.

She was sitting at the table with the guys, going over plans for the next job. Emily was across the room trying to stay cool by watching a movie in front of the fans.

Without warning, Asher, exhausted and bloody, fell through the door. Maggie and the others leaped to their feet.

"My God!" Jake screamed.

Asher was trying to say something but he had no breath. Mickey scooped him up and carried him to the couch in the middle of the floor.

"He's in shock. Thad, get him some water," ordered Jake.

Asher lay unmoving where Mickey had placed him. His dirty face was streaked with tears, his eyes wide and fixed. Suddenly, before their eyes, his face contorted into a terrified mask, his breath coming fast and sharp. Then he screamed into the air. Maggie suppressed the rise of panic within her.

Thad returned with the water. They forced Asher to sit up and take a drink. His eyes remained fixed.

"What happened?" Jake asked.

"Eh... I... wha..." was all Asher could muster.

"Enough!" Seth shouted, pounding his fist into the arm of the couch. "Goddammit! Where's Barak?"

At first, his older brother's shout brought Asher back to where he could catch a breath but at the sound of his other brother's name, he screamed, "BARAK! Oh my god, I... he... oh, Barak?"

Seth grabbed Asher and shook him. "What the fuck's going on? Where's Barak? Is he hurt? Does he need help?" Seth's voice croaked as he shook the limp form in his hands.

"Come on, mano," Jake said, pulling Seth away. "He doesn't need that!"

"He needs to tell us what happened!" shouted Seth, shoving Jake's arms aside.

"Shut up!" Mickey yelled, looking down at the shaking boy on the couch. "Everyone, just shut up, so we can figure this out!"

Thad sat next to Asher and placed his arm across his back. He gently rubbed Asher's neck. "It's okay, just start from the beginning... you and Barak went out hunting..."

Asher took a deep breath and then in a halting voice said, "We were hunting... in the south end."

"South end? What the hell were you doing there?" Seth interrupted.

Jake and Mickey glared at Seth. Then, Thad gently encouraged Asher. Asher breathed deeply and started again. "Someone told us some alcohol was in this old warehouse. When we got there, there it was. Like twenty of these big cartons. We counted 16 bottles in each. We thought we were rich and then...these guys showed up."

"Who were they?" asked Thad.

"Three-twelves."

"Jesus Christ!" Seth exclaimed.

"They... they... were mad because we were tress... tress..."

"Trespassing," Thad finished gently.

"We tried to run but they caught us. I hit my head on something... I heard Barak yelling... some big guy was kicking him... and then... and then... there was this other kid... like our age... he was standing over us... and he looked scared but he was holding a gun and... and... then the big guy told him to choose..."

"Choose? Choose what?" Seth demanded.

Yet Asher said no more. Like hot coal being passed from one to another, the realization of what came next hit each of them individually until the whole room was struck with a tidal wave of grief, confusion and despair. Screams of horror and disbelief erupted. Seth smashed a small table against a wall on his way to his bedroom. Emily screamed and ran to her room.

Maggie's mind was numb. She knelt next to the crumpled heap, reached out and put her hand on his shoulder. Asher lay limp and exhausted, his thin body shaking with every breath.

Seth came back into the main room. There was a pistol tucked into his belt.

"Oh, no," Jake said, standing between Seth and the door.

"Get outta my way."

"Look, we're not gonna let you go down there. You heard what he said, that's the Three-twelves. You know who those guys are."

"He's my brother."

"I know. But number one, you have another brother and you won't help him by getting yourself killed. Number two, we're not sure what happened. I mean, I believe he believes what he saw, no doubt about that, but he's a kid. Maybe, he just thinks he saw it. You know what I mean?"

"So?"

"So, let's find out how much of this is true, first. Okay? We'll go down, check the warehouse out. But let's go quietly, mano. You know. That's who we are. Ninjas."

Seth reluctantly agreed. "I'm taking the gun."

Jake relented. "Fine. Okay, here's the plan. Mickey stays here with Asher and Em. Thad, Maggie get your working clothes on, you come with us. This is seriously enemy territory. We have no friends so we avoid everyone. Clear?"

A couple of hours later, the four of them stood on the roof of a nearby building overlooking the abandoned warehouse. The warehouse itself appeared dark, the only light came from a few exterior bulbs but they could see several groups of young men milling about.

"We sure that's the right building?" Seth asked.

"Fits the description," said Jake.

Seth took the gun out of his belt. "I'm going in."

"Easy, Seth," Jake said. "Look. The place is swarming."

"Makes sense," said Thad, "If the story's true, they'd probably be guarding the booze... or moving it."

"Fuck this, I'm going in," Seth repeated.

"Come on, Seth, you won't make it five feet past the gate," insisted Jake.

Maggie took a moment to survey the scene. The activity seemed to be centered around the front of the building; behind it looked dark and quiet. "I'm going in," she said.

"Will you just calm down, Night Warrior. We need to think about this. Come up with a plan."

"No time for that," Maggie said, nodding to Seth. "We need to get close enough to find out what's going on, and only one of us can do that without getting caught."

"Maggie, there's no way I'm gonna let you..."

"It's not about letting me, Jake. And this isn't about thrills. Barak could be seriously hurt."

Jake looked to Thad who gave a barely visible nod. "Okay," Jake said, "but promise me you only go as far as it takes to find out what happened. Maybe you can overhear someone talking. And don't take any chances. If it even gets warm, you get your ass back here."

"Absolutely," she confirmed, "I won't even go into the building."

Fifteen minutes later, after several leaps across rooftops and a couple of slick stealthy moves, she was on the roof of the warehouse. She figured the gang would not be expecting anyone sneaking in. After all, who would be crazy enough to try such a thing in Three-twelve territory? Despite the gravity of the situation, Maggie smiled when she mentally replied to the question. She sure had no pretentions about what would happen to her if she were caught. She also prayed. *If there is a God, please let me find Barak, at worst, tied up inside.* But underneath all that, she had to admit, she loved sneaking around in the shadows and outsmarting the foxes.

On the roof, she found an access hatch held closed by an ancient chain; the lock was easy to pick. Keeping the old rusty chain from making any noise, however, was next to impossible. She was relieved to find the hatch itself was not rusted shut...

Squeeeeeeak.

The old metal parts protested as she lifted the lid. She froze and waited. How loud was that? Was there anyone on the floor below her? She decided she better explore her options. She crept along the roof top and cautiously looked over each edge. She found the west side of the warehouse had no one standing around. There she also found a drainage pipe. Vowing never to admit the whole story to Jake, she climbed over the roof, grabbing the pipe with her gloved hands and shimmied down. She came parallel with a filthy window.

She perched on the ledge, one hand still firmly grasping the pipe. She waited and listened. She heard nothing. She used her free hand to wipe the pane. She could see the room had once been an office but was in total disarray. The file cabinets and antique desks stood like skeletons of a bygone time. She carefully studied every angle; the room was empty.

Now, she reached for the tools in her vest and pulled out her glass cutter. The warehouse must have been built in the twentieth century and no one had ever upgraded the windows. She cut a circle in the glass big enough for her hand. She stood on the ledge so that she could get the right angle to reach through and flip the antique window latch. The wooden window groaned in protest but opened. Seconds later she was creeping quietly through the room.

At the door, she listened intently. Nothing. She opened it slowly. There was no change in the light. Encouraged, she opened the door faster. She was in the office at the end of the hallway. Across from her was a door leading to the stairs. Asher had said everything had happened on the second floor.

Maggie checked her internal fear gage. Fine. She felt fine. As a matter of fact, better than that, she felt cool as a cucumber.

She got to the door of the floor below. She closed her eyes and focused her mind on listening. She wanted to be able to hear a rat scurrying across the floor. She slowed her breathing down so that it, too, would not interfere. She could hear movement within. Footsteps.

She cautiously pulled the door ajar. The floor was completely open. About half way down she could see people. She studied them. There were three young guys picking up boxes and carrying them over to an elevator.

She no longer had any idea what she was going to tell Jake without him flipping out but she had not yet gotten what she had come for. Deftly she used what cover there was strewn about to make her way across the floor.

"Come on, we're almost done," she heard one gang member say.

"I hope so. It's fuckin' three in the morning."

"He said he wanted this out of here tonight. You gonna argue with him?"

"Nope and I'm not complaining either. Just tired."

Maggie crept as close as she could. She could see there were a few boxes left. Then, would they go? She tried to look around but could see nothing in the deep shadows. Maybe, she thought, she should go downstairs, that might be where they were holding Barak. She debated with herself for a few moments and then heard one of the boys say, "Last box!"

"There's no fucking room for us in the vator," another voice said.

"Take the stairs."

"What are we gonna do with that?"

"Leave it, I'm not touching that shit."

Maggie melted even further into the shadows as the three boys walked right past her on their way to the stairs. Soon their voices were nothing but muffled distractions. She started to explore, maintaining her stealth, but fueled by a rising panic.

Then she found Barak.

His soiled bloody clothes covered his lifeless crumpled body but as her eyes moved up from his laces-free shoes to his favorite T-shirt, she saw the true horror. Half of Barak's head was gone. Where it remained was a gushing bloody goo. He had only one eye left which stared at her vacantly.

Her heart stopped and she gasped for air. True. It was all true. Everything Asher had told them was true and he had been there, he had seen it all, he had witnessed his brother's head…

Maggie needed to vomit. She fought the urge, yet it was no use. She ran to a corner and fell to her knees retching. When her stomach was empty, she found herself convulsing with dry heaves.

Get yourself together! she scolded. She would allow herself to fall apart later, right now, she had a job to do. No longer overly concerned with stealth, she looked around the floor until she found some large sheets of paper. Cloth would have been better. She went back and wrapped up Barak's body as best she could. Barak was dead but he didn't deserve to be treated like a discarded pile of trash.

His body was not as heavy as she thought it would be as she carried it up the stairs. She found the ladder to the hatch she had opened and climbed up. The way up was slow with his body over her shoulder. The hatch squealed again but she did not care. On the roof she found a long coil of cable. Using it, she lowered Barak's body down the side of the building and soon she was working her way back to the guys.

"Fucking sons of bitches!" Seth screamed, waving his gun.

"Put it away," Jake said.

"The hell I will!"

"What are you gonna do? Go down the road shooting? Take out as many as you can? Jesus, Seth, don't make us bring both of your bodies back to Asher."

"Fine. What are we gonna do? Cause I'm not gonna do nothin'!"

"First, we're gonna bring Barak home. Then we'll decide what to do from there, but we're gonna remain stealth."

"Sounds like nothin'," spat Seth.

"I promise you, we'll take care of this but you need to put your mind on Asher."

"Don't fucking tell me what to do!"

For two days, the Office was as silent as a morgue. After a ceremony of mostly tears, they anonymously delivered Barak's body to a hospital. Seth moved in with Asher and the two stayed in their room. The only sounds emanating were quiet murmurs and occasional outbreaks of tears. Maggie and Emily tried to keep their routine of gymnastics and school, but neither of their hearts were in it. Jake and Thad spent the days away while Mickey took the whole thing with a quiet solemnness that betrayed anything he was truly feeling.

Then one day, Jake took Seth and Maggie with him to meet the leader of the Kellies, a young man known only as 'Z.' They met in what had once been a family style restaurant, but now served as the Kellies official war room.

"Thanks for meeting with us, Z," Jake said.

"You're straight, Jake. What's the word?"

Jake explained what happened. When he was done, Z sat thoughtfully. He took a sip of coffee. "And what exactly would you like us to do about it?"

"Kill 'em all!" Seth shouted.

"Whoa, that's some jihadist shit, mano."

"No," Jake said. "We'd like you look into it for us. Find out who did it."

"Yeah," Seth said, "Let me know who it is so I can kill him."

"And why, exactly, would we help you? None of you are Kelly."

"True," Jake acknowledged. "But, we're good tenants." Jake offered Z an herbal smoke.

Z thoughtfully puffed on the j. "Okay, but there's gonna be a rent increase."

"How much?" asked Jake.

"Twenty-five."

"Dollars?" Seth laughed.

"Percent," corrected Z.

"Ha! No fucking way!" mocked Seth.

"For six months," Z continued, "and this is my guarantee, if we haven't found him by then, we'll give you a full refund."

Jake turned to Seth and pleaded. "Let them find him. They know what they're doing."

Maggie caught Seth's eyes. "He's right, Seth. Think of Asher."

It was obvious Z was not used to being questioned. "We're gonna find this guy. I guarantee you. It might take a week, a month, but it's not gonna take six months. I've no intention of giving you your money back."

In the end, Seth relented.

At first, Seth was constantly asking Jake if he had heard anything but, as Asher and he grew into their life without Barak, he asked less and less. About four months later, a photo of a dead boy mysteriously arrived under their door. Attached was a note. "I know we told you we'd take him alive, but he refused to cooperate. This is the guy. Z." Seth looked at the photo and read the caption then tossed the picture back on the table. It was tucked away in Mickey's office and the subject was never brought up again.

Life went on for the little family but it was never the same. For the rest of them the incident was a reminder that survival in the city was not a game. Their successes as burglars had gone to their heads. Barak's death was a reality check. For Maggie, the lesson was different. It was a realization. Sure, in the last couple of years, she had seen more death and violence than she had ever imagined, but it remained at a distance. The occasional dead drug addict or gang member she would see on the street was more the environment in which she lived.

Now, it had come directly into her home.

Nothing felt as safe as it did before. It was her suggestion that they get some money together and get out of Columbus. They could go live in the woods, maybe near a lake, or maybe up in the mountains. Someplace where the only thing they would have to worry about is the occasional bear. It became an idea they would expand on and talk about late at night. They had heard about small communities of people that were living outside of the cities, outside of the government. At first it seemed crazy to Maggie that there would be such places. It was hard to imagine any place in America not controlled by CAP.

Mickey showed her one night with satellite photos. America was a big place. A very big place. "The Christians may control their fucking Seven Mountains, but they can't control the land. There's just too much of it."

Chapter Fourteen

Josh found himself alone, hiking through the forest in search of a portable camping hut. He had no access to GPS and instead had to rely solely on a compass and an age-old topographical map. That morning, he was advised the hut was about two hours away. He had been hiking for more than three. It was the damn map. How in the world can anything only two dimensional be seen as three? Or maybe, it was just him. The sinking feeling of despair weakened his knees. His pack felt three times heavier and he quickly scoped out a safe place to collapse.

He dropped his bag and fell to the ground exhausted. In a few minutes, he was able to breathe normally again. He shifted to look over the forest. He decided he did not like the smell of woods. They all smelled the same, like decaying leaves… like death.

Josh took a long swig of water.

Getting to the hut was supposed to be the easy part of this adventure. He just had to hike to it. Then, he would live in solitude for four nights. That was supposed to be the hard part but Josh had failed… again… before he even got to the starting line. Tears welled up in his eyes and he wiped them away with his filthy fingers. This was all just babel.

The whole summer had been babel.

It began with a chronic rumbling in his gut as he waited to hear from Mrs. Marone to let him know he had flunked out of JOT. The call never came. He learned she was away on speaking engagements so he thought he would at least hear from the church office. Nothing. So, while all the others were excitedly talking about the Senior Camp as it was one of the most exciting events of their lives, Josh could only go through the motions. What was the point of looking forward to something he would not be able to go to?

As the days grew into weeks, he thought how unfair it was that they would not let him know. He continued to receive all the posts about camp as if there was no problem. His mother saw this as a good sign. He tried to convince her his grades were too low and Mrs. Marone never budged on anything. Peter, like Josh's mother, was one hundred percent positive and assured him he would be going. "I asked in prayer, *And whatever you ask in prayer, you will receive, if you have faith.*"

As the final weekend before camp arrived Josh was angry. It was completely unfair he would be required to go to camp if he was just going to be removed from the program. Peter, of course, looked at it differently.

"I have a confession to make," Peter told him on Elmer. "I didn't ask God to keep you in JOT. God's Will be done on that. I asked God to let you go to camp. See, this isn't a school camp. It's a spiritual pilgrimage. For a month, they're gonna challenge us in every way Jesus was, culminating in a solitary retreat where you just might get baptized by the Holy Spirit. If that happens, who cares if you're removed from JOT or not."

Josh could not argue with the logic but that did not help with the fear of public humiliation. When and how would Mrs. Marone lower the boom? He imagined her, through her megaphone, announcing his failure right there in the camp lodge.

Mrs. Marone based her idea of the individual retreat on Jesus's time in the wilderness just before beginning His ministry. *And he was in the wilderness forty days, being tempted by Satan. And he was with the wild animals, and the angels were ministering to him.* The campers were given just enough food, a Bible, and daily readings. They were told to spend their time communing with God, seeking His guidance for their lives, and asking for the Holy Spirit baptism. Mrs. Marone said the experience would help open spiritual pathways so that if God willed it, the students own brains would not resist this most sacred of gifts.

Josh went through the camp's activities as invisibly as possible. He was afraid if he brought attention to himself someone would ask the question "What's he doing here?" Peter was on him at times about loosening up and having some fun but Josh could not escape the burden of the question: why did he have to do this if he had flunked out anyway?

Now, sitting there lost in the woods, it seemed he would no longer need to answer that question. His back ached, his legs were throbbing, and his spirit was broken. Why couldn't he do anything right? He smacked his thigh with his fist, his leg screamed in protest. He hit it again and again... each time harder than the last. "Silence!" he screamed at the pain. "You don't have the right to complain!" His sob seemed loud in the quiet forest as he buried his face in his arms. He gave into the tears and felt them quickly soak the sleeve of his camping shirt. After a few moments of complete surrender, a thought struck him like a bullet from a sniper...

Was he being watched?

Perhaps a camp counselor had been secretly following him, making sure he got to the cabin alright. Now that student was witnessing Josh's breakdown.

The thought jerked his head up and his eyes were hurt by the blinding light. When his eyes adjusted, he scanned the forest slowly. A forest that looked the same in all directions and nothing like what the map said it should.

God is our refuge and strength, a very present help in trouble. The passage popped into his mind; he was at the end of his rope... there was only one thing to do... surrender. His knees and legs groaned as he forced them to kneel. "Dear Lord, *for in you I trust. Make me know the way I should go, for to you I lift up my soul.* I'm lost, Jesus. Please help me." He repeated similar appeals for several minutes. Finally, he ended his prayer with "Thy Will be done."

He opened his eyes and it seemed God had adjusted the color levels. The deep greens of the pines, the golden floor of their needles, and the rich blue sky all shone brilliantly. Josh, marveling at the newness, scanned the forest again and this time he saw someone looking back.

A stag stood majestically on the slope. The woodlander gazed as any true resident stares at a tourist having a meltdown... with stone cold amusement.

Then the stag did something Josh had never seen before with nobly silent deer. He snorted. It looked and sounded a bit like a sneeze but the buck did it with intent. He, then, trotted up the hill ten more yards, now nearing the top, where he stopped, turned and studied Josh keenly.

Was he trying to tell him something? There certainly was no reason to think he was not. Josh had just finished asking for God's help and there was the Biblical example of Balaam's donkey.

There was only one way to find out. Gently, so as not to startle the deer, Josh lifted his pack, barely aware of his muscles' screams. He kept his eyes locked on the stag who continued to have his own eyes fixed on Josh. Josh took several steps toward the buck who then trotted gracefully up and over the hill.

Maybe the deer wasn't a messenger after all. Maybe it was just angry with Josh's trespassing. Josh had to know.

As he crested the hill he saw what it was the stag was trying to tell him. Sitting neatly, looking a bit like a lunar landing module, stood the portable camping cabin. It was the sweetest thing Josh had ever laid eyes on!

He verified the number. Yep, this was his. Josh realized he had just witnessed a miracle. Maybe not on the scale of the Red Sea but God had used the stag to save him; there could no doubt of that.

In front of the hut, he knelt. "Thank you, Jesus, for delivering me. I'm sorry for my lack of faith. In the name of Jesus Christ, I pray a hedge of protection over this dwelling. Thy Will be done."

Only then did Josh open the door. The room was smaller than one of his closets, consisting of a simple cot, a smell-proof cupboard with his food, and a bio-toilet but it was a welcoming home to this exhausted traveler.

Josh dropped his pack and stretched out on the bed. He had been less than a hundred yards away and was about to turn back. How embarrassing would that have been? God had saved him from serious humiliation. "Thanks for that too, God."

He laid on his bunk for a long time drifting in and out of states of light unconsciousness as he regained his strength. He felt like he had walked fifty miles with all the zig-zagging. Then at his greatest moment of despair he had turned to God and God delivered. A voice, sounding very much like Mrs. Marone, scolded him, "If you'd turned it over to God from the beginning you never would have been lost in the first place." The voice was right, of course, yet the fact of the matter was God had saved him. God was here with him in this place. This was not a vacation but exactly what everyone told him it would be: a sacred communion. The thought sent goosebumps down his spine. *God, You got me. I turn the next four days over to You.*

When he was energized, Josh busied himself in making his temporary location a bit homier. He easily collected enough wood for the campfires and neatly stacked it next to the portable fire pit. He unpacked as best he could. There was no place to sit so he found a couple of logs and erected a make shift lounge chair next to the fire pit. He even went so far as to hang a small clothes line between two trees for later. Then he hiked back down the slope to the creek where he collected water from a stream. He carried the heavy container up the hill and used the purifying supplies. He soon felt like he had stamped out his territory for the next few days. All his needs would be met and he could simply focus on opening himself up to the Spirit.

Josh took a deep breath of the forest air. It smelled so good, so alive. He was ready. If God had a message for him, he was going to be open to it. He was tired of his life. Tired of struggling just to be mediocre. Tired of always feeling like a drowning man. Maybe, if God revealed to him the path He had planned for him then all that might go away.

Josh sat soaking in the world around him in his makeshift chair. It was odd not to hear the steady stream of sounds he was accustomed to: the commentators, the music, even kitchen appliances. Here, there was merely the rustling of leaves caressed by the wind. A small chorus of birds entertained him in surround sound. As he allowed his breath to slow even further, Josh's heart embraced the awareness of a more vivid world. Peter was right, in JOT or out, this was going to be a fantastic few days.

Far too soon the shadows of the trees grew heavy. He built a small campfire, secured his flashlights, and returned to his seat. He was reminded of the family camping trips. The whole extended family surrounded a single fire. They sang and shared stories. Often, Josh felt the family had been lifted to a spiritual plane, perhaps a visit to Heaven itself, where laughter was easy and everyone praised God. The memories were as warm as the reflecting fire.

A gust of wind caused the flames to dance viciously. He shuddered. The sky had become a dazzling array of grayness as the last of the sunlight danced off the clouds overhead. It gave the whole woods an eerie haunted feel.

A rustling came from deep in the woods. His head screamed as his heart jumped into his throat. A scratching sound, no, his mind corrected, more like footsteps in leaves. Quickly, Josh grabbed his flashlight and aimed the bright beacon at the source of the sound. The ray of light revealed nothing more than a dark forbidding forest.

He heard the rustling again. Someone… or something… was there. Josh leaped to his feet and quickly scanned the woods. A racoon? A skunk? A bear? It was not that he was unfamiliar with forest animals but this was the first time he was encountering them alone. Raccoons had rabies and skunks had odor; neither of which he wanted to take back with him. Bears he had no interest in seeing at all. He decided he had enough of campfires and reminiscing. He hastily put out the fire, grabbed his things and retreated to the safety of the porta-cabin.

Inside, his anxious mind went even further. Was it someone trying to sneak up on him? Peter? There was no way Peter would dishonor this sacred experience. Maybe, it was a counselor checking on him? Doubtful, not after dark. Oh, but perhaps it was a lib or backslidden coming to rob him. He did not have an immediate argument against that and it worried him. It was a state park and probably protected as best it could be but throughout his childhood he had been warned of bands of uncommitteds, no longer living in the Light, wandering through the woods at night. Impossible, his mind argued but he was not reassured. State park or not, it was possible for someone to be out there.

He peered out his small window. "C'mon, Josh," he scolded, "you're on a school function." He may feel alone but there were another hundred campers scattered around the forest and a base camp full of counselors. There was no way a bunch of libs were out there? But maybe, just one or two?

He heard the rustling again. This time closer. It was coming lightly from several directions.

Racoons. That had to be it. Three, maybe four. Josh could imagine them coming into his camp site, sniffing around a bit, finding nothing but a lingering scent. Inside the cabin, he felt safe. He also knew he wasn't being visited by libs, backsliddens or… zombies. How quickly his mind always went to the worst-case scenario. *Trust in the Lord with all your heart, and do not lean on your own understanding.*

He crawled over to his cot and laid down. As he tried to escape the darkness through unconsciousness, his mind whirled, bouncing from one memory to another, and to the voices of various people in his life scolding him for every mistake he had ever made. His earliest memory was being four and taking a sucker out of a grocery store. He remembered vividly his father's rage at his sin and encountered the depth of that word for the first time. But, it was Stephen's vivid and detailed description of Hell that was truly embedded in his brain.

Outside, there was no more shuffling, just an eerie stillness muffling the many noises from deep within the woods.

The shadows in the cabin projected by the light of the moon took on a three-dimensional quality as they floated slowly about. He used to play the "what do you see in the clouds" game with his cousins. He found himself playing it again. Only the shadows were not taking the forms of cute little lambs or furry huggable bunnies. These shadows were nefarious doppelgangers of cumulus clouds forming a murder of crows circling overhead, snakes slithering up his walls, and evil demons dancing.

Josh buried himself as deeply as he could in his sleeping bag. He forced his eyes closed and assured himself it would all be solomon in the morning.

❖

The man's face was impossible to see, Josh could only make out he was older. Maybe his dad's age. Josh should know him but just as he was about to make identification the face skirted away amongst a heavy layer of dark floating bubbles. The man was trying to say something to him. Josh reached out to pull the man's head closer so he could hear but it was like trying to catch a leaf in a windstorm.

"Come here!" Josh shouted. "I can't hear you."

The man struggled against the current. Josh desperately tried to reach him but to no avail. Then with a massive rush the head was on a direct course for Josh but it was moving too fast… it was going to crash into him… Josh threw his hands up to protect himself and the man's face slithered by him.

"What's going on?" Josh screamed in panic but the only answer was a swirl of dark bubbles and then the man's face, out of nowhere, bright as the sun, was inches from Josh's own. The man screamed something but the volume was so extreme Josh could not make out the words.

"What?" Josh shrieked. The head floated around in a chaotic orbit. As it came back again, for a split-second, Josh was able to catch his eyes. They were brown, like his, only older and deeply pained.

A blanket of darkness engulfed him.

⋈

He awoke paralyzed with fear, his sleeping bag soaked in sweat. A dream. No, a freaking TERROR!

It was pitch black outside. Had he been asleep for hours or minutes? He had no way of knowing. Wow! He reflected on the dream, a floating head giving him a warning. Was there a message in it? What was God trying to tell him? Was it God?

Josh no longer wanted to sleep but was struck with the fact there was nothing else to do. He was trapped in a tiny box in the middle of a deep dark nowhere.

The Lord will fight for you; you only have to be silent. That was it. Why did he not see it before? Just like Jesus was tested in the desert by Satan, Josh was being tested now. A Spirit from God would not be deceptive. He would have been able to understand what the man was trying to tell him. That's the Devil's strategy. *He was a murderer from the beginning, and has nothing to do with the truth…for he is a liar and the father of lies.*

Comforted, Josh rolled over and tried to sleep. He was successful until the nightmare came back with a vengeance. Josh could only endure the terror as the head floated around and around in a whirlpool of gloomy bubbles, spinning closer and closer. Then, when the head was right in his face, it shouted its incomprehensible warning. Josh forced his eyes shut and with a vicious mental push, he jumped out of his dream back into consciousness.

It was Deja-vu as he awoke in a cold sweat, heart drumming in his chest in the otherwise silent night. Again, it could have been hours or minutes, he had no way of telling.

Hey, Satan, I didn't like the program the first time, there was no need for a re-run.

He heard more scratching noises outside.

"That's just great!" he gasped. "If I go to sleep I have nightmares, if I stay awake I hear noises."

That is how he remained the rest of the first night, drifting between a terrified unconsciousness and an equally petrified conscious. As the black sky slowly turned to a deep grey, it began to rain. A gentle soothing rain that calmed Josh's nerves and he slept undisturbed for a few hours.

When he awoke, the watery remnants of the shower were being lifted by the powerful morning sun creating a natural steam room. Josh surveyed his campsite to see if any damage had been done by his nocturnal visitors but everything appeared to be in order.

He shook his head in disbelief. What a night!

He filled out his Bible study for the day. It was the story of the Original Apostles on the day of Pentecost. Peter preached citing the prophet Joel: *"In the Last days, God says, I will pour out my Spirit on all people...."* At the end of the study guide, there was a note from Mrs. Marone:

"Dear aspiring Joseph,
 In this Awakening, God is pouring out His Spirit but we must be a vase to catch it.
 This week, be that vase. God Bless You. Justjudy"

After the lesson, Josh took a hike but did not get far. The woods looked the same in all directions and he had no desire to get lost again. He returned to his camp. He cleaned some more water, which was not needed but he was having trouble finding anything to do. Eventually, he settled into his makeshift chair. Why did he have to do anything? There he spent the rest of the day. When he was not napping, he would pray or more likely allow his mind to drift. Time ticked by; nevertheless, when the sun was beginning to dip below the western horizon, Josh faced the inevitable darkness with a sense of dread.

Still, God was not about to alter the sun and moon just for him. Night was coming and he needed to ask God for the strength to overcome his fear. The romance of a campfire was gone. He thought it would be better if he just went to sleep when the sun went down.

He took his time preparing for bed, brushing his teeth thoroughly and cleaning himself with a shower towel. Maybe if he felt clean his mind would be more at ease. He had thought about the nightmare much of the day. If the nightmare was from Satan, Josh prayed a hedge of protection around himself. If it was from God, he prayed, despite his fear, for the messenger to return and this time... please, God... let him hear what the man says.

The nightmare did not return that night. Instead, Josh was yanked from his sleep by a high-pitched wail emanating from the forest.

He jumped to a sitting position. What was that? A scream... a human scream... a lady's scream.

Josh's heart revved.

"HELP!"

There it was again, screaming for help. Is that what she said? Josh was no longer sure. Was he dreaming again? Was Satan trying something new?

He looked around as best he could. He was awake in a portacabin in the middle of the Mohican Forest and a lady was screaming for help. There was no way it was a female camper as they had their retreat the previous week. His mind returned to the idea of a backslidden or lib. But she was screaming, probably in pain.

She screamed again. She was closer. Should he call out? He was not sure if revealing himself was a good idea but he could not just sit there and do nothing!

Again, the silent night was injected with the piercing scream.

Wait a minute. Josh's mind screeched to a halt. Is that a human voice? If it was it did not sound at all like the word "help." This was no English word; in fact, it was no word at all. It wasn't even any kind of normal syllable. It sounded more like the first "caw" of a crow being squeezed followed by a sizzling steaks-on-a-grill sound.

Oh, dear God! It was a demon! An actual demon!

Josh froze in panic. He was hearing what he was hearing. Josh knew raccoons and skunks did not make those kinds of noises. He did not think they made any sounds at all. And there was no way a bear sounded like a screeching woman. What else could it be?

When he could move again the first thing he did was grab his Bible. He had wrestled with the temptations of demons all his life, but they had always been the normal mental ones. Yet on TV and in speakers' testimonies, he heard of battles with the physical demons of Satan and learned there was only one way to fight them.

His heart raced like he had just sprinted a mile. His hands shook as he knelt, holding his Bible to his chest. He prayed, his voice a mere whisper. *"In the name of Jesus Christ, Lord of Lords, depart from me, you cursed, into the eternal fire prepared for the devil and his angels."* His voice felt engulfed by the night. He repeated his prayer, this time at a conversational tone. *"In the name of Jesus Christ, Lord of Lords, depart from me, you cursed, into the eternal fire prepared for the devil and his angels."* His voice was a rock thrown into the lake of darkness. Josh raised his voice to a shout. *"In the name of Jesus Christ, Lord of Lords, depart from me, you cursed, into the eternal fire prepared for the devil and his angels!"* Empowered by his bold voice, he shouted his command again and again, determined, resolute, a warrior thumping his chest before his enemy on the field of battle.

As the sounds of his shouts faded into the night, he listened.

No screams, no footsteps, and no loud thumps against the door of the cabin. Nothing but the eerie silence of the night. Moments turned into minutes. The demon had retreated.

"Yeah, that's right! *Get behind me Satan! You're a hindrance to me*! I'm armed with the full armor of God. I have the helmet of salvation and the Sword of the Spirit." He bounced about the cabin in victory.

Submit yourselves therefore to God. Resist the devil, and he will flee from you.

Chapter Fifteen

He awoke reliving his victory as the sun made its initial poke through the trees. He exited his cabin and took a deep gulp of the morning air. There was no early morning fog this day. Josh found himself walking in the general direction of the screams. He wondered if the demon had left any tracks but found nothing.

As he ate his breakfast and treated himself to the mature act of preparing coffee, he reminded himself that, despite how wonderful the victory may have been, it was still a lesson on how real all of this was. He was not a kid on summer camp. He was a warrior in battle. *When I became a man, I gave up childish ways.* In so many aspects, he was trying to hang on to being a child. He spent as much time complaining about the JOT workload as he did actually doing the work.

The lesson popped into his head: that was why school was so hard for him. Deep down he was not just resenting the work, he was resisting it. The truth sat before him as if it had been there all the time. He felt guilty. He had just been playing games; how respectful to God was that? How was that *loving the Lord God with all your heart and soul?*

As he meditatively drank his coffee, he thought about what to do that day. The devil had attacked him in more ways than one but Josh had beaten him back. Now, what? *But he would withdraw to desolate places and pray.* That felt right to Josh. He would spend the day in prayer, asking for God's guidance for his life.

Several hours later, when his daily Bible assignment was complete, he created a small altar out of the pile of wood and placed a makeshift cross at the top. There, he alternated between reading his Bible, praying, and when

114

he ran out of things to say, he would sit in contemplative prayer, "listening to the Lord."

As the day went on, he became emboldened. His thoughts turned to the baptism of the Holy Spirit. *The fruit of the Spirit is love, joy, peace, patience, kindness, goodness, faithfulness, gentleness, self-control.* That sounded like a shopping list for the things he needed in his life. Joy? Josh was too busy trying to stay afloat to experience joy. Peace? Yeah, right. Faithfulness? He remembered the film from the first day of the JOT program. Had he ever given that kind of effort? And self-control? He wasn't anywhere near having that. But, what if he received the baptism of the Holy Spirit? His deepest feeling was one of fear. The idea of being touched by almighty God was terrifying but… that was what he was out in the woods for. That was why he was being challenged. It was time to rise above his fear.

Josh directed his prayers towards asking for the gift of the Holy Spirit. Still afraid, yet he was ready. *Ask and you shall receive.* Again and again, he pleaded for the Holy Spirit to descend upon him. For the first time, he knew, with the kind of faith that could move mountains, he was asking with a sincere heart. He was ready to be a Joseph.

He went back to the idea of a campfire and continued his prayers long after dark, his kneeling body providing a motivating shadow from the flickering flames. Eventually, Josh moved into his cabin. He continued to pray on the floor, even entertaining ideas of pulling an "all-nighter" just like Jesus but finally gave into the sleepiness that enveloped him.

That night, he slept undisturbed.

The next day was his last full day at the cabin. Over breakfast, he finished his final Bible lesson and thought about what to do. He felt too restless for another day in prayer. Hiking? And, get lost again? Then an idea occurred to him, he could follow the creek bed. There would be no risk of losing his way.

With a small pack containing water, a few energy bars and his Bible, he set off to see what he could see. His strides were no longer those of a timid tourist but of a seasoned resident. Birds were singing their songs above him and he would occasionally stop to watch a squirrel hastily going about its business. The scent of the forest was heavy yet rejuvenating. The shallow creek was easy to follow as he made his way through acres of rolling forest. Josh found himself with an all too rare quiet mind as he lost himself in the walk. For once in his life, he seemed to have little to think about. He hiked… and looked… and on occasion, took a deep gulp of the clean forest air.

He discovered what looked like an ancient road and decided to explore it. It was another hundred yards when he saw the roof. A building? Out here? Maybe, it was a ranger's station. Josh slowed his pace. As the antique building was revealed, Josh could see he had nothing to worry about. It was obviously from the early twentieth century, maybe even the nineteenth. The ancient bricks were a combination of baked-pink from decades of hot Ohio summers and bleached white by the offensive winters. The windows were long gone, replaced with now dilapidated boards barely clinging to their original purpose. It was a two-story structure with a simple box-like architecture, a front porch and straight roofing. Built by hand right where it stood.

At first Josh thought it was a church but there was no attempt at a steeple or any kind of cross on the outside. As he approached he saw what it was… or had been… a school house. A simple one-room school house. How triumphant!

He looked around the area but there was no sign of civilization anywhere else. He imagined himself to be an archeologist uncovering a long forgotten historical site.

Josh picked his way up the crumbling steps and came to the front door. The door protested as it was forced to swing on its brittle rusty hinges. The room was empty and in many places the floor boards were nothing more than a rotting mess but Josh could imagine the children all sitting in the one classroom with one teacher. Josh could even imagine what the young pretty teacher looked like with wire rim glasses and her hair up in a bun. Her magnificently white blouse and long skirt demonstrating her modest dedication to her students. Ah, those were the days.

Watching his step, Josh explored the room. On the far side were the remains of a ladder that led up to whatever was on the second floor. Josh calculated it had probably been the living quarters for the teacher. He wondered if anything was up there but could see the ladder was in no shape to be used. He had no desire to break his leg on the last day of his retreat. Furthermore, he imagined the dark walls upstairs would be covered with sleeping bats.

The idea of bats turned Josh completely around and he went outside. He stood on the porch picturing the farm kids in their overalls and homemade dresses traipsing through the woods on their way to school. How the pretty school teacher would be standing right where he was, ringing her bell and welcoming all the eager students.

Josh noticed a warm inflation expanding his chest as if a balloon was being blown up inside his rib cage. When the balloon reached its fill and his chest could expand no more, the balloon dropped into his gut. Josh waited, terrified to move. The balloon was suddenly punctured by a multitude of tiny holes. The heavy liquid seeped over his internal organs. His testicles crawled but it wasn't sexual.

Josh's knees weakened and he dropped to a kneeling position; there was a rumbling deep in his gut. It started as a slow gentle turning of thick liquid but the pace quickened causing a whirlpool. The liquid began splashing against the inside of his skin. He felt light-headed and in the next instant wholly dizzy. Was he going to pass out? Was this what death felt like?

The next instant, it was over. A wave returning to the sea.

He sat motionless, anticipating more. Was he okay? Absolutely. What in the heavens was that? But he knew exactly what it was, the only logical conclusion, he had just been baptized by the Holy Spirit.

The realization resulted in a stream of tears. "Thank you, Jesus."

He lay in a heap reliving the sensation over and over in his mind. This was not the tingling sensations he had at church and youth concerts; this was an all-powerful flat out assault on his senses. It had been overwhelming, scary, and comforting all at the same time. *Tongues as of fire appeared to them and rested on each one of them.* Yes, that was as good a verbal description of the indescribable as anything else. He thought of the paintings he had seen of Jesus and the Apostles and how they were often depicted as radiating light. That was how he felt, illuminated.

He could have sat there for hours soaking in the sensation... in the daylight. Yet, that was ending and he did not think to bring a flashlight. Reluctantly, he left his sacred site and headed back to his cabin which he found effortlessly.

That final night, Josh found it impossible to sleep. This time it was not because of nocturnal visits or nightmarish warnings. This time it was excitement. Josh found the hours dragging as he anticipated his return to camp a victorious warrior complete with the Holy Spirit's baptism. When he closed his eyes, he could still feel the comforting ball of energy down deep in his gut. *Therefore, if anyone is in Christ, he is a new creation. The old has passed away; behold, the new has come.*

The walk back to the base camp was a triumphant march. Every bird was singing just for him and every squirrel saluted him with its long bushy tale.

When he arrived at the bustling camp, he immediately sought out Peter, finding him sitting uncharacteristically alone on a picnic table.

"How was it?" Peter asked.

"Triumphant!" Josh shouted, hugging his friend. He launched into his tale.

When he had finished, Peter responded by saying, "A bobcat."

"What?"

"It wasn't a demon; it was a bobcat. I heard it too. Rare around here. Sounds like a lady screaming."

Josh's spirit deflated with the simple explanation. A bobcat? Seriously? Peter studied him. "Hey, whatever, you got baptized, right?"

"Yeah, I mean… I need to verify it with Mrs. Marone."

"Well, yeah, but that certainly sounds like it."

"What about you?" Josh asked, no longer desiring the conversation be about his experience.

"Spent four glorious days in the woods."

"No baptism?"

"Four glorious days in the woods," Peter repeated with a bit of a smirk.

The solitary campers met individually with Mrs. Marone who had arrived for the last week. Waiting for his turn, Josh found himself mulling over his experience. If that had been a bobcat and not a demon had he won a spiritual victory? If he had not, did that make the rest of his experience dubious? The questions were crushing to his spirit as he wondered if the adventure, in the end, was just something else he had managed to screw up.

When Josh met with Mrs. Marone in her makeshift camp office, he told her everything, beginning with being lost in the woods and almost quitting. He told her all about the nightmares the first night and then the mysterious sounds he took to be a real demon the second night. He explained what Peter said about the bobcat and told the rest of the story with the caveat of doubt that this was indeed a spiritual baptism.

When he finished his tale, Mrs. Marone stared at him for several long moments while he remained motionless, a defendant waiting for a verdict.

"How did you find your way to the campsite?" she asked.

"A stag. Well, I mean… I thought… I guess maybe it was just a coincidence."

"Is coincidence Biblical?"

"No."

"How is it you can give credit to God for the deer but can't hold Satan accountable for the bobcat?"

"I guess I didn't think of it that way."

"I want an answer to my question. How do we answer questions?"

"Biblically."

"Has Satan ever spoken through an animal?"

"Of course. The serpent in the Garden of Eden."

"So, the bobcat being a bobcat and not an actual demon changes what part of your story?"

"So, you think it was sent by the devil?"

"Of course. Satan attacked you and tried to scare you. You fought back as a Joseph. That's the story. Joshua, real demons are extremely rare. Especially in this area of the world. Think of it this way, Satan's a brilliant general but as vast as his army is, it's nevertheless limited. So, he uses his resources based on the need. A stronger foe requires a stronger attack."

"You're saying he sent a measly little bobcat to scare me?"

"Satan's been at this for centuries. You're a seventeen-year-old kid out in the forest by himself. What kind of fire power would you send? But then look at what he did after you thwarted his attack, he placed the seed of doubt in you by questioning his choice of weapons. That way, he wins by convincing you he was never playing. Bottom line is- you stood like a warrior for Christ and showed God you were ready the Holy Spirit."

"So, it really was the Baptism?"

"Absolutely. I've heard that description a thousand times. I think you've missed one major point however. Have you asked yourself, 'Why there?'"

"Well, yes. I figured it was the last day, and…"

"Joshua, don't waste my time. I asked, 'Why there?' If it was just a matter of the last day, why did He lead you to that schoolhouse?"

"The schoolhouse?"

"Nothing's coincidental."

"I should work harder in school?"

"God doesn't need to tell you that, I do that every day. He took you to that schoolhouse to tell you what Mountain is your destiny."

"Education? He wants me to be a teacher?"

"Oh, He was far more specific."

Josh thought. A schoolhouse, in the middle of nowhere… but that may not have anything to do with it. It was the schoolhouse itself. It was small. The kids that went there were probably young.

"An elementary school teacher?"

"That's what I thought at first but for you I think God has a different message. When you went into the school, you said you had a vision of the students and teacher as they had been in history. Is that correct?"

"Yes."

"Don't you think that's fairly significant?"

"Is it?"

"Of course, it is. So, what do you think God's trying to tell you?"

Josh thought again and smiled. "A history teacher? I mean... a history teacher."

"Considers all the evidence, don't you think?"

"Yes, ma'am." A history teacher. Yes, he could see himself in that role, like Mr. Dillon. Triumphant.

"So, leaving room for the Holy Spirit," Mrs. Marone concluded. "We'll put you on course for the Mountain of Education. Understand something, my young Joseph, this is not the end of anything, this is just the beginning. Being called to the Mountain of Education is a huge responsibility. It's the teachers who train the next generation of Josephs. What does the Bible say about teachers?"

"I... I don't know."

"James 3:1, *not many of you should become teachers... for you know that we who teach will be judged with greater strictness.* What's that tell us? First, it tells us God calls few to become teachers. Why? Because teaching is more than a job, it's a lifestyle. A righteous lifestyle. A teacher needs to always be a role model for his students because when a teacher sins, it isn't just God who sees it but all of the teacher's students, indeed the whole church community. Follow me?"

"Yes, ma'am."

"And the second thing that verse says is teachers will be judged with greater strictness. Do you know what will happen when I get to Heaven? I will be standing before God Almighty and He will hold me accountable for each and every student who has ever passed through my doors. Every single one of them. That's the cross I carry and it's the cross you'll have to carry. Don't take this calling lightly. Go forth and walk the path righteously."

"Yes, Mrs. Marone." As he turned to leave he remembered something. "Mrs. Marone? One more thing..."

"Yes?"

"Am I still in JOT?"

"Of course."

"But my grades..."

"Not many of you were wise according to worldly standards. But God chose what is foolish in the world to shame the wise; God chose what is weak in the world to shame the strong."

"Yes, ma'am. And thank you!" he shouted as he dashed away to find Peter.

Chapter Sixteen

The group did their best to move on after Barak's death but there was a change in everyone. Seth and Asher spent all their time together and Asher's lifestyle altered dramatically. He was no longer the wild jungle boy but firmly under the wing of his elder brother. By far the brothers' favorite activities were fishing and camping where they would often be gone for days, sometimes weeks. They reported meeting wanderers, people quietly moving around the country, under the government's radar. It added to the dream of getting out of the city permanently.

Mickey became even more reclusive and would often not show up for the evening meals. He used the kitchen to get his food, his room to sleep, but, other than that, he stayed downstairs claiming he was researching the next job. Emily treated the whole thing as something she simply did not want to talk about. It made Maggie wonder what other things Emily had seen and who else she had lost. Jake and Thad tried the hardest to be upbeat but there was no denying, an unspoken somberness clung in the air.

Then, one crisp autumn night, the Office was flooded with bright lights and wailing buzzers as they were yanked from their sleep by the screeching of Mickey's security alarm. As Emily sat up screaming, Maggie leapt out of bed to comfort her. Soldiers, dressed from head-to-toe in black uniforms, carrying rifles, stormed into the room shouting. Two soldiers appeared in the doorway of their partitioned bedroom and pointed guns at them. Maggie's own scream was trapped in her throat.

"You two! Hands on your heads! DO NOT TOUCH ANYTHING!"

In a dazed petrified state, and clutching Emily's hand, Maggie was led, along with the others, into the back of a black van. Everyone, that is, except Mickey, who was taken by himself in a smaller car.

Once at the station, she identified herself as Margret Anderson from Cleveland. They put Emily and her into a holding cell with a bunch of older women. The place smelled putrid of urine, body odor, and disinfectant. The two girls stayed huddled in a corner by themselves. Maggie did what she could to comfort Emily. How did they know? Her mind went through their string of burglaries trying to determine which one was the one that gave them away. All their jobs had been so meticulous. She tried her best to stay strong for Emily but she was nauseous with her powerlessness.

Eventually, she was taken from Emily and brought into a small interrogation room, where she was handcuffed to a chair. Across the tattered old desk were a couple of chairs and a large mirror where, she knew from the cop shows, people could be watching. The waiting was intense but she played it cool. She spent most of her time staring into the mirror, imagining she was having a stare down with whomever was behind it. Inside she was terrified, but she was not going to give any of them the satisfaction of seeing that.

After what seemed hours, two men dressed in suits came into the room. One was an old guy, his face wrinkled to the point of a permanent scowl. The other was much younger, meticulously groomed.

"Hello, Margret," the younger one said. "Don't be scared. We're from Homeland Security. This is Agent Hollinger, and I am Agent Matthews. But I'll tell you what, we don't need to be formal here. Just call me Thomas. How's that?"

Maggie stared with disgust at the young man's act.

"Solomon," Thomas said. "Well, the first thing I want to say is, you're not in trouble."

Oh, brother, this guy was a real gem. "Yeah, the handcuffs certainly led me to believe that."

Thomas looked up at his partner. "I believe we have one with a sense of humor."

"Even the devil laughs," the angry man spat.

"I'm sorry about the cuffs. It's just procedure. We'll get them off very soon. We just need to ask you a few questions."

Initially Thomas asked stupid questions. How many people lived in the Office? How many were minors? Did any have a church membership? From there, he asked about the conversations that went on. What were the groups' beliefs? Maggie thought the questions odd. "Group beliefs"? They believed in survival. She was as evasive and uncooperative as she dared. The one thing he did not ask about was the burglaries.

It was the angry man who brought the subject up when he asked what they were doing to survive. "Stealing, I bet. I know what these gutter rats do, unless this pretty one is into something else…is that it?" He bent down, grabbing her chin and pulling her face towards his. His breath was atrocious, like her father's. She yanked her head from his grasp and resisted the urge to scratch his eyes out. "Yeah, I've seen rats like this my whole life. Running the streets, no church. If it wasn't for this filth, this whole country could be delivered up as a righteous nation unto God. So, what is it? Stealing? Drugs? Or are you offering other services?"

"Mind the log in your own eye." She regretted her retort as soon as she uttered it.

The old agent smacked her across her face with the back of his hand. "See what I mean," he shouted. "*Unchained demons*."

Maggie held up her hand that was cuffed to the chair. Thomas could not control his chuckle and held his hand over his mouth. The old agent glared at him. "You think this is funny? Fine. You sit with the devil. She's either talking when I get back or I'm casting her into the pit." He slammed the door as he left.

Thomas smiled. "I'm sorry about that. He's a good Joseph, really, four kids, grandchildren, and a beautiful wife."

"Happy for him."

"Look, I feel like we got a little off topic. We really don't care what you've been doing to take care of yourselves. That would be a police matter. We're from Homeland Security. You do know the difference?"

"It's all the same to me."

"Well, yes, I can see where you might say that." Maggie noticed Thomas had an annoying way of pulling at the skin between his nostrils as he spoke. It was like he was picking both nostrils at the same time. It was gross. "The police are interested in people who break…what I like to call… normal laws. Drugs, gangs, robbery, stuff like that. But Homeland Security, we have a different focus. We keep people safe by going after those who are trying to poison the Awakening. Some of them are remnants of the past, libs mostly…"

"Look," Maggie said, "I'm not stupid. I know what you guys do. And I can't help you. I don't know any libs. I just know a bunch of kids who are trying to live in this fucked up world of ours."

"There are more than enough social services; you kids just don't take advantage of them. So, when you use words like that to describe our God-ordained society, I get a little antsy about it. Know what I'm saying?"

Maggie heeded the warning. She was tired and scared and tired of being scared. She wanted to get Emily and the boys and get the hell out of there. And if she could not get that, she just wanted to be back with Emily in that smelly cell. "What do you want from me? I don't know anyone."

"Ah, but you do. You know one, a Michael Barto."

Mickey? "What about him?"

"I need to know what you know about him."

Maggie thought for a moment. Were they asking her to rat Mickey out? Why just him? Sure, he did all the planning but they all did the burglaries. But wait, that would be a job for the police. Was Mickey doing something else? She realized she did not know what he was doing most of the time and how little she knew him. She certainly was not going to talk about his anti-government rants and especially of his condemnation of the Christian establishment.

"I don't know much. I'm not even sure where he's from. He keeps to himself. On his computer, mostly."

"He spends a lot of time on his computer?"

"I don't know. His office is downstairs. I don't go down there."

"Office? Have you ever been down there?"

"No. Me and Emily don't have reason to. Look, I don't know what you think he's done but he's a good guy. We all are. We don't deal drugs and we aren't part of any gang."

"See, there you go, back to those other kinds of crime. I've already told you, I'm not interested in that stuff. I'm interested in crime against God's Will for this country. And your friend Michael has been…well…shall we say, 'up to the devil's work.' No, what Michael's doing is far worse than selling drugs, or running a gang, or even… organizing burglaries." He winked.

"But…"

"It's okay, Margret. It's pretty obvious Michael was working on his own. You'll not be charged. However, as a minor, you will be turned over to social services. A social worker will be in shortly." With that the agent abruptly left, and Maggie, still cuffed, was alone with her fears. Mickey? What was going to happen to him? What was going to happen to her? And Emily? Will they split them all up? Will she ever see them again? No doubt they were going to discover who she really was, would they send her back to her family?

Though she was soaking in anxiety, she forced herself to show no emotions. She was not about to give them the pleasure. Nevertheless, after a long agonizing wait, she had to make something happen. "Hey," she shouted at the mirror. "Excuse me... I'd like to use the ladies' room."

A few moments later, a female officer took her to the bathroom. When Maggie finished, she was taken to another room with a smaller desk and no mirror. Here she waited for just a few minutes before the door opened again and a lady walked in.

Maggie noticed there was something different about her right away. First, she was young, just a few years older than Maggie. Second, she was not dressed like the others who wore dark-colored business attire. This lady was wearing a brightly colored blouse and a skirt that reminded Maggie of Native American clothing. Third, she did not move like the others. Their walk was heavy, determined. This lady's shuffle was more like a student late for class. She did, however, have a smile that struck Maggie as the first genuine one she had seen since she was arrested.

"Hi," the lady said as she walked in the door. "I'm Becca. I'm with Child Protective Services. And you're Margret...or do you go by Maggie?"

"Whatever...Maggie."

"I thought so, you look like a Maggie. So, I've moved you into this room back here so that we can talk. We can talk freely here, and it'll stay between the two of us. Follow me?"

"Sure."

"I'm gonna cut right to the chase, okay? Now, before I begin, I want you to hear me all the way to the end. Don't freak out on me. Agreed?"

Maggie nodded. Becca knew something, the question was how much?

"First, I know you're not from Cleveland, and I know your last name's not Anderson."

Maggie's stomach rolled with panic.

"I also know you're from right here in Columbus and I know who your father is. Oh, and I know you have a little brother. But, don't let any of that scare you. I have to say, whoever falsified your records did a pretty good job."

Every neuron was shouting at her to flee but there was nowhere to go.

"Would you like to know how I know these things?"

Maggie nodded, hopelessly.

"Maggie, I'm Rebecca."

At first, the name met nothing to Maggie. Then she remembered, the babysitter who promised to help, and never came back.

"I saw you in the holding pen and immediately knew it was you. I'd recognize those eyes of yours anywhere."

"Just so you know, if you send me back, I'll…"

"Maggie, I assure you, I have no intention of sending you back. The only plan I have is to get you out of here. I'm gonna fix your paper work and then you and Emily are gonna move in with me. We're gonna get you off the streets and into church and school."

Maggie shook her head.

"Now come on, don't argue. You know that kind of life can't last. It's not good for either of you."

"It's been working just fine."

"Really? The little guy, Asher, said he had a twin brother. What happened to him?"

Maggie glared at her.

"I'm not saying that to be mean, Maggie. But, you must be honest. Think of Emily."

What gives her the right to lecture? "Still safer than here."

"Maybe, but I'm not talking about here. I'm talking about setting you and Emily up in my extra bedroom. You'll have a room to yourselves…and your own bathroom. You can be clean all the time. We'll just be three girls sharing an apartment together."

"No, I just want to go back to the Office."

"Maggie, Michael's been arrested for domestic treason. The others are being held on other charges. Your age is the only reason you are not being charged with them. They aren't coming back. Asher's already been sent into foster care. There's no Office to go back to. It's over. You really have just two choices. Plan A, come live with me or Plan B, be referred to social services for real."

With the two options in front of her, Maggie saw it would be easier to run away from Becca than from an orphanage, or worse, her old family. She felt even better about her decision when she was reunited with Emily. Becca obtained temporary passes for the girls so they rode the ET. This was almost a new experience for Emily as she only had ridden it those few times she was able to sneak on. Maggie had not ridden it since she had run away and then it had always been tier four, never tier one. When she was a kid she had always thought of tier one as the car for the poor people. Now, she was no longer so naïve.

Becca's apartment was on the east side, ironically not too far from the Office. Maggie felt comforted by that. It would not be difficult to make a visit or two… or three.

The apartment seemed small after living on a whole floor all that time in the Office, but it was clean. There was a small living area with a couch and entertainment system, a kitchen with a real dishwasher, and two bedrooms each with their own bath. A sliding door from the living room opened onto a small balcony. From there, the tip of the Columbus sky line could be seen. Maggie had to admit, she was impressed.

Becca asked Emily if she would like to freshen up. "I've never taken a real shower before," Emily said as she looked over the bathroom. "Just the hose." Becca showed her how to use everything and laid out some towels.

"We'll be out in the living room. Just yell if you need anything," Becca said, leaving the door ajar. She turned to Maggie. "Would you like anything? I have some great tea."

"Yeah, sure,"

"Great," Becca said and went to the kitchen. She returned with a tea tray and the two sat on the couch. "How's she doing?"

"No screams yet."

"I can't believe she's never taken a shower before. How long has she been on the streets?"

"I don't know. Longer than me. Look, I need to know something."

"Of course."

"No bullshit."

"On my honor, I shovel no shit."

"How come you're doing all this? I'm not stupid. I know what you did could get you in a lot of trouble. At the very least it could get you fired. You could lose your church membership. So why are you risking that? Because you were my babysitter? It doesn't make sense."

"Do you know how God puts people in our lives for a reason?"

Maggie shrugged. And here comes the bullshit.

"Well, I believe it. I believe when we're walking our paths God puts lamps to light our way. You're one of my lamps."

Maggie laughed. "Sorry, it's just been a long time since I've heard that kind of talk." Just then, Emily yelled. Maggie headed to the bathroom. "When I get back, maybe you can just tell it to me without all the 'heavenly lights.'"

Maggie found Emily cowering against the far wall of the shower. "I don't like it, turn it off."

Maggie chuckled. "Yeah, kind of weird the first time." It turned out Emily was far from ready to get out, however. Instead, what she wanted was to fill the bathtub. When Emily had all she needed, Maggie returned to the living room.

"Okay," Becky said. "Do you remember the night you told me... what... the things your dad did."

"Not really." And that was the truth, Maggie only remembered the babysitter doing nothing.

"I do. I remember everything about it. I even remember the pajamas you had on. Oh, Maggie, I was so scared. I knew I should do something, I prayed and prayed about it. Finally, I told my mom. She told me I did the right thing but not to tell anyone else. She said she'd take care of it. I never got called to babysit again. A few years later, I heard you had disappeared. The church said you'd been tempted away, and that it was a lesson on how Satan attacks everyone's families. But I suspected you left for a different reason. I've carried the guilt of not helping you ever since. I should have done more and I didn't. You're the reason I went into social work. I thought if I could help others...and then...out of the blue...I look up and see you. I truly felt the hand of God."

"If you're breaking the law, aren't you going against God?"

Becca smiled. "We'll see about that."

That night Emily and Maggie lay in their new beds. Emily nervously chattered as she recounted the evenings events. They relived every terrifying moment with Emily's constant acknowledgment that if Maggie had not been there, "I would have freaked!"

Emily asked repeatedly about the others, especially Jake, but Maggie could offer little in the way of comfort. Eventually the ramblings turned to Becca. Emily asked if Maggie liked her.

"She seems nice," said Maggie.

"I like her too. And I like this apartment. I've never lived in a real apartment before. Are we gonna stay here?"

"It looks like we can. But if something goes wrong, just tell me and we'll leave. Together. Okay?"

"Deal. But just until Jake gets back. Then we'll all leave... together."

Maggie hoped Emily was right.

Chapter Seventeen

J osh's senior year in the JOT program was the best year of his whole academic career. With both history and education as focal points, Josh found his choice of classes much more to his liking. He still had to work hard to stay on top of the heavy load of assignments and he maintained a strict discipline in keeping himself organized but everything from the Bible classes to calisthenics was easier and far less stressful. After all those years of struggling to simply stay afloat, Josh finally had a raft. The raft of the Holy Spirit.

Peter had been unanimously elected class president. Adults and students alike agreed, he was a living example of the Bible's directive: *Let no one despise you for your youth, but set the believers an example in speech, in conduct, in love, in faith, in purity.* As a result, though Josh was no longer slinking from class to class, he still saw little of Peter at school.

There remained, however, the Saturday afternoons on Elmer.

"So, what do you think?"

"I think it sounds triumphant," Josh answered.

"It would be, wouldn't it? Right on the front lines of Jehovah's Revolution."

In school the previous day, the seniors had a special assembly where a guest speaker promoted a year of missionary work. The youth were sent overseas to live at outreach centers where they would spend half their time working on various improvement projects and the other half acting as missionaries.

"Where do you wanna go?" Josh asked.

"Well, anywhere God sends me but I think the Middle East would be amazing. You can't get more involved in Jehovah's Revolution than there. Africa's where most of the youth go. I don't know. I'd like to help with construction. When I was a kid, I went through a real carpentry phase. Following in the footsteps of Jesus."

The first semester flew by. Stephen came home for Christmas. Matthew and Ada announced their engagement with plans for a July wedding. Matthew said it had not been easy regaining Ada's parents' trust but eventually they gave the young couple their blessing. They planned on staying in Columbus and attending university together. They also heard from Luke, through a picture, in uniform, looking older but with the same tight-lipped expression. The caption read simply, "Seniors."

Shortly after the holidays, Josh received the news he had been accepted to the Ohio State University. His parents were beyond proud; he may not have followed his brother to West Point but he was accepted to the most prestigious school in Ohio. Peter found he had been accepted to all three schools he had applied to: Harvard, Princeton, and Liberty. Mrs. Marone was overjoyed and made a huge deal out of it one morning at the Justjudy show. Peter himself was excited but his true focus was on the mission year.

For most high school students, graduation is a day, a big day full of ceremonies and parties. For JOT students, graduation lasted a week. The students were paraded in front of the church, of course, but then again at an Elder's meeting, followed by the State House, the Capitol, and visits from all kinds of Apostles. There were dinners sponsored by various groups all "sending off" the new Josephs. Josh saw nothing of Peter that week as Peter spent most of his days with Mrs. Marone as she introduced her top students to all the dignitaries. Peter himself cleaned up nicely in his suit and neatly trimmed hair. Still, the way he wrestled with his sport coat made him resemble Tarzan after he was brought back to England.

The Saturday after the graduation ceremony, Josh's mother threw a massive party at one of the club houses at American Harvest. The whole Conrad clan came from Canton. It had been a busy four years, so busy he had rarely had time to return to Canton. He had seen his extended family exclusively at holiday get-togethers and a couple vacations. There had been only one Ohio State/Michigan party.

Josh basked in the attention and the remarks of how developed his body had become and how confidently he stood. As for his old friends, Jared and Jesse, he had seen them even less. When they showed up at his party, they critiqued every new video game and were surprised Josh was not at all up-to-date. From Josh's perspective, their conversation was childishly boring.

That summer, Peter and Josh spent as much time together as they could. Church and YF continued but for the first time in four years, they found themselves with long periods of free time. They lounged around the pool, hiked in the nearby state parks, and spent evenings on High Street. They even squeezed in a white-water rafting trip in nearby Ohiopyle, Pennsylvania. But, the main event of the summer, by far, was Matthew's bachelor party.

Bachelor parties were not the drunken orgies of long ago. Even before the FGA, Christians were more likely to celebrate by taking the groom camping. In a few generations, it had become the tradition. The guest list was twenty, including Matthew. For Peter, the best man, that was a divinely ordained number, making it ten-on-ten.

"Remember the way we used to play *Capture the Flag*?" Peter asked.

"Sure."

"How about a bachelor party playing *Capture the Flag*?"

"Sounds fun...I guess."

"Ah, but I sense a lack of true enthusiasm. Perhaps, it's because you don't see the big picture. See, we're going to Michigan. This guy turned his four-hundred-acre ranch into the premier laser tag site. You're divided into armies and you go to war with each other all weekend." Peter brought the site up on his cell showing the promises of the latest laser gun technology and the "world's greatest game of *Capture the Flag*."

"It looks triumphant," Josh agreed. And it was. For three days and nights, the boys crawled around a forest and slept under the stars.

A week later, Matthew was a married man. Two weeks after that, Peter and Josh sat on Elmer for the last time. Peter was leaving the next day for a six-week training program.

For a long time, they lay quiet, each of them lost in his own thoughts. Josh finally broke the silence. "Do you remember the day I first met you?"

"Sure. Oh my, you were hilarious, standing there in your swimsuit and towel, telling us you were taking a walk... in the woods!"

Josh joined the laughter. "Yeah, the part I never told you was my mom kicked me out of the house to find friends. I was supposed to go to the pool but thought I could hide in the woods for a while and then just go home."

Peter rolled with giggles. "And you walked right into us! Oh my, that's so triumphant! You can't trick God."

"Solomon. I'll tell you something, I thought you were the weirdest joe I'd ever seen, and now, you're my best friend."

"Solomon, joe"

The two stayed out on Elmer long after the sun went down. They reminisced about the years spent and dreamt of the future God had in store for them. Eventually, with great reluctance, they climbed off Elmer and picked their way through the woods. Peter prayed a hedge of protection, gave Josh a long warm hug, turned and walked away.

PART II

Chapter Eighteen

Was it her? Yes, yes it was. At first, he had not recognized her in her neatly pressed white dress shirt, yet her eyes were unmistakable. They were wide in the middle and narrowly Asian-like on the ends beneath long thick lashes. She looked like an Egyptian statue come to life. And she appeared to have that effect with the use of very little makeup.

She was working as one of the bartenders.

He had first noticed her months before when she walked into the student lounge. He was sitting in his favorite morning spot in the back when she breezed in and up to one of the counters. No one else paid any attention to her but, for him, the world had stopped. It was not just because she was triumphantly gorgeous either. The university was filled with beautiful women. It was the fact that her beauty defied convention. Her hair was much shorter than the fashion, as if she had little regard for the fashion at all. Her clothing likewise was more for comfort than style. Her pants were baggy and her shirt was at least two sizes too large. Yet, if she was trying to conceal her beauty, she was failing miserably. He watched her as she engaged with no one, ordered her breakfast, and found an empty booth. She proceeded to eat but her true attention was given to whatever textbook she was studying. Josh was hooked.

For months he watched from afar as she came in every Monday, Wednesday, and Friday becoming the highlight of Josh's mornings. One day, he dared himself to talk to her but chickened out as he got close to her booth. He did, however, get a closer look at her rich ebony eyes and his knees almost buckled. After that, he did not make another attempt, and now, here she was right in the same room.

Josh and his parents were making their way through a formidable crowd, Josephs and Apostles from all the Mountains gathered together in celebration.

Josh had not wanted to come to the party but his mother insisted. In the last two years, he had enjoyed many freedoms living in his own apartment but, when it came to a certain tone in his mother's voice, there was no negotiation. So, once again, he put on the mantle of "son-of-our DHS Director," donned his tuxedo, and dutifully attended.

He appreciated the fact that the men and women in the room were the instruments of God's history but that did not help with the claustrophobia he felt in situations like these. He had been going to parties all his life, mostly at his family's church. When he was younger, he would get through the initial greetings and then meet his cousins in the back. That continued to be his strategy long after there were no longer any cousins to meet. He would attend to his family obligation, slip away the first chance he had, and find a spot.

In between handshakes, Josh noted the oasis of another bar on the opposite side of the room, far away from the girl. Having a drink of some kind was a necessary prop for these get-togethers.

"So, I understand you're a student at OSU," some man Josh should know was saying to him.

"Yes, sir, the Mountain of Education," Josh said, maintaining a firm handshake out of fear of getting his hand crushed.

"What a blessing… such a blessing. I heard your brother's doing well."

"Yes, sir."

"Such a blessing. And your father. We're so blessed to have him…" The man's voice trailed off as he found someone else's hand to squeeze.

Josh's parents were engaged in dialogue with a couple. This was his chance to slip away. Moments later, feeling like a slick operative, he arrived in the short line for the bar. As he waited, his focus was across the room. The girl was busy and the few seconds she had between patrons she stayed focused, keeping herself organized. Nice work ethic.

"Yes, sir?" the young bartender asked, shaking Josh from his thoughts.

"Orange juice, please."

"Make it a screwdriver," said a voice from behind him.

Josh whirled around to see his father. "Really?"

"Sure, private party, college student. Enjoy yourself. But do me a favor tonight, mingle a little. Network. These people just might be people you'll teach about later."

"Yes, sir." Josh was more focused on the bartender pouring vodka into his glass. Seconds later, he handed the drink to Josh. "Thanks, Dad."

His dad ordered a drink for himself and then lifted his glass in toast. "God's Will be done."

Josh repeated the words and clinked his glass against his dad's.

After they finished their sips, his dad turned to him and said, "I've wanted to talk to you about something. You're now eligible to be an intern. How would you like to work at my office this summer?"

"Really?"

"On the third floor. Level one clearance."

"You mean like real security clearance?"

"Well, yeah, but don't get too excited, it's not like you're gonna be James Bond. It'll be good. We'll be able to spend more time together and having DHS on your résumé will be quite a blessing."

"Yes, sir," replied Josh.

Moments later, with his father once again engaged in conversation, Josh worked his way into the furthest corner of the room. He was pleasantly surprised by the smooth taste of the vodka-laden orange juice. As he sipped his drink, he surveyed the room. His father was right, he should socialize. The whole idea of blending into the back was quite stupid. The fact he was the only one in the room not talking to someone made him stand out more.

Fear not, for I am with you; be not dismayed, for I am your God. Years ago, when he had been baptized by the Holy Spirit, he had hoped all his fears and insecurities would go away. However, as he learned, he still had to struggle with Satan's attacks. Only now, he had divine help on the inside. "So, by standing in a corner who's winning?" The voice in his head was that of Mrs. Marone. He could just imagine what she would say if she saw him standing there like that.

He was surprised to see he had only ice cubes in his glass. Well, that went down quickly.

He returned to the bar where the line was surprisingly short. He doubted he would get another real drink without his father present, but he had to have something in his hand. He gave his glass to the bartender who asked, "Another?"

"Um, yes, please." Nothing more was said as the bartender proceeded to mix his drink. Josh squelched a giggle.

The first drink had not affected him at all. If anything, it woke him up. He went back to his spot to plan his strategy. He saw a group of people his age talking in a corner. He recognized a few of their faces. That would be the logical choice yet as soon as that thought crossed his mind, his stomach quivered. He would be much more comfortable mingling with the adults who knew him through his parents.

A bold challenge entered his head. "Talk to her."

Now that would be gutsy. Yet, like an annoying fly, the thought would not go away. Why shouldn't he talk to her? He was a successful, Spirit-baptized college student. His professors respected him for how hard he worked and his classmates knew they could count on him. Even without being the son of a DHS director, even without being a Conrad, he was an impending Joseph in his own right.

He watched the girl gracefully go about her work. She professionally smiled at just the right times but did not engage any of the patrons directly. She was not at the party; this was a job.

He was already half-way through his drink.

The situation was perfect of course. Here he had a reason to talk to her. He just needed to order a drink. It was the perfect opening line. Why it wasn't even a line at all. It was just something to be said. Then... then what? Then, he would trust the Spirit. He was cognizant the plan had an air of desperation, like jumping in the water and then learning how to swim. Nevertheless, he was feeling emboldened.

He got lost in taking short sips until he was down to nothing but ice, his courage not quite strong enough to reach his feet. "Come on, joe." It was as if he could hear the voice of his long-lost friend, Peter. "God leads you to the door but you have to open it."

He was half-way across the room before his mind caught up to his body. Oh shit, he was going to actually do this.

As he approached, he became aware of a noise, it was a rattle of some kind, as if something was... clinking? Then he realized his hand was shaking, causing the ice in his glass to jiggle.

The next thing he knew, she was looking directly at him.

Spellbound by the depth of her eyes, he froze. *Just forget it!* his mind screamed. *She's so far out of your league. Just get your drink, turn around, and crawl back to your corner.*

"May I help you?" Her voice seemed more mature than her young face should produce.

"Um, orange juice...please," he was barely able to mutter.

"Sure," she said. "That all you want in it?"

At first, he did not understand the question. "Well, um no, you could put some vodka in there if you want."

She smiled and proceeded to expertly mix a screwdriver. With a neat flip of a small napkin to act as the coaster, she placed the drink before him.

He did his best to sound nonchalant. "You don't look old enough to be serving alcohol."

"You don't look old enough to be drinking it," she said with a grin.

Josh felt his face flush. "It's a private party."

She smiled teasingly but, unlike what she delivered the other guests, it was genuine. How could God have sculpted such a perfect face? "I work for the caterer. Twenty-one to drink, eighteen to serve. Who would police a party like this anyway?"

"Good point," answered Josh. His mind raced for something to say. Something suave and debonair. "You're a student at OSU, aren't you?"

"Nursing school." She wiped the counter with a dry dish towel.

"I've seen you in the student union... I mean... sometimes."

"I know. You're the guy who's always sitting in the back watching everyone."

He could feel his cheeks growing warm and knew they were beyond his control. "I like people watching. I'm a history major. It's kind of what we do."

She remained busy wiping the counter. "So, what's a budding historian doing at a CAP function like this?"

"My parents like to drag me to these things."

"Oh, your dad's one of the big shots?"

"I guess you could say that, he's..."

The girl's attention was turned abruptly away to wait on a customer who had come to the far end of the bar. Josh took a sip of his drink and smiled. He was doing it, he was in reality... REAL Reality... conversing with HER. Okay, so maybe it was just a few words but he had done it. He had approached her. A couple of years ago, he would never have had the courage to come this far. Things were changing, he was changing. School was going great. He was growing up, conquering his fears, why shouldn't he start to look around for the next step in his life?

Two more customers came, as Josh waited patiently. No way was he going anywhere.

Then, she was back.

"Don't think I introduced myself... Josh Conrad."

"Maggie Anderson."

"It must be tough to be a student and have a job. Especially nursing school. I've heard the tales."

"Yeah, it's not easy. Keeps me busy."

"Righteous work. You stay on campus?"

"No. I'm a commuter. I share an apartment with my cousin and sister on the east side. You?"

"Apartment but it's on campus."

They were interrupted by what appeared to be her boss. The chubby old man glared at Josh disapprovingly. He reminded himself she was working and he sure didn't want to do anything that would get her in trouble. When she returned, Josh drew in a deep breath. "Look, I don't want to keep you, but… well… I was hoping… maybe… if you'd like to… maybe you'd let me buy you a cup of coffee… sometime." He had meant to swing away and ask her out but in the end he choked. In the second she used to mull over his question, he could see she was just as inexperienced as he was.

He was relieved to see her smile. "How about we meet Monday morning? Your booth."

"Solomon."

◈

"Who was that cute bartender you were talking to?" his mother asked in the car on the way to dropping Josh off at his apartment.

"A girl from school," he answered.

"She's adorable. Petite."

Josh hid his smile with his hand. For an evening he thought would just be something he had to endure, it turned out to be…possibly… the best evening of his life. She was the most perfect girl he had ever met. Her beauty was overwhelming but she did not flaunt it. She wore her clothes modestly with simple earrings and a beat-up old bracelet. *Likewise also that women should adorn themselves in respectable apparel, with modesty and self-control.* She was smart and what more nobler profession is there than medicine? She also laughed, she laughed so easily and there was something about it. It was casual, natural, so… she laughed like Peter. Oh my Lord, that was it!

The thought of his old friend brought both joy and sadness to his heart. It was the one flaw in what had become an almost perfect life.

A life that had just gotten better. He knew he should not jump to any conclusions. Let this all play out in God's time as part of God's plan but it certainly did seem strange that out of all the students at OSU, the millions of people living in the Columbus area, they would end up at a party together.

And for him to find the courage to approach her? But, whoa, *it is the purpose of the Lord that will stand*. He needed to slow down his thinking, leave room for the Holy Spirit. He would relax and wait for Monday morning.

Sure, his anxious mind whined, *no problem.*

Chapter Nineteen

When Maggie got home that night, she accidentally woke Emily up.

"How was work?" Emily croaked.

"Fine. Bunch of bureaucrats stroking each other. Talked to a boy for a while."

"That's good." Emily rolled over. Abruptly, she sat up, snapping on the light. "Wait… what?"

Maggie smiled sheepishly as she climbed into bed. "I talked to a boy. No big deal."

"No big deal? No big deal? I thought you were a nun or something."

"Ha, ha." Maggie threw her stuffed bear in Emily's general direction.

Emily used the stuffed animal to lay on for support. "So, do tell. I want all the details."

"Not much to tell. His name's Josh. He's a sophomore. Studying history and education."

"Fine, nice résumé but get to it… is he cute?"

"Yeah, yeah he is. Boyish looking. He has nice eyes. Oh, you should have seen it though. He stood in the back of the room for an hour. Then he comes up shaking his glass. Clinking his ice together, making sure I could see it was empty."

Emily laughed. "No way, did he really do that?"

"Yeah, it was so cute."

"So, when's the date?"

"Oh, no date, we're meeting for coffee Monday morning."

"Morning coffee?" Emily was clearly unimpressed.

"It makes sense since he's been staring at me all year."

"What? You know this guy?"

"No. I've seen him in the student lounge."

"He stares at you? Isn't that a little weird?"

"Not for him. He's just too scared to approach."

"Sounds like a wimp."

"Maybe. Or maybe, he's just gentle."

"Is that the kind of guy you like?"

"Honestly, I don't know what kind of guy I like. And it's not like I'm marrying him. Besides, I tell him about you and he'll shout, 'No way, I'm outta here!'"

"Really?" Emily grinned, throwing a pillow at Maggie's head.

"See what I mean?"

Though it had been a long day and she was dead tired, Maggie found herself having trouble sleeping. So much so, she waited for Emily's breathing to grow deep and then slipped out of the apartment. The cool night air splashed her. Dressed in her Night Warrior clothes, slinking through the shadows she quickly worked her way back to the rooftops surrounding their old Office. She had not done this since starting nursing school. It felt good.

Two years ago, Maggie surrendered to her new life. Becca was right, it was what was best for Emily. Maggie only had to glance down at Barak's bracelet, most of its glass stones having long disappeared, to be reminded of that fact.

Becca had used her social worker connections to establish both girls. Emily was easy as she had no reason to lie. She could simply be brought back in under the Prodigal Son Edict. Maggie was a bit more complicated and she was sure Becca took a bigger risk than she admitted to. Becca explained nothing was foolproof but, in the end, Maggie had all the paperwork she needed to go to school, get a job, and... attend church.

That was what had terrified Maggie the most. She could fake the rest of it but church? Church was where people would get in her face, lock eyes with her, ask her questions she did not want to answer. Becca assured her Maplewood Christian was "not that kind of church."

Maggie had no idea what Becca meant by that until she arrived on her first Sunday. The church was only one building, consisting of a dozen classrooms, a basement for the children, and a small sanctuary, which was packed with a few hundred people. Nevertheless, Maggie entered with her defenses up. To her surprise, there were no overreaching smiles or insistent questions. People welcomed her with sincere warmth and a gentle acceptance. The congregation was mostly young adults in their mid-twenties. There were lots of little babies.

The pastor was also a young man who spoke with a Texas drawl. His sermon was funny as he relayed stories from his childhood and being raised a preacher's kid. When she met him after the service, he did not appear formidable but was a down-to-earth guy, with the willingness to laugh at himself. She found herself drawn to his tender sincerity even as alarms went off in her head.

The real difference in the church showed up most when they started their Bible classes. This was where she was sure to be exposed, but the teachers did not pry. They asked the required questions and seemed content with Maggie's shallow rehearsed answers.

That was when Maggie questioned Becca, asking whether it was a legitimate church. "Oh yeah," Becca said. "All legal and everything. We get through all the required stuff and focus on loving each other. That's what churches used to be about until they decided they could take over the world!"

Maggie did not allow herself to get too close to anyone and she made it clear the doors the church membership opened were something she could live without. Nevertheless, two months later, Emily and Maggie were official church members and their lives changed completely.

Public school was now available. At first, both girls chose online classes but after a year, Emily opted for an actual school. Maggie felt like a fretting mother, sending her daughter off for the first time. Her worries were unfounded as Emily surrounded herself with a good group of friends and blended right in with the other students. Maggie respected how well Emily adjusted. She was a real chameleon.

Maggie alone was privy to the nights when Emily, usually stressed for other reasons, would ramble on incessantly about Jake. Information was scant, but Becca found out he had been shipped to a school out west. Emily liked the sound of "school," rather than "prison." She spoke of how she thought Jake would be back as soon as he graduated. Maggie knew there were no promises.

Maggie stuck with the online classes. Partly because she could set the pace but mostly because she had no interest in the drama of high school. Even the idea of being around so many people sent her into a state of quivering nausea.

But, it was not just school. Because of their church membership, a world they had long been cut out of now welcomed them. The two girls could easily hop on the ET and go anywhere in the city. They could also go IN anywhere in the city. All the security gates that had been impassible were now nothing more than minor inconveniences. They could go to High Street, see movies in theaters, and though money was tight, they could go shopping. For Emily, it was a wondrous new world. For Maggie, it was all too familiar and brought a secret consternation.

Becca was busy with her job and taking classes for her continuing education. She also had an active social life with a group of other young ladies from the church that treated Maggie and Emily nicely. There was one lady, Sherah, that Becca was particularly close to. Sometimes, Becca spent nights at Sherah's house, which was just fine with Maggie.

It was into the six month of their stay with Becca when Becca caught Maggie sneaking back into the apartment late at night.

Becca was waiting for her on the balcony. "Where have you been?"

"Out."

"Maggie, what the… are you still stealing?"

"No."

"Then what are you doing?"

"Just letting off a little steam."

"In the middle of the night? Dressed like a ninja? Maggie, you've got to put that behind you. What would happen if you were caught? Do you think I'd be able to get you out of it?"

In truth, since she wasn't stealing, or even breaking in to anything, the thought of getting caught never crossed Maggie's mind. That was the point of the game, to slink through the shadows and not be seen.

The resulting argument led to their first major bone of contention. Becca, using the "best-for-Emily" argument, made Maggie promise not to go out at night anymore. It was a promise Maggie kept… when Becca was home.

Many times, Becca and Sherah took the girls away for the weekend. Sometimes it was in a large group, other times it was just the four of them. They hiked and camped which led to backpacking, white water rafting and other outdoor adventures. Emily adored those weekends. To Maggie, they were fun escapes but lacked the adrenaline rush of a night of parkour.

When Maggie turned sixteen, she obtained the job with the catering company through one of Sherah's friends. She felt good about being able to contribute to the monthly expenses. When she obtained her high school diploma, she came up with the plan to go to nursing school while Emily finished high school. With the skills always in demand, a nursing license would open the doors to go anywhere.

All in all, everything was going according to plan. So why was she talking to a boy? Because if she were not too proud to admit it to herself, she was lonely. Becca had Sherah and the others, Emily had a whole circle of friends, and Maggie had nobody. Yeah, but this was not just somebody, this was a boy. Well, yes and no. Josh was obviously a boy but he was different. Maggie saw him day after day sitting in a booth by himself. He appeared to be a simple, kind person and he was a loner. Like her.

Besides, she told herself, it was just a cup of coffee.

❖❖❖

When she arrived Monday morning, she found a far more nervous Josh than the one she had met on Saturday. Maybe because the student lounge did not sell screwdrivers, she mused.

"Hi... Hello..." Josh said, trying to gallantly stand up and almost knocking the table over.

"Hi, Josh."

"Can I get you something? Breakfast? Coffee?"

Maggie held up the coffee in her hand. "Already took care of it." She realized she had disrupted his plans and felt bad about it. She sat in the booth across from him. Silence.

"You gonna get something?" she asked.

"No... um... yeah. Yeah, I think I will. Sure I can't get you anything? Muffin?"

She declined. As she waited, she tried to study the bones in the human hand but it was futile. He was nice. Overthinking himself like crazy, but still a nice guy. Yet she was not all sure what she was doing there. Did she really want to open this door? She knew she shouldn't but she also knew if she did open it, it would be with someone like him. Quiet, nervous, but a thinker. She liked that about him.

Josh came back with coffee and several muffins which he set on the table to offer. He apologized for the wait. Maggie decided she liked his voice. Even in his nervousness, it had a calming tone.

For an awkward moment, they sat in silence.

She was the one to break it. "Okay, let's not be weird. What shall we talk about?"

"You," blurted Josh. "How do you like OSU so far?"

"It's fine. About what I expected... nursing school though..."

"Hard?"

"It's hard but... well... if you want to know the truth... I think it's pretty gross."

"What is?"

"The human body."

Josh's laughter was filled with irony. "That's a pretty interesting conclusion for a nurse to make."

"I know. I decided to go into nursing because I wanted the skills that would be in demand. But now that I'm studying what goes on under our skin, it's pretty nauseating."

"And this is your first year?"

"Quite a predicament. I worked my ass off to get into a university and now I'm not sure I want to be here. Not in nursing any way."

"Why you hippie!" Josh laughed. "Imagine, a college student who doesn't know what to major in."

"That's okay, isn't it?"

"Solomon."

The air in the room felt lighter. She made sense to him. That was relieving. She was not at all sure she made sense to herself. "I'm thinking maybe forestry."

"Forestry?"

"I love the woods. I go backpacking a lot. State Parks mostly. I think I'd like to work in one."

"Yeah, that would be solomon. You'd make a great ranger. Nicer than most of them. There was this ranger once, when Peter and I were hiking..."

It was the way he said his name that made her ask. "Who's Peter?"

Josh stopped. Had she upset him? No, but she did drudge up something.

"My best friend. My best friend who's disappeared."

"Disappeared?"

"Yeah, he went on a mission trip after high school. He was solomon for the first, I don't know, six months maybe, and then he dropped off the face of the earth. He stopped texting and calling. And not just me but everyone. His mom came over one day when I was home. She was crushed. She didn't want to believe he wasn't talking to me either. He was only supposed to be gone for a year; now he's been gone almost two."

"That's a long time. Is it possible he's..."

"Dead? No, actually he's sent his parents a couple of 'don't worry' telegrams."

"Telegrams?"

"Yeah, believe it or not. The best theory is that somehow he got caught up in a cult."

"What do you think?"

"It's hard for me to think he's in a cult. He's the most Christ-like guy I know. I mean, I'm sure Satan attacked him, but I don't see Peter losing that battle. No way."

"So, what do you think happened?"

"I have no idea. In truth, sometimes I'm angry at him. We're best friends, closer than I've been with anyone else my whole life. Including my own brother. And then, he just disappears."

"Understandable."

Their conversation turned to life at school and far too quickly their time ran out.

As she gathered her things, he stumbled through his question. "So… I've enjoyed talking today and I was wondering… maybe… we could… maybe… do it again?"

She could tell that was not exactly the question he wanted to ask. She found herself relieved he had not had the courage. Still, she had to admit she enjoyed the conversation as well. "Yeah, Mr. Conrad, you're alright. I have a lab tomorrow… Wednesday?"

Josh beamed. "Solomon."

On Wednesday, he asked her out for Friday night. She was forced to hold back a giggle as he struggled through his over-rehearsed invitation. She had to work. When he quickly postponed it to Saturday, she had to turn him down again as Becca and Sherah were taking Emily and her on a backpacking trip. She could tell he was crushed. When he changed it to a concert on High Street the following weekend she was both relieved and terrified to say "yes."

On the backpacking trip, Emily made the big announcement by challenging Sherah and Becca. "Guess who has a boyfriend."

"You?" they asked simultaneously.

"Nope," answered Emily. Sherah and Becca's faces registered disbelief. "Yep, she's got a date next Saturday."

Maggie felt her cheeks flush. "It's just to a concert."

"A concert and dinner," corrected Emily. "That's a date. Yep, the wannabe nurse that doesn't like people now has a boyfriend. Life just gets weirder and weirder."

Emily enjoyed teasing Maggie throughout the week but danced around like a bridesmaid when it came time for Maggie to get ready.

Josh arrived at the door with flowers for Maggie and candy for Emily, who giggled uncontrollably at the gesture. Maggie wasted no time leaving the apartment and the embarrassing girl behind.

They walked to the ET, where at the first available interchange, Josh brought her to the Tier 4 car. It was the first time she had ridden in that tier since she had run away. The plush environment appeared to her as overused stage furniture. She sat close to Josh and looked no one in the eyes.

They took the ET to the furthest outreaches of the city, where they had dinner in a historic restaurant named the Buxton Inn. The dinner itself was perfect and served by a pretty young server dressed like she was from the eighteenth century. Maggie was sure Josh meticulously planned every detail of the evening.

After dinner they took the ET back to High Street. Josh's tickets were for seats in the VIP section just a few feet from the stage. The thunderous volume reverberated throughout her body and the glitzy highly choreographed multimedia showcase left her feeling claustrophobic. She swallowed her feelings. The dinner had been wonderful and she did not want to cast a shadow on the evening.

On the ET ride home, Josh was pensive. "You sure you liked the concert?"

"It was good." Maggie could see she had not convinced him. "Well, to be honest, I guess it was all a little loud for me."

"I'm sorry..."

"Oh, no. The evening's been wonderful. Believe it or not but that was my first concert. I guess I'm just into quieter things."

"How do you feel about theater?"

"You mean like actors?"

Josh laughed. "Yeah, like real life actors."

Maggie felt her cheeks flush with embarrassment. "I haven't been since I was a little kid..."

Josh looked astonished. "Really? Not even with your YF?"

A wave of guilt rolled over her. She did not want to lie to her new friend and yet she was not ready to come clean. "Um... no."

"Well, that's something that'll have to change. There's a comedy on campus. We could go next weekend. I heard it's hilarious and... not too loud."

"Sounds great. Thanks, Josh."

At the door to her apartment building, it became quickly obvious what he intended as he hem-hawed around. When he finally made his awkward move to kiss her, she met his warm gentle lips with her own. The first kiss was a quick peck to test the waters but it was followed by a second try that was held for just the right amount of time. His eyes locked on hers questioningly. She smiled reassuringly. And they kissed again.

"Thank you, Josh. Thanks for a wonderful evening."

"Thank you," he said with a slight bow.

Emily, met her at the door and insisted on all the details. She giggled as Maggie relayed the evenings events. "Maggie kissed a boy! Maggie kissed a boy!"

The teasing led to a pillow fight that lasted until the adrenaline burned off.

As they lay in their beds, Emily asked, "You really didn't like the concert?"

"No. It was too much."

Emily remained quiet a moment. "Maggie, are you still mad at God?"

"Mad at God? Why do you ask me that?"

"Jake said that's why no one in the Office talked about God or went to church, 'cause everyone was mad at Him."

Maggie had no idea where to begin. Should she come clean? With Emily, it was not a matter of trust. It was more a sense of responsibility. As her virtual older sister and role model, should she tell Emily her real feelings? Or was there a higher responsibility? Emily was changing from the urban wild child she had been. She liked school and was learning things from it, and she enjoyed going to church. "I guess there was a time when I was angry. But I don't think I'm as mad anymore."

Emily pondered her words. "I don't think I was ever mad at God. I hated Him because my brother hated Him. I didn't even know Him. All I ever knew was Jake and he always told me that we had to stay hidden, that it wasn't safe to be caught, that they would send me away to some horrible place. But, none of that was true. We weren't sent anywhere. We have a great apartment, we joined a church, I'm in school, and we get to do everything normal people get to do. Jake was wrong, we should've gotten caught a long time ago. We were lost lambs in the forest, all we had to do was come home... maybe then Barak would still be alive."

"Wow, you've been doing some thinking."

"Yeah, I guess. But, you know what I mean, don't you?"

"I certainly can't deny we're in good shape but we've had a real guardian angel."

"That's true. Do you think Becca was God's way of saving us?"

"Can't rule it out."

"Exactly. So doesn't that prove He wants what's best for us? Everything does happen for a reason. We just need to go to church, get right with God and follow the path He has for us. Then there's nothing to be afraid of."

"There certainly shouldn't be," said Maggie.

"I'm thinking I'm gonna become a social worker like Becca and try to help all those kids back there. They don't need to hide anymore. And when Jake gets home, I'm telling him how wrong he was. I'm telling him all about God."

"Sounds like a noble idea."

Maggie's mind would not let her sleep that night as it raced along a pendulum of turbulent emotions and self-doubts. What was she doing? This was never to be about her, it was about Emily. And Emily was doing great. She was finding safety and security in the society around her. Was that not exactly what society was meant to do? So, why did the thought make Maggie feel like she was losing her? All these years, it was Emily providing her a way to stay grounded. When she was swinging high on the rooftops she told herself it was all about Emily. When she stopped, joined a church and went to school, it had been all about what was best for Emily. Emily had always provided her a reason, a reason beyond the anger that simmered deep within her. So, how did going on a date and kissing a boy protect Emily? To that, she had no answer.

The following Wednesday, Josh arrived for coffee with the biggest grin she had ever seen. Without a word, and with shaking hands, he handed her his phone. The screen showed a written text: *Elmer Sat Too.*

Maggie gave him a confused stare. "I don't get it. Who's Elmer?"

"Elmer's not a 'who,' he's a 'what.' It's that tree we used to hang around. It's a code, we… they had… I'm to meet at Elmer at two o'clock on Saturday. And there's only one person in the world who would send a message like that… Peter! He's back!" Josh's eyes grew moist.

"Why all the secrecy?"

"He's babel. He always does stuff like this." With that, Josh, in a complete reversal of his normal subdued self, danced… right there in the middle of the student lounge.

Maggie laughed even as she glanced about embarrassed.

Chapter Twenty

As he waited impatiently for the days to pass, Josh began to think maybe there was more to this than just Peter being babel. Why had he not heard Peter was coming home? Josh had not been to American Harvest for several months but news like that should have been all over the church. Why did his parents not tell him?

As he walked back through the woods, he was struck by the nostalgia of it. He had not been back there since Peter had left. He noticed there were some new homes in the area. Someday soon, the houses would envelope the woods. Would they cut the old tree down? As he approached Elmer, he was shocked. In his memory, Elmer was a huge tree. Now it seemed smaller, barely capable of holding the young boys who once lounged around it. The old rope was right where they left it. Before climbing, Josh paused. Was Peter already up there?

"Peter?" Some birds chirped loudly. "Peter, if you're trying to scare me… after two years… I'm just saying, that's not solomon."

Josh had barely slept the night before as he lay awake thinking about this moment. He wrestled with the tornado of emotions rolling around in him. He should be happy Peter was back but he was not. Not yet anyway. Too many questions needed to be answered. Sure, he wanted to know why all the secrecy with his homecoming but he wanted to know a great deal more than that. Now, he realized if he climbed up and Peter jumped out laughing, Josh was most likely going to punch his old friend in the mouth. "I'm serious, Peter, please don't be funny."

Josh's ascent was cautious. Elmer was empty. He breathed a sigh of relief as he stood to look around. The memories of those years came flooding back to him. Even though he had been an insecure scared kid working his ass off, in some ways, they were the best years of his life.

Tap, tap, tap. What was that?

Tap, tap, tap. It was rhythmic.

Tap, tap, tap, pause. Tap, tap, tap, pause.

Josh whirled around and looked high in the trees, the source of the noise. Nobody was there. He looked higher. There it was. Someone, higher in a tree than seemed possible. "Peter?"

"Check this out!" a voice called. With a thrust of both his legs, the figure jumped out of the tree. Josh could not stifle his scream as he watched the figure fall and then grab hold of the top of a pine tree. The pine tree was violently wrenched over but slowed as the added weight caused it to continue to bend. The figure was brought effortlessly to the ground. As the figure let go, the pine tree snapped back to its upright position like an angry adult happy to be putting down an overly enthusiastic toddler.

Seconds later the figure was atop Elmer. "Man, oh, man, I can't believe we didn't do that when we were kids!"

There before Josh stood a shaggy long-haired young man with a scraggily beard and bare feet. Yet, the minute he smiled and his eyes lit up, it was clear who it was.

"Peter!" All anger evaporated from Josh's heart. He half-reached, half-fell into his arms.

"How are you doin,' mano?" Peter laughed breaking the hold and then pulling Josh in again for another long hug. Josh didn't even try and fight back the tears.

"I… I can't believe you're here," Josh choked. His lips quivered uncontrollably. As much as he said he missed Peter, he had missed him far more. Now he was a tiny boy again, hugging, crying freely. Neither of them said a thing for a long moment. The only sounds were of Josh's sobs.

They stood apart and looked each other up and down. Even through his tears, Josh could see Peter was a disheveled mess. His hair was so long it had become golden curls dancing all over in an impenetrable mess. It was impossible to tell if the beard was on purpose or just a result of him choosing not to shave. His skin was deeply bronzed by the sun. He was in good shape, his muscles seemed even more pronounced than Josh remembered. His clothes, however, belonged at a second-hand store. His grin was bright, warming, and… beautiful.

"I've got a million questions, joe, a million of 'em. Where've you been? What've you been doing? What brings you home?"

"They caught me," Peter answered.

"Caught you? Who?"

"My parents. I got sloppy. I stepped out of a coffee shop in Madrid, two big guys grabbed me and threw me into a car. That was last Saturday night."

Josh cackled until he realized, Peter was serious. "What're you talking about? How was the mission trip? Why didn't you come home after a year? And why didn't you contact me? After two years, you can't start with the end of the story, you pean!"

Peter laughed. "Oh, Josh, I missed you. I left the mission trip about six months in. I wanted to contact you but I couldn't. I knew my parents had hired deprogrammers. I couldn't bring you into it."

"Deprogrammers? Were you in a cult?"

"Hell, no. That's what my parents want to believe. I was just traveling around, seeing stuff, thinking."

Josh's mind was trying to make sense of it all. Talking with Peter was like walking with Peter... training a puppy on a leash. "Traveling around and seeing stuff? What? Why'd you leave the mission trip?"

"That, mi mano, is a long story."

"We've got all the time 'til the Revelation."

Peter's smile broke for the first time. "I'll save it for another day. Okay?"

"Solomon. So, I don't understand, even if you left the mission trip, for whatever reason, why'd you have to hide? Why not just come home?"

"I hid because leaving a mission trip's a big deal. They treat it as a rebellion against the Holy Spirit. And...I wasn't ready to come home."

Josh reached out and hugged him again. "Well, I, for one, am thrilled you're home. I missed you."

"I missed you too, Josh, but you understand why I couldn't contact you."

"Yeah, I guess. So, you've just been what? Traveling around the world incognito or something?"

"'Incognito,'" Peter repeated and whistled. "Vocabulary of a college man. Yeah, I mean not the world. Mostly I stayed in Europe. Made it to India for about six weeks."

"Peter, I still don't get it. So, the mission trip didn't work out, why didn't you just come home?"

"That's hard to explain, Josh."

"Hey, pean, you would think after two years you'd have something to talk about. How about... are you going to stick around awhile?"

"Can't go anywhere. Wardens won't let me."

"You make it sound like you're in prison."

"Not yet but we're getting there."

"Joe, you in some trouble?"

"Well, according to my parents I've been rescued. I'm just sort of stuck here."

"Go to college. Liberty..."

Peter laughed. "No, my friend, those days are gone. I abandoned a mission. No university will accept me, at least, not until I finish a stint at one of those so-called rebaptism schools."

"Well... that's..."

"Not a chance."

"So, what are you gonna do?"

"I have absolutely no idea, Josh. No fucking idea." As he spat the profanity, he threw a stick viciously into the trees.

Josh's mind raced trying to think of one time he had ever seen his friend upset and could not come up with any. Still, Josh felt sure Peter's predicament was not nearly as hopeless as Peter was making out. He was probably getting the ideas from his parents who were hurt and angry at him. Whatever was going on would be worked out for the best. God's Will be done.

"So, enough about me. What've you been up to?"

Josh had no problem starting at the beginning. "Well, after you left for your great adventure, my parents felt bad for me so..." He went on to tell Peter about his parents renting him his triumphant apartment. He explained what it was like living on his own, going to classes, attending the campus services, living the life of the typical college student. None of it seemed all that exciting until he reached the climax of his story. "And...a couple of weeks ago... I met a girl."

"You did? Good for you."

"Her name's Maggie. Peter, she's amazing. I think she's the one God's chosen for me. She's triumphantly miraculous. She's funny and beautiful and smart and beautiful and she's got these eyes. They're amazing... And then, there's Emily."

"Two girls?"

"Silence, Pharisee! Emily's Maggie's sister. They live with their cousin and Maggie's studying to be a nurse. And now you're back. I'm so blessed. I can't wait to show you around. We've got to take you to High Street. It's a whole different experience at the college level..."

"Yeah, not right away."

"What? You grounded?"

"Something like that. I can't leave The Gardens. Officially, I'm in intervention but you can come here."

"Solomon. It'll be like we're kids again."

For the rest of the afternoon, the two young men lay across the dilapidated boards just as they had done for so many Saturdays. Josh caught him up on what he knew about everyone else. He told him of Matthew and Ada's apartment and how he seldom saw them. Both were in school and doing well. The last he had heard of Luke was that he had joined the military. "He was never much for communication, was he?" Peter chuckled.

"Look who's talking!"

Peter, for his part, spoke of the places he had been seen. He spoke of walking through Greek ruins, Roman cathedrals, and the natural wonders of Europe. He spoke of the cities he had been to but his greatest activity had been going to libraries and lectures at universities. "It was like I was in college, just not getting any credits."

Josh loved listening to the stories Peter told. Ancient Rome, Berlin, Athens, Sparta. All the places Josh had read about. Israel? No, Peter shook his head. Heavy Security. His tales of India were completely foreign to Josh. Nevertheless, Josh found himself wrestling with jealousy. Peter had seen so much. Josh had barely left home.

Like old times, they walked back up the hillside together. At their usual parting of the ways, Josh grabbed his friend in a hug again. "Praise God, you're okay," he whispered. "I don't know what's going on, but I love you, joe. I was mad at you for dropping off the face of the earth but all is forgiven. I'm here for you. As David was knit to Jonathan."

Peter's eyes grew glassy. "Thanks, Josh, I'm not sure what's going on but I know I need a real friend."

As Josh started walking towards his driveway, Peter called. "Hey, Josh!"

"Yeah?"

"Nice car!"

"Thanks, joe. Christmas present."

"Have a good time on your date!"

"Hedge, Peter."

"Nos vemos, mi hermano."

Chapter Twenty One

The following week, as Maggie was leaving class, she was approached by Ruth, a girl from one of her classes. They had never spoken before and Maggie only knew who she was because she was one of those girls who often orchestrated herself into being the center of attention. It was the kind of social tom foolery Maggie purposely and methodically avoided.

From the moment the young lady spoke, Maggie's defenses went up. "Hello, Maggie. How you been?"

"Fine," Maggie answered.

"You are, aren't you?"

Maggie was growing alarmed. This girl knew something.

"I saw you at the concert the other night. Are you and Josh dating?"

Maggie did not know how to answer even if she wanted to. She gulped in fear. "Josh? How do you know him?"

"We went to school together. His friend's married to my friend. Josh is a nice guy. Quiet."

It was the way Ruth said the words that kept Maggie on guard. What was she getting at?

"So, are you dating?"

This was the reason Maggie preferred to be alone. People were so noisy. Enough. "I'm not sure why you need to know that."

Ruth took a step back. "Hey, I'm just in fellowship. And he's quite a catch. His dad and everything."

His dad? Maggie made a move to walk away.

Ruth was not deterred. "You do know who is dad is, don't you?"

Maggie scurried away as quickly as she could. No. She did not know who his dad was. She never asked about his family to avoid him asking about hers.

So, who was Josh's dad? A big wig that brings his family to CAP parties. A senator? The governor?

Maggie followed politics like she followed yacht racing.

Once she was far enough away, she found an empty bench and used her phone. In a matter of seconds, she had her answer. Oh. My. God.

The next morning, she was waiting for him at their booth. "Do you know who Timothy Conrad is?" she asked him coldly.

"Yeah. He's the Midwest Director of Homeland Security. He's also my dad."

"Why didn't you tell me?" She stood up.

"What? Where you going? What's the big deal?"

"Homeland Security?"

The words caught the attention of those around them.

"Come on, please, sit down, talk to me." Reluctantly, Maggie sat back down. "I'm sorry. I'm sorry I didn't tell you. I actually started to a few times but I don't know…." He reached out to take her hand, she pulled it away. "I wasn't deliberately trying to hide anything from you. All my life I've lived in the shadow of my dad, of my brother, the whole Conrad family. Since coming to college though, I've just been another student, a nobody. Even the students in my study group don't know what my dad does. Then I met you and, well, you seem to like me, the Josh part and not because of the Conrad part."

Maggie shook her head. "You said your dad was a big shot but a Homeland Security Director? Jeez, Josh, that's… beyond…"

"To me, he's just my dad. He's gone a lot and, when he is home, he yells at me for leaving my dirty socks on the sofa."

Despite herself, she smiled. He reached for her hand again, this time, for reasons she did not know, she did not pull away. "This isn't about my father. This is about you and me. The Bible says in Ephesians *therefore a man shall leave his father and mother and hold fast to his wife, and the two shall become one flesh.*"

"You're not proposing, are you?"

Josh laughed. "No, I'm just saying that it's God's course for our lives to grow up and leave our father's house, our parents' home, to create our own. My dad's my dad. God led him up Mountains He will never lead me to and that's solomon. My dad's living the life God planned for him and I'm living my life according to the plan God has for me."

Maggie felt the sincerity in his voice. Even with all the "God's plan stuff," he was right. She had no business judging Josh through his father. And, Maggie mentally smacked herself, who was she to judge someone for keeping secrets? Josh was a nice, unassuming, young man that liked her without being pushy. She enjoyed the time they spent together. Still, she knew she was going be in no hurry to meet his parents.

Maggie felt Josh studying her. He was waiting for a reaction. She did not know what to say.

"So," Josh said lightly. "Let me tell you about the whole family…"

When he finished telling her, she certainly felt she understood Josh better. She was afraid he would ask about her family. If he did, she was not at all sure how she would answer. He deserved the truth but she was not yet ready to tell it. Instead he asked an equally uncomfortable question. "So, can I ask why my father's job is such a concern?"

She had no idea how to answer that question. "Maybe, fear of DHS gets instilled in us at a very early age."

"Really?"

"Sure. In school, kids didn't threaten you with DHS?"

Josh sat pensive. "I don't remember that. That's a shame, though. I mean, I've heard the stories. They make DHS sound like the Gestapo or something. But, DHS is just doing its job. Keeping us safe. The only ones who need to be afraid are the ones working to undermine the Awakening." He took a sip of his coffee. "Now that we're on the subject, I should let you know, I'm gonna intern there this summer."

"Really?"

"Just an office boy but I think it'll be interesting. I should get a few good stories to tell."

As their time ran out and Maggie began to gather her things, Josh reached for her hand again. "So, are we solomon?"

"Yeah, Josh. We're fine."

Maggie walked away in a daze. What was going on? "Night Warrior dating son of DHS director. Good News at Eleven!" What was Emily's favorite expression? "Life just gets weirder and weirder." Wait until she hears this one.

Chapter Twenty Two

For once, Josh was the first to arrive at Elmer. As he climbed to the platform, he noticed how rotten the wood was becoming. Maybe Peter and he could spend some time fixing it up. For nostalgia sake.

He sat down and waited. It had been a wild week: two exams, a presentation for Colonial History, Maggie's confrontation about his father, and the ever-growing excitement about spending time with Peter.

His thoughts were interrupted by the sound of the desperate spring of a forest animal or an adopted brother. Peter came bounding through the woods. He did not use the rope but instead leaped for a branch and proceeded to perform a back-hip circle to a mount. A few deft moves later, he was high in Elmer without ever touching the platform. Peter said nothing as he jumped from one limb to another, like a caged animal looking for a hole.

At the branch, which was a bit more level than the others, Peter stopped. He slowly rose to his full height and screamed. The anguished call reverberated throughout the quiet woods. After the outburst, Peter engulfed a lungful of air and spouted a tirade of profanity in a variety of languages. Josh sat shocked at not just the sinful words but the unmitigated ire of his dear peaceful friend.

When he was played out, Peter bent over and took several recuperating breaths.

"Peter?" Josh called hesitantly.

Peter stood high on the branch. Silence now hung in the woods. When Peter finally turned around, it was obvious he had been crying.

"Peter, just tell me what's going on?"

"How can they keep me here? I'm an adult, right? A full-fledged citizen! Why do they have the right to keep me here?"

"I don't know."

"Cockamamie bullshit! What the fuck's the 'Prodigal Son Edict' anyway?" He turned and shouted to the trees. "I got news for you… I'm not the Prodigal Son! I didn't come home with my tail between my legs! You kidnapped me!"

Peter was on the move again, bouncing from one massive branch to another. "What they did was against international law! That's why they had to drug me to get me through the airport. How can they keep me here? I don't want what they're offering! I had friends… I had a life. What right do they have?"

Once again, Josh was overwhelmed with the feeling he was coming in at the end of the story. "Can you stop climbing around like a monkey and talk to me?"

Peter halted, drew in a deep breath and deftly dropped to the platform. "It isn't right. I'm an adult. They shouldn't have the right."

Peter may have been correct, maybe taking him was against international law, but *the whole world lies in the power of the evil one.* Just because it was against a Satan-controlled law did not make it wrong but Josh decided to go a different direction. "Yeah, I get that, but my question is, what's so bad about staying here? This is your home, your family's here, your sisters, your friends… me!"

"Ah, Josh, you don't know what it's like. My mom wakes me up at 5:30 every morning for prayer and Bible study. It just gets worse from there. My dad hardly says a word; he walks around like a zombie. She ends up yelling at him. It's chaos."

"And your sisters?"

"Oh, they aren't even there. They're staying at my aunt's house. When my mom isn't in my face preaching at me, she sits in the sunroom and wails these long, anguished prayers. It goes on all day and half the night. Even grace is twenty minutes long. I tried to talk to her but she's not hearing me. Her mind's fixated. I feel terrible watching her suffer but I can't help her. She goes on and on, blaming herself for everything and asks God to punish her, not me. Meanwhile, I spend all day reading and taking tests over stuff I know backwards and forwards but I'm not answering their questions like a sheep anymore. I'm done. Which is really what's pissing everyone off."

"I don't understand. What do you mean, you aren't answering their questions like a sheep?"

Peter dropped his head. "I don't know if I can explain it to you. I think you need to see it to really understand it."

"See what?"

"The world. The real world."

"The 'real world'?" Josh chuckled.

"Yeah, Josh, I wish I could show you what I've seen. I wish you could talk to who I've talked to…" Peter paused. "Do you know in Genesis where God created the world? On the second day, after creating light God said, '*let there be an expanse between the waters to separate water from water.*' And the Bible says, *so God made the expanse. And He called the expanse- sky.*"

"Yeah, I'm familiar with it."

"It's never a passage anyone asked us to memorize because it's wrong."

A Bible passage "wrong"? Alarms went off in Josh's head but he did not want to do anything that would stop the flow of words from his friend.

"It's an inaccurate description by an ignorant mind. A human being who simply didn't know any better because the Earth's place in the universe had not been fully understood. People stared up at the sky and tried to explain it. Blue waters down below, blue sky up above… maybe the same blue… maybe the same water… separated by an invisible magical dome. Why not? Makes as much sense as anything else from a simple human perspective."

"But, what does…"

"When it turned out the dome wasn't true, the Apostles built one over this nation. The Seven Mountains aren't mountains at all, they're pillars for a dome that's keeping us all trapped inside. They've taken control of everything to keep us ignorant…. To keep us blind to their corruption… and to hide the fact, there is no Jehovah's Revolution."

No Revolution? What in the world was Peter talking about? Vid clips and news stories on its progresses and trials were an hourly event in the news.

Peter had not lost his ability to read Josh's mind. "It's all lies, Josh. Propaganda. Plain and simple. The lies told by any authoritarian government."

"What lies?"

"Everything the government's telling you is smoke and mirrors. There's no Jehovah Revolution. Oh, they like to pretend there is but it's just our government pushing and bullying its way into portraying itself as a leader. It's a way of unifying the nation, getting us to believe in a higher cause so we ignore what's really going on, greed, corruption, and, most of all, incompetence. Meanwhile, the rest of the world's tip-toeing around our Apostles' lunacy and praying one of them doesn't push the damn button and nuke the whole world."

"Peter, that's babel!"

"That's what my parents think and I get it. A couple of years ago, I would have thought it was crazy too. But, it isn't. The phony Apostles have used the tools of society, the so-called Mountains of Influence, as a means of cutting our nation off from the rest of the world and mentally enslaving its people."

Josh shook his head. Mentally enslaving people? America was the most righteous nation on earth… with the most freedom. "Our nation's run by righteous men, baptized in the Holy Spirit, and given the gift of leadership."

"Our nation's being run by a bunch of deluded lunatics."

"PETER! That's… that's…"

"Blaspheming the Holy Spirit? My soul damned forever? It's all bullshit, Josh. They say they're being led by the Holy Spirit and so to question them is to commit the only unforgivable sin. They're not following the Bible, they're using it. They took control of their Seven Mountains not because of a special anointing but by hook or crook. The Dominionist movement lied and deceived to place people into positions of power. As the FGA became more and more consolidated, and their influence on the Seven Mountains became more fixed, it became a necessity for people to join their movement or be ostracized. Business owners either joined a church or lost their licenses. Educators signed on or lost their credentials. Athletes, politicians… everyone. They either played ball or were denied the game altogether. Once the Christians had control, they turned on everyone they labelled an enemy, meeting them with the *righteous sword of a vengeful God.*" The last few words dripped with sarcasm.

Peter read Josh's confused face. "If you go outside of the CSA, you'd be able to see for yourself. You know, when I first left the mission trip, I had no idea what I was doing or where I was going. I wandered around in a daze. I went from café to café, park to park, listening, watching. Eventually I came to my senses and I tell you it was like being born-again. I started going to lectures, read everything I could get my hands on. I spent months and months going to libraries, first one in, last one out. For the first time in my life there were no filters. I could see it all. Science, history, philosophy, religion, it was all right there in front of me, as natural as the air we're breathing. Oh my god Josh, the things they're keeping from us."

"Set your minds on things that are above, not on things that are on earth."

Peter waved his hand dismissively. *"Whatever is true, whatever is honorable, whatever is just, whatever is pure, whatever is lovely, whatever is commendable, if there is any excellence, if there is anything worthy of praise, think about these things.* Not everything outside our Apostles' dome is ugly and evil. That's the lie they use to control us, the fear they instill in us. There's truth in other people's ideas, there's honor, and justice, and purity. But, because it doesn't fit into our Apostles' mind control, they're keeping it from us."

Josh found his mind spinning. Peter was back up again, moving amongst the large limbs.

"Take evolution, for instance. For the first time in my life, I didn't recoil at the word like it had been spit out of the mouth of Satan. I sat down and looked at the evidence and I'm telling you, Josh, it's overwhelming and everywhere. It's in the geological record, the archeological record, genetics, linguistics, historic…"

"Historic?"

"Sparked your interest? Yeah… just think about it for a minute. Evolution's the idea we developed through natural processes from simple life forms to more and more complex. Well, look at human history, even Biblical history… Abraham wasn't riding around in a car, Joshua didn't use machine guns… They were riding on camels and fighting with swords. As a human race, we've learned more and created greater technology. That fits the model of evolution far better than God creating man in His image and then not bestowing in him all the knowledge there is. Why not at least give humans the medical knowledge, the knowledge about the need for sanitation? Why'd we have to discover thousands of years later that there's something on this planet called 'bacteria' and it can kill us? Why wasn't that in the Bible?"

"For my thoughts are not your thoughts, neither are your ways my ways, declares the LORD."

"Sorry, but that's a cop-out. Why shouldn't we question God? Frankly, He has a lot to answer for. Starvation, disease, war… the Dark Ages, the Crusades, Native American genocide, the Holocaust, the Final Great Awakening." Peter paused lost in thought. "You know, in amongst those horrible evil atheists spread out all over Europe, I met many Christians. But you and I wouldn't know they were. They're not nation building, but building the Kingdom of Heaven. They aren't spouting gross misinterpretations of Revelations but trying to live their lives according to the Sermon on the Mount. For them, Christianity isn't about loyalty to a despotic God, it's about demonstrating love."

"For by grace you have been saved through faith. And this is not your own doing; it is the gift of God, not a result of works."

"You see that a person is justified by works and not by faith alone…." We can do this all day, Josh. There's a passage in the Bible to support any position you want. The Nazis used it, the Southern slave owners used it, and our Final

Great Awakening is a bunch of heretics using it for power. They say God ordered us to take dominion over all the earth but if you read Genesis outside of this dome of deceit, you might see it's just a poetic way of saying humans are responsible for the planet. They cherry picked the Bible, pulling passages from the Old and New Testaments to combine it into this nationalistic vision that justified everything they did.

"You can see it again and again. Especially the three Abrahamic religions. When they combine governmental power with religious faith, it leads to oppressive violence, even genocide. Read the Old Testament, look at the way the Israelites are described conquering Canaan. They attacked cities who did not comply and performed the most horrendous deeds of murder, slaughtering every man, woman, and child in the name of Yahweh. The Muslims did it too. And Christianity? The religion of the Prince of Peace? Time and time again they showed no mercy as they conquered nation after nation, sometimes whole continents. Then they did it again in the FGA. The only way to temper religious irrationalism is with the rule of law. That's what the United States tried to do. That's what the Constitution did.

"Want to know what happened to the Puritans? Why their experiment of establishing a New Israel really failed? It wasn't a Satan inspired liberal agenda. They were simply flooded by diversity. Immigrants. People were coming to the colonies in huge numbers, bringing with them their own ideas. It was just too overwhelming for the Puritans to keep up with. The guys who wrote the Constitution for the United States weren't the evil interlopers into God's plan that we were taught. They were geniuses who recognized the diversity and sought to establish a nation based on both order and liberty."

Josh sat dumbfounded. Peter was denying everything they had ever been taught. Is this the result of living among the atheistic Europeans?

"The delusion is the sickest part of The Christian States of America. From the moment we're born, we're indoctrinated. We're told what to see, what to hear, and what to think, even when there's no evidence to support it. In fact, the real evidence is against it, that's why they're keeping it from us.

"Christian America pats itself on the back for getting rid of the idea of separate races, *All in Christ*, but they treated a symptom, not the disease. They simply replaced racial intolerance with religious intolerance; they replaced White privilege with Christian privilege and they did it at the point of a gun. It wasn't the result of an outpouring of the Spirit; it was a military and political coup, simple as that. They took the divine judgement threatened by

Christianity, mixed it with the nation building theology of the Jewish religion, and came up with this amalgamation that led to this fascist police-state."

As he continued to climb among the trees, Peter's voice grew louder and faster. "I can't begin to describe to you how overwhelming it all is. When I left the mission trip, I felt like I walked into a whirlpool. Everything I thought I knew about the world was false. So, I did what I always did, I turned it over to God. I prayed, 'God, the Bible tells us whatever we ask in faith You will provide. I'm asking for nothing more than the truth. Show me...And that's when I set out to question everything."

"And God led you to accepting evolution?"

"God led me to see He doesn't exist."

The statement hung between the two of them. Peter understood the depth of the statement, that was obvious, but he did not seem to grasp its stupidity. "That doesn't even make sense," declared Josh.

"It's a house of cards. Once you question the infallibility of the Bible, you discover how fallible it is. The universe isn't six thousand years old, it's billions. That's not a satanic idea perpetrated by a conspiracy of scientists, it's observable fact. The distance between stars and time it takes light to travel is proof alone. The Babylonians and Sumerians were already brewing beer at the time of our supposed creation. There was no worldwide flood; there are records from civilizations that were kept before and after the flood. They seemed to have forgotten to mention they were all wiped out. There was no Moses, no Exodus."

"Peter?! That's outlandish." Josh stared into Peter's face, hoping to see his friend was pulling his leg.

"It's true, Josh. I know how hard it is to hear, but it's all a myth. Yahweh did not reveal Himself to Abraham and promise his descendants the land of Israel. Nor did they march across a parted Red Sea to claim it. The Jewish people evolved as a nation right where they were, and from a polytheistic culture. If you look at the Old Testament closely you can see it. References to all kinds of gods and goddesses. Even the name 'Israel' comes from a reference to a Canaanite god named 'El.' Yahweh was not a single monotheistic god but in a family of gods. Records show the idea of an all-powerful single god who created the heavens and earth was not consolidated until the Babylonian captivity. That's when monotheism was born. The Jewish leaders combined nationalism with religion, just like Mohammed did. And now, the Christian States of America is doing it again. To insult the nation is to insult God Himself. What better fear to instill into a people you're governing?

"You'd see it for yourself if you could get away from the Net. It's all right there. That's what the Net's really doing. It isn't filtering out evil messages. It's keeping Christian America from knowing the truth. Jesus was one of the first things I researched. Lo and behold, do you know what I found out? Jesus was born again and again and again, there are Jesus stories all over the world and they predate our Jesus."

"Jesus is one of the most established historical figures of all time."

"No, he isn't. It's just shit they taught us in school. Fact is there's no evidence, no contemporary collaborating historian; and there were historians in Jerusalem at that time. They were there reporting on more trivial shit than a Messiah riding into the city on a donkey, or a movement that fed over five thousand people from a few loaves of bread, or how about the five hundred dead people that got up and walked out of their graves? And what happened to those people? Did they live another life? Did they go back to visit their families? No one else mentioned it? Not even as a story going around, like in the tabloid section, 'oh, and by the way, there's a bunch of nuts saying five hundred people walked out of their graves the other day, wish I had seen it… ha ha ha… More Good News to come.'

"Then there are the first Christian documents, the letters of Paul. We've been reading them all our lives but do you know only half of them were actually written by Paul? And nowhere in them does he talk about an historical Jesus. When he talks about visiting the Disciples, he doesn't mention how he's excited to learn from someone who talked to Jesus. No, he just says he knows everything about Jesus through a divine revelation. Why? Because that's all it was, a revelation supported by Jewish scripture. As the movement grew, it needed to solidify so they historicized the whole thing. Mark, or whoever he was, wrote his fable using various tales from other traditions. Read Mark's version carefully. Jesus is low-key, reluctant to even perform miracles… and on the cross? He's screaming, 'My God, my God, why have you forsaken me?' Then Luke and Matthew, some twenty years later, add embellishments to the story. Miracles and teachings that were not in Mark's version. By the time you get to John, the last gospel, Jesus is a dazzling miracle worker that supposedly is known throughout Judea and Syria. On the cross he's now saying victoriously, 'I commend my spirit.' Jesus, like God, evolved. That's why it took over forty years to record the events. There were no events to record, there were just stories to make up."

"Really? It's that simple?"

"Actually, yes."

"If the story's that flimsy, how in the world did it become the world-wide religion that it is? I suppose the Holy Spirit had nothing to do with that?"

"Good question. And one I've asked myself. It turns out, there were a lot of factors, not least of which was people, under the oppression of the Romans, were ready for a god of love rather than one of sacrifice and strict obedience to rules. Paul was quite a good franchiser. He established churches all over the place, kept tabs on them through letters, and, gave the brethren a place to stay in their travels. Commerce was a huge part of the Roman empire and Christian churches, which were often rich people's houses, offered safer places to stay than the inns. That's another great myth. Christian persecution. There were a few times Christians were persecuted but mostly they were tolerated by the Romans. Then Constantine gave his blessing to Christianity, more for political reasons than spiritual ones and Christianity, the apocalyptic movement born of revelations and myth, became a major religion. From there, Christianity was spread through military conquest or, should I say the politer term, 'colonization.' It was exactly what we accuse the Muslims of. Powerful people used inspired people to their own advantage. That's how Christianity spread and might I also add… no offence… that you use the argument of a world-wide spread of Christianity when it meets your needs but you don't have much respect for the Christianity south of the border."

"That's because they're Catholics, their beliefs have been corrupted by…"

"Yeah, and they say the same thing about us. That's another fail in the house of cards. So many denominations arguing they have the right interpretation. Here's God's eternal truth, our eternal souls are dependent upon it, and God can't make it at least plain enough for all believers to believe in the same things?"

"That's not true anymore, not since the Awakening."

"Not since the Apostles took control and made everyone conform, you mean. When faced with deportation or death, most people simply fall in line. We aren't free at all… we're sheep locked in a pen and taught to fear everything outside. Now…" Peter picked up a small branch and snapped the dead wood in two. "Here I am again." He threw the pieces, like knives, sharply into the woods.

Josh watched his friend. What could he think? In his whole life, he had never spoken to anyone who denied Jesus as the Son of God. He had read about it in his history classes, been warned about it since he was four, but he had never spoken to anyone who was not a believer. Now, here was Peter, the most Christ-like person he had ever met, denying Christ completely.

"Josh, I didn't let it go lightly. I prayed God would give me the key to put it all back together but the more questions I answered the more questions I asked, and I never accepted the answer 'God's Will be done.' I told God that too, I told Him that was no longer acceptable."

"Blessed are those who have not seen and yet believed."

"So, I'm a doubting Thomas. I'm asking for evidence. Jesus may have scolded Thomas for his lack of faith but He still showed him the evidence. But He didn't show me the proof. The Bible says, *we destroy arguments and every lofty opinion raised against the knowledge of God, and take every thought captive to obey Christ.* But we don't. It's just another fake promise. Christians not only don't destroy arguments or hold every thought captive, they can't even win an argument. Denying science, denying logic and denying morality. In the end, all Christians can say is, 'it all boils down to faith.' Tell me, how is that *destroying every lofty opinion raised against God*?"

The question remained unanswered. Josh had no idea where to even begin to make sense of what Peter was saying. Peter continued climbing around on the branches. "There's a Chinese fable about a frog that was born at the bottom of a well. He couldn't leave his whole life but he had plenty to eat and was completely protected. As far as he knew the well was the whole world and he was quite content. Then, one day, a big storm came through and a long branch was tossed into the well. The frog was able to hop onto the branch and crawl out of the well for the first time in his life. Now, there are various endings to that story, some say the frog was so overwhelmed by the vastness of the world that he exploded; others say he hopped off to live happily-ever-after."

Josh stared dumbfounded at his friend. What in the world did frogs in wells have to do with anything?

"If you get out of here, Josh, you'll see what it's like to be that frog. Six months. Six months in a library... a real library... with an open mind. Six months suspending your belief that every historian, linguist, geneticist, astronomer, archaeologist, anthropologist, and all other real scientists are part of a worldwide conspiracy to destroy religion. Six months of reading peer reviewed scientific works that do not begin with the premise of proving the Bible right, but begin with the premise of going where the facts lead them. Six months and you will see for yourself, all religions, Judaism, Islam, and Christianity are completely based on mythology that is no more akin to reality than Zeus, King Arthur, or Superman."

Peter was running out of steam. Josh noticed Peter was clean shaven and his hair was shorter, still an uncombed mess, but it was obvious he had seen a barber. His face was streaked with dirty tears and his eyes appeared older and strained.

Peter then did something Josh thought he would never see, right there on Elmer, his boyhood play fort, a place of comfort, Peter took an afternoon nap. Josh nodded off himself a few times but mostly he just watched his dear friend's stomach rise and fall. Asleep, Peter was no longer angry... no longer suffering... he again looked like that carefree kid that had brought Josh to Elmer for the first time.

❖

Josh had seen Mrs. Marone several times when he attended church with his parents but had not really spoken with her since he graduated. As he arrived at the door of her office, he noted the familiar smell, which brought a smile to his lips. As he opened the door, he noticed the office appeared more cluttered than he remembered but other than that it looked the same.

"Hey, Joshua," Mrs. Marone said, coming around her desk.

"Hi, Mrs. Marone," Josh said and the two hugged with Mrs. Marone not letting go. Eventually, she released her grip and stepped back, her eyes tearing.

"It's good to see you again, Mrs. Marone."

"You, too, Joshua. Come in, take a seat. Catch me up."

"Well, I'm finishing up my sophomore year. Still doing the double major. Gets tough sometimes."

"But, with the power of God..."

"Yes, I can handle it."

"And that's where you feel God's leading you?"

"Absolutely. I've felt the Holy Spirit's guidance all the way through this."

"You're so blessed."

Josh smiled. "And, there's another blessing."

"Oh? Who is she?"

"Her name's Maggie. She's studying to be a nurse. We've been seeing each other for a few weeks now. Mrs. Marone, she's wonderful. I'm sure she's the one."

"Joshua, that's great. Do you see the kinds of blessings bestowed upon you when you're a righteous man?"

"I do. Sometimes, I feel like I'm standing in the palm of God's hand and He's just taking me places. I know I told you before, but thank you, Mrs. Marone. Thanks for believing in me."

"It was never me, Joshua. You give it all to God and He delivers. It's as simple as that." Mrs. Marone smiled but grew silent. A thickness in the air was cultivated as each of them realized it was time to talk about what had really brought them together.

Josh took a breath and began. "I need to talk to you about Peter. I assume you know he's back."

"Yes, I've spoken with him several times."

"He didn't mention that. I spent some time with him on Saturday. Mrs. Marone, I'm really worried about him. He's so angry. So angry at… everything."

"Yes, I've had that experience."

"And the things he said…"

"What did he say?"

"All kinds of things, blasphemous things about how Jesus never lived, that He was just a story people made up from other stories. God's an unjust despot, if… if… He exists at all. I'm telling you, Mrs. Marone, I've never heard anything like it. And to be coming out of Peter's mouth?"

"Did he tell you what happened on the mission trip? Why he left?"

"No, I asked him but he said he didn't want to talk about it anymore."

"Anymore? From what I understand, he refuses to tell anyone."

"How can we help him?"

Mrs. Marone thought for a moment. "This is exactly why we need to stop letting high school graduates go on these trips. We give in to their youthful exuberance, but they are not spiritually mature." She stopped speaking for a moment and quickly typed something into her tablet. When she concluded, she began again. "So, where do we go from here? Right to the Bible. James 5:20 states: *Let him know that whoever brings back a sinner from his wandering will save his soul from death and will cover a multitude of sins.* Know what that means?"

"I'm not doing this for my…"

Mrs. Marone held up her hand to stop him. "I understand your motivation. It wouldn't be a righteous action if you did it for your own gain. The point in my bringing up the verse is to illustrate the enormity of what you're undertaking. The greatest rewards come with the greatest of risks. God will not grant so great a reward if the task itself isn't dangerous.

"Whatever Satan did to trick Peter into leaving the mission trip also led him into the wilderness of atheism that plagues Europe. He thinks he found freedom but he just found chains. The chains of unbelief. *The Lord is my Shepard.* Peter shows what happens when a sheep without a shepherd gets lost in the wilderness. He's open season for the carnivores. I don't know what happened on the mission trip but, instead of coming and asking for help, he ran off with no guidance, no spiritual teacher at all. Can you imagine the filth and lies he was exposed to? And the euro-peans don't label things as true and untrue, they just throw it all out there. *For God is not a God of confusion but of peace.* Look at Peter, look how confused he is; he's so vulnerable..."

Josh nodded in agreement.

Mrs. Marone leapt at him and shouted. "And that is exactly what Satan wants to lull you into thinking. He wants you to feel sorry for him, to walk over and hug him, but when you bend down to offer your friend comfort... the demon shoves a sword into your spirit."

Josh was taken aback by the intensity of her words. "So, how do I help him?"

"You can't drop your shield. I know you want to help your friend but that's one of the Devil's strategies. He picks one off then the friend who tries to help him. So, you need to be a Joseph, you need to approach this with the warrior's mind. *For the weapons of our warfare are not of the flesh but have divine power to destroy strongholds.*"

"That's what I'm worried about. The things he was saying. I don't know how to answer them. It's stuff I've never heard before."

"Don't try and answer at all. It's better for you not to battle Satan on his terms. Peter's expressing age-old heresies that he had been sheltered from until he decided to leave God's protection. The circular arguments based on a web of lies can draw anyone in. Here's what I want you to do. Ignore all that gibberish. Don't listen to it, raise your armor, and protect yourself. Be compassionate but guarded. Listen to his feelings but not his words, for it is in the words that lie the deception. Stay in touch with me and report directly to me if he says anything of any real importance, like what happened on the mission trip. Is that clear?"

"Yes, ma'am."

"I can't begin to tell you how dangerous this is. You're taking on demons, you must be on guard at all times."

"Yes, ma'am."

She stood and raised her hands over Josh's bowed head. "Dear Lord, I pray a hedge of protection for this Joseph. As You declare in Your word: You are our refuge and fortress. Deliver us *from the snare of the fowler and from the deadly pestilence.* cover us with Your pinions, and under Your wings may we find refuge; so that we *will not fear the terror of the night, nor the arrow that flies by day.* In the name of Almighty Jesus. Amen."

Josh left Mrs. Marone's office with a chest filled with energy. It would be three more days before he would be able to meet with Peter again but he would be ready. He spent extra time in prayer each day asking for the courage and wisdom needed for the upcoming battle.

Then, on Friday morning, he received a vid call from his mother, her furious face masked her tears. "Did you know about this?"

Josh, who was still in bed, answered groggily. "About what?"

"Peter. He's gone."

"What? No."

"I just got a call from his mother. She went to his bedroom this morning and he's gone. Security has no record of him leaving. Now I need to know something, *speak the truth in love*, did you know anything about this?"

"No, Mother. Nothing. I had plans to see him tomorrow, last time I talked to him was Saturday."

"And that's it. I can assure his mother you know nothing else."

"Nothing."

Josh hung up the phone. His first emotion was concern but it was quickly swept away by anger. Why? Why couldn't Peter take the help being offered? And to just drop out of sight... again? A thought occurred to him, one he followed as soon as he was done with class. He hopped the ET to his house and hiked the short trail to Elmer. There, tucked in a crevice of a thick layer of bark was a piece of paper. The letter was handwritten and Josh had trouble deciphering the words but eventually he could read:

> *Josh,*
> *I hate to say goodbye like this but I didn't want to draw you into anything. I hope you can forgive me for leaving. It obviously isn't you and it isn't my family either. I know they can't love me in any other way. But no one can put the frog back into the well. I hope life brings you happiness.*
> *Brothers forever,*
> *P*

Josh slumped, defeated. Peter had been gone for two years, was home for just two weeks and was gone again. There would be no battle, no great warrior Joshua stepping up to drive the demons from his friend.

There was only the stillness in the long-abandoned woods.

Chapter Twenty Three

For the next few weeks, Josh tried to maintain his attention on finishing up the school year as Peter's parents frantically looked for their son.

"How do you feel about it?" Maggie asked at their morning cup of coffee.

"Honestly, I don't know. A turbulence of emotions, I guess. I'm concerned for him spiritually just like everyone is but, mostly, I'm mad at him. He had plenty of support right here to work through all this and he thumbs his nose at it all. His parents may have been driving him crazy but they were doing it out of love. We all were. A soldier goes into battle and is wounded, he should accept the medics help, shouldn't he? I know part of it is personal though. I was gonna hang out with him again, hiking, boating, all kinds of stuff. He could have gotten his head straight and enrolled at OSU. Maybe, we could even have moved in together, you know? And… I was gonna introduce him to you. Now, he's gone and it's like he's given a big 'up your wazoo' to everyone who tried to help him. Then, I think, how solomon he is. I mean, to ride a pine out of The Gardens is one thing but to get away, to just disappear without a trace? My dad even had him put on the NBL… um…do you know what that is?"

Maggie shook her head.

"The National Backslidden List. My dad said it's the quickest way to corral him. All he needs is to show his ID once, even get a clear picture of him on a camera, and DHS will round him up in no time. Still, it's been three weeks and you know something? Part of me is proud of him for giving everyone the slip. I mean, how's he doing it? What's he living on? Where's he sleeping?"

"I'm sure there are all kinds of little pockets he can hide in. And he certainly sounds smart enough to find them."

"Yeah, he is," Josh answered proudly. "Although, I went to church with my parents last Sunday and, well, needless to say, he's the hot topic. His mother was there, she looks like she's aged fifty years. And his dad? His dad used to smile all the time, has the same big grin as Peter, now he barely even looks up. It's sad. It's so selfish of Peter to leave. He has to realize what his parents are going through, doesn't he?"

Maggie did not answer his question. Instead, she changed the subject. "Getting nervous?"

"About Monday? Yeah, I am. When my dad first told me about this internship, I was solomon with it. I mean, working at Homeland Security! On the other hand, it's like I told you. I like being away from my dad a bit, but, if I go work there, everyone's gonna know I am the head chief's son."

"So, you're not happy about working there?"

"I don't know. I guess it's just another thing that's giving me mixed emotions."

In the end, what would be the big deal about working at DHS even if his dad was the boss? It was just a summer, an experience few school teachers ever had. A couple of uncomfortable lunches with his dad and co-workers, and voila… the summer would be over. Josh also had a recurring fantasy of somehow uncovering something that would help find Peter. "Intern succeeds where agents didn't. Good News at 11."

The first thing that indicated how different things were going to be was when Josh arrived at the DHS building Monday morning and tried to go through the security system he always used. He was stopped by Officer Christopher who, from the first day they met, had always called him "Josh." But, not this day…

"Mr. Conrad?"

"Hey, Christopher, I can't seem to pass through."

"Well, sir, that's because this security system is set up for the Director and his family. You, Mr. Conrad, are an employee. You need to go back over there and walk in like everyone else." Christopher stated everything in a tone that suggested he was resisting the urge to chuckle.

"Really?"

"Yes, sir, Mr. Conrad. Order came from the Director himself. Welcome to the working class."

The two shared a laugh. Christopher led him over to another security guard. "This is Zeke. Zeke, this is Josh, the new guy I told you about." Zeke led Josh through the security check where he was officially registered as an employee of Homeland Security. Zeke explained his clearance was "Level 1, intern" which was the absolute lowest level. Zeke proceeded to read the definition of what that meant, which as far as Josh could tell, meant he could do nothing special at all except report for work. Zeke went on to explain any attempt to breech his designated security status, including incredulously, going beyond the fifth floor of the building, would be a felony punishable by loss of church membership and/or prison time.

Josh could not stop grinning through the whole procedure.

The new employee orientation took an hour as he went through the process of having his retina scanned, his picture taken dozens of times, and his prints placed on all the proper forms. When he finished, he was sent up the elevator to the third floor.

When the doors opened, Josh was immediately greeted by a young man in his mid-twenties. Dressed meticulously in a blue suit and appearing quite nervous, he stuck his hand out as he said, "Hi Joshua, it's so good to meet you. I'm Adam. I'll be your trainer, but, not that you really need one. I'm sure you know all about it."

"Hi, Adam. Call me Josh, and I doubt it, but we'll see."

"Can I get you anything? No... I mean... why don't I just show you around."

Adam led Josh over to the desk in the middle of the room.

"You're about to meet the most important person in our office. This is Marie. Marie, this is Josh, our intern for the summer."

Marie, an elegant thin woman in her mid-sixties, stood up and extended her hand over the partition. Josh found her shake both femininely thin and professionally firm. "Hello, Josh. Welcome. I believe your father to be a righteous Joseph."

"Thank you," Josh replied.

"If you need anything, any question, whatever, Marie's the place to go. She's been with DHS for.... how long now, Marie?" asked Adam.

"Long before the Lord knew you in the womb, young man." Marie's laughter was light and welcoming. "See what I have to put up with? Children... nothing but children."

Adam walked Josh around and introduced him to everyone. There were only nine active offices on the whole floor. Adam explained it used to be much busier but things were quiet, "and that's a good thing." The men were around Adam's age and all dressed the same. They greeted him with great enthusiasm.

From there, Josh was led to a small desk at the far end of the room. "This is normally the intern's desk," Adam said apologetically. "Um, so I guess you can have a seat, until you have something to do."

"So, what exactly does this department do?" Josh asked.

"Oh, I'm sorry, I thought you knew that. Well, come into my office and I'll show you."

Moments later, Josh was seated in Adam's small office looking at a holograph of Ohio and the surrounding states. "We consider ourselves the main line of defense. I mean, sure, we're only Tonies, but we're the ones who notice Satan's movements first."

"Tonies?" Josh asked.

Adam glanced at Josh unbelievably. "A Tony's someone with Tier One security clearance. Tier One… T-One… Tony."

Josh smiled. "Solomon. So, I'm a Tony, too? Tony the intern?"

Again, Adam's face showed disbelief. "Yeah, more or less." Adam paused a moment and then questioned, "May I ask you something?"

"All one in Jesus."

"Well, I heard that you're Director Conrad's son…but you… forgive me, but you don't seem to know…"

"Oh, I don't," Josh interrupted him. "My dad got me this internship because it would be a good experience for me but the Lord's led me to a different Mountain. I'm training to be a history teacher."

A look of relief flooded Adam's face. "Well, that explains a lot. We heard you were being fast-tracked."

"Oh, no. I think it's all triumphant, but I don't know anything about it. My dad was never allowed to talk much about what he does."

"Of course, that makes sense. Well, okay, solomon then. Let me show you what we do. See all those red dots on the hologram?"

"The one's that look like towns?"

"Well, yeah, but if you look closer you'll see, they aren't towns but small communities, sometimes even just one house. Here's how our system works. The DHS monitors the whole Net, the majority of that done by computers monitoring communications. Downstairs there are Tonies who pose as libs, engaging people in conversations. Looking for the heretics. When they get one on the hook, they refer it to us. We gather all the background info. That's what those red dots represent, places where there may be heretics of one kind or another."

"What's the number on the dot?"

"That's the Security Threat Level, STL. Lowest number's a one. That means they pose no real threat. But if we receive information that would lead us to believe something's going on, we raise the STL and send it to the fifth floor."

"What's there?

Adam smiled. "You really don't know anything, do you? That's where the agents step in and the real investigation begins."

"So, you guys are kind of like birddogs?"

"Yeah, I guess you could say that. We think of ourselves as being proactive so that the agents can be reactive."

"Solomon," agreed Josh. He studied the hologram. "It looks like everything in Ohio's a level one."

"There's a few places in the big cities we have to keep an eye on. One or two right here in Columbus." Adam moved the cursor and highlighted a red dot that had a "3" on it. "That's an area where there's gang activity. A gang called the Three-twelves, nothing counter-revolutionary, just a bunch of punks dealing drugs."

"Are there any 'fives'?"

"Oh, my golly, no. The whole Midwest is safe these days. We used to have 5's, long before my time. Marie remembers those days. She'll tell you about them if you ask her. Now, out west and in New York and some of the other big cities" With a few taps, Adam brought up a map of America. "There are some 4's but if it gets moved up to 5, the DHS agents are probably on their way."

Adam let Josh look at the hologram for a moment. "Why do some of the numbers have an 'A' next to them?"

"Agent."

"You mean, undercover?"

"Best way to mind the gaps."

"So, I have a question. Are you… I mean… we… able to get information on someone who's being looked for?"

"You mean, intel on an active investigation?"

"I mean someone who's on the NBL."

"The NBL? Oh, no way, I mean, not an active investigation, but, in the archives, there's vids of arrests being made. I'll show 'em to you sometime. Some of it's real solomon."

Adam undoubtedly put the word out that Josh was safe because everyone was quite friendly to him. In fact, for the most part, except when his father's name would come up or his father himself would drop in to pick him up for lunch, the other guys treated him almost like one of them. They were still a bit guarded when he was around, especially about making sure to look busy. Josh quickly learned, however, that the nine men had little to do. They spent much of their time moving from one office to another speaking in pairs or threes. The greatest topic was not any kind of current investigation but more likely on their common studies, as they were all studying to be promoted. In some ways, Josh concluded, they were all interns.

As bored as everyone else was, Josh found himself even more so. Occasionally, he would get a request to run an errand of some kind. When the alerts came, there was nothing for Josh to do. As a matter of fact, the alerts were so seldom that it was a cause for all the guys to gather in one office and watch. Josh talked to Marie a great deal, mostly about college and Maggie. Other than that, Josh was left to sit at his computer. He immediately regretted not taking a summer class. He did not think he would have the time and as a result missed the deadline. Instead, he found himself looking things up. Mostly, he researched things on history, watched vids, or took virtual tours of historical sites.

One other thing that kept Josh busy was planning dates with Maggie. Maggie was taking summer classes, working full time, and had Emily but the two of them had developed a nice routine. There was coffee in the Student Center two times a week and a standing weekend date where Maggie would find a way to have time with him.

Throughout the summer, the dates became more and more precious. Josh wanted to spend as much time with Maggie as he could but made up for it by trying to be the most romantic boyfriend in the world. He would send her a gift basket of flowers on Wednesday with a "cordial invitation to accompany me to…" and then lay out his plans for the weekend date. Josh learned early on Maggie was not impressed by fancy dinners in swank restaurants. What she did like was variety. So, one weekend, Josh would plan a simple dinner for two in an exotic out of the way restaurant, followed by a musical theater. And the next Saturday, he would plan a hike at Old Man's Cave followed by hotdogs from a street vendor on High Street. Week after week, Josh prided himself in surprising her with new experiences.

One evening, he cooked her dinner in his apartment. She could not believe the spacious luxury. She teased him about posing as a "normal" student when in fact he lived in a virtual paradise. He laughed and begged her not to give him away.

By mid-July, Maggie decided it was time to include Emily in an activity. Josh went all out. He picked the two young ladies up in his car and zipped them off to Salt Fork State Park where he had rented a motorboat for the day. Both girls were thrilled as they spent the day taking turns being whisked around the lake on an inner tube. Later, Maggie accused Josh of deliberating trying to impress Emily. Josh did not deny it. "As a matter of fact, my lady," he declared, as he bent down in an exaggerated bow. "I will do whatever's necessary to win your fair hand. Fight any dragon."

"Oh, is that what Emily is?"

"I believe you may have suggested that a time or two," he answered with a smirk.

Josh was thrilled the afternoon had gone well. Emily had given her approval. He knew he would have to meet Maggie's parents someday so it was nice to have one member of the family already in his corner.

Josh decided the next step was to introduce Maggie to his parents and as it turned out, there was the perfect opportunity just a couple of weeks later. Mrs. Marone had officially taken a job with the Department of Education in Washington D.C. The JOT program was going to become a part of the national educational curriculum. Josh made plans to take Maggie and his parents out to the Granville Inn for a casual lunch and then zip them to the church for the party. A perfect blend of the formal introduction and the informal party time.

"I'm sorry, I'm just not ready for that," Maggie stated, squeezing his hand.

"Ready for a party?" Josh asked incredulously.

"You know, ready to meet your parents. Go to your church. It's a big step."

Josh had decided there was more to this reluctance than just the fact his father was a DHS director. He thought maybe she was intimidated by his family's wealth. Whatever it was, he was not about to push her.

Love is patient and kind.

Chapter Twenty Four

Maggie spent the summer juggling. The nursing classes were a storm of perpetual craziness. She spent many late nights cramming the names of body parts into her head. There were lectures, labs, and hours of research. For a full-time student it was a rigorous program, yet Maggie had to work too. She spent thirty hours a week, much of that time on the weekends, working for the catering business. Then, to top it off, she had Emily and the apartment upkeep. And, of course, there was Josh.

Working to squeeze time with Josh was a bit tricky but she was always glad when she did. She enjoyed his company and found him easy to talk to but it was also the one thing in her life where she did not have to be in charge. She could allow herself to relax, and enjoy the experience.

As fun as the dates were, Maggie found the morning coffees were the most enjoyable. It was comforting when they could sit in the booth and silently study together. When she was not studying, he would share his perceptions of the things he uncovered. When he did, he demonstrated his fascination with the subject matter. She especially liked the fact he seemed most interested in the everyday lives of people. He would often show her pictures of the tools, household utensils, and other items and they would imagine what life was like in the old days.

Josh's plans allowed for only a small amount of alone, intimate time. It was obvious he deliberately planned it that way. When they were alone, they spent the time talking, holding hands, and occasionally kissing with some gentle petting. For him, he was avoiding putting them in a position where they might sin. She had her own reasons to avoid the situation. While she liked kissing and his tender touch, the idea of intimacy with a man was a source of chaotic emotional confusion. She was happy to have found a boy who was in no hurry.

Despite her heavy schedule, Maggie added another activity. Running. It was great exercise and, though lacking the adrenaline rush, it was quite a bit more socially acceptable than parkour on rooftops. She began getting up in the early morning hours and running along the Olentangy River. Most mornings, she was under a severe time constraint but Sundays were special. Emily and she did not attend church until the eleven o'clock service and the catering company was always closed on Sundays. So, it was the one morning run Maggie could take her time, relax, and enjoy.

On one particularly humid Sunday in early August, she exited her apartment and started to stretch when she noticed a young man staring at her from a nearby bench. God, she hoped she didn't have to put up with a pervert. Fine, let him look at her butt, she would be well beyond him in…

He stood up.

Oh, no, fear gripped her as her muscles coiled. If he takes even one step…

"Maggie?"

Shocked her brain dropped into freeze mode. She knew she should know him but…

Then it hit her. "Jake?"

"Hi, Maggie!"

Her knees were no longer controllable as she propelled herself into his embrace. Tears burst freely forth when she pressed her face to his chest. "I can't believe it? What? How? When?"

Maggie pulled away and looked at him closely. His hair was shorter than it had ever been and cut neatly. He seemed a bit taller or maybe he was just carrying himself that way. His clothing was new, and worn with precision. His grin, however, was the same.

"Emily's upstairs, still sleeping. Come on!"

"Yeah, I will but I need to talk to you first, solomon?"

The last word was odd coming out of Jake's mouth. "Sure, what's up?"

"It's kinda complicated."

"Is everything alright?"

"Oh, yeah, better than it's ever been. I just need to fill you in before I see Emily. Can we go somewhere and talk?"

"Well, sure, it's Sunday, but we can sit in the park."

Moments later, they were seated on a bench overlooking the river.

"This is so weird," Maggie said.

"It is." He searched for the words to begin.

Maggie thought of a way to cut the ice. "There's something I've been thinking about and wanting to ask you…"

"Just one thing?"

"That time you took Seth and me to see Z about Barak's killer… was that a set-up?"

Jake smiled. "Z and I worked well together."

"So, the photo of the dead boy?"

"Yeah. Well-staged. Seth needed his focus on Asher, not revenge. *Hatred stirs up strife.*"

"I knew it! I always thought that seemed a little too perfect. And the rent increase?"

Jake laughed heartily. "Oh, that part was real. Z never did anything for free."

She always suspected Jake had their backs more so than he let on. "So, tell me what's going on? Why all the secrecy?"

"It's hard to know where to begin," Jake said.

"The last time I saw you was the night we were arrested, start there."

"Wow, yeah, the night we were arrested. What a night that was! I was so terrified… for all of us. Mickey took the heat for everything but they sent me to a military school. I was there about two years. I was angry… bitter… always in trouble. Over time, I think I just grew weary of fighting. I had this one counselor, Sean, who… I guess he saw the good in me before I saw it in myself. I started to talk with him, I mean really talk. I cleansed a lot of that bitterness and my heart softened. It opened me up to hearing God's Word. For the first time in my life, I understood it. I knocked down all those walls and accepted Jesus' plan for my life. After jail, they sent me to a school in New Mexico. I studied to be an electrician, but mostly I learned God's Word. It wasn't easy. I had a lot of bad ideas I had to get rid of. Anyway, they let me out a couple of months ago. I have a good job in Florida. I belong to a wonderful church, it's amazing, a real contributor to the Awakening."

It was obvious Jake had gone through a thorough transformation from the herb-smoking thief she had known, but it didn't matter. He was still Jake.

Jake took a deep breath. "Which brings me to why I am here. When I was at the school in New Mexico, God gave me a vision in a dream. He told me to get myself straight and then get Em."

"What? What do you mean? Take her to Florida?"

"Families belong together and we're all we've got."

Maggie resisted the urge to feel hurt, but she could not let the statement stand. "Well, I'm no stranger…"

"Maggie, you've done an amazing job but it's time to get Emily out of this."

"What do you mean? We got out years ago."

"Sort of."

"What does that mean?" Maggie felt her pulse quicken.

"Oh, come on, Maggie. Look around you. You haven't really left the streets. Living here, amid all these people. I bet if you investigate any one of them, you'd find they falsified their commitment."

"We have a church membership."

"Yeah, I know. That's not a proper church."

"That's not true."

"That shack or whatever it is, is just like the people, barely able to meet the qualifications. Even the pastor. The son of a minister in Texas but isn't working for his father's church? C'mon, Maggie, Em needs to be around anointed people."

Maggie sat in disbelief. "She may not want to go with you. She's going to school… she has friends."

"She'll come with me. I have the documents here. She's a minor and I'm her family."

"But she's happy. Why are you doing this?"

"I know this is difficult and it probably feels like I dropped out of the sky but we have to trust in God's plan."

Maggie fought back the tears. "I don't understand. Why can't I go too?"

Jake put his arm around her shoulders. "My vision said Em alone. I'm sorry."

"Your vision?" Maggie lashed out, shaking her shoulders from his arm.

"Yeah, and maybe that's why God didn't include you in this plan. You aren't right with the Lord, are you? Whatever sins that brought you to the Office are still holding you prisoner. You took the first helping hand offered, without asking if it was a hand from God."

"Who? Becca?"

"Yeah, Becca. She's just one of those playing the system but those who deceive the Lord are always brought to light."

"She's a social worker."

"And has had a lifelong friend and never married. Oh yeah, I've done my homework. Come on, Maggie, don't be so naïve. Look, I'm gonna take Emily and if you or anyone does anything other than encourage her to come with me, I'm gonna turn over to DHS everything I've discovered which includes Becca falsifying government documents."

Maggie jumped up, who was this man? "Why? We're just doing what we need to do in this fucked up world."

"See, that's just the kind of thing we said in the Office. You still have one foot in that Godless slum. Get right with God, Maggie, and a whole new world opens. Come to Jesus for real and you'll see it."

Maggie lived through the rest of the day in a fog. Jake came into the apartment and woke Emily up. There were tears and cries of unbelievable joy. The rest of the afternoon was spent together. At first, Maggie was reluctant but Emily insisted so Maggie did not want to show her anything was wrong. She listened as Emily filled him in on everything that had happened. Maggie hoped Jake might be swayed by how wonderfully Emily was doing but it was obvious his mind was made up.

Jake told them what he knew about the others. Seth was still in custody but was also enrolled in an electrician program. Asher had been adopted by a family in Kansas. He was a standout on his high school soccer team. Thad had joined the military and was stationed somewhere overseas. When Emily asked about Mickey, Jake merely shook his head.

By evening, Maggie was more than ready to get away. She made a beeline for Sherah's apartment and emergency tea with Becca.

When Maggie finished her story, Becca sat for a long time. Her face drawn with fear. Finally, she asked, "So, what are you gonna do?"

"What can I do? See if Jake's bluffing? Expose us all to an investigation? Maybe, the whole church? C'mon, you know nobody'll win that. He holds all the cards. How would I fight him? What? Take him to court? They would expose me as an uncommitted in a second. Oh my God, what am I gonna do without her?"

Maggie spent the next few days in a mind/body disconnect. At one point, Jake explained everything to Emily. Maggie did not hear what he told her but Emily appeared fine with the idea. "Living in Florida?" she exclaimed in delight. As for her friends, Emily did not see it as leaving them at all. "Most of the time, we talk through our phones anyway. What's a few hundred miles? Besides this is a chance to make more friends." She felt the same way about Maggie. "I'll miss you, but we'll always be sisters. Jake said, once you finish your nursing program, you'll be able to move too. We can get another apartment together just like we planned."

Only Maggie knew, looking at Jake, two years was a long time.

Then, just like that, Emily was gone. Each morning, Maggie awoke, she relived the sadness of Emily's absence and each night she had to stop herself from waiting for her to come home. Emily kept her abreast of every exciting move she made but that just made things worse.

Maggie explained to Josh her parents had called Emily home. She hated to lie again but was not emotionally ready to reveal the truth.

As for Becca and Sherah, one could say the stadium lights turned on. Everything made sense. The amount of time Becca stayed away, the fact Sherah never sat with them at church, everything.

The subject came up only once.

"I'm not an uncommitted at all," Becca explained. "I'm a Christian. I believe Jesus' fundamental teaching is to love God and love my neighbor. I do my best at both of those things. Sherah and I've been together since we were in high school. They're wrong, that's all. They're just wrong."

The revelation was a bit unsettling for Maggie but, in the end, made no difference. After what Becca did for the two of them, she was free to love anyone she wanted.

Maggie decided to take extra classes in the fall. If she continued with summer classes, she could be done with the program in another eighteen months. What the hell, she thought, she would have all kinds of extra time now that Emily was gone. Maggie remembered the day they had first met. She had been living in that tiny little hole in the wall, terrified of her own shadow. Emily, with her eager determined smile, had given Maggie something to care about, something to live for, something that always needed to be done. And now? Maggie grieved. No amount of forced thinking, telling herself Emily was in a better place, a more secure environment, could overcome the fact… she was going to miss her.

Two weeks and three days went by. Maggie was spending the evening, alone in her dark silent apartment looking through the weeks' worth of texts and pictures from Emily. She was startled from her thoughts by the door chime. Who? She went to the screen in her kitchen.

"Josh?"

"I'm sorry, Maggie. I know we didn't have any plans but I've got to talk to you. It's Peter!"

Once inside her apartment, it took several moments and a glass of water before he could speak. "I was on the Net, doing some research, when this ad popped up from nowhere."

"An ad?"

"Yeah, I didn't pay any attention to it. I deleted it. But it popped back up. I got rid of it again and, within seconds, it pops up. Now, I'm irritated so I look at it and it's for some tiny lumber yard near Denver, Colorado."

Maggie glanced at Josh quizzically.

"My thought exactly. What's going on? So, I looked closer."

Josh brought the image up. The advertisement appeared amateurish, with a simple grainy black-and-white photo of a wooden building surrounded by a chain linked fence. Across the top of the page was a banner that read, "Come to Martin's Lumber" in large letters. Below the photo was what looked like an antiquated coupon for a ten percent discount.

Whatever Josh was so excited about, Maggie did not see it. "So?"

"That's what I thought. Even went so far as to restart my session but you know what happened? The ad popped up again."

"It's a virus."

"Yep!" He could no longer sit, he bounced around like a little kid going to an amusement park. "I looked at the ad closer and that's when I saw it. At the bottom of the coupon."

Maggie was beginning to think he was having a mental meltdown. She looked again, and saw a tiny sentence just below the "10% Off" caption. It read, "Mention Elmer for your discount." Helplessly, she looked at Josh who stood there drunk on emotion.

"This isn't an ad at all. It's a message from Peter!"

Maggie looked at the ad again. "Are you sure? I mean Elmer's not exactly a common name but…"

"I looked it up. Martin's Lumber. It's a real place. Small. A local business. But, it's not even an advertisement, like you said, it's a virus… it's a virus sent by Peter."

"Did you show it to anyone else?"

"No, I made a bee-line over here. I came to tell you, I'm going to Denver tomorrow."

She did not want to bust his bubble, but she felt she couldn't keep quiet. "Josh, you have to be realistic. I know how much finding Peter means to you but…"

"But, I prayed about it. Leaving room for the Spirit, I believe this is real. And even if it's not, so what? I take a train to Denver, show up, nothing there, I come home. No big deal. But even if there's just the slightest chance this is him, I've got to find out."

Maggie stared at him. He was right. "Of course, you do. You should go and I'm going with you."

"What? No, I'm a big boy."

"I know. I'm not going as your mother, silly. I need this. Since Emily le...went home I've been climbing the walls. A little trip might be just what I need. The semester starts next week so let's end our summer with a trip to Colorado."

Josh pondered the idea. "But, I don't think that would be... you know... proper. If it is Peter, I was planning on staying the weekend."

"Oh, come on, it'll be okay. We're just traveling together."

"I don't know, Maggie... I'm not sure what I'm getting into. It could be dangerous."

Maggie chuckled. "Josh, it's Denver." He remained hesitant. She placed her hand gently on his arm. "Please, I really need this."

In the end, Josh agreed. The rest of the evening, he stayed to make the arrangements. He ended up paying for everything which, since he insisted on first-class, she had to be okay with. Despite his vocal apprehension, Maggie was aware of how much he was enjoying himself. Here he was on what he considered a divine mission to save his friend and he was traveling as an unchaperoned adult with his girlfriend. Josh was also thrilled when he found out his Tony status was finally good for something. When asked on the application for the tickets if he had security clearance, he could say, "Yes." From that point on, the whole process was expedited. Josh danced around like a big shot.

Chapter Twenty Five

The next day, bright and early on Friday morning, she found herself, overnight backpack at her feet, waiting at the main train station. Next to her, Josh fought to maintain a dignified composure.

They sat across from an elderly gentleman with the longest beard Maggie had ever scene. The way it lay across the slouched man's chest made it look big enough for a whole family of birds to make a nest in.

The man caught her staring and smiled. "Do you travel a lot?"

"No," she answered shyly, "just a few times."

"Wow. Lucky you. I've been traveling for almost forty years now. Seems like all I do. I'll tell you what, when the Apostles first built these trains they were really something. Sleek... fast, this train system was a shot in the arm to the whole nation. Everything was alive... people were on the move... like *tongues of fire*. Not that way anymore, is it? People've grown complacent. We're missing that revolutionary spark. These are hard times. It's those heretical international sanctions... that's what it is. Atheists and heathens imposing their Godless morality on us. What business is it of those libs how we conduct our country? There's only one morality and it's found in God's Holy Word. We've created a righteous nation open to all Christians who want to live in accordance with our divine covenant. It's exactly what our Puritan Founders intended." The man realized his raised voice had garnered the attention of those around him. Sheepishly, he slipped a bit lower in his chair and leaned closer to Maggie and whispered, "Oh, but you should have seen these trains back then... so vibrant and new... and clean...spotless." He winked. "Let me tell you."

The ride from Columbus to Denver would take about five hours. Josh had obtained a private non-sleeper room. It consisted of a couple of adjustable

191

chairs, a foldout table and a stocked kitchenette. As they took their seats, Josh laughed. "That guy was babel. And there he is talking about cleanliness and he's got at least three meals in that beard."

Maggie nestled into the snug soft chair. To her left was a massive window that at the moment showed a bustling crowded train terminal but would soon be displaying wondrous sites. Maggie had a few memories of traveling with her family on vacations but she had not been outside of Ohio since then. Now she felt like that girl again, giddy with enthusiasm, excited by every detail of the upcoming adventure. Josh was doing his best to play it cool but it was obvious he was as thrilled as she was.

As they waited for their train to depart they raided the small cupboards. Maggie was amazed at the deliciously healthy options. Though it had been years since she had to worry about where her next meal would come from, she wasn't so far removed that she'd forgotten this type of food had been like gold to everyone at the Office. It was so valuable that they rarely ate it themselves, but would use it to trade for a cheaper and more abundant option. Now she sat munching away on the treasure as nothing more than a mere snack.

"Thanks for coming, Maggie," Josh said. "I was pretty nervous about it, but this is solomon and I'm glad you're here."

She leaned over and kissed him. Keeping her face close to his, she smiled. "I'm glad I'm here, too."

Soon, the train was on its way. At first, the scenery was the same as from the ET only in a larger format but eventually the urban sprawl gave way to small towns, farmland, and woods rolling over the slowly sloping land.

Josh turned out to be quite the tour guide and their remarks about the landscape were often supplemented by his reflections on history. As they neared Cincinnati, he spoke a great deal about its involvement in the abolitionist movement and the Underground Railroad. Mostly, he spoke of the exploits of Harriet Tubman, ("like Moses"), sneaking slaves out of the South and to freedom in the North. They watched the terrain as they imagined what it must have been like for those fugitives, having to walk, mostly at night, through the deepest of woods, moving from one safe house to another, terrified of being caught at any second.

As Josh proudly displayed his knowledge, Maggie listened not for content so much as for Josh's feelings. He spoke as a proud messenger. It was obvious he loved history, speaking with deference for those who stood up to make a difference. Maggie imagined him standing in front of his class enthusiastically relaying the stories.

They had a feast for lunch in the dining car followed by tea in their private room. After tea, Maggie moved over to Josh and curled up next to him in his chair. There they continued to talk and share their thoughts on the changing landscape unfolding before them. Eventually, they dozed off.

It was early evening when they arrived in Denver. Josh had meticulously organized the whole itinerary. The plan was to arrive at the lumber yard first thing in the morning. So, he had arranged rooms in one of the finest hotels in Denver with a gorgeous view of the mountains. After a light dinner at the hotel's posh restaurant, a taxi whisked them off to the Gethsemane Theater where a traveling show of the reworked "Jesus Christ Superstar" was playing.

The show itself was an amazing VR extravaganza set ablaze with some of the hardest pounding pulse-charging music they had ever heard. Yet in the end, Josh expressed his disappointment as the story was not at all a reworking of the original script but the fictionalized version of the making of *Jesus Christ Superstar*. It was the story of a liberal Hollywood upcomer who wanted to draw people away from Christ so he wrote the musical to distort the truth of the Gospel. Some true Christians exposed his deceit and he lost everything. At the end, in the man's suffering and despair, Jesus revealed Himself and the man was saved. "The story was powerful," admitted Josh, "just not what I was expecting."

As they kissed in front of Maggie's hotel room door, things began to heat up. Josh's kisses grew fervent as they crushed their bodies together. Perhaps it was being far from Columbus, or maybe just the adventure itself, but for the first time, his hands went exploring. She felt a warm pleasurable wave as his hand, hesitantly, squeezed her rear end. She found herself returning his passionate kisses in kind.

For good or bad, they were interrupted by a group of hotel guests, exiting the elevator.

Josh pulled away from the kiss and turned slightly away from the approaching people. "I should probably say 'good-night.'" She nodded reluctantly and he offered one last embarrassed kiss.

As Maggie lay in her hugely extravagant hotel bed, her mind danced from one topic to another. This was just what she needed to distract her from missing Emily. Josh was going out of his way to show her a good time. Then, the kiss at the door. The idea of real intimacy was still not something she wanted to explore, even mentally, but she had to admit, the passion was exciting. Even if they got to the lumber yard the next day and it all turned out to be a wild goose chase, she was having a great time.

The next morning, they arrived at the lumber yard by taxi. Even at the extreme outskirts, the heavy wooden building appeared out of place in the technologically advanced city. "Reminds me of an Old West saloon," remarked Josh.

Josh's hand was shaking as he helped her out of the cab. The yard was quiet. They walked through the unsecured front doors but saw no one. As they walked toward the back, they heard planks of wood dropping to the floor.

"Hello?" called Josh.

From the back emerged a woman somewhere in her forties, dressed in jeans and a T-shirt with the sleeves rolled up. She was covered from her neck to her calves in a heavy safety smock. She was wearing a yellow helmet, goggles, and thick gloves she struggled to remove as she entered the room. Her face was dotted with sawdust but her youthful smile was brilliant. "Hey, there, how's it going? Sorry, my mom had to step out." She removed her goggles to reveal delicate hazel eyes. "Name's Vanessa. May I help you?"

Josh appeared unsure what to say. "I'm…. I'm…. I'm here to meet Peter."

Vanessa looked for a second like she was sizing Josh up and then answered, "Peter? Sorry, no Peter here. Just me and my mom, Priscilla."

"But he sent me a message to meet him here."

"Well, I don't know about any message. I know a whole bunch of Peters. If someone told you to meet them here, you're welcome to wait for a few minutes but this isn't a coffee shop either, you know what I mean?"

"Of course," answered Josh.

Vanessa paused again, then, laughing at her own irony, she invited them to a cup of coffee. "It's fresh, first pot of the morning."

They politely helped themselves. "So, it's just you and your mom running the whole yard?" Maggie asked.

"Well, I don't know if you can call it a yard anymore. Business went kind of bust after my dad died. We do the best we can but, to be honest, I'd rather be climbing a mountain."

"Surprised a business like this has the money to advertise," said Josh.

Vanessa shot him a glance. "Oh, you saw one of our advertisements?"

"Yeah, the one with the discount if I mention Elmer."

Vanessa smiled. "So, take your time, enjoy your coffee. I need to take care of something in back."

When Vanessa left the room, Maggie asked, "What was that all about?"

"Just wait," he assured her.

Moments later, Vanessa reemerged. "Come back tonight," she said with a smile. "When it's dark." With that, she disappeared again.

Josh's face beamed. "I knew it."

They took the cab back to the city and consumed a long leisurely lunch. Maggie watched as Josh hopelessly tried to play off the time as no big deal. After lunch, they talked about taking in a movie but Josh said he would feel trapped in a theater. They had no hotel to go back to, so, they stowed their things in a city locker and decided to see Denver by foot. They spent their time marveling at both the differences and similarities to Columbus. Occasionally they would find a park and sit for a while on a bench watching the city life. Time passed slowly, but it did pass. Eventually, Josh called for a taxi.

As they pulled into the shadowy deserted parking lot, the taxi shut down. The area sunk into an eerie quiet. Josh and Maggie sat together, unsure what to do, realizing this was as far as their planning had taken them. Then...

BANG! BANG! BANG!

The taxi shook with the blows from outside. Maggie felt her heart slam against her chest. Josh catapulted into the air, his fists ready in instinctual defense.

"You in there! Out!" a voice ordered.

Maggie felt light-headed and dizzy as the blood rushed from her head. It was the last night in the Office all over again.

Josh looked just as scared and then his face altered into a grimace. "Oh, it better not be," he said, pushing the button to open the door of the cab.

As the door slowly opened, Maggie expected to see a squad of robot-looking soldiers, rifles at the ready. Instead, she saw only the dim empty lot.

Suddenly, a figure leaped into view. "Ta-da!"

"You Philistine!" Josh screamed, lunging out of the cab. In an amazing display of courage, if not athletic prowess, Josh leaped onto the figure. In a flash, Maggie watched them fall to the ground wrestling, she was vaguely aware of her scream.

"You're a pean!" Josh was shouting. "A fucking pean!"

Perhaps it was the shock of her straight-laced boyfriend dropping the "f" bomb, or perhaps it was the sound of laughter, but the scene suddenly became clearer to her.

"I can't believe you did that!" Josh shouted. "You scared the crap out of me!"

The figure howled.

"It's not funny, really, you gave me a heart attack. And Maggie... oh my Lord... Maggie!" Josh came running up to where she sat frozen in the cab. "Are you alright?"

"Yeah, I guess so. I'm assuming this is Peter."

Peter was exactly the way Josh had described him: shaggy, unkempt hair and beard. His clothing was just short of being tattered and he had no shoes on his feet. The only area Josh had not done his description justice, perhaps because there were no words to describe it, was the young man's grin. It was both handsomely masculine and beautifully feminine; both boyishly devilish and compassionately gentle. It was with that complexity of spirit he looked into her eyes. Graciously, with the manners of a southern gentleman, he extended his hand to her, offering help out of the cab.

"I am Peter," he said. "You must be Maggie. I've heard a lot about you."

"I've heard a lot about you, too."

"Some of it might be true," joked Peter.

"Apparently, a lot of it is."

Peter's eyes held hers for a moment as he assessed her comment. He smiled with respect at her sense of humor. Or was it something else?

"You see that, you pean, you almost killed my girlfriend!" Josh wailed.

"I'm sorry," Peter said directly to her. "It was a very immature thing to do." Then Peter turned to Josh and defended himself. "I figured you'd be expecting me."

"Expecting you to walk up and say 'hello!' Yes! Expecting you to act like an ass, NO! Why do you have to do things like that?"

"I've no idea. These things just come to me. So, I'm glad you made it. Welcome. And welcome Maggie. And you, mano, look at you, figuring it out."

Josh smiled with satisfaction. "How'd you send that ad anyway?"

"What can I tell you? DHS needs to tend to their gaps." Peter's laughter echoed in the silent lot.

"And why'd we have to come back at night?"

"Hey, I had no idea you'd show up. I told Vanessa to call me if and when you did. Took me all day."

"So, what are we doing here?" asked Josh. "At night, in a scary parking lot, outside a lumber yard? After four months?"

"I wanna show you something. Follow me."

They removed their packs from the taxi and Josh sent it back. Peter led them around the building and over to a dilapidated barn. Inside, he held up a small light to reveal an antique vehicle.

"What's this?" Josh asked.

"This is what's called an S-U-V," announced Peter. "It's how we're getting up the mountains."

"Do you even know how to drive one of these things?" Josh asked incredulously.

"Sure, no big deal, just think of it as a big SV."

"Only a hundred times more dangerous and…wait a minute… S-U-V? The 'S' doesn't stand for 'solar,' does it?"

Peter laughed. "'Sport,' actually. It's okay, Josh. Despite what you may have read, gas engines were the norm for well over a century and the world didn't blow up."

Josh looked at Maggie. "You solomon with this?"

"Sure, I've never ridden in one, it'll be like the olden days."

It took Josh a moment to figure out how to open the door for Maggie. Once inside, Maggie was overwhelmed with the smell of fresh cut lumber and confronted with a large pile of boards taking up the whole cargo area and half of the back seat. Her next dilemma was learning how to use the antiquated seat belt. There was no way, she thought, that thin piece of cloth was going to help her in the event of a crash.

"Everybody buckled in?" Peter announced as he took his seat behind the wheel.

"Aye, aye, captain." Josh laughed.

With a tumultuous flurry of spinning wheels shot-gunning a blast of gravel, they were off. Peter exited the main streets as soon as he could. Maggie could not believe how bumpy the ride was. How in the world did anyone stand these things for more than a quick trip to the store?

Josh was on the same train of thought. "Jeez, Peter, how long's this gonna be?"

"Well, if we don't stop at all, about four hours."

"Four HOURS! In this thing? Over these…I don't even know what to call these things… roads? At night? Peter, this isn't safe."

"It's fine Josh. Trust me. Sit back, relax. Let me tell you a story."

Chapter Twenty Six

"From the moment they brought me back, I knew I could get out anytime I wanted. When they explained to me that they were gonna send me to one of those prisons posing as a school, I was gone. So, I rode a pine over the security fence."

"I knew it!" exclaimed Josh.

"Once on the road, I thought it would be easy but it wasn't. The government's cracking down on wanderers. There were times when these trucks would pull up to campgrounds, soldiers jumped out and rounded everyone up. Shit was intense. My plan was to work my way west and then figure which way was safer, north to Canada or south to Mexico. From there, I figured I could get back to Madrid. Public transportation, however, was out of the question so I had to hike it…"

"You walked?"

"Mostly. In Europe, there's a whole network willing to help but here… it was rough. I stayed in the woods and cut across farmlands. I avoided everybody, especially when I saw I was on the NBL."

"My dad told me it was the quickest way to pick you up."

"I'm sure. The further west I went the tougher it got. There were these so-called militias, unemployed guys that blame uncommitteds for the economy. They drive deep into the woods looking for wanderers. I had a group practically drive right up on me once. Fortunately, they were louder than a stampeding herd. I learned to camouflage my campsites, but I never felt safe. Toughest months of my life."

Maggie listened from the backseat. Josh always talked about Peter in a way that made him larger than life. She could see why he did. Despite his disheveled appearance, he had an aura. On the other hand, he was, in the end, simply human.

"I knew the longer I stayed on the road the more likely I'd get caught but there really wasn't anyplace to stop. Then, I came across this trio living deep in the woods: Tirza, Mari and Gustavo. They told me there were safe places to hide in the mountains. They let me join them. Gustavo's a major survivalist, knows his shit. Mari's his sister and Tirza's her friend. Beautiful people. We didn't know where we were going, we talked about finding a safe place as high up as possible and maybe build a cabin. We went days without seeing anyone, not even other wanderers. I mean we were out in the freaking boondocks and I was loving it. For the first time in months, I was able to relax."

"What'd you survive on?" Maggie asked.

"We all had supplies but it was Gustavo's hunting ability really. He's amazing with a bow. Water's not a problem, easy to clean. Just think basics. It's primitive but liberating, know what I mean? Anyway, it was just another day when out of freaking nowhere, at the crest of this hill we look down, and a magical kingdom pops up..."

"Disney World?" asked Josh.

"That's what it looked like to us. It looked a bit like an old-fashioned motel. The kind with the office in the middle and the rooms in wings on each side. It was perched there with a spectacular view of the mountains. It was pretty rundown and it looked empty. But we still approached cautiously." Peter paused, reveling in his tale. "I took the lead, the two girls walked one on each side of me and Gustavo followed in the back with his bow ready. When we got to the courtyard in front, I'm telling you, it was like something out of a western. This guy, biggest guy I've seen in my whole life, steps out the door with a shotgun in his hands. And he says, 'Okay, folks, that's far enough.'"

"Seriously?" asked Josh.

"Yep, I probably looked like you did when you hopped out of that cab back there."

Maggie chuckled. Josh threw up his hands in feigned exasperation. "Thanks a lot!"

The vehicle hit a bump and Maggie felt catapulted upward, the restraining belt was the only thing that kept her from slamming into the ceiling.

"Peter!" exclaimed Josh as he righted himself.

Peter laughed. "It's alright. This thing's built solid."

"Well, I'm not," said Josh. He turned around in his seat and looked apologetically at her. She gave him a thumbs-up, so he turned back to Peter. "Solomon, so Paul Bunyan's holding a shotgun to your head and..."

"We all freeze in our tracks. I say something like, 'Whoa, brethren, fear not. We simply seek a place to rest the night.' And the big guy said, 'Well, dis here is our place so you's gonna hafta find yourself somewhere else.'"

"Did he really talk like that?" asked Josh.

"Well, I reserve the right to embellish. So, I turned on the charm. 'My dear chap, I'm sure you are aware of the story of Lot. Lot lived in this town and had two daughters. Some strangers came to town and Lot invited them to stay at his house. Now the townspeople smelled fresh meat so they came over and demanded Lot turn the strangers over to them so they could rape them. Lot said, 'My, that would be immoral so instead, I'll give the townspeople my daughters to rape so that they will leave the strangers alone.' I pointed to Mari and Tirza and said, 'Now these two young ladies with me aren't my daughters but I'll give them to you for a place to stay.'"

Maggie went into shock until she was able to see Peter's face. It was a joke? The guy her boyfriend looked up to more than anyone else was making jokes about rape? And what exactly was the joke?

"What happened?" Josh asked.

"There was this stunned silence. I could feel the girls' eyes on me. They must have thought I'd gone mad."

Maggie agreed with them.

"The big guy's staring at me like I'd just spoken Swahili or something. Then, I hear laughter from inside and this other guy comes out and tells the big guy to put away his gun. He's still laughing which caused me to start laughing and the next thing you know we're all holding our guts. I swear we all spent fifteen minutes howling our heads off before we even got around to introducing ourselves."

"Wait a minute..." Josh interrupted. "I'm not sure I get it. Why were you all laughing?"

"Josh," Peter said, turning to him. Maggie bit her lip to keep from gasping. *Eyes on the road, buddy, eyes on the road.* "Is that the story you would pick if you were trying to convince a committed Christian that you were too?"

"Well, no... I guess not. But he knew you weren't serious about the girls?"

"Yeah, Josh, that's kind of the point."

Josh shook his head. "I'm not sure I get it."

"Think about it, mano. Anyway, the big guy's Ed. You'll like him. He doesn't talk much but you can count on him. The guy who came out of the house laughing is Levy. Smartest guy I've ever met. He's the old man of the group. He's teaching me carpentry. There were three, well, four, others inside the lodge. They said they'd been living in there since early Spring. It's great, wait 'til you see it. There's the main building with a living room, the kitchen and a dining room overlooking the mountains. But get this, there are these little huts built up the hill a bit. Levy has one, I took another one and we're working on fixing up a third one for Ed. Roof still needs major repairs. So... um..." Peter lowered his voice, but Maggie could still hear. "That leaves just one repaired room open at the lodge. I've got an old air mattress and room on my floor."

"That'll work," Josh answered. "So, what is this? A hippie commune?"

"No, mano, just people tired of being sheep."

Maggie remembered the time in the Office, after Barak's death, when the dream was to run into the mountains and find a community living off the grid. It looked like she was the only one who would make it to such a place. And then, it was just for a visit. She imagined Josh was probably freaking out a bit. She was sure he never anticipated driving off to some remote lodge in the mountains. If he had he probably would have resisted her companionship.

The drive was long and eventually they sunk into silence. Maggie checked her phone and found another new text from Emily.

Emily continued to send her daily texts. She was doing great. She said Jake's apartment was bigger but "not as clean" as theirs. It also was within walking distance, "long but worth it" to the beach. Jake had taken her to the school and it was "really big" but "not too scary." But it was the church she was most excited about as she described it as "gorgeously beyond huge" and filled with "millions of really nice" people. She concluded with how wonderful it was to be in a "real church." It was the writing on the wall.

Was that really so bad? Emily was right where she needed to be, in the safety of the social net. What could she offer Emily really? Life on the fringe? Emily deserved better than that. And so what if she became a committed member to a real church? That was better for her. No, Maggie concluded, she had just been holding Emily back for her own selfish reasons.

She drifted in and out of consciousness as the vehicle continued its long twisting journey. She had thought she had things well mapped out. She had not seen Jake coming and never would have dreamt he would drop in just to swoop Emily away. Where did that leave her? And then, there was Josh. Another thing she had not planned for. Her whole life she had a plan of one kind or another. Now she felt an ominous emptiness without one.

When the vehicle came to a halt it was unclear to her if she had been asleep or not. After regaining her focus, she could see they were parked in front of a large ancient wooden building.

"Hey, Maggie, we made it," Josh whispered. "Peter didn't kill us after all."

"What time is it?" Her throat and lips felt dry.

"After two. He says there's a room in here where you can stay." Josh carried her backpack while she robotically followed. A bed of some kind would be a relief after the hours of being bent out of shape in that contraption.

Josh insisted on checking out the room. When he was convinced there were no boogie men under the bed and the locks were of sufficient strength, he took her in his arms. "I'm so sorry about this. Peter, the ride in that death trap, this… this barn to sleep in…. I never should have…"

She interrupted him with a gentle placement of her finger on his lips. "Whoa! There's nothing to worry about. Remember? I've been backpacking. This place is like a palace compared to places I've slept. Trust me."

"You sure?"

"Absolutely. I have no idea where I am, but I've never been more excited to see what tomorrow brings."

"Knowing Peter, he's probably gonna have us hang glide off a cliff!"

"Count me in."

Chapter Twenty Seven

Maggie came to consciousness. It took her several moments to collect her thoughts and organize her memories to realize where she was. It was difficult to determine what was real and what was simply a product of her overworked mind. She was still in her clothes from the night before; they now left her feeling grimy.

The bed smelled funny, a musty burnt wood odor. It was not unpleasant. Maggie listened, but there was no sound. A moment later, a distant bird sang a "Good morning," and then nothing. She could not remember being anywhere, ever, that was so silent.

She went to the window. She pulled back the blinds and the room was ablaze with early morning sunlight. After several heavy blinks, she looked and beheld a painting, the most beautifully detailed painting she had ever seen. There were intricate layers of heavily forested green trees on top of layers of mountains. The details gave it a 3D effect… Then she realized, it wasn't a painting. She could see wisps of clouds moving. The VR games with the highest pixels paled in comparison to the majestic mountains that stood before her. It was overwhelming. She had one desire, to be there.

She freshened up, changed clothes, and threw open the door. Encased in a dazzling light, she felt like she walked inside a rainbow. Every color imaginable splashed against the tapestry of the deep rich blue sky. Above her were two perfectly white fluffy clouds, resembling turtles, making their way across the horizon.

She took several long breaths and enjoyed the sensation of the clean crisp air streaming through her nostrils and into her chest. As she breathed out, she imagined she was expelling the old stale air of Columbus.

Maggie stood for a few moments taking it all in. The whole mountain was waking from a night's sleep. There were some birds up and welcoming the new day but mostly there was a gentle heavy stillness, like a snuggly flannel blanket.

She was brought out of her mesmerized state by the sound of walking feet on gravel. She felt a slight rush of adrenaline as she focused down the hill. There were two people walking. Peter and Josh? No, the gait was wrong. They were girls.

The girls, engaged in a conversation, sauntered slowly up the slope. When they saw Maggie, they both stopped, smiling simultaneously.

"Buenas Dias!" one of them greeted.

"Hi," Maggie said.

The girls looked to be about Maggie's age. The one who had spoken was her height. Her hair was long and dark; her ebony eyes nestled beneath thick eyebrows. The other was tall, maybe taller than Josh, her shoulder length orange/blonde hair fell over her strong athletic shoulders.

The shorter one spoke again as she approached the porch. "My name's Mariposa but you can call me, Mari. This is Tirza."

Maggie was struck by the accent. She had been around people from a Hispanic background all her life but very few of them ever spoke anything but good ole Ohioan. She decided the accent made Mari sound like a chirpy bird.

"I'm Maggie. I'm here with a friend. We got in early this morning."

"Yeah, I heard you guys," Tirza said with an obvious southern influence. "No offence but Peter said you were a guy."

"Oh, I'm not Peter's friend. I guess I should say I'm a friend of the friend of Peter... Josh... I mean the friend's name is Josh and I'm Maggie, but I said that, didn't I? ... Could we just start this over?"

The two girls laughed. "You're gonna fit in around here," Tirza said. "We're gonna get some breakfast. Want some?"

The girls led her into the main building and under a large sign. The lettering burned into a thick piece of wood read: ABHAYAGIRI.

Sunlight exposed a living room from another century. None of the cushioned chairs and sofas were any less than a hundred years old. Against the walls stood shelves piled high with antique books. The room smelled of fresh pine and burnt wood from the old-fashioned fireplace.

"So, was the room bien?" Mari asked.

"It's lovely. I love the way it smells."

Mari agreed, opening a set of doors leading into another room. As she entered, Maggie saw a good-sized kitchen to her left and to her right was a dining area with two neatly arranged tables. The dining room's far wall was a glass window revealing the majesty of the mountains.

"Fantastic!" Maggie exclaimed.

The girls giggled at her enthusiasm.

"You make everyone breakfast?" Maggie asked as they entered the kitchen.

"Oh, my no." Mari laughed. "Think of it like your kitchen back home. Over there's the walk-in, everything's self-serve."

"And self-clean-up!" added Tirza.

As the three women prepared their breakfast, Maggie told them the story of their drive in and how it was her first time in a car needing a driver. She talked about how she was sitting in the back seat trying to keep her body from shaking with fear while listening to Peter, who was not only not keeping his eyes on the road but talking as casually as if he had been sitting in his living room. The girls laughed at the story and assured her of his driving qualifications.

Soon, they were seated at one of the dining tables. "How many people live here?" asked Maggie.

"We're ten," Tirza answered. "Counting Gustavo and the baby."

"Gustavo's my brother. He was in the Army. Since he's been home, he prefers to be solo... alone."

"He camps out there somewhere, but he comes and sees us once a week or so, brings us meat. He's like our guardian angel."

"And there's a baby?"

"Nesta. Eight months. He's Josiah and Ayesha's. Ayesha's twin sister is Manda. Then there's Ed and Levy."

"Oh yes, Peter told us about them. He also told this crazy story about how you all met." Maggie went on to reiterate Peter's tale. The girls cackled at the memory and assured her Peter's version was more or less accurate.

Her mind struggled with a description of the two girls and decided on "naturally nice." There was no pretense, no weighing of social position, they had the demeanor of young children, innocently playing together. Maggie was enraptured. "I saw a sign on the way in... Abba-something."

"Abhayagiri. We aren't sure what language it is, but we know it translates as 'Fearless Mountain.'"

"We found some records in an old file cabinet," said Tirza. "Originally, there were only two buildings. This and the big garage outside. The guy who built it was a rich movie star who would come up here to get away from everything. The guy donated the place to a group of Buddhist monks."

"Buddhists?" Maggie asked. "In America?"

"All before the FGA, of course," replied Mari. "They came in and renovated. They expanded the kitchen, turned the bedroom into the dining room and added the wings. They made the garage into a meditation hall. The monks built small cabins higher up the hill. They called them 'kutis.' We've found about a dozen of them. Most of them are beyond repair but Peter and the others are fixing up the salvageable ones. Simple places, no more than bedrooms. The monks lived humble lives. We think the wings with the bedrooms were built for guests to stay in. The place acted as a retreat center until the Awakening shut it all down. Judging from all the books and stuff still around, we're guessing the monks left in a hurry."

"The best thing about the place is its self-sufficiency," Tirza said. "There's a stream where we pump our water and a green house where we can grow food."

"The whole place is like a fantasy world," said Maggie.

"How long you've been a wanderer?" Mari asked.

"Me?" Maggie asked. "Oh, no, I'm not a wanderer. I'm a student. Nursing school."

Mari stared at her, clearly skeptical.

A part of Maggie wanted to open up and tell her new friends everything about herself but years of conditioning trapped the words in her throat.

Their quiet breakfast was abruptly interrupted by Peter's grand entrance followed by Josh.

"I told Josh we'd find you here!" Peter exclaimed. "Good morning, you beautiful people."

Josh was grinning broadly. "You solomon?" he asked softly.

"Yeah," answered Maggie. "The eggs are delicious. Want some?"

Josh took a bite and exclaimed his approval. Peter then introduced Mari and Tirza to Josh.

As Josh and Peter went about making their breakfast, the rest of the little community made appearances. The first to come through the door were the parents, Josiah and Ayesha. They too looked to be in their early twenties. Josiah seemed a bit wary of strangers in the house but Ayesha was thrilled that Maggie was a nurse.

"Will you look at Nesta? Please? He's not been to a doctor since he was born."

Maggie tried to explain she was only a student and a first year one at that but the young mother heard very little. In the end, nervous but smiling,

Maggie looked the little guy over. As far as she could tell, the smiling fat kid was healthy as a horse.

A while later, Ed entered. Maggie couldn't believe it; the guy was enormous. He stood unsure in the doorway until Peter went up to him and told him he wanted to introduce him to some friends. He moved slowly as if he were afraid of what his steps might do to the floor. As he smilingly engulfed Maggie's hand in one of his own, he gently placed his other on top. Maggie now felt like she knew how Nesta must have felt when she took him by the hand. Ed took a larger chair at the end of the table. Maggie noticed Peter began making breakfast for Ed. Apparently, there were exceptions to "everyone fends for themselves."

Manda stopped in for just a second. In some ways, she was the spitting image of her sister: dark, short hair, stern eyebrows, but in other ways she was the exact opposite. Ayesha was thin and feminine in her dress as well as her mannerisms. Manda was dressed more like a man in overalls and boots. She had a handkerchief tied around her head and she was carrying a pair of well-worn work gloves. When she was introduced to the newcomers, she merely gave an annoyed nod and then asked Peter about the supply of lumber. Peter told her about the wood in the SUV and she was satisfied with his answer. She kissed her nephew and left without another word.

Levy was the last to make an appearance. He was a good bit older than the rest but with a boyish smile and a handsome chiseled face. As he took her hand Maggie noticed a kindness in his eyes. He welcomed the guests and joined the table. He asked Peter if it all went well and Peter responded. "Except for these two being in an SUV for the first time, it was perfect."

Josh jumped to defend. "Hey, it wasn't the vehicle, it was the driver!"

The whole table laughed and from there, the two men bantered back and forth in telling the story of the trip up the mountain.

After cleaning up, they took a short walk around the compound. Peter showed them the buildings including the green house. Maggie stood in the misty air breathing in the deep odor of the growing plants. From there, Peter took them up the road to his kuti. Maggie was amazed at the simplicity of the community's life. There was no access to computers or phones. The electricity needed to run the refrigeration and necessary lights was provided by solar panels. It was a life based on a simple paradigm: if a person doesn't want much, he doesn't need much.

After the tour, Josh took Maggie aside and explained he needed some time with Peter. Maggie knew the talk was the real purpose of the trip. So, she asked Mari and Tirza if they were up for a "serious hike." The two girls were quite happy to join forces with a kindred adventurer and the three young women set out to find an old fire tower at the top of the nearby slope.

As they left the grounds they went almost straight up a steep hill. At one time there had been stairs carved out of the stone and reinforced by wood braces but the disintegrated steps were now more an obstacle than a help.

When she reached the top, she was stunned. There before her, sheltered by a decrepit wooden gazebo, sat a larger than life golden statue of the Buddha. He was sitting in a serene lotus position. And he was headless. As she followed the girls up the path closer to the statue she noticed how torn up the statue was. There were huge chunks missing. Across the chest someone had painted "False god!!!!" in bright red paint. The statue was haphazardly surrounded by a ring of large rocks.

"Can you believe it?" asked Mari. "They actually went to the trouble of gathering stones."

"Whoever blasphemes the name of the LORD shall surely be put to death. All the congregation shall stone him," Tirza quoted, sarcastically.

"Pendejos," said Mari.

From there the elevation continued but not nearly in such a dramatic way. The well-worn path wound its way up the remaining slope. After which, the path became a snaking weave through large boulders. At every elevation, a new vison of paradise emerged. Occasionally, a hyperactive chipmunk scampered by or an eagle glided lazily through the flawless blue sky. At times, Maggie stopped and breathed in as much as she could of the crisp air, as if it were cold water after a good long run.

Eventually, they arrived on what appeared to be the top of the highest mountain in the area. It was still dwarfed by the distant peaks, but it stood proudly as king of a massive domain. Yet, they were not done. There stood a primitive fire tower, its old boards sagging in their dilapidation.

Maggie found herself giggling as she made her way up the tattered antique structure. Mari and Tirza were quite impressed as she effortlessly navigated the maze of ramshackle boards.

On top, Maggie could only stand... bewildered.

All around her, in a complete panoramic view, was the most dazzling sight she had ever beheld. Even with all that she had seen that morning, even with all she had seen with the hike up there, taking all that into consideration, this was still by far the most breath-taking thing she had ever witnessed.

"It's like an ocean of forest!" Maggie exclaimed. "Look at how all the different trees being blown by the wind make it look like a current. A green ocean. And the tree line. That looks like a beach with the waves of the forest lapping up to it. Even the sunlight looks like water bubbles."

The three women lost themselves in the splendor. Maggie had the sensation her breath was a tributary to the river of breeze sweeping by her. She was overwhelmed by the paradoxical feelings of being a part of the vastness before her and feeling completely insignificant in it all.

Maggie could not believe these people were living with this majesty every day.

Mari and Tirza were from Florida. The two met when they were in first grade and stood next to each other for the church choir. They had been friends ever since.

Mari was the sixth child of a couple who, after being born-again in their native country, Ecuador, came to America. As a science teacher, Mari's father was greeted with many opportunities. When her brother, Gustavo, returned from the military, explained Mari. "I knew something was wrong. My family kept saying, 'Pray and he will be healed.' But I knew it was not that at all. Gus was not sick, he had changed."

It had been Tirza's idea to leave. They stayed in Atlanta's underground for six months before Gustavo talked them into trying the deep wilderness. Mari had been the most reluctant but when she spent her first night under a star-filled sky, a sky not at all effected by the lights of a city, she was hooked. "If it's just a matter of what wolves you choose to sleep with, I'll take the animal kind."

That made sense to Maggie. As she lost herself in the natural wonder she thought of Mickey. What was it Mickey had said? "They can't control the land, there's too much of it." Mickey had been right. She wished he had been able to see it. And the twins. Oh my god, would they have loved being up here. A whole new world to explore. And Emily? How much fun would she be having right now? But that was the reason Maggie was there. Because there was no more Emily. Nor Asher. Nor Mickey, Nor Barak.

Maggie caught Mari staring at her. She was searching for a question to ask. *Please, don't ask*, Maggie inwardly begged. Some things were just better not talked about.

Mari found Maggie's hand. She did not pull it away. "You okay?"

"Yeah, just a little emotional." Maggie wiped her eyes with her shirt. "Thinking of some friends."

"Abhayagiri is a good place to think."

Chapter Twenty Eight

While the girls were away, Josh and Peter climbed a nearby hill and found a place to sit that overlooked the buildings of Abayagiri. Beyond, the lines of tree-covered hills extended into apparent infinity.

"Pretty amazing place you found," Josh said.

"Triumphant, wouldn't you say?"

Josh had prayed about this moment. He had asked God to give him the words to help his friend. Now, he sat there, his stomach trembling with a nervous queasiness, as no great words of wisdom arrived. The mountains were beautiful, of course, but...

"Peter, you know this isn't real, don't you?"

"Look around you, mano. This is as real as it gets."

"No, Peter, it's an illusion. You can't stay here. I've seen the kind of surveillance DHS has. Believe me, you aren't hiding from anyone."

"Yeah, I know it's only temporary, but DHS is looking for counter-revolutionaries. Levy says, if we keep our heads down, we won't be bothered. Getting out of the country's tough right now. I've got... someone... working on it."

"Why not just come home, do whatever you have to do and..."

Peter shook his head vigorously. "Not an option."

"Then you owe it to me to tell me why," Josh stubbornly said. "I promise, I will *incline my heart to understanding*." At that moment, it seemed to be the best strategy. He needed to get Peter talking, maybe then his guard would drop and Josh could find a way to get past it and into Peter's heart and soul.

"Not much to it. I can't go back to that, Josh. And don't get the idea this is an easy decision. It isn't. I'm fully aware of what I am walking away from. I know I'm hurting my family. I know I'm hurting you. But I can't live my life there. Not knowing what I know. Do you want to hear how the whole thing got started?"

"What whole thing?"

"God, religion."

"Absolutely." As he mentally lifted his spiritual armor, Josh was overcome with sadness. Why did he need armor with his best friend?

"Okay, so we begin with the idea, homo sapiens developed in the Rift Valleys of Africa. At least that's what the scientific evidence indicates. But it was no Garden of Eden. You okay so far?"

"Solomon." Josh was familiar with the basic delusion of evolution.

"So, suppose homo sapiens, us, developed in Africa with no God involved. The world around us is hostile, wondrous, violent, and majestic. Indescribably awesome in both its beauty and its viciousness. It's the same way all animals experience it. But, our brains have developed to the point where we can communicate with each other. Now, a species can share personal thoughts and experiences and… and this is important… collect them as a community consciousness. We could tell each other stories of our experiences and, in a world we didn't at all understand, try to explain, collectively, those experiences. We learned to use symbolic language to describe indescribable concepts and we could pass those explanations on to each new generation until the concepts themselves became solidified.

"Those early people looked up at that blinding circle in the sky. They had no idea what it was and no scientific mindset to answer the question, instead they had to use their own minds. Those wondrous curious creative fallible irrational human minds that sought an explanation. They knew the sun was vital to their survival. They could see it, feel it, but didn't understand it. It's not hard to see how they might give it a conscious mind of some kind. Thus, religion is born."

"So, religion is all a product of sun worship?" asked Josh incredulously. He looked up towards the big yellow ball reigning supreme above the grand peaks. *And beware lest you raise your eyes to heaven, and when you see the sun… you be drawn away and bow down.*

"Yeah… more or less. I've seen how, just like we can retrace our biological history, or retrace the history of tools, for instance, we can retrace the concept of religion back to a common source. From there, religion evolved just like people. When groups were cut off from each other, they not only no longer reproduced with each other, they stopped telling each other the same stories. So, the stories evolved in different directions but all from the same common ancestor- the sun. Eventually, they were able to better understand their natural world and the nature of the sun but the idea of a great and powerful being never left the human psyche. It just transformed from something observable into something not observable. So, generations after generations, centuries and centuries, the stories were told, spread, altered, and the people were conditioned. The stories gave each new generation a label, an identity, a means of defining themselves and the world around them."

"Come on…"

"How is that more fantastic than all the world's animals walking two-by-two to spend the next year floating on a large wooden boat? Or an invisible man floating around us with the power to end our suffering and choosing not to? Or that the tricks of our minds and coincidences are actual messages from a god personally intervening in our lives?"

"So, you really believe there's no God?"

Peter took a long breath. "When I was a kid, I loved Him. He was my Heavenly Father; Jesus was like an older brother to me. They were as much a part of me as my mom and dad. And as real. That's hard to give up, really hard, and deep down inside I don't want to give it up. But the answer's 'yes,' not in the way you're defining God. I believe in spirituality, an energy in nature we can tap into, but after an exhaustive search, I can unequivocally say- the God of the Bible does not… thank God… exist."

Josh knew he should be shocked, but surprisingly, he found his greatest emotion was an overwhelming sense of sadness for his friend. A Godless world was so pointless. "Do you believe in anything?"

"I believe in that breeze that just passed through. I believe in the heat of the sun against my skin. I believe I'm alive and am gonna enjoy every breath I take. I believe in the miracle of life and am amazed at its infinite diversity of forms. I believe in the miracle of humans and how we've taken our ability to manipulate our environment from simple wooden tools to magnificent machines. I believe in art, in music, poetry and theater. I believe in the intellect that can create such things and applaud it, not denounce it. Because it's exactly *our own understanding* that has had the power to do such things."

Not surprising, Josh thought. Peter's arguments sounded like the liberals pointing to Man as God. Why wouldn't Peter come up with such ideas? Living up here like a hippie.

"I believe we're all right here. Alive in this moment, sharing this moment, and then our moment will be up. I think deep down inside, everyone knows it's true. That's why we're willing to fight so hard to defend it, why it's such a big deal if someone loses it. If we really believed this measly hundred years of life was just a prelude to an eternity of bliss, why would anyone fight to stay alive? Better yet, why would anyone kill to stay alive?

"I believe in the indelible human spirit that has had the curiosity and desire to take on the challenges of this world and master them. And I believe it's that spirit that unites us all. If we really want to connect to our roots than we need to go beyond the Puritans founding our Christian America, we need to go beyond our identification to a national ancestry, we need to go beyond the establishment of nations, beyond the divisions of religion and race, beyond all the labels we've put on ourselves. Back to that first tribe of homo sapiens. Back to the time before we all forgot we are of one clan. That's where our true ancestors are. They're the well from which we all sprung."

Josh was about to argue that is exactly what the Bible teaches. Mankind was created, male and female and placed in the Garden of Eden. Instead, Josh opted to keep his thoughts to himself. Peter was not speaking in anger as he had done before, but from a soft heart.

Peter turned to Josh. Their eyes locked and Josh found himself thinking of the first time he had seen them. The first time Peter had dropped down out of that tree only to light up the whole woods.

Peter spoke in a voice that seemed to dance in the sunlight. "The world came without lines, without borders, and our minds did too. There was a common singular purpose: survival. That's what united them then and that's what should be uniting us now. When we do that, virtually all the reasons we use to justify killing each other dissipates into the abyss, whether it be loyalty to the illusion of nationality or the myth of religion. No one is superior to anyone else because they've been chosen by a god or are reading the right book or are marching to patriotic glory.

"It's time we started seeing ourselves for what we have revealed ourselves to be. A conscious communicating species on a tiny speck of dust in the middle of absolutely nowhere. And, if we don't get our act together, we may become an unconscious species on a tiny insignificant ball in the middle of nowhere. See, the true danger of our lunatic Apostles and their Jehovah Revolution is that they just might create a self-fulfilling prophecy and nuke the whole world into oblivion. What happens then? What happens when there's no triumphant return of Jesus but just a world-wide nuclear winter?"

The two sat quietly for a while. Josh mulled over Peter's words presented with such sincerity and conviction. He was left with a single question...

"Peter, may I ask you something?"

"Of course."

"What happened on the mission trip? Why'd you leave?"

Peter smiled meekly. "Yeah… that's a toughie." Peter paused, picked up a good-sized rock and threw it over the edge. "The first stop was a few months of training. We learned a little first aid but mostly it was the JOT program all over again. Only, we lived it every minute of every day. Since the guys in my group were all just high school graduates, our jobs were gonna be as assistants to engineers, nurses, and ministers. We were at the bottom and I loved it. *Blessed are the meek, the poor*, all that. I spent most of my time under what I called radical spiritual training. I prayed for hours every day, studied my Bible, and even went on a twenty-one day fast. I was determined to be the best soldier in Jehovah's army.

"I was assigned to this little village called Tukania. I was with a team of three other guys. We worked on projects, irrigation, sewage, stuff like that and to act as missionaries. We'd wake up each morning at the crack of dawn and have a long morning Bible study. Then we'd eat a little breakfast and go to work. Pretty hard work most of the time but we only worked until noon. Then we'd break for lunch, have a couple hours to ourselves and regroup for mission work. Often, we would go door-to-door, offering Bibles and talking to people about Jehovah's Revolution but what we mostly did was market one big rally after another. You know, those huge CAP-sponsored crusades we see on TV. The kind where thousands are brought to Jesus and everyone's miraculously healed.

"Anyway, the guys and I kept a strict schedule, to keep us spiritually strong. In two months, I was completely hooked. It was amazing, everything I did I felt like I was doing in the Spirit. I'd be digging a latrine and I'd feel God was right there with me. I'd be taking a hike and I'd feel Jesus walking next to me. Every morning I awoke to this… this… lightness of being.

"And life went on like that. It was great. Until one day… it all went kaplooee…"

Peter paused as if he was mustering his courage to reach back into the deepest part of a dark dank closet.

"I swear, Josh, a few seconds before it happened I felt something, like the air went out of everything. I saw a huge bolt of lightning come up from the ground. A few seconds later there was this earth-shaking BOOM! As if a hundred cannons were shot simultaneously. It stopped my heart for a second. The next second, my captain gets a call and tells us there was an explosion, maybe a bomb, in the nearby city. We were being called to help in any way we could. All four of us leaped into our Jeep and raced away like superheroes, bringing God's glory."

Josh sat frozen in place, so as not to do anything to disturb the conversational waters.

"It was like driving into Hell itself. Half a city block had been blown to bits. The smoke was so thick it was choking. Dead bodies lay all over the place and everyone was running around trying to save the survivors. I swear by this time I don't think my feet were even touching the ground. I had no idea what was happening but I knew I was prepared to do whatever it took. This girl comes running up and says something to the head guy. The guy looks over at me and my friend and tells us to follow this girl to the hospital. I was like 'Thy Will be done.'

"As we got to the hospital I realized what it really was. It was a church, only now all of the pews were filled with bloody wounded people. I can't describe what it was like to rush into that chaos. Everywhere I looked there were either screaming people or the people running around trying to help them but all of them were covered in blood and the black dirt from the smoke. There were men, women, old people, and… kids. I realized I had already lost my companion. I didn't know what to do and then it struck me. This is what I had been preparing for my whole life.

"I saw this one kid, he'd lost half his body. I mean right down the middle. His right arm and leg were gone and the whole right side of his face had melted away. He looked up at me with his one eye and I could not only see his fear, I could feel it."

Peter took a pained breath. "I prayed. This was the moment. This was the moment God was gonna perform a miracle through me. I closed my eyes and breathed deeply. And then, with absolute faith, I reached out and touched that little kid. I had no idea what was gonna happen. I guess a part of me expected to see him sprout a new arm and leg, hop up, and run out the door. What I got instead was… he recoiled from me like I had shot him with electricity. Then, this nurse runs over and yells at me, 'What're you doing?' I said, 'I'm trying to help.' She straightens him out on the bed. I just stood there. I didn't know what to do. She hollers at me again to get out of the way. I stepped over into a corner. My mind went to the time Peter and John walked to the temple and they stopped to heal a man who had been crippled all his life. I prayed again. 'Jesus, use me as your vessel.' I then walked out of the corner and over to the first pew. On it was this man, maybe my dad's age. I looked at him and quoted, *Silver and gold I do not have, but what I have I give you. In the name of Jesus Christ, be healed.*

"The guy looks up at me and do you know what he did?" Peter was openly crying. "He thanked me. After I ordered by the power of Jesus Himself to be healed, he looks up at me, his dying eyes squinting in anguish and... thanks me... before flopping back down onto that blood-soaked cushion. Then, that nurse walks up with a bucket and mop and says, 'If you want to be of real help, do what you can to get the blood off the floor.'

"And so, I did. I was still trying to figure this out. There were, I don't know, a hundred people in there; most of them screaming in pain. These people needed healing. They needed their suffering to stop. So, while I'm mopping, I'm praying, begging really, for God to heal them. I said, 'Don't do it through me, I don't want any glory, but please, God, please heal these people.' I quoted the Bible to God. I reminded him Peter's shadow had the power to heal. I told him these people were Christians. It went on for hours. I stayed bent over the mop so that no one could see me crying. All the screaming, the yelling, the smell, my God, Josh, the smell... all that suffering... and all I had the power to do was mop up their blood."

Peter stopped, took several pained breaths and wiped the tears from his eyes. "There was a service that night, only it had to be outside because the church was still occupied. All these exhausted doctors and nurses attended, singing praise songs and asking God to continue His healing. I'm sitting there surrounded by these people who've spent the last twelve straight hours working their asses off, doing shit I can't even begin to describe to you, and these people are giving God the credit.

"It made absolutely no sense to me. Why didn't God just heal them? I'm this pathetic little kid and my heart's breaking for these people. How can God, who's Love itself, and has the power to alleviate these people's suffering, how can He choose not to? It was the doctors and nurses who did all the work. It was their guts, their knowledge, **their** love, that pulled those people through and now they were thanking Him?

"I didn't recognize it then but, looking back on it, that was the point. That was the point I lost my faith. I spent the next couple years looking up all the science, the philosophy, the history but I realize now I was just searching for the god I had already lost. See, I realized at that moment, as Christians, we have absolutely nothing additional to offer. We're not anointed. The Bible promises us gifts so we convince ourselves we've received them but we haven't received anything. We're not special. Christians not only do not have the power to perform miracles, they aren't different in any way. It's just another false promise of the Bible.

"I withdrew from the guys; none of them seemed to be affected by the experience. Suddenly, it all felt stifling to me. The whole routine that had been so holy now seemed utterly foolish. I had to get out of there. So, I left them a note, told them I was gonna commune with God for a few days. I was three days in before I realized I was no longer looking for someplace to spend some time alone. I was traveling... searching... and I guess I've never stopped."

Peter turned, staring fiercely into Josh's eyes. "I'm gonna get out of here again, Josh. I'm gonna make it back to Madrid. I want you to get out too. That's why I asked you here. It'll be easy for you. You don't have any negative record. When you're ready, book a flight, a boat... whatever. Get to Madrid and contact me through LAN, that's the Lost American Network. Use 'Elmer' as the contact word. We'll meet up again there. Don't worry about it if you don't understand it all, get out, and you'll see for yourself."

Josh did his best to listen intently but so much of what Peter was saying was absurdly foreign to him. The implications of Peter's ideas made Josh's whole world sound like a fairy tale. Yet, Peter was speaking with such logical conviction that Josh found himself following... thinking... questioning... however, when Josh heard the request to leave America, he was snapped back to reality. His shield had given but held. It was time to draw his sword.

"No, Peter," Josh declared. "I won't. You need to come home with me. I can't begin to understand what you went through but I do know this is spiritual warfare. You can't see it now, but the devil's wounded you. Deep down, you know God's real. That's why you said it's so hard to let go your belief in Him. This is exactly what they taught us in school. They told us about the attacks of Satan. Remember? Remember the *Screwtape Letters*?"

To Josh's annoyance, Peter laughed as he said, "Ah yes...Wormwood."

This was no laughing matter. "And you're wrong about the Holy Spirit. I know it's true. I know the Spirit's guiding me every day. You've been away from God's protection, Peter. You feel caged only because you're lost in the wilderness but when you come home, and stop running, you'll see we weren't meant to live without a Shepherd. *The Lord is my Shepherd; I shall not want.*

"Look, back home, we can find people who have the answers. That's what our ministers and youth pastors are for, to guide us. I spoke to Mrs. Marone, and she likened you to a sheep who got out of the pen. At first you think you're happy and free but, without a Shepherd, you're prone to get tangled in the briars and become prey for the carnivores. Spiritually speaking, that's what you went through. Away from the mission, away from the Church, you got your mind all twisted. But, I believe, in the end, this search is gonna make you an even stronger Joseph… but you have to stop running."

Peter simply shook his head.

"Peter! You're meant for so much more than this. Look at you, living in a tiny shack, hiding out on a mountain until you can slink away. That isn't the life God has intended for you. Maybe, He showed you those things so you can fix them. Maybe, our government is off-track, I don't know, but I do know running away isn't gonna fix anything. Come back with me, get your education, become a Joseph and eventually, you'll be in a position to make a difference. Someday, you're gonna be an Apostle."

"Like I told you before, Josh, you can't put the frog back in the well."

What ensued next could only be defined as an argument as Josh's fear and pain quickly turned to anger. However, in the end, the two could only stare in despair at each other, each resolute in his convictions.

To make matters even worse, on the way back down, Josh slipped on one of the boulders, fell and twisted his ankle. The pain was drowned by his fury.

Chapter Twenty Nine

M aggie returned to the lodge to find Josh, looking hurt and defeated, propped up on a porch chair.

"I think we have a patient for you, Maggie." Peter chuckled.

It was obvious Josh was in no mood for Peter's humor.

"What happened?" she asked.

"Like a pean, I slipped. Peter had to practically carry me back."

Maggie examined Josh's foot. As near as she could tell nothing was broken. It was, however, beginning to swell. Mari came with a small bag of ice and they found an inflatable brace and pain pills in the medical supplies. Maggie's prescription for him was to stay off the ankle.

"We'll set you up a chair on the porch and you can still enjoy the mountains," Maggie said.

"I'm so humiliated."

"Don't be. It can happen to anyone."

Peter arrived with a pair of ancient crutches. "They're still solid."

Maggie served a late lunch to a sulky Josh on the porch where Peter and she joined him for an impromptu picnic. Afterwards, Josh said the painkillers were making him tired and he thought he could take a nap. He insisted Maggie did not need to stay and that he would prefer that she not waste the time tending to him. Maggie did not need too much coaxing. Josh was a big boy with a sprained ankle. He'd be fine and she had no idea when she would ever be back to such magnificence again.

The ever-energized Peter offered to accompany her.

As the two walked away from the lodge, Peter asked, "Where to?"

"Someplace challenging."

"Oh, it's gonna be like that, is it?" Peter laughed. "I believe I have just the place."

He led her down the hill slightly and then veered to the right. They moved quickly as Maggie stayed determined to keep up with him. When he saw her level of commitment he squealed with delight. The puppy was off the leash!

Their pace quickened to an all-out run. For the last twenty-four hours, her senses had been on overload and unable to grasp the multitude of inputs. Running created a whole new experience. The path was rough and rocky. She had to pay attention to the placement of each foot. Sprinting through the mountainous forest caused her to have to focus on what was right in front of her. Her mind became absorbed by the task at hand. At first, it was laborious but, as she found her rhythm, it too became a sensuous experience. Now, instead of feeling like she was standing on the shore looking out across a magnificent green ocean, she felt like she had joined that ocean and found the flow of the current itself.

The altitude and pace pushed her to her limit but she showed no weakness as they at last arrived at what looked like a sheer wall of rock.

Catching her breath, she studied the awesome challenge.

"I'm just kidding." Peter laughed. "But there are some climbable places on the other…"

Maggie was no longer hearing him. She could see it in her head. It was possible. She walked over to the rock, reached up and found the first handhold.

"Are you serious?" His cackles were amplified by the rock wall.

They spent the rest of the afternoon challenging each other, climbing all over the face of the cliffs. When they were exhausted, they sat on a ledge with, yet again, a miraculous view.

"That's pretty amazing!" Peter said, after taking a long gulp of water.

"It is."

"No, I mean, you. Where'd you learn to climb like that?"

"I'm a bit of an adrenaline junkie. I was a gymnast when I was a kid but… I really learned to climb by breaking into buildings."

Peter sat dumbfounded.

"I ran away from home when I was thirteen. Made a living through burglary. Offices, warehouses… churches, we mostly stole techy stuff." As the words exited her mouth, she was shocked. What was she doing? She had often reminisced about these things with Emily, but never had she told someone new. Yet, for reasons quite unclear to her, she was not afraid. If felt right. Was it the mountains? Or Peter?

There was no judgment in Peter's eyes. "Josh know?"

"Not yet. I feel badly about it too. It's just that…my whole life is a lie and when you meet someone under a lie, it's hard to know when to tell the truth."

"Well, Josh can handle it, trust me. It won't make a difference to him."

Won't it? How about if he knew why she left? "I'm actually from Columbus. My father was the pastor at American Harvest."

"I thought you looked familiar. That was my church."

"I know. You recognized me?"

"I wasn't sure, but your eyes are hard to forget. You're Pastor Mike's daughter, aren't you?"

Maggie nodded.

"I remember seeing you in front of the church. You had long tight braids. We probably shared a few picnics together." Peter laughed until he saw her feeble attempt at a smile.

"He was… abusive." As soon as the words were uttered she realized they were a mistake. Even amongst these majestic mountains and this odd but compassionate young man, there were places her mind did not want to go.

Peter processed the new information with a slow deliberate breath. "I'm sorry. Is that why you ran away?"

"Yes… no… I thought so at the time, but now I realize it was more than that. It was everything. The pretense. The show. One night, I just decided I had enough."

"I can't imagine being brought up as a preacher's kid. The whole family's treated like royalty."

"Worse than royalty. My father was seen as a prophet of God, speaking the Truth through his special anointing. But I knew the truth. Right after my parents taught me about Jesus, they taught me how to lie. I got tired of living the lie. But in so many ways, I simply replaced one lie for another."

The conversation paused in comfortable silence. It dawned on her this was the first time she was alone with Peter the Great. Josh was right. There was something uniquely different about him. He was handsome beyond description, of course, but that was not the true uniqueness. If he was aware of his beauty he showed no recognition of it. He had no pretense. No show. He had an air of openness and warmth shared with a constant smirk. Unlike the students she saw every day who took themselves so seriously, Peter acted from the view that underneath it all, life is an inside joke.

"May I ask you something?"

"Open book."

"What's it like out there? Outside of America."

"Something you need to experience for yourself." His gaze was intense as he stated the words. Then he stared out over the mountains. "The first thing I noticed was the silence, the next thing I noticed was the noise. The silence came from the absence of all the Good News. They have monitors in public places, of course, but it's not the constant barrage of propaganda making sure we all see the world the way someone else wants us to see it. Then, there's the noise and I don't just mean audible. There's the multitude of languages all around you and the abundance of different styles of clothing. The diversity of cultures is celebrated and people aren't forced into conformity. I saw arguments erupt in public, people raising their voices and criticizing the government. Stuff that would get someone arrested here was just normal every day happenings there. And the music. The sheer diversity of it is incredible. Instruments and rhythms not based on some Christian criteria but coming from the minds of the artists themselves. Some of its loud and angry, but all of it's art."

Peter tossed a couple of rocks over the edge of the cliff. Maggie turned her attention to the breeze blowing through and how it contrasted on her skin with the warmth of the sun.

"Don't get me wrong, it's no paradise. Life is life and sometimes it's ugly. But it's an honest ugly. And you lose the feeling of everybody watching you all the time, waiting to catch your sin. You live your life being responsible for yourself. I don't know... it's hard to explain. I think my favorite word to describe it is 'doused.'"

"Doused?"

"Yeah. You ever been to Niagara Falls?"

"A family vacation. When I was a kid."

"Remember standing on the Hurricane Platform?"

Maggie laughed. "I do. It knocked me over."

"That's what it's like outside of Christian America, only instead of water, you're doused with freedom."

Maggie snickered.

"I'm serious. It's overwhelming. It's like being blind, deaf and mute your whole life and having those senses for the first time." Peter paused. "Did Josh tell you about our conversation this morning?"

"No, with the injury we didn't really talk."

"He's mad at me because I'm not going back with him."

"Oh, so there was more to the grumpiness than just the ankle?"

"Not only that, I tried to talk him into leaving America. You, too."

"I'd never be able to get a passport."

"You don't need one. You can come with us. It looks like it won't be until next spring but we're all getting out of here. We've got someone working on it for us. We'll probably end up going into Mexico. Once we get there, you'll be amazed how easy it is. People all over are willing to help Americans who get out. Hell, it's big business. The twenty-first century version of the Underground Railroad. You'll never have to lie again… about anything."

Maggie pondered what a life without a protective shell would be like. Could she really be somewhere where she could live authentically? Peter made it sound simple.

"Maggie, I asked Josh to come here because I couldn't leave without at least trying. But, I don't think I made much headway. How do you explain the world to someone who hasn't left the cave?"

"I'm not sure you can."

"You figured it out. What did it for you?"

"My father, of course. Anyone who claims to represent God and then… does what he did… there's something far more wrong there than just one bad apple. Once I lost my faith I never found a reason to have it again. But if we're talking about evidence… I think it's all around us. We claim to be made in the image of God. More divine than animal. But we aren't. Look at the digestive system."

"Okay?"

"Do you have any idea how gross all that is? Oh, people spend millions trying pretty it all up but, essentially, it's the same thing all animals do. Put plants or flesh into our mouths, start grinding away at it. The saliva begins to dissolve the food so it can be passed down this narrow tube into what's essentially an acid filled compost bin. That's when things start getting gross. Stomach acids breaking it all down until, in the end, whatever our body doesn't absorb gets pushed out in this ball of decomposing fecal matter. And we want to claim humans alone were made in the image of God? I bet if the apes could talk they'd say, 'Yeah well, your shit smells just as bad as mine, you pompous mammal.'"

Peter burst into applause. "Yes! That's perfect! I think the same thing every time I see a dog owner picking up shit in a little plastic baggie."

"Exactly." Maggie joined in the laughter. "And let's not forget the reproductive system. I mean, we're taught to glorify this thing as a gift from God. A means of passing on His Love to a new generation. Two becoming one flesh and all that bullshit, and, then, we use the same parts we piss with?"

Peter rolled with laughter and for the briefest of moments she was alarmed he might roll off the cliff.

She was feeling lighter and it was not just the altitude. So many thoughts dancing in her mind could finally be articulated. "I've got a theory. You know, how in the Garden, Adam and Eve covered up their nakedness after eating the fruit?"

"Sure."

"Well, I don't believe people started wearing clothes out of a sense of modesty for their sexual organs. I think they started wearing them because people got sick and tired of seeing each other's plumbing. No toilets, no toilet paper. At some point some chieftain said, 'Jesus, people, would you cover up that shit."

Peter's guffaws echoed across the mountainous ocean. When the last of them disappeared into the current of forest, they sat in silence for a moment.

"But I think the greatest link between humans and animals came to me when I was hiking once. We took a break on this hillside and I noticed there was this doe, with two fawns, walking through, not more than twenty yards from me. They took a few steps and then would pause, listening. Especially the mother. I realized then what unites us with animals more than anything else."

"What's that?"

"Fear. I mean it's simple really, an animal born without fear in this world would never live to reproduce. So, its ingrained in us, at the most primitive level. Animals create shells and other defenses because of fear. Humans create societies, nations, and religions for the same reason. Everything from crossing the street to wars between nations. It's all about fear. The same fear every other animal on earth experiences."

Peter nodded.

"We try so hard to distance ourselves from the animals, from nature. We cover ourselves in fancy cloth, build elaborate houses and cities, do whatever we can to insulate ourselves from the natural world. Religion does it for us too. Creates an alternative world because the real one is too scary to deal with."

The two sat in silence, sharing their moment of bonding. The fact was not lost on Maggie that Peter was probably the first person in her whole life she had been completely honest with. Honesty felt good.

"Then I started nursing school. The diseases, the birth defects, all of it. There's no godly explanation why a baby is born without legs or hands or can't walk. When I saw those babies… impossible to believe in a loving God."

Peter nodded. "Yeah, I came to a similar understanding. Every year millions of kids die before their fifth birthday. I can imagine every single one of their parents are praying with everything they have for God to save their children. If there is a God, He either can't help or doesn't want to." Peter picked up a stone and threw it over the edge of the cliff. "But I don't see any of this convincing Josh."

"Probably not. I don't think he's capable of seeing the evil but he has a great heart."

"That's why if we could just get him out of there. Get him into a library, a real library, and his heart will show him the answer."

But Maggie knew it was not that simple and Peter should have realized it. He was naïve, or had simply forgotten, how deeply rooted the delusion was.

Chapter Thirty

That evening the whole gang insisted on a campfire as a going-away party. At first, Maggie balked at the idea saying she did not want anyone making a fuss but Peter assured her. "Oh, you guys are just the excuse. Levy's wine is ready."

At the campfire, Levy arrived with a hefty sampling of his "fruit wine." He introduced it with a smirk and acknowledged "wine" was a gracious term for what was actually in the bag but he went on to explain he didn't think it was "hooch," either.

Tirza showed up with a guitar at which she quickly demonstrated how adept she was. But, to both Josh and Maggie's utmost surprise, when Tirza started to sing, it was with a deep yet tender voice, in total contrast to her usual sarcastic demeanor. Her vocals were strong, yet vulnerable, like a gust of mountain air swirling before dissipating into the surrounding forest.

It became obvious that the little community had done this many times before as they were almost choreographed. Peter had a wooden box that he sat on helping to tap out accompanying rhythms. Many of the tunes were bluegrass with a crowd favorite being about some guy named Dooley who had a still. Each time the name "Dooley" came up in the song, the whole group, in a gale of laughter, would drink a toast to Levy.

Other songs were strictly folk. "Songs from a by-gone era." One such song sent eerie tingles up Maggie's spine as it was a story of Valley People rising up and killing all the Mountain People for the buried treasure. The treasure turned out to be nothing more than a plaque with a wish for "Peace on Earth." When the song ended the group grew silent, their pensive faces illuminated by the flickering fire.

Between songs, the wine was passed and stories were told. Maggie noticed few of the stories were about their families or anything that happened prior to their arrival at Abhayagiri. Most of them had to do with the maintenance and upkeep of the place. The trials and errors of trying to repair the ancient plumbing which often ended with someone covered in mud and howling at the moon. They politely teased each other, prodding Mari about her sing-song Hispanic accent and goading Manda for being as strong as a bull. Ed was teased for barely talking and Levy was labeled the "old man." It seemed everyone had something but no one took it more than Peter. Peter was often portrayed in the stories as having to be moving all the time. There were running jokes that he was on cocaine but too selfish to share with the rest of them. It was all done with loving humor and Peter took it in stride with his persistent grin and dancing eyes.

It was a makeshift family just like the Office had been. A group of people, partly by happenstance, partly by choice, bonded together to help each other and by doing that they created something more. This group was reveling in their freedom. It was very much like when she had first started living at the Office. How comforting and warm the place had felt in the evenings when they were safely locked away, circled up around an old space heater, teasing one another as they shared stories. It was the kind of activity that created a family. Each of them had their reason for being there, each of them had their hidden suffering, and yet, there was the unacknowledged acceptance that no matter how they might have been misfits elsewhere, here each of them belonged. So, as Maggie sipped on a bottomless glass of wine, she found herself floating between nostalgic sadness for a lost time and the gratitude of being able to feel that same warmth again.

At some point Josh reached over and took her hand. There, they sat together silently as they settled into the ancient yet surprisingly comfortable camping chairs. Often, they would catch each other's eyes and smile; other times they would lightly squeeze the other's hand.

The wine came around and around in a seemingly never-ending rotation. Maggie completely lost track of how much she drank but did recognize the light-headedness when it arrived.

Eventually, however, they began to leave. The young parents were the first to go, taking with them their precious cargo, who had fallen sound asleep at his mother's breast. Manda followed soon after, leaving without a word to anyone. A few moments later, Levy stood up, he thanked everyone for a wonderful evening and they verbally applauded his wine. Then to Maggie's shock, for there had been no previous indication, Tirza stood up and, carrying her guitar with one hand, she interlocked the other around Levy's waist and the two of them walked off toward Levy's cabin. Maggie looked around the small group and caught Mari's eyes. "Shhh." Mari smiled and held a finger over her lips. "They like to pretend we don't notice."

Silence now enveloped the campfire as there was no more guitar. It was a silence like the final scene in an epic movie when all the characters had made it through whatever they had to get through and they were sighing with relief and hope. For a long time, they simply stared into the mesmerizing flames. Maggie quietly wished time itself would stop and they could stay like that forever.

Mari was the next to stand and, as she did, she warned the others of not doing so too quickly. On shaky legs, she turned and tried to bend down to give Maggie a hug. She lost her balance and the two of them almost went tumbling over in the aluminum chair. Laughing, Maggie worked her way to her feet and found herself dizzily looking directly into the moist eyes of Mari. There they hugged properly.

"I know we just met," Mari whispered. "But I'm gonna miss you. I made a new amiga only to lose her."

Maggie began to cry. "Me, too."

"Maybe we see each other again?" Mari asked.

"Maybe," was all Maggie could mutter. Mari then kissed Maggie on the cheek and used her to help her move over to Josh. She bent down a bit and gave Josh a quick hug. She thanked him for coming and said she decided he was a "buen hombre." She then made her way, stumbling a bit and giggling at herself, back towards the lodge. Ed followed her, silently nodding to Maggie and Josh as he left. They heard Ed offer to carry Mari which caused her to cackle. "No, I'm fine… just point me… which room is mine?"

They heard the door open and shut, ending their slight concern Mari was going to make it there safely. Then they all listened to Ed clump his way to his room.

A heavy stillness hung in the air.

Finally, Peter stood and clasped Josh at his elbows. The two of them stared at each other for a long time, each looking like the words they had to say were locked behind closed lips. Peter then turned to Maggie and gave her a warm hug. The campfire danced in his sparkling eyes, giving them the appearance of a trick photo taken into a mirror where the images are reflected repeatedly into infinity. "It's been an absolute pleasure getting to know you, milady."

"The pleasure was all mine."

"Well, I'll see you two in the morning. I'd kind of like to leave right after breakfast, okay? I've got a couple stops to make on the way back."

"Sure, whatever's best for you," answered Josh.

"Great. Then, the SV is there so you don't have to walk, there's some more wood over there if you went to kick up the fire again, otherwise I'll be off. See you in the morning."

And just like that, Josh and Maggie found themselves alone... by a smoldering campfire... beneath a star-filled sky... on the top of an isolated mountain.

It took but a moment for Josh to turn in his chair so he could place his hand on her forearm. Gently, he caressed the tender skin on her inner arm; she was flooded with waves of warmth. She turned in her own chair to move closer to him. She felt his lips on hers, ever so gently at first, but quickly becoming a series of longer and stronger kisses. His free hand was roaming over her neck and shoulders as he urgently pulled her closer to him. Her aluminum chair was up on only two legs but Josh's chair was preventing her from falling over. His hand touched her left breast. Accidentally? She felt it again, this time his hand grazed over it longer. When she felt his hand begin a third time she grabbed his wrist and placed his hand on her breast. At first, his hand resisted but, seconds later, it gave into a far more powerful instinct.

She rode the wave of passion as they explored each other's faces and necks. She became aware of his now emboldened hand finding its way down her stomach and under her shirt. She had never been one for any kind of lacy underwear and that included her no-nonsense choice of bras but when she felt his fingers caressing every fiber, she realized it all meant something entirely different to Josh.

Increasingly passionate, his hand found its way under her bra. The sensation was like a tsunami crashing against her insides. She involuntarily gasped and felt him slightly increase the pressure, encouraged by her response. She felt the evening air sensually touch her breast as he gently lifted it. He then bent down to kiss it but the camping chairs were not built for such acrobatics.

For a moment, both wobbled. Josh stopped and, with stifled annoyance, righted their chairs. She fixed her clothes and took his hand.

"I think I've had too much to drink. I'm sorry," he said.

"For what?"

He shrugged his shoulders and stood up on his one good leg. The fire was nothing but embers at this point and safely inside the ring. Josh picked up his crutches. Somewhere deep inside her was a voice warning her to just let him go to his room but, whether fueled by alcohol or passion, she did not want this enchanted night to be over.

He began slowly, awkwardly, to make his way toward the SV. Maggie stood up and reluctantly followed him.

She thought of Peter and how he had described himself feeling doused in freedom. Then, she had an idea. "Stay with me tonight," she said. "You're in no shape to go hobbling up the mountain anyway, even with an SV."

Josh paused in his efforts. She came around to the front of him and looked into his tired bloodshot eyes. "It'll be okay. Let's just spend this last magical night in these magnificent mountains in each other's arms."

Josh's voice croaked something incomprehensible as he nodded and turned toward the lodge. Once inside her room, Josh let her lead him over to the bed. They kicked off their shoes and laid across the top of the cotton bedspread. There was a light blanket folded neatly at the bottom and Maggie used that to lay across the two of them.

"Sure, this is solomon?"

"Wonderful," she answered placing her head on his chest. She always avoided physical contact, especially with males. But somehow this seemed okay. Deep inside her, she was aware of the potential for a panic attack but the anxiety seemed asleep… or drunk.

Moments ticked by as Maggie listened to Josh's heart beat return to normal after the exertion. Gradually, however, she could feel it increasing in its beats again. She lifted her head and was met with his lips on hers. His kiss was urgently passionate. She returned it in kind.

Now, there were no camping chairs to get in the way. His hand moved freely from one breast to another. She in turn slipped her hand under his shirt and felt the heat of his skin against her palm. His hand was soon under her shirt and was again fumbling with the unfamiliar article of clothing. Without a word, she pulled away, propped herself up on her knees and removed her shirt. He said nothing. She unclasped her bra and took it off as well. The only light in the room was provided by the moon through the window but it was enough as Josh stared transfixed at her naked breasts.

She reached out and removed his shirt and then snuggled next to him. Seconds later, they were again kissing. He was now unencumbered in his caressing. She murmured as he took her nipple between his thumb and finger. For the first time in her life she felt the passionate kiss of a man on her breast; a kiss as much concerned with her pleasure as his. Somewhere in the darkest corner of her mind, a shadow lurked yet her focus was on the warmth and softness of the present moment. This was what intimacy was supposed to look like... to feel like.

As his hands softly explored her body, every nerve was brought to attention. She allowed her own hands to explore his, running them up and down his chest and back. They continued like that, touching, caressing, stroking, yet no more clothes came off. In the end, the lateness of the night and the wine allowed the passion to cool like the embers from their campfire and they fell sound asleep in each other's arms.

Listening to Josh's heavy rhythmic breathing in her last moments of consciousness, Maggie went over in her mind what she had just done. She had made love. Maybe not the complete act, but they had gone far enough for her to know she could if she had wanted to. What had she told Peter? The thing that united all living beings more than anything else... fear. She realized she had been carrying her own fear. A fear she suppressed deep within. It was the fear that her father had damaged her, if not physically than mentally where she could not feel... what she had just felt. As she lay there, her sobriety returning, she knew she was okay. Her father had not taken that from her, when the time was right, she would, not only be able to, but enjoy it as well.

Maybe the human body wasn't so gross after all.

Chapter Thirty One

Maggie awoke, the dawn's sunlight pouring in through the skylight. Something was different. Hangover? No, maybe she was a bit groggy but she was feeling fine; she was feeling better than fine. Then, she remembered.

She reached her hands up into the air, in a celebratory grab for the heavens. She was naked from the waist up, save for the thin blanket, and it felt as if every exposed cell was breathing in the mountain air. She closed her eyes and inhaled slowly. As she breathed in, she could feel her stomach rise, as she breathed out, her stomach fell. She paid attention to this process, experiencing it as if for the first time. While she did, she became aware of another sensation. It was a tingling of sorts but she decided a more apt description would be a glistening of her senses. The way a light spring rain enhances every color. Is this, what a woman feels?

Then, it occurred to her, she was in bed alone. With the reluctance of having to get up on a cold winter morning, Maggie brought her attention off the glow she felt and turned it to her surroundings. Josh, fully clothed in the previous night's wardrobe, was seated in silhouette in the chair across the room. Though she could barely make out the features of his face, he was exuding an aura of pensiveness.

She guessed what it was about. "Good morning," she said cheerfully.

"Morning," he murmured, and then asked, "You solomon?"

"Wonderful. Maybe a little hung over."

"I mean, about last night."

"Yeah… I am."

"Oh, Maggie, I'm so sorry. It was a moment of weakness…"

"Josh, last night was perfect. Think about it. The fire, the music, the mountain, the wine…"

At the mention of wine, Josh smacked his forehead with unsettling force. "I know, I had too much. I never should have had any after the pain pills."

"What I meant was, the setting was perfect. We were surrounded by all these wonderful people, up here in these mystical mountains. Maybe, we had a little too much wine but come on... how perfect could everything be? And we didn't actually... you know..."

Josh sat quietly for a moment replaying the words. "No. It was a sin. We need to ask for forgiveness." He quickly knelt next to the bed and before she could say anything else he prayed. "Dear Lord, please forgive us for our sins. Your word tells us to abstain from sexual immorality, that each one of us knows how to control his own body in holiness and honor. Please forgive us, Lord, and know that we will do everything in our power to make sure we don't sin again. *For the wages of sin is death.* In Jesus' name, Amen."

Maggie found the prayer to be disconcerting. Josh just needed to calm down.

When Josh finished, he lifted his head but the sternness of his face was fixed. "It'll be fine."

He excused himself to allow Maggie to get dressed. Maggie cleaned up as best she could with a shower towel before putting on a new outfit. She packed her few things and tidied up. Before leaving, she stood at the door. She had felt welcomed by this room, and, here, she had discovered something about herself. Now, saying goodbye, she was surprised to find sadness to be a secondary emotion. Mostly she felt grateful.

She met Josh in the dining room along with Mari, Tirza, Peter, and Ed, who had all pitched in to provide a delicious gourmet breakfast. During the morning conversation, concerning mostly the bonfire and Levi's contribution, Maggie savored every moment, knowing she would soon be leaving this serene environment. Josh, however, spent more time mindlessly playing with his food than eating it.

After breakfast, Peter took Josh, still hobbled and complaining about the pain, up to his cabin in the SV to get his things. Maggie was left with Mari and Tirza. They did their dishes first and then returned to the table to sip tea.

"Everything okay?" Mari asked. "I mean between you and Josh?"

"You noticed."

"Like a gosling among ducks," said Tirza.

"Pretty obvious," said Mari. "And I could tell it wasn't about leaving."

"No, that would be me. With Josh, it's something else." Maggie looked at the two young women who had so quickly become her friends. "We... um... last night, we got caught up in things and... ended up sleeping together."

"For the first time?" Tirza laughed and then, realizing she was being rude. "I mean, really?"

"We didn't even... actually... but we definitely crossed a line for Josh." Maggie took a deep breath. It was the second time in less than a day she was being open and honest. God, it felt good.

"Yeah," Mari acknowledged. "How do you feel about it?"

Maggie felt her cheeks flush and an involuntary grin crept across her face.

Mari giggled. Tirza cackled.

After a few moments, where Maggie was aware of her face returning to normal, Mari reached out and placed her hand on top of Maggie's. Mari looked deeply into Maggie's eyes. "Peter talk to you yesterday? About coming with us?"

"Yeah."

"You can, you know."

"I couldn't. I've got school and a job. And Josh."

"I don't see how you can go back into that hypocrisy."

"Tirza!" scolded Mari. She turned to Maggie. "Don't listen to her. You do what's best for you... and Josh."

"Josh would never... his dad's a director of DHS."

"So?" Tirza asked. "My dad's a fucking general."

"It isn't just that, it's Josh himself. He'd never..."

Mari silently studied Maggie. "Well, the door's always open."

Shortly thereafter Peter and Josh arrived. Josh was no longer using his crutches but was limping gingerly. "I'm fine," he said with angry determination.

The goodbyes were simple but tearful. Maggie found herself overwhelmed by emotions. Mari especially was difficult to leave. They promised to find ways to keep in touch but they were hollow statements. Mari was cut off from the world; Maggie was about to go back into that very watchful world. It was going to be impossible.

The ride back down to Denver was horrendous. Not only did Maggie have to deal with the jostling of the antique vehicle, which no longer felt quaint, she also had to deal with a sulking boyfriend who was upset with both Peter and her. Then, there was Peter who rambled on and on about the plans to finish reconstruction by winter. The more Peter spoke, the more annoyed Josh grew. Maggie shut them both out and spent as much time as she could napping and staring out the window. The views were nothing but magnificent yet, from the point of view of a vehicle taking her away from it all, she already felt cut off.

Gradually the signs of civilization returned. First, a few houses high up in the mountains and then more and more of them until they began to pass through the villages that were dotted through the Colorado Mountains.

Finally, something looked familiar as Peter brought the SUV to a halt behind Vanessa's lumber yard. A cab, Josh had called for, was waiting for them.

They all got out of the vehicle. Maggie felt out of place as the two men stared intently at each other. Josh was the first to speak. "So, what do I need to say to get you in the cab with us?"

"I was just about to ask you what I needed to say to get you to come back with me," said Peter.

"This isn't a game, Peter."

"I know. It's okay, Josh. I'm happy."

"And, that's what life's all about?"

"Yeah, Josh, near as I can figure."

"This isn't a life, Peter, it's a vacation."

It looked as if Peter was going to say something else but he swallowed his words. Maggie could only watch as they embraced, looking like two anchored boats hopelessly trying to come together. When Peter was finally able to pull away he turned to Maggie, tears streaming down his face. "It was wonderful to get to know you."

"And I, you. I'm gonna miss you, and Abhayagiri." Maggie bit back the tears herself. She knew even having just met him, this strange young man had made a serious impact on her life. One she would never forget and always be grateful for.

With that, Peter climbed back into the vehicle. On his way out, he spun the tires in the loose gravel and blared the horn.

"No wonder so many people died in those things," Josh said with an attempt at a grin that did nothing to conceal his broken heart. "Dangerous."

Maggie reached out, putting her arm around his back. The possibility that he would pull away crossed her mind but he did not. Instead, he put his own arm around her. "I think my hangover's finally faded."

She smiled and kissed his tear-soaked cheek. "It'll be okay."

Shortly thereafter they found themselves once again on the train. It would be another long ride but, this time it would be in the lap of luxury.

As they settled into their seats, Josh let out a sigh. "Oh, this is nice, haven't sat in a decent chair all weekend."

Maggie had to admit it felt good, for, what the Abhayagiri community acquired in freedom, they gave up quite a bit in comfort.

"We need to talk," Josh said when the train was on its way.

She did not want to as the emotions and thoughts in her whirled in confusion but she nodded.

"I'm not sure how to put this but, the bottom line is, I don't think we should so easily dismiss our sin last night."

"What do you mean? Should we do some penance?"

"This is serious."

"What we did last night was an expression of… how we feel about each other. And you're tainting it."

"It was a sin. If we don't live a righteous life, God will not bless our union. *Let the marriage bed be undefiled, for God will judge the sexually immoral and adulterous.*"

"Yeah, I get that, but can't we be human as well?"

"Of course, we can. We are human, that's why we must overcome our evil nature."

"Our evil nature?"

Josh rolled his eyes and took an exasperated breath. "When Adam and Eve ate the forbidden fruit, sin was introduced into the world and that sin is what we carry with us. Why don't you know this?"

"Yeah, I get it, Josh. Original sin, but doesn't the Bible say people are made in God's image?"

"Yeah, *So God created man in his own image, male and female.* What's the point?"

"It seems to me something made in the image of God can't possibly have an evil nature."

"Where do you learn this stuff?"

"It's in the Bible."

"You're not interpreting that correctly."

At that precise moment, Maggie was struck with the memory of Becca often referring to "lamps on the path of life." For Maggie, Josh's comment became one of those lamps.

It was the conviction in his statement.

In that instant, she realized she could not stay with him. She could not love him, certainly not in the way he needed her to and not in the way she needed either. The thought popped into her head as much a matter of fact as the grasslands being flat. The thought brought a deep sense of sadness that distracted her from what he was saying. All she could think as she sat there was, she was going to have to find a way to break up with him.

At some point, Josh noticed she was not mentally present and he pulled up his Bible on screen. He spoke with a rapid nervousness, citing passages to go along with his points. "The Bible says in Colossians three verse two: *Set your minds on things that are above, not on things that are on earth.* We haven't been doing that. I mean think about it, we barely talk about God at all. But, a relationship's only going to work if God is put in the center of it. See? The Bible teaches us: *But each person is tempted when he is lured and enticed by his own desire.* We gave into that temptation because we weren't *sober minded and watchful.* I'm saying all these things because I… I want this to work, you know? But, a relationship needs to be built on righteousness. *Sow for yourselves righteousness; reap steadfast love.* If we don't live in righteousness, we will not create real love. So…."

She wanted to stop. To tell him there was no reason to go any further but she could not find the words.

Josh paused to take a deep breath. "I think last night was a wake-up call. We need to seriously heed this warning. Now, I'm not dictating but I've been thinking about this all morning. First, I think when I come and pick you up for our dates, before we go out, we should take a moment to pray, maybe a reading from the Bible. I also think we should end each night in prayer. Pray a hedge of protection from the temptations of Satan. And… and I think we should be going to church together. We could start going to the student services on campus. The music's fantastic and they have Bible studies that are geared toward the needs of college students and… young couples. Their credits are okayed for transfer to our home churches. It'll be the start of something we create ourselves, from the beginning."

He really believed he was her knight in shining armor come to rescue her. In a way, she had always known this, perhaps even encouraged it, but now it seemed condescendingly arrogant. This was not the path for her. She had just been fooling herself into thinking that it was. Jake was right she had never left the Office but it was not because she had been afraid to, it had been because she never wanted to. Going to church, to school, were just turns in a game. A game she never wanted to play. A game she only played because it was the best way to take care of Emily. A game… she no longer needed to play.

Yet there was Josh. Good decent Josh who never asked for this. He was searching for a clean Christian woman whose past was church, youth groups, and praise concerts; not streets, burglaries, and rape. What had she been thinking? Why had she even opened the door a little? She could have stopped it at any time, at coffee, or even before. Why had she not ended it when she found out who is father was? Or what church he attended? Why had she even let it get that far? The night of the party... when she was bartending, she could have... should have... fixed his drink and pretended to be too busy to talk. Instead, she had let herself enjoy his attention, then enjoy his touch and then... it had been selfish of her. She had lost herself in her desire, she had not thought of what it would mean to Josh. Now she had dug the hole even deeper.

It was not even Josh himself. It was the life he offered. The life of church services, praise concerts, jubilant celebrations of Christian America. It would be a life of wifely duties, maintaining a house for him, raising children. She would be required to serve on committees at church and school, smilingly endorsing all the "right" things while keeping her real thoughts private, even from Josh. It would be an extremely comfortable life with every one of her physical needs met with luxury and health and wealth... and it would be a return to the life she had fled.

She could see it so clearly now. Everything, that is, except the words to say to Josh.

He was slowing down, like a hungry man who had received his fill. Now, he was beginning to slouch a bit lower and starting to twist his body. He took her hand and murmured. "Good night."

She did not think she would sleep but soon succumbed to the plush chair. When they awoke, they went to the dining car. Maggie found the train food less exciting this time than it was on the way out. Then, it was fuel for an adventure. Now it was just fuel.

Josh began the conversation at dinner by apologizing if he had come on too strong earlier. "I was feeling like the whole trip was a bust. I came out here to bring Peter home or to at least get him to seriously consider it but I failed. I don't think I made a dent in his thinking. Then, I sprained my ankle and looked like a fool in front of you and then the wine and... I just failed. I left Ohio feeling like a Joseph and now I'm coming home defeated, dragging my shield behind me."

"Hey, Josh, you never looked like a fool in front of me. I haven't seen you in any other way than the sweet man that you are. As for Peter, I'm not sure what your expectations were but I wouldn't be surprised. He seems really happy."

"Happy running around wild on a mountain top?"

"Yeah, I think he is."

"You've only just met him. You didn't know him back in high school. He wasn't like this. He was committed. I can't just leave him, that's not what friends do."

"What're you gonna do?"

"Not sure beyond talking to Mrs. Marone again. She'll know."

Once back amongst the buildings and congestion, Maggie felt her stomach shrink. After the spaciousness of the mountains, the city of Columbus seemed small and suffocating. Just a few days before, it had been her whole world. Now, it seemed like nothing more than a shed in the back of someone's yard.

Josh accompanied her all the way to her apartment. It was early evening and yet the sunbaked humidity clung heavily in the air. At the door, he apologized again for "being overly zealous" and promised that they would talk again soon. He kissed her and held her for several moments.

As he walked away, Maggie was overcome with sadness. She was going to have to hurt him.

Chapter Thirty Two

Josh slumped onto the bench overlooking Maggie's apartment. He had just finished yet another long loop as he painfully survived the endless night. All night, he had felt like his internal organs were exploding over and over in his chest. Sitting caused the feelings to intensify but walking was only a temporary distraction. Increasingly temporary as his throbbing ankle demanded more and more breaks.

It had been a couple of days since Josh and Maggie had returned from Fearless Mountain. Days they had spent apart, communicating only through vague texts. Days he spent thinking. They had fallen off the path but it was a sin God would forgive... if they repented. Judging by Maggie's near silence on the train ride home, Josh had decided he had come on too strong. He knew it was up to him to lead but he had to lead with honor, in ways that sanctified her. As Josh replayed their dates and time together, he realized she never talked about her relationship with God. He wondered if her distance from her family might also be a distance from God. He used the DHS computers to check her church and was shocked to see how small it was. Why would she choose to go there? Still, it was a church in good standing as far as DHS was concerned.

Maggie, of course, was not the only thing on his mind these last couple of days. There was Peter. Josh had failed in his quest to rescue his friend. Failed miserably. At the office, he found Fearless Mountain on the map. Just as he suspected, DHS knew the little community was there. As a matter of fact, Josh was shocked to find that there was an agent there. Who was it? Levy? He was the oldest and best candidate. Ed? Josh doubted he had the intelligence, unless the whole gentle giant thing was a ruse? Manda? She had certainly acted strangely but, as a girl, it was unlikely. Or how about the mysterious Gustavo? Josh had never even seen him but Mari said he was ex-military.

Whomever he was, it was just a matter of time before the agent discovered Peter was on the NBL and then it would be vacation over. It would be so much better for Peter to turn himself in, accept his family's help, give the loving arms of the Lord another try. If Peter would only stop running. Peter claimed not to be the Prodigal Son but, maybe, he just had not yet hit rock bottom. Josh prayed Peter would lose his stubbornness long before then. The question for Josh was how to help him. How does a soul knitted to another help when the other soul is dying?

Josh was not at all sure he had an answer to that question. He put a call into Mrs. Marone to see if she would meet with him again. He found out she had made the move to Washington. In his message, he stated he urgently needed to talk to her about Peter. He prayed she had the time to return his call.

So, it was with a head full of worries, Josh entered the restaurant only to be confronted by Maggie's sad sullen face. She did not make it far into the conversation before beginning to cry. She acknowledged the timing was sudden and maybe inappropriate, knowing what they had done just a few days earlier, but she felt it would be wrong to lead him on for even a minute. She went into a long explanation of how she was completely unsure of where she wanted to go in life. She no longer felt a desire to be a nurse. She talked about how she missed Emily and she made it sound like Emily had been her sole responsibility. She talked about enjoying the trip and how she wanted to see more of the country.

"Are you breaking up with me?" Josh asked, not wanting an answer.

"Uh-uh-m…" she stuttered and then more tears. "I'm so sorry, Josh."

From there, the conversation disintegrated into a chaotic rumble of tears, jumbled sentences, and incessant waves of irrationality. In the end, however, she had held firm. She was ending their young relationship.

Josh insisted on walking her home and it was in front of her door she gave him the letter. She explained she had not known if she would be able to say the things needing to be said so she had written them down. She told him how sorry she was and knew she was hurting him but also hoped he would be able to forgive her someday. She kissed him on the cheek and went into her apartment.

He stood outside for a few minutes hoping she would come back but to no avail. So, he started to walk the streets of Columbus, the same streets Maggie and he had strolled together. At first, he had no plan, but the later it became, the more walking he was doing, and with his constant prayers for guidance, he started to realize one. It made a lot of sense. Her sister had to move back home, Becca was never around, so Maggie was feeling alone. He should have seen that a long time ago. She was going through all this, questioning a lot of things and he took her to some fantasyland. Yeah, real smart. Then, he got drunk and was immoral with her. No wonder she's so confused.

Husbands, love your wives, just as Christ loved the church and gave himself up for her to make her holy, cleansing her by the washing with water through the word.

Maggie may not be his wife... yet... but he had to help her, not abandon her.

He pulled out the letter and read through it again. It seemed her biggest argument was she needed time to find herself. Wow! Did that sound like a fucking hippie or what? Sounded like something she picked up at Fearless Mountain. Maggie had spent a great deal of time with those two girls. What had they said to her? And Peter? Maggie and Peter had their hike together when Josh was laid up on the porch. Had Peter told Maggie what he had told Josh? Had he filled her mind with his heresies?

What a mistake it had been to bring her! He smacked his palm against his forehead. The whack of flesh upon flesh seemed loud in the stillness of the night.

This was a ludicrous idea too. What was she going to do, wander around looking for God? The best way to find God was to be a member of a church... a real church... enroll in the best Bible studies and prayer groups and voila! God reveals Himself. There's no need to go on some cockamamie search for Him! For whatever reason, whether her parents failed her or she had just drifted away, she was a child spiritually. It would be just like a child to go and wander but it takes the child's parents to show her the way. This was not about dominating her, this was about loving her.

He walked another giant loop, this time with some conviction and lessening of pain. The real problem, he decided, was just like everything else in his life he had failed to step up. This was why God had set it up this way; it was to teach him a lesson. When the time came for them to get married he would need to become the head of the household. *The head of man is Christ, the head of a wife is her husband.* They were like two little kids playing together but not having responsibilities. Well, a relationship was a responsibility and they needed to start acting that way.

The city took on an air of eeriness. All around him, people were sound asleep, rejuvenating themselves before another day. It was the cycle of life and at this time of night, a time he rarely experienced, he could feel the history. Every night for hundreds of years, right there, in that exact spot, people slept, the seasons changed, the architecture changed, the people changed. The young replaced the old only to be replaced by the young once again. It was history. And now it was his time. His time to step up, to live his life as a man, a Joseph.

As the blackness of the night slowly became gray and the lights in the surrounding buildings began to flick on, Josh found himself energized. He had survived the night without sleeping and his mind felt clearer for it. It was time to step up.

He stood for a moment and said one final prayer asking for the strength to be the spiritual warrior he knew he could be. At the door entrance, he buzzed and waited. There was no answer. He buzzed again. Nothing. At this point, Josh called. No answer. A young woman Josh knew lived in an apartment on Maggie's floor came bopping out of the door. She recognized Josh. "Hey, she's not answering?"

"No and I'm sure she's up there."

"Well, come on in," she said with a smile, holding the door. Josh hesitated but then leaped up the steps. Once inside, he took the elevator to her apartment and knocked directly on her door. No answer. He pounded the door. Still nothing. He pounded again, this time louder than he had wanted to. He heard the elevator door open and was hopeful for just a second it might be Maggie but saw it was a security officer. A young man who looked to be about his age.

"May I help you?" he asked.

"Oh, I'm sorry. Maggie's not answering, I know she's in there."

The young man knocked on the door. Josh fought his irritation, how was his knock any different? "Do you have a pass key?"

"Yeah," the guard said and reached for his belt. A second later the door was open. "I'll ask you to stay here, solomon?"

"Um, yeah, sure," Josh said.

Josh heard the officer call Maggie's name as he walked about the apartment. A few seconds later, he was back at the door. "No one's here."

"What? That's impossible." Josh forced his way into the room. The guard shouted his protest. Josh ran through the apartment, shouting her name, checking every closet, behind every curtain. The apartment was serenely clean and organized, all beds made, not so much as a spoon out of place.

"I dropped her off here last night. I never went home, so where did she go?" Josh thought for a moment and then turned to the officer. "Cameras. You must have cameras."

"Of course, we do. How do you think I saw you banging on the door?"

"Let's go see 'em."

"Now wait a minute, joe. Look, I get it but there's no sign of any struggle here. I'm not gonna start a full-scale investigation over a girl who just wanted to get away from her boyfriend. I'd lose my job."

The words were biting. Why would this guy think Maggie wanted to get away from him? Then, something occurred to Josh. It was a thought he had only entertained as a joke but he flipped open his phone and showed the man his DHS ID. The blood drained from the young man's face and he suddenly looked like a six-year-old boy dressed up in a police uniform. "Oh my God... I mean, goodness, I am so sorry but I didn't know, I mean, you didn't identify yourself... and you're so... so... young... I mean young looking, of course..."

Josh had a feeling the apology would have rambled on for another ten minutes if he had not interrupted it. "The cameras," he said, concealing the quiver in his voice.

"Oh, yes, sir, down in the office. We can watch them from there. This way."

Josh followed the young man to the security office and they pulled up the video. They quickly found the point Maggie had come into the building and entered her apartment. Her neighbor, the girl who had let Josh in, came in an hour later and once again the cameras showed nothing but a safe and secure hallway. They sped through the vid as fast as they could and then the guard shouted, "Wait, there!" There she was, leaving her apartment with a backpack stuffed to the brim. Josh glanced at the time: 2:38. The cameras followed her down the hallway, into the elevator, and again as she walked out of the building. That was it.

Josh slammed his forehead with his palm. "Dammit. I should have just stayed. If I hadn't walked all over the place, I would have seen her leave."

"Easy, joe, I mean, sir. She looks solomon. No one abducted her or anything."

Josh barely heard what he said, his mind was reeling with thoughts, questions. Becca? Maggie mentioned Becca was always staying with her friend, what was her name? Sheba? Maybe Maggie went there. What about her parents? Maybe she just went home. After all Emily had to go back, so, maybe, Maggie just needed some time to be with her again. But, why the middle of the night? Josh then realized something even more important. He did not know where her parents lived or even what church they belonged to. All he knew was she was from Cleveland. Well, this was something that had to change as well, he would no longer be cut out of her family.

At this point, for most people, Josh fully understood, the trail would be cold, but Josh had just been introduced to what it meant to have that special ID in his possession. Being DHS opened doors. The first being to simply report to work.

As he walked into the office, Marie remarked, "Sleep in your clothes?"

He went back to his cubicle and turned on the computer. Seconds later he was in the DHS program. He started with her name, Maggie Anderson. Then, went to Margret Anderson. Then, stared at the screen. Something was not right here. Maybe, he did not understand the program. Marie was the only one he trusted enough to take into his confidence. "I have to talk to her!" he pleaded.

With an assuring smile and the expertise of a long-time veteran, Marie went exploring. Soon, she uncovered nothing. The address in Cleveland was phony, and the listed church had no record of a family of Andersons with daughters named Margret and Emily. From all indications, Maggie Anderson seemed to appear out of nowhere in Columbus when she was fifteen years old. Poof! Josh's mind went numb. What did this mean?

They went to Maggie's current church site. Josh read through the names as quickly as he could. There it was, not "Sheba," but "Sherah." Sherah Easton.

Twenty minutes later, he was standing in front of Sherah's apartment building. He realized he not only didn't get any sleep, but he had not eaten anything either. His hands were shaking uncontrollably and his stomach was exploding but he prayed to keep his spirit strong. He had to find her.

"Um...hello?" he heard a female voice through the intercom.

"Becca?"

"No."

"Rebecca Sanders. I know she doesn't live here but I have to talk to her."

"Who are you?"

Josh was reaching for his ID when a different female voice asked, "Josh?"

Josh knew his face could be seen, he forced a reassuring smile. "Becca? Yeah, it's me... um nice to meet you, I've heard a lot... look, I really need to talk to you."

From the moment he walked into Sherah's apartment, he felt he understood Maggie better. Both Becca and Sherah had their hair short, like Maggie's. Also, judging from all of the outdoor gear scattered about the apartment, he could see the girls shared an interest in athletics. Josh made a mental note that once this situation was fixed, he was going to be sure to do more sports with Maggie...even if it killed him.

Both women seemed nervous at his being there but he could not have cared less. He was there for Maggie. "Is she here? Do you know where she is? I just want to talk with her."

"Josh, I haven't seen Maggie since before her trip with you. I spoke to her a couple of times. She never said anything about going anywhere."

Josh could not stop the tears from forming in his eyes. "Please, tell me where she is."

"Honestly, Josh, I don't know. I'm sure she's okay. Maybe, she just needs to be alone for a while."

"Yeah, maybe," Josh said but it was not enough. "So, perhaps you can answer another question for me..."

"Sure, if I can."

"When I looked her up, I couldn't find anything and then, suddenly, like a miracle, she arrives at your apartment a full-fledged teenager."

Becca remained quiet, but he could tell he was scaring her.

"Don't try and deny it. I work for DHS. The... um... agent that helped me said someone did a thorough job creating a person out of thin air. Someone who had some connections, like a church secretary... or, maybe, a social worker?"

The statement hung in the air.

"Are you gonna turn me in?"

"I don't want to get anyone in trouble. I just want my girlfriend back."

Sherah spoke for the first time. "Ultimately, it's her choice."

Josh glared at her. Another pean, he thought, but he was too tired to care. He spoke directly to Becca. "Of course. I'm not going after her like some babbling Pharisee. I just want to talk to her... with her. Can you tell me where her family is? I get it, Cleveland was a ruse for whatever purposes, but maybe she went back to her family. Maybe she just needed to be with Emily."

Becca looked at him like he was a little kid who had just dropped his ice cream.

"What?" he shouted more forcefully than he intended.

She teared up. What was she crying for? He was the one who should be crying! She took a deep breath. "Maggie's a runaway."

"But, she has to be from somewhere!"

"True, but, I can assure you, you won't find her by going into her past. There's nothing there she'll go back to."

"Do you know?"

"I do. I hope you'll respect the promise I made."

Josh thought for a moment. A runaway? But, she seemed so... normal. If Maggie lied to him about who she was, what else had she lied about?

Becca was studying him. "Josh, the reasons Maggie didn't tell you had nothing to do with you and, I can assure you, her feelings for you have always been sincere. You just don't understand. I grew up in a neighborhood like you did but... but... since I've been a social worker, I've seen what it takes for some people to survive. Especially runaways. To get help, they have to expose themselves to the risk of being returned to the families they ran away from."

A runaway? That certainly explained her reluctance to talk about her family. What had she gone through? Why had he not seen it?

"Josh, do you want some advice?" Becca asked.

"Sure."

"Give her some time. Let her do her thinking. It's what she needs."

"People shouldn't run from their problems."

"Maybe not but it's who she is. Call it a family legacy. It could be a few hours from now or a few days but she'll contact you. Trust me."

Josh wasn't sure about that as he left Sherah's apartment. Maggie could be in real trouble, if not physically, then spiritually. A runaway. All his life, kids were occasionally reported having run away. Not many, mostly he heard about it on the news. He recollected a lesson way back in kindergarten that was burned in his memory. It was video about all the horrible things that can happen to a kid who leaves the protection of his family and church. If she had somehow survived the streets and got herself back into church and school- that was something to be proud of.

Josh was unsure of his next move so he walked. Block after block he mulled things over. He was exhausted but there was no way he could stop. He bought a couple of energy bars and forced himself to eat them.

Things were beginning to make sense. Why she seemed so guarded all the time. She had secrets. What she did not realize is none of that was important to him. What did he care where she came from? What he cared about was Maggie, in the here and now. That was the woman he was... in love with. He would straighten all the rest of that stuff out later.

His phone rang. Maggie? No, Marie. "Hey love, I think I found a line on your girlfriend."

"Really? Where is she?"

"I had to visit a friend on an upper floor, but her ID was used to take an ET in Denver."

Denver? Fearless Mountain! What a pean he was! Why hadn't he thought of it before?

"Does that sound reasonable? Does she know someone there?"

"No," he lied and felt Marie's disappointment. "Thanks, Marie. Thanks for everything."

"Sure, love, anything you need. A hedge of protection for you both."

Josh's first impulse was to hop back on a train for Denver. Then, what? Contact Vanessa? That's probably what Maggie did. He checked the time and calculated, by that point, she was already in Denver and probably well on her way to Fearless Mountain. Josh knew how foolish he would feel showing up on Vanessa's doorstep asking for transportation. Would she even help him? He thought of a way to bypass Vanessa and just go up the mountain himself. He could rent a vehicle. Yeah, sure, like some old flammable SUV he didn't even know how to drive? Maybe, something smaller… Josh had a vision of himself running willy-nilly all over the mountain on an ATV only to miss a turn and go careening off the edge of a cliff. No… there were no "resets" in real life.

But, he could not do nothing. He was the one who had agreed to take her into that Godless place. He should have said, "No." Instead, he let her laugh when he mentioned it could be dangerous. As it turned out… it was.

It was his failed leadership that led her into an environment where she was obviously ill-equipped. Then, instead of being a good warrior and protecting her, he allowed her to be exposed to all their Godless ideas. He never should have left her alone with any of them. To top it all off, he drank the wine. *Wine is a mocker* and he had let it lead him astray. Instead of maintaining his wits, he allowed the drink to lower his shield of righteousness.

Flee from sexual immorality.

Abstain from sexual immorality.

But each person is tempted when he is lured and enticed by his own desire.

The passages were coming at him like cannonballs. Maggie's confusion was God's punishment for his sin. This was all his fault.

She had placed her trust in him, as a man of God, and he had violated it. Now, instead of drawing her closer to God, he had driven her away. She was confused; she had been a runaway which probably meant she had not been going to church… how many years? He had no idea. He realized he knew almost nothing about her… but that did not matter. If she had been a lost sheep, if she was still a lost sheep, God had placed her into his life for a reason. The reason was obvious, to bring her back to Him, and Josh was blowing it.

He had been up to bat twice. He had left the protection of his home and family to come out to the wilderness to do battle as a spiritual warrior and save his best friend from Satan's snare. He had not only failed at that, but in doing so, he had taken his eyes off the innocent heart God had placed in his life and he had struck out with that as well. Two outs.

Mindlessly, groggily and robotically, Josh found himself taking the ET to American Harvest. Once there he borrowed an SV at the gate and drove to the top of the hill overlooking the grounds. He remembered vividly the day Peter and Matthew had first brought him there. He remembered how he had been so terrified of his new life. Deep down, he was simply afraid he would fail. Well, that certainly appeared to be prophetic.

Yet, looking out over the vast city-church grounds, Josh, as exhausted as he was, felt a surge of inspiration. This was his church, his fortress. Here he had been trained. He sweated, he cried, he despaired and he triumphed. American Harvest had provided the armor. It was through this church he had been baptized by the Spirit. It was here he had become a warrior for Christ.

Josh thought back on his favorite love story, Jacob and Rachel. How many years had Jacob worked to earn her hand in marriage? Seven years. And then, her father forced him to marry the older daughter first and he had to work seven more years to get Rachel. Fourteen years he worked, unable to have the one he loved, but never giving up on her. Never quitting. That was true love. Josh had to rise to that level.

He had two outs… his back was against the wall… yet he was not defeated. He could not be… this was his best friend and… probable… future wife.

So, what was his next move? He was tired, so very tired. No sleep, almost nothing to eat. He should just go back to his apartment and recuperate. Yet, he could not until he had seen this thing through.

As he sat on the picnic table, he weighed his strategy. Driving up the mountain in some crazy attempt at rescue seemed ludicrous. Even if he did make it without killing himself, what would he do when he got there? He had already failed trying to talk Peter into coming home. Why would another trip up the mountain be any different? Now there were two of them and, while Maggie may not have the spiritual where-with-all to discuss things like Peter, would Josh be able to find the words to convince her?

Maybe, he was not the right guy to be at bat. Maybe, he needed a pinch hitter. A plan began to formulate in his head. At first, the plan was alarming but, the more he pondered it, the more he realized it may be his only option if he wanted to help his friends.

Yet, was the idea from the Holy Spirit? *Test the spirits to see whether they are from God.*

He bowed his head and whispered a prayer. "Dear Jesus, you know the number of hairs on my head so I know you know my situation. I know You want me to do what is necessary to save my friends but I need to be sure I'm doing the right thing. Please, send me a sign. Thy Will be done… Amen."

He was hoping to see clouds shaped in an arrow pointing but he did not. The sky was an intense blue with only a few wisps of white desperately clinging to maintain a coherent shape.

At that moment, a hawk glided gracefully into his view. It held its wings aloft effortlessly riding the gentle wind currents. The hawk glanced at Josh as it passed by.

Josh smiled. "Thank you, Lord."

For the first-time, Josh noticed how far west the sun was. Was it really that late? After hours. That was solomon, where he was headed was never closed.

Josh hopped back onto the SV and made a mad "Peter-esque" dash down to the main gates. On the ET ride, he forced himself to down another energy bar.

At 7:45 in the evening, the DHS building was less populated and quieter than it was during the day but as Josh walked in the main doors and stood before the giant emblem of CAP, he felt a sense of calm.

The security officer mentioned Josh looked tired but did not seem to be wondering at all what he was doing there in the evening.

Once on the third floor, Josh appreciated he had never been alone in the office. The first thing he noticed was the comforting sign of Marie's sweater draped carefully over her chair.

Josh sat down at his desk, logged in, and went right to the map. There it was, a tiny little dot amongst hundreds, thousands, of others. The security level was only a "1." That seemed low to him as a community like that, cut off from any kind of real oversight, should be at least a "2." Maybe it was because there were so many red dots in the Colorado mountains. Or, maybe, it was because the agent was keeping tabs on them. But why had he not discovered Peter was on the NBL?

Josh tried to open the icon but was denied. Josh then tried the "known inhabitants." He was denied that too. He clicked through other icons but nothing opened. His Tony the Intern clearance was once again useless.

"ACCESS DENIED. IMPROPER SECURITY CLEARANCE." Dammit. Josh slammed his hands on his desk. The hawk came into his mind. The Holy Spirit had left him with only one card to play.

Mrs. Marone's warnings were sure on point. Josh was encountering forces he had never had to deal with before. What did he know about the demons of atheism? He had never met an atheist in his life… until Peter. One thing was clear, Peter needed far more help than Josh knew how to provide.

Slowly, he directed his finger as a cursor and hovered over the number. A slight push forward with his finger and a small chart popped up. Numbers "1" through "5" appeared with all numbers being dimmed except the "1."

Josh could not imagine what Maggie may have gone through far removed from a family… a church… and quite possibly God's Word altogether. That's probably why she had such strange ideas about things. To think, she did not even have a complete grasp of Original Sin! Whatever that little rinky-dink church she was going to was, it was not providing quality teaching. Now, she was running around in the spiritual wilderness. A confusing wilderness that had overcome Peter, what chance did Maggie have?

For some reason, he found himself thinking of the dream he had on his solitary retreat. The memory of which was faded and muddled. It had been the head of a man… an unrecognizable man. The only thing he was sure of was that it was a man, decades older… maybe in his forties… even his fifties. Was the age of the man significant? More importantly, who exactly was it and what had he been trying to tell Josh. Was it a warning? That was the way it felt but a warning about what?

Perhaps, Josh had already missed the moment at which he was supposed to heed the warning. Perhaps he had taken Peter's words and reckless attitude too casually. He had been so focused on his friendship with Peter, on their vow to be brothers, that he had ignored what Peter really needed. Peter needed everyone who loved him to help reign him in. Instead of offering Peter any real wisdom, Josh had allowed himself to be captivated by Peter's sincerity and then allowed himself to be confused by Peter's ideas. He had already failed Peter… again and again. Maybe then, it was this moment the dream was warning him about. Maybe the man, whomever he was, was telling Josh to not let this moment go by without doing something.

There were two small moves left. He made the first, the cursor was now hovering over the "5."

Alarms were going off all over his body but they were a chaotic jumble of mixed messages. As if a tornado alarm was going off at the same time as a fire alarm, Josh had no idea what to listen to.

How many times had Mrs. Marone told him he needed to step up? *Here I am, Lord, send me!* Now, Josh was seated in a dark office with his finger on the button. Does he let this moment pass only to regret it later? Or is this the moment Josh stepped up, righteously and decisively for the Lord?

The Spirit had been tested. He had seen the hawk.

This was for their own good.

Like a muddied spring or a polluted fountain is a righteous man who gives way before the wicked.

Josh had to step up.

Click.

Part of Josh was shocked with the stillness. He had not expected alarms and whistles but he had expected something... not this eerie silence... not after he...

Oh, God, what had he done?

Chapter Thirty Three

The first obstacle Maggie had to overcome after leaving her apartment that night was the train. She emptied her bank account but had no permission to travel. She sat in the train station, observing for more than two hours before she chose an employee to approach. He was a member of the maintenance crew, mid-twenties and did not seem especially close to the other employees. At first, he was wary but when she started talking money his interest grew. For a hefty bribe, he smuggled her onto the train with no questions asked. The accommodations in the baggage car were far less extravagant than her last train ride but they got her to where she was going.

Once in Denver, Maggie took the ET to the last station possible and then hiked the rest of the way to Vanessa's. Vanessa did not seem surprised to see her.

It turned out there was another customer headed up the mountain and could get her close. Vanessa contacted Peter through some old radio-thing and told him where Maggie would be. The ride up was in a modern pickup and far more comfortable than the SUV had been. The heavy-set middle-aged man, gratefully, was not much of a talker and so Maggie spent most of her time staring out the window.

School was starting in a few days. She had no intention of being there. Why was she walking away from it? Maybe, for the same reason she had left home in the first place. She was tired of living the lie. Maggie thought about all the people she knew. Other than Becca and Emily, of course, no one else knew her at all. Her fellow students, her professors, her college advisor, even Josh, saw her not for who she was but for who she portrayed herself to be. Abayagiri offered a place to be real.

The man took her as far as a small village high in the mountains. She waited for several hours at a community park until she saw the beat up old SUV heading down the street. She found herself relieved to see it was Mari and Tirza who had come to pick her up. Mari greeted her with a tearful long hug; Tirza, with a knowing grin. "I thought we'd be seeing you again."

Tirza drove the SUV while Mari sat in the back with Maggie. Maggie filled them in- the revelation she had that she did not want to go back, her heartbreaking discussion with Josh, and her trip back out. By the time they reached Abayagiri, it was dark. The two girls forced Maggie to have a decent meal which caused her to descend into drowsiness. She had barely slept for two days. They gave her the same room she had before and Mari tucked Maggie into bed.

Maggie drifted off to sleep to the crisp fresh mountain air and the underlying scent of cedar.

She awoke at the dawn's first beams thrusting through her window. A smile was already on her face. She was back.

She freshened up as best she could and found the whole gang already in the kitchen. They greeted her like a long-lost relative returned. Peter was overjoyed to see her, though he remarked he had hoped Josh had "come to his senses." Peter insisted on making her a "coming home breakfast."

As he put the plate in front of her, Maggie felt the blood drain from her face.

"Hey," Peter protested. "It isn't that bad."

"It's not that. Something's wrong."

Every hair on Maggie's arms was standing straight up and the air in the room collapsed to the floor. She was transported back to the terrible night when the agents broke in and… and…

No!

The doors of the dining room burst open and soldiers, dressed head to toe in mountain cameo, their faces covered behind deeply tinted visors, rifles at the ready, stormed into the room. Chaos erupted as the soldiers barked at them.

"What the….?" Maggie heard Levy exclaim.

"Everyone remain seated and put your hands on the table. Anyone who fails to do so will be shot," shouted one of the soldiers.

Levy started to stand up. "What are you men doing?" A soldier slammed the butt of his gun against the back of Levy's head, dropping it like a brick onto his plate. Tirza reached for him but another soldier hit her outstretched hand.

"Any other heroes?" the soldier shouted.

Maggie looked over at Peter who tried to give her a reassuring smile. She was aware of her racing heart, the sweat seeping in her hands, and the painful fluttering in her stomach but it was a detached awareness. Mind and body had once again divided to save the other. Mari held her eyes closed and was taking long deliberate breaths. Tirza sat rubbing her arm and glaring at the soldiers. Manda was calculating. The parents were huddled over their child. Ed was breathing deeply, as if charging himself.

"Ed," Peter said in no more than a whisper. "Easy does it, buddy, just stay cool. Everything's gonna be okay."

"No!" said the main soldier who had been shouting the orders. He was a good deal shorter than the others with a body that looked to Maggie like a jelly bean with legs. "It's not, but you keep telling your..." The soldier stopped himself and stared at Peter for a long time. "...self... that."

"Hey," Tirza shouted.

"Cállate," hissed Mari.

"Request permission to remove this man's face from his breakfast, sir!" Tirza said with a satiric salute.

"Got a live one here," a soldier said.

"Yeah. I can see that," said the one that looked like a jelly bean. He addressed those at the table. "All right, listen up. This facility is now under the jurisdiction of the Green Mountain Patriot Militia. Under the articles of the declaration of Martial Law by the Righteous Apostles, we assume complete and total control of the contents and residents of this unregistered thereby illegal community. I assume no one's stupid enough to come up with a question, so understand something.... We have the authority to use whatever means necessary, including lethal force, to subdue this populace. Squad One, you'll remain here keeping these prisoners under guard. Squad two, we'll conduct a search of this entire area, beginning with those shacks we saw on the way down."

Peter and Ed were ordered to carry Levy into the living room where they placed him on an overstuffed chair. Ed and Peter sat in the other chairs while the three girls, with Mari in the middle, were pushed to a sofa. On the other sofa, Manda sat on one side and the parents on the other. Four soldiers stood guard over them.

"It's gonna be okay," said Peter. "They're just get off harassing us for a while, maybe take some food. They're not DHS."

"Are you sure?" Maggie asked.

"They would've identified themselves as such. The Green Mountain… whatever? It's just one of those militia groups. They'll go hard ass but they can't touch us." His words were reassuring but Maggie could see the fear in Peter's eyes. Maggie was not sure of the status of the others but Peter, being on the NBL, had to be especially vulnerable.

"Tell that to Levy," Tirza said angrily.

"Solomon," the soldier who seemed to be in charge announced. "New rule: you talk, the person you talk to eats his own teeth."

Time ticked by in an agonizing crawl. Mari had taken Maggie's hand and would sometimes squeeze it in terror. Peter spent his time looking from one of them to another and smiling reassuringly.

Levy eventually stirred. At first, he tried speaking with the soldiers but they would have none of that as one of them walked over and raised the butt of his gun. Tirza screamed, "He's had enough!" which halted the soldier. As if speaking to the new kid in a classroom, he explained the rules to Levy.

Maggie, for her part, did her best to keep her breathing at an even pace. She did not know what to make of any of this. Last night, she had been so happy to arrive safe and sound. She had felt as light as a bird coming to rest in the safety of a nest. Then these wanna-bes show up. What were they doing? How did they know the lodge was there? Did they stumble upon it? And the big question? Was the timing of this raid coincidental or did it have something to do with her arrival? Josh would not deliberately betray her, she was sure, but he could be flipping out, perhaps using DHS equipment that was being monitored.

She should have stayed in Columbus, at least for a while to help Josh not have a meltdown. But, she had not considered that. There he was surrounded by loving parents and a big family. He would be fine, she had told herself. As a result, she had not only hurt Josh but may have brought this chaos on her new friends.

She looked around at the group of captives, fear showing on each of their faces in their own way. She wanted to apologize to them, explain to them that this was all her fault, but she dared not. It would not have helped anyway.

Maggie heard Tirza whisper, "What the fuck's taking so long?"

"Shhh," Mari hushed. Then after a few seconds, she whispered, "I believe Gus is killing them all."

Gustavo. Maggie had forgotten about him. Where was he? Was he aware of what was going on? There had been no gunfire, no shouts. Peter said Gus was good with the bow. Maybe he was killing them all.

The front door flew open. Jelly Bean stomped in followed by the other soldiers. "We've stumbled into a jackpot here, joes. Bring 'em outside."

The captives were marched to the courtyard where they were forced to stand in two straight lines. Maggie found herself at the end of the first row; beside her was Mari, behind her was Levy.

"On the ground," Jelly Bean ordered. "Cuff 'em."

"Now this has gone far enough," Levy said. "I'm sure you've discovered who I am so you should know you are interfering with…"

"I assure you, we know exactly who you are," Jelly Bean interrupted, pacing back and forth in front of them, relishing his power. He stopped in front of Maggie. He put his gloved hand on her chin and lifted her head. That close Maggie could make out the young man's eyes behind the face shield and smell his grotesque body odor. He studied her for a long time and then said just to her, "Well, this day has one surprise after another."

She yanked her face away from his hand.

He addressed the group. "So, what do we have here… a bunch of hippies communing with nature? Or so that's what they want us to believe. Certainly, that's what the local agent wants us to believe."

"Agent? DHS?" one of the soldiers exclaimed.

Jelly Bean nodded and a couple of the soldiers grabbed Levy and dragged him, by his elbows, to the front where they unceremoniously dumped him in front of Jelly Bean.

Levy lifted himself up to his knees. "You're making a big mistake."

"Oh, I don't think so, Agent Man," Jelly Bean said. "See, joes, what we have here is a Dancer with Wolves. Back when the Christians were first conquering this land and bringing those lost souls back to the flock, sometimes the missionaries or soldiers would get lulled away. Enticed by sin, they would backslide and join the Godless heathens. Oh, I don't know, maybe they liked the food, or hell, maybe they succumbed to demons. Is that it, Dancer? Is it demons? Well, let me exorcise them for you." Jelly Bean grabbed Levy by the hair and slammed his fist into the cuffed man's face.

Maggie screamed but it was Tirza's wail that raised attention.

Jelly Bean paused and looked over at her. "Or sometimes it was something else. Is that it baby doll? Do you like the way this guy dances?"

"Fuck you," spat Tirza.

Jelly Bean cackled. "A righteous woman *remains quiet for Adam was created first.*"

Levy tried again. "I'm underco…"

Jelly Bean stabbed him with his fist. "I'd call that resisting. Wouldn't you call that resisting?"

The soldiers nodded.

Jelly Bean addressed his captives. "From the vacant look on your faces I can see this is all quite a shock to you. Well, let me enlighten you. We all know the Awakening's not over. The Light's been brought into the deepest crevices, only to scatter the rats. DHS closes the gate behind them but they don't have the resources to chase them. That's where we come in. See, we have a covenant with DHS. They give us the equipment to tell us where the rats are and we exterminate them. *Behold, I have given you authority to tread on serpents and scorpions, and over all the power of the enemy.* We roam these mountains searching for serpents and scorpions. Then, just last evening, we pick up a notification that this little community, that never made so much as a blip before, jumps four levels in its security factor. To Level Five! After a few calls, we find out, though there's an agent present, he wasn't the one who adjusted the levels. Now, I'm intrigued, so we decided to investigate. And lo and behold what do we find? An agent dancing with wolves."

"I'm undercover."

"Oh?" Jelly Bean chuckled. "Where exactly in the agent handbook are the instructions to make moonshine? And the books we found in your shack? Shame, shame, shame. And what about the false reports about the number of people here? Part of your cover? Falsifying records is a blaspheme of the Holy Spirit!"

"There are reasons. A security matter, I'm sure you're not cleared to know about but you have to let me… us… go."

"No, Satan, I don't." Jelly Bean took a couple of grand steps backward and then with the gusto of a kicker scoring the winning field goal he catapulted his foot into Levy's ribcage. Levy plopped to the ground.

"For God's sake, stop it!" Peter screamed and started to his feet. One of the soldiers knocked him down with the butt of his rifle.

Jelly Bean appeared overwhelmed by his power-fueled adrenaline. *"For God's judgment is swift."* He paused to kick Levy again. *"And true."* Kick. *"And righteous."* A heavy final kick.

"STOP! Please!" Peter cried, "Okay, so you got him, he's not following protocol. Turn him in and let him work it out."

Jelly Bean whirled around at Peter. "Ah, *even the demons believe—and shudder!*"

He walked around Peter like he was merchandise for sale. "Would you look at this, joes? Have you ever seen anyone more perfect? I bet David himself wasn't this pretty." He grabbed Peter by the hair. "So, you think maybe we've gone too far? Think our methods might be a bit... I don't know... severe? Well let me ask you something... don't you really want to know? ... How far are we willing to go to bring God's Righteousness to this Earth?"

Seemingly out of nowhere, two soldiers dropped a lifeless body into their midst. There was a stunned silence, broken by Mari's anguished scream, "GUSTAVO!"

The body was caked in blood. Mari crumpled into a sobbing heap. Peter, kneeling the closest to the body, cried, "Why?"

Jelly Bean walked over and knelt next to Peter. "Oh, because I'm really good at what I do. I learned a long time ago, playing in the woods as a kid, stealth gives you the advantage because you see them before they see you."

Peter raised his head with a quizzical look. "Luke?"

Jelly Bean removed his helmet. He was a young man, as Maggie had thought. His head was cleanly shaven save for a tiny wisp of red beneath his lip. "Hello, brother," he spat.

From that point, everything instantly both sped up and slowed down. Ed roared like a lion struggling to get his massive cuffed frame off the ground. His efforts were met with a slew of blows as three of the soldiers unloaded on him. Manda made it to her feet and was able to kick two of the soldiers in their groins before a third one bashed her head. The soldiers did not stop hitting Ed until he too lay unmoving, the giant of a man reduced to resembling a bison carcass left to rot. During the ruckus, Josiah managed to move closer to Ayesha, draping his body as best he could over his family, repeatedly crying, "We're not resisting... we're not resisting." Mari was bent completely over, her face buried in the ground. Peter was sobbing uncontrollably. To Maggie, the whole mountain had burst into flames.

Luke ordered two of the soldiers to drag Peter over to an old stump near Maggie. The stump stood several feet high and was riddled with ancient bullet holes from hours of target practice.

Luke goose-stepped over to Peter.

Peter, now restrained to the target, his face streaked with tears, pleaded, "Luke, why? We're brothers."

"And a person's enemies will be those of his own household." Luke found a stick on the ground. He began smacking his new prop against his palm.

When Luke was in front of him, Peter tried again. "Luke…" But his appeal was met with the crushing force of the stick against his cheek.

"Silence, Pharisee! I don't have to listen anymore. You have nothing over me. *For false prophets will arise to lead astray the elect.*"

"I'm not a false prophet. I'm a nobo…"

Luke's swing of the stick shut Peter up as it connected hard against his ribcage.

"Stop it! Asshole!" Tirza shouted. "He hasn't done anything to you."

"Somebody put something into that whore's mouth before I do!" Luke commanded. When one of the soldiers stuffed a dirty rag from the porch into Tirza's mouth, Luke said, "I assure you, little lady, my anger at this antichrist is justifiable and righteous." Luke swung at one of Peter's legs. There was a heavy thump and a yell of pain followed by a second dose of each as Luke teed off on the other leg. "Oh yes, I SEE YOU, SATAN!"

Even the soldiers seemed uncomfortable at their leader's unbridled fury. One of the soldiers nervously asked, "You know this guy, sir?"

"Know him? Believe it or not, I grew up with this sack of shit. He was the golden boy of my church, people thought he was gonna be the next Paul or something. But I heard what happened, guy goes off to bring Jehovah's Revolution to the world but didn't have the balls to sustain. *Therefore, we know that it is the last hour. They went out from us, but they were not of us; for if they had been of us, they would have continued with us.*"

Luke's sermon was cut off by one of the soldiers holding a monitor before him. "Other than the agent, not much here. Although that guy's docs are a little questionable."

"Really? I'm not surprised. Run him again but, this time, under the name Peter Albrecht. A-L-B-R-E-C-H-T. From the American Harvest Church, Columbus, Ohio." Luke looked at Maggie and asked, "She checked out?"

The soldier glanced at his screen. "Yes, sir, Maggie Anderson, missed last week, but her memberships in good standing, Maplewood Christian, Columbus. Originally from Cleveland."

"Cleveland?" Luke grinned at her. Maggie looked away in disgust.

The soldier stepped back and began tapping at his computer. "Oh my God, the guy's on the NBL."

"No way! So, the Dancer was hiding a Backslidden. Oh, how the plot thickens!" Luke turned his attention back to Peter. "NBL? Now I'm impressed.

I heard you backslid, but to make it to the NBL. My, you must have been one busy little devil."

"It's not like that." Peter forced the words out through his pain. "I was put on because..."

"Get behind me, Satan!" Luke raised his stick to strike Peter again.

"Sir, the reward," a soldier shouted.

The statement annoyed Luke. He stormed about, then stopped in front of Peter. "I honestly can't believe you're here. This is a fantasy I dared not even dream. I do have a confession to make... when we were kids I idolized you. You became more important to me than God Himself. That was my sin."

Luke marched about tapping his stick against his palm. "See, I didn't last long at the military academy. Anger issues... you know. I was sent to what was affectionately called a 'Youth Intervention Camp.' A fucking prison. I was too ashamed to tell you. I spent a lot of time in solitary, what we called 'the Tomb.' Twenty-three hours a day, alone with nothing but God and my Bible. I prayed for God to fix me, turn off the tap of anger, but it never went away. I was beginning to believe I was possessed. Then, one night, an angel appeared before me. I saw him as plainly as I see you now. He looked at me and said, '*The LORD is with you, O mighty man of valor.*' Then, the angel picked up my Bible, opened it, and handed it to me. The pages were all blank except for one bold verse: *Whosoever is born of God doth not commit sin; for His seed remaineth in him, and he cannot sin, because he is born of God.*

"It was like a blindfold came off, my whole cell was doused in a heavenly light, and the words literally rose from the page. There it was in front me as plain as day. Once a man is born of God, he cannot sin. Everyone was wrong. They saw my anger as a sin, they didn't see it for what it really was... what it really is... my gift! *I will execute great vengeance on them with wrathful rebukes.*"

As he spoke the last sentence, Luke placed the tip of his knife against Peter's face and flicked it across his cheek. At first it looked like it had just been for show but gradually a red line appeared and seconds later blood seeped from the gash.

"Luke," the soldier warned tentatively.

"Silence, Pharisee!" Luke whirled around on his subordinate. "I have only dreamt of confronting this heretic. Do NOT spoil this for me."

He took a deep breath to compose himself. "That was the night I honestly found God. I joined the military after JD but they didn't understand my anointing. They feared me, so they kicked me out. At first, I thought I had failed God. I spent months going from one shitty hotel to another, too ashamed to go home. Then one night the angel came back. This time he levitated my Bible into my lap and without even touching it, opened it to the passage: *Every tree that does not bear good fruit is cut down and thrown into the fire.* The angel told me to stop being a Jonah and accept my anointing. That's when God led me here, to these sacred mountains, and to these righteous brothers, where we can walk God's righteous path. *Then I heard another voice from heaven saying, 'Come out of her, my people, lest you take part in her sins, lest you share in her plagues.'* God isn't done with this nation. As those Apostles in Washington grow more corrupt, God's people, God's truly righteous people will rise up. We'll take dominion over not just the Seven Mountains but every aspect of society. We'll drive Satan out of this land once and for all. *Blessed be the LORD, my rock, who trains my hands for war!*"

At the culmination of his fiery speech, Luke rained down a cascade of blows all over Peter's body. Hammering away with his club, he looked like a butcher tenderizing a side of beef, seeking patches of flesh that had yet to feel his wrath. The first blows were a loud thump followed by a scream of anguish from Peter but, as the clubbing continued, Peter grew silent and there was only the thump-thump-thump of wood hitting flesh.

The soldiers were frozen, hypnotized by the rage. Maggie realized if someone did not stop the madman, Peter was going to be killed. With the dexterity of trained muscles, she leapt to her feet. As she ran forward, her handcuffed arms made it difficult to keep her balance but she quickly closed the distance. She leaped in the air and threw her feet into Luke's chest. Luke was catapulted away and Maggie fell hard to the ground. Her shoulder screamed in pain. Luke came up to a crouch, his pistol at the ready.

"A woman?" he laughed. Maggie was grabbed harshly by her shoulders. Luke waved his hand. "Let her go."

The soldier did as he was told. Luke stood up and announced, "*A gracious woman gets honor, and violent men get riches.*" Luke then turned and asked the soldier, "He alive?"

The soldier was examining Peter like a corpse at an autopsy. "I think so. Jesus, Luke, you almost beat him to death."

Luke smiled nervously. "He had it coming. Fucking backslidden piece of shit."

"But, when we take him in, they're gonna ask…"

"You leave the answering to me. *The LORD has a sword; it is sated with blood;* no sin was committed here. Now, get what's left of this heretic into the truck. And the Dancer. Take Goliath over there too, he's too fucking big to be running around up here unsupervised. Throw the dyke in too, she probably needs a hospital. Grab the body, make sure we've got all the evidence. I want a word with Angel Eyes here before we go."

When Maggie realized he was referring to her, her brain snapped into survival mode. Never again! "You touch me," she scowled, spitting out each word as if it was a flame. "I'll eat you alive."

"I understand you're afraid of me, and you should be. *Let a woman learn quietly with all submissiveness.* I can assure you, however, my intentions are nothing but righteous."

Her mind was aflame with fear but she also saw the possibilities. He may take the cuffs off. If he did she would show him what a five-foot ball of ninja fury looked like.

She let him lead her into the lodge and back to the dining room. At the table, he pulled out a chair for her. She refused to sit. "Please," he insisted.

"Can't sit in cuffs. It's uncomfortable."

"Oh, yes, well, to be brutally honest," he said, rubbing his chest. "I'm not ready to remove those yet. I'd like to talk to you first."

He turned the dining chair sideways. She sat, searching for her opportunity.

"Thank you," he said in his sardonic voice. "Allow me to introduce myself. My name's Luke Mayle. And you are?"

She did not answer but just stared at him coldly, imagining herself digging her claws into his face.

"Maggie, right? Maggie Anderson? From Cleveland? Or was it Columbus?"

She was not going to play his game.

"I grew up in Columbus, same church as your friend out there... oh, but you heard all that. It's interesting that you and he are both from Columbus. What are the odds you would both be here? You and he aren't...? You know.... together? Well, that's not important... he'll be out of commission for some time. What I wanted to talk to you about was this: American Harvest, that's the church Peter and I grew up in. The place is huge. Thousands of kids. We had a pastor. Pastor Mike. He had a daughter. She was a couple of years younger than me but I saw her sometimes around church. I believe her name was Margaret, but everyone called her Maggie. I remember she had these cute tight braids all around her head but what really struck me were her eyes."

Maggie stared at the floor.

"I'll never forget her. I guess you could say I had a boyhood crush on her.

I think the last time I saw her was when I was in the eighth grade… maybe ninth. Rumor was she ran away." He paused. "You are her, aren't you?"

As she glared at him she imagined herself ripping that cocky smile right off of him.

"Yeah, I understand. I'm sure what you saw out there was quite unsettling. But, think about it. Was it really any more violent than the slaughter at Jericho? Was it any less ruthless then Peter confronting Ananias and Sapphira? Or God sending a flood to wipe out everyone and everything on the whole planet? We can sing our lullabies to Jesus all we want but this is war and I'm *the servant of God, an avenger who carries out God's wrath on the wrongdoer.*"

For a second, Maggie was afraid he was going to begin beating her but he took a deep breath.

"I had a teacher once, best Sunday School teacher ever. He loved the Old Testament, especially all the battles. He'd always get so into reenacting them. By the end of the story we were hooting and hollering, cheering God's people to victory. But I remember he always saved time at the end of each class for us to calm down. He told us how the Jewish law made strict provisions for washing weapons after battle, but God had something else in mind than just having clean weapons. The ritual washing also served for the warriors to wash their minds. It isn't easy going from the blood of battle back to being just normal, maybe a husband, a father. I believe in that too. You only know me as the soldier I am but there's another side of me. A side that's kind, gentle, even funny. A man devoted to the Lord. A man that would be a good father and a good husband."

He paused to see if there would be a reaction, she gave him nothing.

"I guess what I'm trying to say, if I could be so formal, is… I'd like to call on you."

He was serious, stating it as if they were sitting on a porch swing outside her parents' house. Maggie was not at all sure if she should feel horrified or laugh at the pathetic idiot.

"Oh, I guess it's nothing I need a reply on right this moment. Look, I've got to take our prisoners down the mountain but I'll be back. Next time I come, we'll just make it a social call. Does that sound solomon? I'll pick up some real wine when I'm down there and we can have a nice evening right here. Maybe, you can cook a dinner. I can't tell you how long it's been since I've enjoyed a woman's cooking."

Luke was interrupted by a soldier in the doorway. "Sir, it's getting late."

"Don't rush me."

"Yes, sir, but, some of the guys are saying… since you get to be in here with her… they're wondering about the others…"

Luke slammed his fist down on the table. *"He is Lord of lords and King of kings, and those with him are called and chosen and faithful."*

"Yes, sir," the soldier answered, saluted, and disappeared.

With that, Luke came around behind her and took her hands. She started to pull away until she felt him uncuffing them.

"Until next time, Angel Eyes." Luke's heavy stomps shook the whole lodge as he left the dining room to return to his men. Maggie sat alone in the dark room, where only a few hours ago, jokes were shared and laughter abounded. Now, it was dead. Time itself felt dead.

It took Ayesha's agonizing wails to snap her back to reality. What now? Had they finally gotten around to attacking Josiah?

As she exited the lodge, she saw Mari was still a crumbled heap right where she had been. Tirza was sitting next to her. Most of the soldiers were standing by the truck. Center stage was Luke aiming his pistol at Josiah who was standing in front of Ayesha, who was clutching Nesta in her arms. Maggie watched as she quietly made her way over to Tirza and Mari. When Tirza saw her, she gave Maggie a relieved yet terrified smile.

"Think," Luke was saying. "Think about the consequences."

"You can't take our baby," Josiah begged.

"Yes, yes I can. I have the authority. More importantly I have the duty. I'm not gonna let you raise this child in this spiritual wilderness. Now, you have two choices. You can continue to hide from the Light, abandoning your baby or you can follow us into town where you can surrender yourselves to God. Either way, we're taking that innocent soul with us."

Maggie watched as the hopeless father turned to his wife and child. Through his tears, he spoke to Ayesha. Ayesha's reaction was an immediate scream and her wrenching Nesta even closer. Josiah squatted down next to her, his hands bouncing up and down, as he presented the hopeless despair of the choices before them. Maggie's heart dropped to the ground as she watched Josiah hold Ayesha's arms as a soldier walked up and took the screaming child from his mother. Ayesha wailed, turned on Josiah, and pounded his chest.

"Nearest agency's in Denver. You'll find your baby there," Luke said. He surveyed the area and for the first time noticed Maggie. He smiled at her and waived. Just go, she silently pleaded.

Instead, he walked over and addressed the three young women.

"As for you three, I'm to advise you that our righteous nation wants you to come home and get right with God. There's no reason for you to think of yourselves as Lost Sheep. If you don't have a church membership, the government will get you reinstated. That's on the record. Off the record, since we've pretty much cleared out this poisonous man-folk of yours, we'll be keeping an eye on this place. I imagine the dad over there's leaving. Three innocent young ladies like yourselves, up here, all alone, are gonna need someone to watch over them. We, of the Green Mountain Patriot Militia, gratefully volunteer our services." With that, he bowed. As he came back up, he caught Maggie's eye, winked, and stated his parting words. "See you around, Angel Eyes."

Chapter Thirty Four

When he adjusted the security level, Josh was not at all sure what he had done, but his mind went right into flight mode. Recognizing, for the first time, he was probably on camera, he, casually as he could, shut off the computer and hightailed it down the elevator and out to the street. Once there, the initial rush of fresh air felt like an escape but, in just a few breaths, he all but choked on it.

What had he done? What had he done? The unanswerable question swirled around his head as he robotically made his way back to his apartment. Once there, he paced throughout the night like a caged tiger. He again felt vividly the sensation of being on that horrible carnival ride with Stephen. Every organ trapped inside his chest was spinning in chaotic orbits. He no longer kept time in minutes or hours but in rambling muddled mental crises as he wrestled with the unknown future.

Had he betrayed Peter and Maggie? If he had, was it for their own good? Was it fair to the others at Fearless Mountain? Were there more appropriate ways to help? Channels to go through?

When his mind could snag the last question, he sunk into deep despair. Of course, there were more appropriate channels! There was an agent at Fearless Mountain and he did not change the code. That would be DHS's first question and they would simply place a call to the agent. Josh could just imagine the conversation. Headquarters would ask the agent if everything was okay. The agent would say it was. Then, HQ would ask if the agent knew why the security level would be changed from Ohio and the agent would respond, "Well, there's a young lady who just left her boyfriend..." Next, a call would be placed to Josh's father who would then be put in a position of having to

---

explain his grown son's behavior, violations of DHS procedure, overstepping security clearance, and who knew what else?

These were the thoughts that started his organs to churn. Josh had put his father into an awkward and embarrassing position. If a leader could not trust his own son, what kind of a leader was he? *For if someone does not know how to manage his own household...* Josh's father would be mortified and hurt.

In the previous day's hazy calculations, he never considered the trail he would leave. The DHS system would know exactly what time and what computer made the change. That would leave Josh with a lot of explaining to do. Why would he have changed that community? How did he know Peter was there? And if he did know, why did he not notify his superiors? For all Josh knew, even his use of his DHS credentials to arrange the trip was against the rules. He knew he was in trouble. The deepening question simply became... how much? The best-case scenario was his father would put the clamps down and just settle this father-to-son. Would his father have to make calls to other directors and ask for a "personal favor"? Being punished like an unruly child was best for Josh but it would be humiliating for his father.

Josh's mind went to the next logical question: what would be the worst-case scenario? The answer for that was far murkier and depended on how much was revealed. Would DHS find out about his abuse of credentials with the security officer? How about his trip to Sherah's? Would the girls claim he had overstepped his clearance? Technically, he had traveled under false pretenses and using his DHS credentials. What would be the punishment for all of that? He most certainly would never be allowed to work for DHS again but would it result in him not being able to be a teacher? Being expelled from OSU? Losing his church membership? Prison?

Oh, dear Jesus.

Sometimes during the night of pacing, he would sit or lie down, convincing himself he might be able to sleep. Yet, it was useless. There was no way his assaulted mind would ever allow him to escape into unconsciousness.

As the long night finally turned to morning, Josh had to make a decision. He could call in sick, which would definitely not be a lie. Yet, that would make him look like he was hiding. The thought of DHS agents, led by his father, coming to the apartment building to officially arrest him made his gut spin. He decided it would be better to have it all handled within the building. Besides, he concluded, there was no way he would be able to pace all day long... waiting.

He took as cold a shower as he could stand and supplemented the rejuvenation with two cups of strong coffee. He found himself dressing as a meticulous officer for a doomed army might just before going into the final battle. He was not hungry but forced himself to eat something to soothe his caffeinated-charged belly.

A quick ET ride later, Josh stood before the massive structure that was the Department of Homeland Security, a righteous arm of the Final Great Awakening. An arm he had tainted. He half-expected to be arrested the moment he walked in the door but the early morning hustle appeared strangely normal.

He took the elevator to the third floor. Marie commented on how tired he looked and Josh muttered a half-truth in response.

He found his way to his desk. He turned on his computer, glanced around to see if he was being watched, and opened the security program. He homed in on Fearless Mountain. There it was, a great big "5" on an otherwise insignificant little dot. Josh stared at it, hoping it would provide him with something, maybe more information, or maybe a way out of this mess. He thought about trying to change the level again but assumed that would be futile and his actions could be traced. With that thought, he quickly turned off his computer.

He did his best to go through the motions of the day. He spoke to the other guys and was surprised to be able to carry on a normal conversation without letting them see the chaos within him. He stayed out on the floor as sitting at his desk waiting was completely excruciating.

Somehow, he made it through the morning. He spent lunch by himself on a park bench. As he took each bite of food and each sip of his drink, he knew this could be his last supper.

When he returned to the office, he again was overwhelmed by the feeling he would be accosted at any moment. He calculated the time. Colorado was two hours behind. How long does it take for an adjustment in the security level to be investigated?

The waiting was agonizing.

As true as that was, however, as the afternoon stretched on and the office began winding things up for the day, Josh found himself with even greater anxiety. He could not go home to that cage of an apartment and spend another sleepless night in debilitating panic. He wanted… he needed… to get this over with that day. "Please, Lord, waiting is just increasing the fire of my suffering. Thy Will be done."

The last four words sunk in deeply. Had a miracle already been performed?

Maybe the reason nothing had happened was because nothing was going to happen. God could see Josh was suffering. God could see Josh repented. Maybe, God fixed things to give Josh the chance to reset.

It was at that moment he received a call from an unknown number.

Uh, oh, his heart skipped a beat. The shit was going to hit the fan after all.

Part of his mind screamed not to answer the call but the other part detested the idea of putting this off any longer. This had to end... somehow.

Josh answered the call.

"Did you have anything to do with this?"

It took a moment for Josh's bewildered mind to comprehend who it was. Maggie's tear-streaked face appeared hardened and exhausted.

Josh's first reaction was one of relief. Becca had been right; Maggie did call. Yet when he processed the question, he did not understand. "With what?"

"With those lunatics raiding the lodge?"

Raid? Lunatics?

"Slow down, Maggie..."

"All I want to hear is- you had nothing to do with that psycho!"

"What psycho?"

"Luke. He knew Peter... he... he... oh my God, what he did to Peter... and Gus... and Levy... he even took Nesta..."

Everything Maggie was saying sounded as if she was speaking downwind in a hurricane. Luke? She doesn't even know him!

"Please, Maggie. I'm exhausted. I haven't slept for two nights. Start from the beginning. Tell me what happened."

"Your old pal, Luke. Said he grew up with Peter... and you, I guess. He's gone totally mental. He killed Gustavo and turned Levy and Peter into... bloody.... He said he found us because of a change in the DHS level, a 'security something'... I want to know if you had anything to do with that."

And *the Truth shall set you free.*

Josh took a deep breath. "I found out you went back. I panicked, I was worried about you, and I was trying to help Peter. It may not have been the best thing..."

"The best thing?" Maggie snapped. "Are you serious? Do you have any fucking idea what you did? Gustavo's dead. Dead! And Peter and Levy probably are too! And you want to say it might not have been the 'best thing'?"

"I don't know what you're talking about. There's no way Luke's leading a DHS raid. He doesn't work for DHS and even if he did, he'd be way too young to be an agent."

"He's not an agent. Levy was... is. Luke beat the shit outta him. Then, he went after Peter."

It still did not make sense. If it really was Luke, what reason would he have to hurt Peter? Maggie obviously did not have her facts straight.

"Maggie, where are you now?"

"Getting out of here. And don't try tracing this call because..."

"Maggie, of course not. I would never..."

"But, you did!"

The words were like daggers. "Maggie, I'm sorry things got so confusing, but, please, come back. You know I only intended to help. We can work this out. We'll pray about it, go to a pastor... Maggie, I... I... love you."

Maggie showed no reaction. Did she hear what he said? She inhaled deeply. "I'm leaving, Josh. Not just you, not just Columbus, but America. I've had all the Christian love I can take."

She disconnected. Josh stared dumbfoundedly at the empty space. He turned around to see Marie standing at the door.

"I just came by to say goodnight. You solomon?"

The question acted as an emotional spigot and he proceeded to douse her with everything that was going on. By the end of the tale, he was holding a wet ball of tissues and weeping uncontrollably. She cupped his chin in her hand and lifted his gaze to hers. "Let's see if we can find out what's really going on."

"Are you able to find out where Maggie is?"

"Maybe."

"But I could be in trouble, I don't want to get you..."

Marie's smile stopped him. "I don't think you're in as much trouble as you think you are, but let's find out what's going on and leave that up to God."

From there Marie went to work. She used Josh's phone to trace Maggie's call. The call had been pirated through several different numbers bouncing around the country and ending up dropping into a black hole. "Wow," Marie exclaimed. "Either your girlfriend's a genius, or she has some serious help. I'm sorry, but this will take a referral upstairs."

It would not matter. Josh was sure Maggie was not going to be sticking around. She was with Peter's group; they knew what they were doing. "Can we find out how much she said was true?"

"If a militia brought them in like she said, there'd be a report."

"Yeah, go there."

Marie was back in her arena, moments later the report popped up.

They read it together. The report was by the Green Mountain Patriot

Militia. There was a licensing number and then the line, "Filed by Luke Mayle." It really was Luke. That still did not make the rest of Maggie's story accurate. Luke was rough, maybe, but he had no reason to beat up Peter.

Josh continued to read. He saw all the names reported, including Maggie's and Peter's. Then, he saw five had been arrested. Gustavo, Ed, and Manda were charged with resisting. Levy was charged with treason and blasphemy. And Peter was being charged with false prophecy, blasphemy, and resisting. False prophecy? Josh didn't know too much about it but he knew enough to know it was a serious charge.

The rest of the report was a concise synopsis of the events the previous evening, beginning with the militia being alerted by the change in security level. Once there, they discovered an agent had gone rogue and was hiding a Backslidden, Peter. While securing the illegal settlement, there were five casualties. Four wounded prisoners and a fifth DOA. No militia suffered any injuries.

Panic creeped into Josh's gut.

The report went on to cite evidence and this became completely confusing to Josh. The lodge was referred to as a "Buddhist temple" The storage facility was called "the meditation hall." There were references to a "library of blasphemous literature." The huts the guys were living in were called "monastic cells." But, most alarming of all... Peter was signaled out and labelled the "cult leader."

"That's babel," Josh remarked. "It wasn't a cult and Peter wasn't the leader."

Unfortunately, the rest of the report was of little help. Because of the nature of their crimes, Peter and Levy were being held under the tightest security. The baby had been turned over to the authorities. Ed was being held in a normal jail. Manda was in a hospital in Denver. Everyone else was set free.

"Where's Peter now?"

"Oh, love, I won't be able to tell... false prophecy's a capital charge."

"What's a capital charge?"

"It's like treason or...murder... it's for those facing the... death penalty."

"Death penalty?"

"I'm sorry, love."

But, Josh was gone.

He made a bee-line for the thirtieth floor, his security clearance be damned. His father's secretary had gone home for the evening but he knew his dad would still be there. He found his father staring out the window.

"Dad?"

"Josh? What are you doing up here?"

"I've come to turn myself in."

"Oh?"

"I violated my security clearance. More than once. I know I'm in trouble, but there's been a terrible mistake. Peter's been arrested, a capital crime."

"Yes, I'm aware."

"You are? Then you know how it happened? What I did?" Josh found himself dancing around the office, both of his arms were shaking uncontrollably.

"I'm fully aware of what goes on in my building, Josh."

"Then you know I'm the one who changed the security level. I thought I was doing the right thing. I'm not sure what happened. Somehow there's a big mix-up. Peter hasn't done anything."

"It's not in my hands anymore."

"You're Director of Homeland Security. Make a few calls, straighten this out..."

Josh was shocked to see his father leap at him from across the room. He was even more shocked when his father covered his mouth with one hand, and with the other bent Josh's arm behind his back. Hastily, his father pushed him across the office and into the elevator. Once in the elevator his father whispered, "I'm going to let go now and you are going to follow me. Do not say anything... nothing... until I speak first. Nod if you understand."

Josh nodded. A moment later his dad relinquished his hold on him. As the elevator continued downward Josh tried to catch his father's eye but was rebuffed. Feeling very much like he was six again, he followed his father out the door.

Moments later they were seated on the same park bench where Josh had eaten his "last supper."

"Don't you ever talk like that in the office."

"I'm sorry if I was disrespectful but Peter..."

"This isn't about disrespect. There is nothing going on in that building that's not being monitored."

Josh saw something in his father's eyes... his face. Something he had never seen before. Fear. Was it because of what he did?

"Dad, if I've done something... this was all my fault... all my doing... I'm sorry if it's going to be embarrassing but I..."

His father looked at him quizzically. That wasn't his father's fear? Then, what?

"Josh, you're not in trouble. A rogue agent was caught hiding a Backslidden. As far as the department is concerned, it was a good bust."

"Then why the manhandling?"

"Because you were about to question."

"But, Dad, Peter's being charged with false prophecy. It's complete babel. We've got to do something."

"I'm afraid there's not much we can do."

"DHS was just supposed to pick him up. That's what you told me. Pick him up and bring him home."

"That was the original plan."

"Then, what is this?"

"His situation has gotten a good deal more complicated. The report…"

"The report's babel. That's not what was going on at all. Peter wasn't the leader of a cult. They were just living there. I know. I saw. I'm a witness."

His father looked at him like he was again that tiny child experiencing the cruelness of the world for the first time. "I'm afraid that's not going to make a difference. The militia are licensed. They have training. You're a summer intern on an ill-advised trip to save his backslidden friend."

Josh buried his head in his hands. "This can't be happening. We've got to do something."

"You will do nothing but pray." Josh pulled his hands away and considered his father's face. What was he saying? "You can't go around questioning. You know that."

"Dad, this is babel. Peter going to trial? For what? For running away from home?"

"He's going to trial for exactly what the report said."

"The report is babel. There must be someone we can tell. Someone I can tell. Tell them what I saw. Let them know what was really going on."

"You will do no such thing. Who do you think you would talk to?"

"Dad… please…"

"Listen to me, Josh. I would love to help, and not for Peter's sake alone, but for yours. But there really isn't anything we can do. Righteous, Spirit-filled judges will make their ruling. And we will not question that… is that clear?"

"Dad?"

"Oh, Josh, you have no idea what you're dealing with."

It was something in how it was said that caused Josh to stop. He had found his father's real fear.

"Dad, help me understand."

"These are powerful people who believe they are being guided by the Holy Spirit. They don't take being questioned lightly."

In one of those rare moments when he was able to see the man next to him as a brother rather than a father, Josh ran the words through his head. "You sound like you don't believe they're being guided."

"It doesn't matter what I believe. It matters the way things are. Josh, you can't be seen as a doubter. Especially now. Things aren't going well and people are becoming more and more afraid. In fear they react."

"But, Dad, we have to do something!"

"We can pray. We can pray that God will direct righteous judges into a righteous decision. *The sentence is by the decree of the watchers, the decision by the word of the holy ones.*"

His father ordered him to go back to his apartment and get some rest. He was so exhausted there were times he actually fell into a deep yet fitful sleep. Other times his unrelenting mind pounded his skull with a tumultuous storm of rushing thoughts. During those times he prayed feverishly for Peter. He prayed the judges would be able to see beyond the report and see what was really going on. Who they really were. Who Peter really was. *For the LORD loves justice; he will not forsake his saints.*

The next day was the last day of his internship. The staff set a festive mood but Josh was drained of all emotions. Marie was able to find Josiah and Ayesha, both having registered under the Prodigal Son Edict. It would be years of supervision but they would get Nesta back. Manda had escaped from the hospital. Apparently, she snuck out during the night. As for Maggie and the others, they were simply gone.

There was no way to find out where they were holding Peter or anything at all about his case. Any effort to do so, Marie assured him, would fail and bring suspicion.

In the afternoon, the staff provided a going away party for him. He did his best to smile outwardly but his heart was not in it. There was a great deal of good natured teasing and several gag gifts. The only thing that meant anything was Marie's promise she would "keep an eye on things."

At first, Josh contacted Marie several times a day. She eventually had to limit him to just once at the end of each day but she would contact him immediately if she heard anything new.

For the next few weeks, Josh, in a mindless state, went through the motions of starting a new year in college. He tried to focus, if not for the sake of his career, then for the sake of his sanity but it was useless. His mind would never stop spinning. It became less of a feeling and more a way of life... an exhausting debilitating way of life.

The one thing Josh did more than anything else was pray. Every spare minute was spent beseeching God to let Peter go. Begging God to demonstrate to the righteous judges that Peter committed no crime. Josh attended church three times a week and went to crisis prayer groups whenever he found them. He was powerless to do anything else; he had to turn everything over to God. *Cast your burden on the LORD, and he will sustain you; he will never permit the righteous to be moved.*

One evening, it occurred to him, there was something he could do. He took his car over to Peter's parents' house. From the moment he pulled into the driveway, he was dazzled in light. Peter's mom had always been a little uptight on security but this was way beyond average. He found himself shielding his eyes as he made his way to the front door. Before he could ring the bell, the door opened. There stood Peter's father, looking old, tired, and... perturbed.

Behind him, partially shielded by a wall, were his twin sisters, now looking like young ladies. A second later, they were hastily escorted away by what appeared to be their grandmother but Josh quickly realized it was Peter's mom. Josh was awash with regret for coming.

Peter's father stared at him, making no move to let him in.

Josh swallowed hard. "I wanted to stop by... and you know... let you know... how sorry I am..."

Peter's father spoke in a pained whisper. "You've nothing to be sorry for, Joshua. I'm the only one to blame. *Train up a child in the way he should go; even when he is old he will not depart from it.* I failed him as a father."

"Oh, no, that's not true..."

Peter's father offered an agonized smile. "Thank you for coming by," he said, and began closing the door. "But... please... his mother's not well."

It was a full month before Marie called him one morning.

"Did you hear something?" Josh pleaded.

"Yes, love, I'm sorry..."

"What is it?"

"Guilty."

"And that means…"

"I'm so sorry, love…"

Chapter Thirty Five

Under normal circumstances, Josh may have taken the time to appreciate Mrs. Marone's new office overlooking the National Mall. However, as he sat in the reception area waiting to see her, his mind was not capable of such ponderings.

In the course of the last few days, Josh had gone on a tirade. His first stop was, of course, his father again but there, his father provided the same fear filled answers. His mother was even less help. Sure, she offered the warmth of a mother comforting her child but that was all. "The Lord's ways are a mystery to us."

When Mrs. Marone returned his call and found him to be a blubbering babbling basket case, she immediately invited him to come to her office in Washington.

Nothing made sense anymore. Peter was to be executed in less than a week. Josh's father either could not help or was too afraid to. His father being afraid only added to the confusion. His father was a veteran and a DHS agent. What was he afraid of? But it was obvious. Apparently, even the head of DHS did not make waves. But what was so wrong with pointing out a mistake? Mistakes happen. Whatever it was, Josh had seen expressions in his father's face he had never seen before. The man was truly terrified.

That realization, however, did not help Josh help Peter.

Josh's father had made him promise not to try and do anything other than pray. There was to be no reaching out to Denver, or the courts, or anywhere. But the praying wasn't working. He had prayed until he felt his lips had fallen off but Peter was convicted anyway. What good would praying do now?

And so, he had committed a sin against the fifth commandment and went behind his father's back. He hoped he would be forgiven but Mrs. Marone was Peter's last resort. She was dedicated to the Awakening, to the Truth. She was also dedicated to her students. For four years, Josh watched her work tirelessly for her students. None more so than Peter. She was an Apostle and she knew other Apostles. She even knew the President. She would be able to make sense out of this fiasco and, when she did, Mrs. Marone had the power to straighten everything out.

"Mrs. Marone will see you now," the secretary said.

Like everything over the last several days, the words' meaning seeped slowly into his thick frozen brain.

"Young man?" the secretary called.

"I'm sorry. May I go in now?"

"Yes," she answered with a roll of her eyes but maintaining her professional smile.

Inside the office, Josh was struck with how posh and ornate the furnishings were, but he also noted the infamous painting of Jesus pointing to the Seven Mountains was hung in the most prestigious place in the room.

Mrs. Marone, dressed in her ever-black suit, greeted him with a gracious smile. It was all Josh could do to get through the gestures of the welcome. Once seated on the new couch beneath the painting, Josh's frozen mind melted. As he unleashed his narrative stream, he knew, at times, he was being incoherent, but she continued to provide an understanding nod and a steady stream of tissues. He recognized she probably knew most of the basics but he told her everything from the beginning. He had to paint the whole picture for her so that she could see- it was all a series of misunderstandings that grew completely out of hand.

He held nothing back, telling her every minute detail, every thought, and every emotion. He told her about Peter's ad, the trip to Denver with Maggie, Fearless Mountain. He told her about his conversation with Peter, the reason he said he had left the mission trip and how he had pleaded with Peter to come home. He told her about the campfire and how he and Maggie had sinned. He told her about Maggie dumping him shortly after their return and how he did not sleep or eat for two days leading up to his decision to change the security level. He explained he had no idea what he was unleashing. He told her about how the hawk had flown by and how he had taken that as a sign from the Holy Spirit. He then came to his phone call with Maggie and how she said Luke had gone psycho.

"Yes," Mrs. Marone mused. "I saw his name on the report. The last I heard, he'd been dishonorably discharged from the military."

"Maggie said he killed one of the guys and beat Peter to a pulp but that doesn't make any sense. What would Luke have against Peter? Before Luke left, he was Peter's friend. More than that, he looked up to Peter. We all did."

"Maybe, that's your answer. Nothing can be more cutting than a leader failing his followers. *Woe to the shepherds who destroy and scatter the sheep of my pasture!*"

Josh had not thought of that before. He had been mad too. Mad that Peter had not taken the offered help. But was that a reason to pulverize the guy?

As always, Mrs. Marone read his thoughts. "As you said, Peter was a leader to you all. And he repaid your trust by turning his back on God. The report indicated Peter resisted."

"See, right there, that shows it. You know Peter, he wouldn't hurt a fly."

"Maybe you don't know your friend as well as you think. The Peter we knew in high school was a committed Christian. I don't know what this new version of Peter's capable of."

Josh had trouble comprehending what he just heard. What was she saying? "Mrs. Marone, he's the same guy. He's just confused. What happened on the mission trip, with the injured people, it really affected him."

"Since when did Peter get the idea he was given the gift of healing? *God opposes the proud, but gives grace to the humble.*" The bitterness in her voice was like a blade. She was angry with Peter too.

"I think it was more than that," said Josh. "Peter felt… let down by God. He kept asking, if God has the power to heal, why doesn't He?"

"For my thoughts are not your thoughts, neither are your ways my ways."

"That was the exact scripture I quoted to him."

"And?"

"He said it was a cop-out and God has a lot to answer for."

Mrs. Marone nodded.

"Yeah, I know, it's blasphemous," agreed Josh, feeling his hand beginning to shake. "I'm not saying Peter's right, he's messed up. Somehow, Satan got around his armor and attacked his soul. But nothing Peter's done is reason for him to die!"

"The court…"

"The court's wrong!"

"Joshua!" exclaimed Mrs. Marone.

"I know the judges are anointed, but in this case, they made…" He took a deep but quivering breath. "A mistake has been made. I read the report. It wasn't anywhere close to what was going on there. They weren't fixing up the place to turn it into a Buddhist temple. It was a temple before the FGA. They were just fixing it up to live there."

"Outside of church."

"Yeah, I know. It isn't right, but you should see the map at DHS. There are communities like that all over the place. They're confused people who need ministering but they weren't hurting anyone."

"Joshua, I know how much you love Peter, but I think that love's getting in the way of you seeing clearly. Here's some facts to consider. Peter was given the gift of leadership. In high school, he used that gift for God's glory. But he has free-will. He could also use that gift for Satan's purposes. Peter spent almost two years away from the protection of CAP, lost in that wilderness of disbelief and heresy. Two years of Satan, untethered, eating away at him. He may appear to be the same friend you had in high school, but that could be no more than a shell covering a dark soul. A soul quite capable of leading others away from Christ's Truth. Now you say they were just a group of people but notice how easily Peter fell in with them. He's completely alone until he meets three confused people. Peter's charming personality wins them over. Next, they make it to the temple and he wins over another group, including a DHS agent. Then, they give him the cabin that's the highest…"

"That was just because it was the furthest away and Peter was the young…"

"Or, it was the cabin of rank. The ranking monk."

"No, it wasn't like that. Peter didn't hold rank over anyone. They thought he was funny… and hyper… just like he was in high school."

"A leader."

"NO! That's what I'm saying, he wasn't a leader because there was nothing to lead."

"Or so it appeared. Look Joshua, you're not thinking like a warrior, but Peter is… or was. He wasn't gonna come right out and show you. Did you ever ask yourself why you had to come back at the end of the day at that lumber yard?"

"What? Well, Vanessa had to contact Peter and then Peter had to drive down to get us."

"How far a drive was that?"

"About four hours."

"Four. So why did it take him over eight hours to get there?"

"I don't know. Maybe he couldn't leave right away."

"Because maybe, he was helping the others hide the evidence of their cult. He knew if he threw a cult at you, you would freak out on him. So, he lulled you in, made it all look harmless. He presented this happy peaceful world where everyone hugs each other. 'And all we have to do to get there,' he suggests, 'is give up God.' Then what did he do? He tried to talk you into leaving God. See Joshua, cult leaders are inherently insecure so they must surround themselves with loyalty. Peter needed you. He knew he had a chance to pull you away from God and if he did, you would be deeply loyal to him."

"No, that wasn't it. Besides, he didn't pull me away from God."

"Then why are you here?"

"I'm here because I need your help to help Peter."

"You're here because Peter got to you. You're here because you refuse to accept an answer God's already provided."

"What do you mean?"

"The hawk."

"I know but…"

"Is coincidence Biblical?"

"No, but…"

"Why?"

"Because all things work for God's purpose."

With a crinkle of her eyebrows she made it clear she chose to ignore his sarcasm. She solemnly quoted the Word. *"And we know that for those who love God all things work together for good, for those who are called according to his purpose.* What was the question you asked God?"

"Whether I should adjust the security level."

"And?"

Josh sighed deeply. "And a hawk flew by."

"So, knowing God is omnipotent down to the birds of the air and flowers of the field, you have a multiple-choice question. A) the hawk flew by to tell you that 'yes' that's what God wanted. B) God allowed the hawk to fly by, knowing that would confuse you. C) It was a coincidence, meaning God does not exist."

He wished there was a "D" with "none of the above" as the option. Josh knew what the answer was but his mind did not understand the reason. If God wanted him to change the STL, then He also knew what the consequences would be and that would mean…

"God wants Peter to die?"

"Joshua, you know the answer to that."

"No… I don't." Josh's right hand was in a constant shake, his stomach was rolling, and he felt his brain splitting in half. Peter was a lost sheep. A wounded lost sheep. He had done nothing to be rejected by a loving God. He had given his life to that God. Was not their obligation, as Christ's family, to reach out to Peter in love? Why was Mrs. Marone taking this tone with him? He had gotten used to her matter-of-factness but she sounded like she was turning her back on Peter. "This isn't right. It isn't right because it isn't based on truth. *The LORD is near to all who call on him, to all who call on him in truth.* I don't understand why God hasn't fixed this."

"For the word of God is living and active, sharper than any two-edged sword, discerning the thoughts and intentions of the heart."

Josh's mind snapped with exasperation. "What does that mean?"

"It means, maybe the cult was small and disorganized, but maybe that was because it was just getting off the ground. God knows what Peter's capable of so He put a stop to it before it even got started."

Josh pondered her words, her voice. It was a voice he had gone to for wisdom and direction. He desperately tried to find that voice again, to lean on it the way he had in high school. He wanted to find the wisdom in it, the wisdom of her words that always had the right answer. Yet he found only despair. This time, he knew, her answers were wrong.

"No," he stated in defiance, hiding his shaking hand. "This isn't right. And it isn't fair. The most he should get is deported. During the FGA, people who didn't want to live under the Covenant were allowed to leave."

"Oh, Josh, don't be so naïve. Not many were allowed to leave."

"But, then, what happened to them?"

"Most found Jesus. If they didn't… the libs are far too dangerous to let loose only to have to fight them again."

"Come on, Mrs. Marone, do you honestly believe Peter's dangerous?"

"Absolutely. The courts have convicted him of false prophecy, but we really don't need to look any further than Deuteronomy 21. *If a man has a stubborn and rebellious son who will not obey the voice of his father or the voice of his mother, and, though they discipline him, will not listen to them, then his father and his mother shall take hold of him and bring him out to the elders, and they shall say to the elders, 'This our son is stubborn and rebellious; he will not obey our voice; he is a glutton and a drunkard.' Then all the men of the city shall stone him to death with stones. So you shall purge the evil from your midst, and all the nation shall hear, and fear."*

"That's not Peter!" Josh screamed.

"Oh, you don't think Peter's stubborn? Rebellious?" Mrs. Marone's voice was growing in intensity. "When his parents saved him from that European cesspool, did he listen to them? Did he obey their voice?"

"No, but he's a wounded warrior."

"And when you were at the fire, what was going around and around, was that fruit punch? First, he gets you nice and drunk, then he turns his little vixen on you."

"Maggie?"

"Absolutely. *Do not desire her beauty in your heart, and do not let her capture you with her eyelashes.* After your little accident, Peter and Maggie ran off together, didn't they? Next, he orchestrates the perfect romantic evening, complete with a campfire, singing, and wine. A few hours later, she's taking advantage of your drunkenness to lure you into bed. Peter offered your girlfriend a place in his group because he needed her to get to you."

"What? No, besides all she did was break up with me."

"Only after you proved your armor would hold. So, when Peter played his last card, ala the allure of a woman, and lost, he cut you loose, and so did she. So, he's a drunkard, rebellious and stubborn. He had all the help in the world right here. He refused it and instead, ran off to begin gathering followers."

"But they weren't his followers! I keep telling you that! Why can't you see I'm telling the truth?"

"Because maybe it's your warped naïve perception that's telling you it's true. Did you ever think Peter's playing you like a violin?"

"Peter's not like that."

"Sure, Joshua, believe what you like. I've been trying to tell you from the beginning. This is a war. People are either on one side or the other. Deceit is a weapon of war. The only question is: is it being used for righteousness or evil?"

"NO!" Josh recoiled. "That can't be what this is about! We have to show love, compassion. Jesus said to forgive seventy times seventy. In John, Jesus showed mercy to the adulteress. *He who is without sin cast the first stone.*"

"That might work for a whore, but we have a war to win. We must fight fire with fire. *For our God is a consuming fire.* We must remain committed and resolute. Our shield is our faith, and His Word is our sword. *So you shall purge the evil from your midst, and your nation shall hear, and fear.* For Peter to be allowed to just go free sends him right over to the enemy. And it would send the wrong message to the people. As a righteous nation, we cannot ignore this."

"But this is what's not righteous!"

"To question authority is to blaspheme the Holy Spirit," she scolded crossly.

Josh felt like he was on a roller coaster car that just slammed into a wall at full speed. This could not be happening. He found himself on his knees before her. His gut needed to vomit. He tried to speak but there was only a guttural sound. He clapped his jaw together and forced himself to take a deep breath. Finally, he was able to sob. "Please, Mrs. Marone, please don't let them do this…. he's only twenty years old… he has his whole life to get right with God… please don't let them do this… please!"

"Sit up like a Joseph!" When he returned, clutching his stomach, she said, "The Word of God says, for the good of this nation and all the people in it, *the evil must be purged.*"

"NOOO! For God's sake! Peter's not evil. I can't believe you're turning your back on him. He's your student! A teacher is called to be righteous."

Mrs. Malone slammed her palm down on the arm of the chair. "Mind your tongue, youth. I am still in authority over you."

"For he has said, 'I will never leave you nor forsake you.'" How can you do this? I know you can help!"

"Do you think this is easy for me? Do you think I don't feel the pain of this to the depths of my soul? I told you many years ago, when I stand before God Almighty, and He judges me for my life, I will be held accountable for each and every student who has ever passed through my doors. God will judge me for every decision I made and every casualty suffered under me."

"But that's my point, Peter doesn't have to be a casualty. We can save him. You can save him."

"Peter was lost years ago. They're just disposing of the carcass."

Josh stared at the stranger in front of him. He was sitting on both of his hands to keep them from shaking, but when he spoke his voice was firm. "I can't believe you said that. Peter's not a carcass; he's a living breathing brother who needs our help against a terrible injustice. And this isn't about you… I don't give a damn about your Judgment Day."

She looked at him coldly. "I will not intervene."

"Then you…" Josh, harvesting a courage built from shattered despair, stated, "are a poor representation of Christ."

Her koala bear-like features morphed into that of a spoiled child who was just insulted by someone younger than her. "HOW DARE YOU! A poor representation? Me? I've given my life to Jehovah's Revolution. I've trained Josephs. I am being quite consistent with everything I have ever taught you.

You simply haven't learned the lessons. Though I am not surprised, you never belonged in MY program to begin with."

She paused with an actor's precision.

"Oh, yes, I got news for you, little Joshua. I only let you in and kept you in my program because I had a teenage crush on your father. I felt I owed it to him. Did you honestly think you made it through MY program? YOU? You were never cut out to be a Joseph. You're nothing but a whiny moby. And now, the one time in your life you decide to stand up, and it's to blaspheme me. Me? An Anointed Apostle of God! How dare you! Get the hell out of here, blasphemer! Into the pits of Hell!"

Josh, shaking and seething with anger, collected himself. He stood and turned from his former mentor.

At the door, he stated, "You know, my whole life, I've accepted what everyone has told me without question. I don't know if Peter was right in all that he told me, but I do know he was right about one thing. There's nothing in us that makes us better people…. nothing at all."

"Question God at your own peril, young man."

"I knew you were going to say that." He slammed the door as he left.

Epilogue

He checked the time. In a few minutes, the office was going to open. He had every intention of being the first one in the door.

It had been two weeks since Peter's death. Thirteen days since Josh had left home. It had not been an easy decision. The thought of leaving his family saddened him. The thought of leaving the future he was building frightened him. The thought of finding out Peter was right, terrified him. Yet, he owed it to Peter. It was the only way he could begin to make it up to him, short of hanging himself.

He knew if he ran off without going underground his parents would easily find him and bring him back. He assumed his father would track him down at some point anyway. Josh was just looking for some time.

The escape itself had been easier than he imagined. He had plenty of money once he raided his bank account. His DHS ID was never deleted, so travel arrangements to Mexico City were simple. On the other side of customs, he was approached by a young man, Ronaldo, who said he represented LAN, the Lost American Network. He asked Josh if he needed any help. Josh was taken aback at how quickly and openly Ronaldo approached him but the Mexican won him over with his knowledge and sincere smile. A reasonable price later and Josh was officially a fugitive.

The first few days Josh waited in a hotel room for his new papers. During those long hours, he practiced Spanish and reflected on his final meeting with Mrs. Marone. All those years of looking at her as a spiritual guide were washed away in a single second. His last image of her was as a spoiled child having a temper tantrum. If she was indeed a spirit-filled Apostle, then what good was it? The Holy Spirit was not leading her into truth. So, was she deluding herself or was there no Spirit at all? That was the question to which he sought an answer.

It was the answer Peter said he had found. And it had cost him his life.

When the Spirit of truth comes, he will guide you into all the truth. No one needed the Spirit of truth more than Peter, but truth had not saved him. No one had, not even his best friend. There were no loving arms into which Peter could run, just stone-cold hearts. *If I have all faith, so as to remove mountains, but have not love, I am nothing.*

Josh felt like nothing.

As for Maggie, he hoped someday she would forgive him but would understand if she never did. He prayed she would stay safe and happy wherever she ended up. She certainly deserved someone far better than him.

A pigeon landed on the edge of the bench. It's green and blue feathers glistened in the morning sun.

Josh studied the bird and asked, "Did God send you to tell me I'm on the right track? Or did He send you to tell me I'm on the wrong track? Or are you just a dumb bird looking for food?"

The pigeon cocked its head and blinked.

"That's what I thought."

He checked the time again. 8:58.

He bowed his head in prayer. "Dear God. I'm not giving up on You... just yet, but... if You do exist then You know why I'm here. Because nothing makes sense anymore. YOU don't make sense anymore. I put my faith in You, in Your justice, Your love, and frankly that faith has been shattered. In a few moments, I'm going in there as an open vessel. An open vessel seeking You. I'm looking to You to show me how to make sense of everything. To show me, Peter's death was Your will being done. And Peter, if you can hear me, you told me I needed to get out of the dome for six months, that's probably about what I have before they find me. Show me what you wanted to show me."

He stood up from the bench and walked briskly along the sidewalk. He strolled as confidently as he could into the building and down the hall to Office 104. "Estudiantes Internationalis." Ronaldo had directed him here.

He was greeted by a young student worker, who was settling into her morning routine. She smiled graciously when he entered the office.

"Buenos dias," she greeted.

"Um... um...," Josh said nervously, afraid he would be reduced to his feeble attempt at Spanish.

"May I help you?" she said in a voice that reminded him of Mari.

"I've come to see an advisor about registering for classes. I'm an American."

"Muy bien!" she smiled. "Que vas a estudiar? What are you going to study?"

"History. World history."

"Historia. Que Bueno. Pues, bienvenido a la Universidad de Mexico." With a warm smile, she handed Josh a tablet with a form to fill out.

Josh took the tablet, smiled, and, with his best attempt at rolling his "r," replied, "Gracias."

⚜

A short bird flight away there was another bench sitter getting acclimated to her surroundings. Maggie was waiting for Mari and Tirza to come back with their train tickets.

After Luke and his men left that night, followed by Josiah and Ayesha in the SUV, Maggie went into a state of shock. Shock, for though she was in flight mode, her means of escape had followed the soldiers down the mountain. Tirza assured her they could take the truck but they found the soldiers had cut the fuel line.

Maggie panicked. What were they going to do? Run? Luke and his boys would have such fun tracking them down.

What Luke had not counted on was Tirza's ability to repair the truck. It was patchwork but Tirza said she was pretty sure it would get them where they were going.

And where exactly was that?

"We know someone who can make us disappear," said Mari.

"Who?"

"Vanessa."

Vanessa as it turned out was into a great deal more than lumber and mountain climbing. She was a real Harriet Tubman. She had already been working on getting the small group out of the country, but when the three desperate ladies showed up, she expedited matters. The risk was high and expensive but the girls resolve was unyielding. Maggie funded the escape for all of them from her savings. It was the least she could do. The girls did not speak of the night it all happened. It was obvious to Maggie that Mari and Tirza each saw escape as the only tribute they could make to the loved ones they lost. Maggie's guilt gnawed at her.

It was weeks hiding in the back room as fugitives, before Vanessa could make the arrangements.

The three girls felt relief when they were on the move again. The actual crossing was through an old tunnel once used to smuggle illegal immigrants into the United States.

Once in Mexico, they found the going became amazingly easy. Mari complained the Mexicans spoke fast, but she certainly understood everything that was being said. They hopped a train to Mexico City and from there decided to head to a small beach village called Puerto Escondido. The place had developed a reputation for being a haven for escaping Americans.

As for Maggie, she was not at all sure where she was going or when she would get there, but, once she was through the tunnel and safely in the sovereign nation of Mexico, she never felt so… so… doused. Freedom was all around her, in the art, the media, the music, and in the lively bubbling joy that is the Mexican spirit.

A pigeon landed on the bench next to her. It's greenish blue feathers glistened in the sun.

"Buenos Dias," Maggie said quietly.

The pigeon cocked its head and blinked at her.

Maggie smiled, and with her best attempt at rolling her "r," said, "Gracias."

El Fin

Glossary of Terminology

Apostle: an anointed leader.

Babel: crazy, absurd.

ET: Elevated Train.

Heart-bump: a gesture of greeting or friendship performed by the youth. One takes his fist and gently taps his own chest twice then taps knuckles with the other person.

Hedge of Protection: a prayer for divine safety.

Hedge: goodbye.

Joe: similar to man, guy, dude, mano.

Joseph: a leader or one who displays leadership qualities.

Leaving room for the Spirit: a phrase meaning to be open to the direction of the Holy Spirit once a decision has been made.

Lib: a liberal.

Mano: slang term based on Spanish word "hermano" meaning brother. Man, guy, joe.

Matthewed 18: v. meaning to rebuke.

Moby: Mamma's Boy.

Morit: a braggart.

Pean: shortened form of the word "European" and slang term meaning idiot, stupid. A general insult.

Silence, Pharisee: shut-up, be quiet.

Solomon: okay, cool, alright

SV: Solar Vehicle. Similar in size and function to a golf cart.

Triumphant: a common exclamation of joy; fantastic, awesome.

Vid chat: facetiming through a cell phone.

YF: Youth Fellowship